About the Book

Dive into *The Whitstable High Tide Swimming Club* - the irresistible feel-good novel from Katie May. Join Debs and Maisie and the high tide swimmers as they make waves in life, love and friendship.

Only the truly devoted manage to swim every day at Whitstable, because the sea's only deep enough at high tide. So when Deb (ageing bikini, sunglasses) and Maisie (black wetsuit, swimming shoes, goggles) keep meeting on Reeves Beach, they strike up an unlikely friendship based on their love of swimming and their recent divorces.

They swim early in the morning and late at night; through sea-fogs, rain and glorious sunny days. Soon, they are joined by other high tide swimmers, each with a crisis of their own to weather. Ann, a bossy organiser, is caring for her elderly mother at home; Julie has somehow (although she's not quite sure how) managed to produce three children under school age; and Chloe, a bright, brittle girl of fifteen, finds calmness in the water. Quiet, anxious Bill is initially thought to be a peeping Tom, before being welcomed into the heart of the club.

When the swimmers discover plans for their beach to be paved over for a leisure complex, they find a higher purpose that bonds them together, and exposes their fragile worlds to public scrutiny.

ABERDEENSHIRE
LIBRARIES

WITHDRAWN
FROM LIBRARY

Aberdeenshire

3221346

THE WHITSTABLE
HIGH TIDE
SWIMMING CLUB

KATIE MAY

First published in Great Britain in 2018 by Trapeze Books
an imprint of The Orion Publishing Group Ltd
Carmelite House, 50 Victoria Embankment
London EC4Y 0DZ

An Hachette UK company

1 3 5 7 9 10 8 6 4 2

Copyright © Katie May 2018

The moral right of Katie May to be identified as
the author of this work has been asserted in accordance with
the Copyright, Designs and Patents Act of 1988.

All rights reserved. No part of this publication may be
reproduced, stored in a retrieval system, or transmitted
in any form or by any means, electronic, mechanical,
photocopying, recording, or otherwise, without the
prior permission of both the copyright owner and the
above publisher of this book.

All the characters in this book are fictitious, and any resemblance to
actual persons, living or dead, is purely coincidental.

A CIP catalogue record for this book is
available from the British Library.

ISBN 978 1 4091 7238 3

Typeset by Born Group

Printed and bound in Great Britain by Clays Ltd, St Ives plc

www.orionbooks.co.uk

For my Grandad Jim,
who taught me to swim in the sea,
and never let on that he was afraid of the water.

Part One

It's not easy to swim at Whitstable beach. At low tide, the sea retreats so far that it almost vanishes, and the water is barely deep enough to cover your ankles. Locals joke that you could paddle all the way to the Isle of Sheppey. I have no idea whether that's actually true, but I do know that you'd have to wade through an awful lot of mud to find out.

Not that there's anything wrong with low tide; all kinds of strange and beautiful things are waiting to be found on the seabed. But if you want to swim, then you'll have to wait for high tide, when the sea rises halfway up the beach and is suddenly deep and tantalising. This only happens twice in twenty-four hours. Miss it by an hour, and you'll find your knees brushing along the bottom as you attempt a front crawl.

No, to swim at Whitstable – properly swim, without your feet touching the ground – you'll need a tide table and a military sense of punctuality. And, probably, a pair of swimming shoes, because the shingle beach is a killer on bare feet. Even then, if you time your swim to perfection, you'll find muddy-brown Channel water rather than the clear, sparkling waves of the Atlantic.

However, if you're willing to brave all of these things – the tides, the shingle, the looming suspicion of uncleanliness – you'll find that the Whitstable sea has its rewards. It's never as cold as the Atlantic, and nor does it have those crashing waves that can suddenly overwhelm you, leaving you spluttering and spitting out seaweed. By midsummer, it's as warm and smooth as bathwater, and you're never far from a cup of tea (or a glass of wine) when you're done. There's a lifeboat station just around the corner, which is a comfort. But best of all, you'll come out of the water with the distinct sense that you've found a secret passageway through life, one that leaves you feeling renewed and restored. It may take a certain kind of person to appreciate the charms of Whitstable beach, but for those discerning souls, it's almost perfect.

So when Deb spotted Maisie swimming at West Beach every day for two weeks straight, she knew they had to be kindred spirits. Granted, this other woman was properly kitted out in a full-length wetsuit, bootees, goggles and a neon orange swimming hat, which seemed a little excessive for the warm weather. Deb was more of a 'throw on a bikini and maybe tie your hair back if you can find a spare elastic in your handbag' kind of a swimmer. She preferred to limp across the stones than to bother with special shoes. Once upon a time, this difference would have been enough to make Deb believe that Maisie was probably a bit too fancy for the likes of her, and that she was best avoided. Not so long ago, she had some sharp words to say about the 'Down From Londons' and their ridiculous Farrow & Ball perfection.

But things were already changing for Deb by this point. She watched Maisie's careful routine for a few days, and thought that this was the hallmark of a sophisticated woman. This was the kind of person she needed to associate with from now on. *Go on, girl*, she told herself, *go up and shake her hand*.

So that's what she did. It was eight o'clock on a Wednesday morning in June, and she had finished her ten minutes of breast stroke (head upright), and was drying off when Maisie waded inland, caught one foot behind her buttocks to perform a neat quadriceps stretch, and then climbed up the beach to find her belongings. This was Deb's chance. She hid her packet of cigarettes under her sarong, slipped on her flip-flops, and crunched over the stones towards a complete stranger, hoping that this would be yet another step towards her new life.

'You're doing the high tides then,' she said, and stuck out her hand. 'I'm Deb.'

Maisie had a microfibre towel draped over her shoulders, and was in the middle of unpeeling her bathing cap from her short-cropped hair. She glanced at Deb, startled. 'Oh,' she said, and took the hand in an unsteady grip. 'Yes, I suppose I am.' She ran the towel over her head and around her neck, looking utterly disinterested. 'And you are too, I take it?'

'Yes,' said Deb. 'Haven't you seen me? I'm here every day.'

'Oh,' said Maisie. 'I'm sorry. I haven't really been paying attention.'

'Don't worry,' said Deb. 'I'm not really very memorable. Or at least, I try not to be, if I can help it!' She laughed, but it wasn't actually a joke. Maisie wasn't even looking at her any more and was instead staring out to sea, vaguely, as if searching for something she'd lost. Or maybe it was just boredom. Maybe she was trying to be anywhere but in this conversation.

'So,' said Deb, when it was clear that Maisie wasn't going to pick up the conversation again. 'Are you a DFL? You look like one to me.'

'A *what*?'

'You know, a Down From London. The enemy of the Natives.' She laughed again, because it was obvious, surely, that this was a joke. No one really cared all that much about the DFLs, except, perhaps, that bloke on Regent Street who had put up a sign in his garden saying 'DFLs Go Home!' But nobody took him seriously, and anyway he'd taken it down after his neighbours complained.

'I suppose I am,' said Maisie. 'But I had no idea that it made me anyone's enemy.'

'Right,' said Deb. 'Can't we all just live together in peace?'

She was beginning to think this was all probably a mistake. She would now have to talk to this awkward woman every day for the rest of her life, or else find a different beach to swim on. Maisie had taken a bottle of mineral water out of her backpack and was using it to rinse out her goggles before drying them carefully on her towel and folding them into a plastic case. She seemed to be almost absurdly prepared, as if she could bear to leave nothing to chance. The bathing cap was rinsed and folded – presumably to make sure the seawater wouldn't rot it – and then she stood on her towel while she removed her neoprene bootees, shook them out in turn, and placed them in a special mesh bag. Everything was carefully brought under her control.

Just then, Deb heard someone calling her name, and she turned to see Derek puffing over the stones towards her, waving a fistful of papers in the air. He had parked his stupid great big red truck over the lane that led to the caravan site, its doors open and the radio still blaring out Phil Collins.

'Oh God,' said Deb, and knew for certain that Maisie would never be her friend now.

'Deb!' shouted Derek. 'Oh, Deb! Darlin'! What are you trying to do to me, babe?'

'Oh God,' said Deb again, and this time she saw that Maisie was looking right back at her, with inquisitive eyes.

'Postie delivered these just now,' said Derek, his jowly face red and unshaven. 'You can't mean this, babe! You can't do this to me!'

'How did you know I was here?' asked Deb as coldly as she could manage. It was hard not to feel sorry for him, but only in the way that you'd feel sorry for the last dog in the pound.

'I texted Cherie, love,' he said, 'and she said I'd find you here.'

'I'll kill her,' said Deb.

'She just wants to see her old mum and dad back together,' said Derek, tears – real, genuine tears – in his eyes now. 'It's ripping her apart. It's ripping all of us apart.'

'She'll get over it,' said Deb. She took in a breath and stiffened her shoulders. 'Anyway, I'm glad to see you got the letter. You need to fill in the forms and post them back. Let's keep it quick and easy, shall we?'

'But darlin',' said Derek, wiping his nose on his sleeve, 'I don't know what I've done wrong! I don't even know where you're finding the money . . .'

Deb had been trying very hard not to snap, but this found her faultline. 'Why don't you just . . .' she began, but then she felt a hand touch her forearm. Maisie gave the gentlest of squeezes, and stepped between her and Derek, her back straight and her gaze calm and fierce.

'I think it's clear,' she said, in a clipped voice that radiated authority, 'that your presence here is not welcome. I'm sure this is an extremely difficult time for you, but you will gain nothing through harassment.'

'Now hang on,' began Derek, but Maisie raised a hand.

'Go home and fill out your forms. Have dinner with your children and assure them that you will no longer expect them to take sides. And if you want to speak to my client in person again, then I suggest you arrange a mutually convenient appointment.'

Derek looked from Deb to Maisie and back to Deb again. *'Client?'* he said.

'Do as I ask,' said Maisie, and just like that, Derek shrugged, turned and slumped back up the beach.

Deb watched the door slam, and then the truck reversed away too fast, leaving a cloud of dust.

'I hope I didn't overstep the mark there,' said Maisie. She was smiling, and Deb suddenly saw that her cheeks were freckled.

'Your *client?*' said Deb. Was Maisie interested in her, now that there was something she could organise?

'Old habits die hard,' said Maisie. 'Shall we get some tea?'

This is how the club began.

1

Deb had tried to insist that the teas were on her, but she got the same solemn raised hand that Derek had received, and it stopped her in her tracks just the same.

Instead, she sat and watched Maisie order at the counter, all the while feeling the last remnants of seawater from her bikini soaking through her clothes. Maisie, of course, had a special garment just for getting changed on the beach, into which she zipped herself, and then emerged, fully clothed, after a few small, efficient movements. Deb had just pulled on her denim shorts and vest top as usual, but then she usually rode her bike straight home and stripped off there. Today, she felt uncomfortably damp, and had just glanced down to notice two wet circles over her breasts, like a child's drawing of a bra. She draped her wrap around her neck, and although that was damp too, at least it hid the impression that she was somehow leaking.

Maisie placed Deb's builder's tea on the table, and then her own, a clear bright green liquid full of floating leaves.

'What's that?' said Deb.

'Fresh mint. I'm trying to cut out caffeine.'

'Don't blame you,' said Deb. 'Makes you jittery.'

'Something like that.' Maisie stirred her tea, releasing the smell of new potatoes on the boil. 'I take it that was your husband then?'

'Ex-husband.'

'Not quite yet, I'd say.'

Deb sighed. 'I thought all I'd have to do was walk out. Turns out that was the easy bit. Thirty years of marriage, and he barely noticed I existed. Now, he's suddenly . . . I dunno, Romeo.'

'You've given him one hell of a wake-up call.'

'It's too late for that. He's had his chances. Hundreds of them.'

Deb fell silent for a few moments as the hurt washed over her yet again. When she talked about her divorce to other people, she always tried to keep it light, to show how well she was coping. It was a Punch and Judy show, except she was damned if she was being Judy. Problem was, she wasn't sure who else she could be yet: the Policeman, the Judge, or maybe just Toby the dog, yapping and chasing its tail.

'So,' she said, trying to change the subject, 'when you called me your client earlier . . .'

'I slipped into role a bit too easily there. Sorry.'

'You're a solicitor?'

'Corporate lawyer. Or I used to be. All that I know about divorce law is from personal experience.'

'You too?'

'Me too,' said Maisie. 'I left my husband when I turned fifty, and moved down here.'

'When was that?'

'Three months ago.'

'Blimey,' said Deb. 'Same time as me. I didn't think you were from round here. Where're you from, originally?'

A slight flicker of Maisie's eyebrows, and a definite tensing of her jaw. 'I was born in London,' she said.

'Oh God,' said Deb. 'I didn't mean because you're . . .' A few months ago, she'd have said *coloured*, and thought she was being polite, but then the tutor at the Adult Ed college had corrected her about it during class, and she still felt ashamed not to have known. She scrambled for the right word. *African-Caribbean?*

'Black,' said Maisie.

'Right,' said Deb, '*black*. Oh God, I didn't mean that. I meant, I didn't think you were from Whitstable. I've never seen you around before and, well, the varnish hasn't quite worn off you yet.'

'Oh,' said Maisie, 'right. I'm not sure what that means.'

Deb wondered if she had actually dug herself into a deeper hole. 'I mean, like, nothing stays perfect by the sea. You paint your windows and six months later it's all peeling off.

You wash your car, and the salt's got to it by the end of the day. It's the same with people too. You can't stay perfect in Whitstable. You'll end up with sand in your hair either way.'

'Well,' said Maisie, running her hand over her head. 'I thought I'd taken care of that when I bought my clippers.' She laughed. 'But I'm sort of glad you think I'm still glossy. We must cling to what little glamour we can.'

'Right,' said Deb, who noticed that Maisie had already finished her tea. She would be moving on soon, to what was certain to be a busy, important life. 'Hey,' she said, 'I thought I might catch the tide tonight too. About nine o'clock. I mean, you've probably had enough of me for one day . . .'

'I'll be there,' said Maisie. 'See you at nine.'

2

Deb's front door was certainly peeling, but it lacked any faded seaside charm. It had originally been red, she assumed, but had faded to pink, with silvery wood showing underneath it. The door was eternally swollen; she shoved against it with her shoulder, and it slammed against the wall inside. That would be another mark on the paint, and another black mark from the landlord.

Nobody ever said 'bedsit' any more, but that was what it was. You could call it a studio all you liked, but that wouldn't take away the fact that it had a bed at one side (single), and a mean couple of gas rings at the other. She supposed she should count herself lucky that there was a door on the bathroom. But it never felt all that lucky when she was settling down to sleep with the smell of dinner lingering in the air, or arranging a throw and cushions on the bed the next morning, just in case she had visitors. Couldn't have people walking in to find an unmade bed where the living room should be.

She never had visitors anyway. Not that she was short of friends – everyone in Whitstable knew Deb – but these days she preferred to bump into people in pubs and cafes, rather than have them round to hers. The flat was in the basement of a town house on Oxford Street, and was accessed through a dark alleyway. It was dingy, tatty, and too small, and she didn't want anyone feeling sorry for her. There was nothing to feel sorry about. She always saw her kids in their own houses anyway, and tried to make herself useful. Cherie, now thirty years old with two kids of her own, was grateful of the help, even if she only showed it by pointing out all the things Deb was doing wrong. Feeding them too much sugar. Letting them watch too much TV. Using the word 'bum' instead of 'bottom'. None of these things ever did Cherie any harm, but then everything had changed since then. Deb couldn't decide whether she was infuriated, proud, or sick with envy when she spent time with her bossy, ambitious daughter.

Cherie had planned her kids, two years apart, starting from when she was twenty-six. A girl and then a boy, who came along a year ago. She announced the pregnancy just as Deb was getting ready to walk out on Derek. It was bad timing, really; she had to shelve her plans for a while. But then she realised she could have waited forever for a good time to leave.

There was no such thing as planning when Deb had her kids. She 'fell' – that was the word everyone used – at twenty, just after she met Derek. Nobody cared very much about her getting married with a bump under her wedding dress, but Deb had just got herself a nice job as a bank cashier, and was thinking that maybe she could end up managing her own branch if she applied herself. She had two A levels, a certificate in Pitman Script and a typing speed of eighty words per minute. Until she started throwing up on her way to work every morning, she was very much under the impression that the world was her oyster.

Derek said he would take care of everything. She had no reason to doubt it. It was 1985, and everyone was having extensions put on their houses. He was never short of work. 'Don't worry, darlin',' he said. 'I'll take care of you, and your baby.' And he celebrated his pledge by going out and getting spectacularly drunk, even by his standards. He came home at two a.m., all sickly breath and wandering hands. 'We could make another baby, just for luck,' he said, and Deb wondered, not for the last time, whether he could really be as stupid as he seemed to be.

She was stuck after that, or at least too busy to imagine a better life. After Cherie came Darren, and after Darren came Rob. They were lovely kids, all three of them. Deb never begrudged them anything. She took them to the clubs they had at the library, and the playgroup at the church hall. Once they were all at school, she went in and listened to the kids in reception class stammer through their first reading books. She joined the PTA, and was always there to go along on school trips, or to get the kids into their costumes at the nativity play, or the end of year concert. She didn't have time to go back to work. Once she'd dropped them all off, tidied up, got dinner ready and done the ironing, it was time to pick them up again anyway.

Derek said not to worry. He said he didn't need her working, that he wanted his kids to be looked after properly. Deb agreed, probably, but it wasn't like there was much choice anyway. Cherie may moan about the price of childcare, but it didn't even exist back then, whether or not Deb could have afforded it. She never gave it a thought. She was too busy, and she was needed. It felt like enough.

Not that everything was perfect. Far from it. Derek carried on his love affair with the pub, but Deb didn't mind as it kept him out of her way in the evenings. The pub was welcome to him. There were his flings, to which he always confessed, tearfully, as if she cared. Sure, the first one stung; and the second was embarrassing. But by the time she heard about the third, she was almost inclined to congratulate him. Rather some random barmaid than her, frankly. What did it matter if they lived separate lives, as long as the children were happy?

But then, one afternoon, everything changed. Cherie had gone off to university. Darren was at college. Rob was doing his GCSEs. Everything felt pretty much on track. And Deb, standing in the middle of her living room, thought: *I'd like a pair of leather boots for the winter.* She had seen them in the window of Marks and Spencer, a smart pair in burgundy leather, a bit like riding boots. And then it hit her: she had absolutely no way of buying them for herself. She would have to ask Derek, and if he was in a good mood, and he'd dragged his fat arse into work enough times this month, he would let her have them. Suddenly, this disgusted her.

All the work I've done, and I've got nothing of my own.
Nothing.
Nothing.

She was cleverer than him. She was kinder. She was better than him. And it all caught up with her, the sense of overbearing horror that she had lost the last twenty years of her life to bringing up his kids – *and she never resented it, because they were lovely kids* – and keeping his house, and keeping in touch with their friends and his family, and making everything all right for all of them, and she still had to go crawling to him if she just wanted a pair of boots.

That was all it was. Nothing happened. It had happened already, and Deb hadn't noticed it.

That was the day that Deb started saving. She asked for the boots, bought a cheap pair in Primark, and pocketed the difference. He didn't notice. She knew he wouldn't. When she emptied the change out of his pockets to put a wash on, she kept 50p coins, and sometimes a few pounds, too. He had no idea what he spent anyway after the first couple of pints. Deb was only rescuing them from the slot machine. She started buying Smart Price tea and yesterday's bread. What would he notice, through the haze of a hangover? All of it went in her special jar behind the now-redundant Tampax in the bathroom cupboard, where he definitely wouldn't find it.

Soon, she had enough to open a bank account. Sometimes, she wondered if it was stealing, but then she thought about everything he had taken from her, and realised it didn't bother her at all. You couldn't steal from someone who had forgotten what they had.

She thought she would walk out when the last child left home, because by then they would all have lives of their own, and she wouldn't have to worry. But Rob suddenly decided, last minute, that he needed to do a Media Studies degree, which gave her no small amount of pleasure, seeing as Derek couldn't come to understand what that even was, try as he might. She couldn't bring herself to leave while Rob was away, because she wanted him to feel like he still had a home to come back to in the holidays. It was only three years. She got herself a job in the chemist's on the High Street, and then she really started tucking the money away, hundreds of pounds a month.

She signed up for a Returning to Education course at the local college, and started sneaking there on Wednesday mornings, hiding her homework under the pile of paid bills in the spare room. She would just be more ready, that was all, when the time came. Derek never suspected a thing.

But by the time Rob was finished, he started talking about taking a gap year in Australia, and Cherie was pregnant for the second time. Then Darren got married. When his wife started talking about trying for a baby, Deb realised she would have to draw the line somewhere. It would never end. There would never be a right time. They would all go on needing her, forever.

Whitstable had gone up in the world since Deb last moved house. The first time she saw what was affordable on her tiny budget, she nearly slammed that peeling door to run back to Derek and his booze-soaked snoring. But then she reminded herself that her sights were set on bigger things. The bedsit – studio, whatever you call it – was just a stepping-stone. No point sitting around, waiting for something to happen. It was a means to an end. She'd put up with far worse.

But right now, with nowhere to be for the rest of the day, she felt the meanness of the place. College had finished for the year, so she didn't even have that to distract her. She hung her wet bikini over the shower rail to dry and made a salad out of a handful of leaves from a bag and a tin of tuna. Bread and butter on the side. As she ate it, she texted Cherie:

U shouldnt hv told Dad where i was it wasnt fair

A reply, straightaway:

He was in a right state. You can't just send him divorce papers through the post like that.

Thats just how it happens love – dont make it harder than it already is

I thought you were better than this.

There was no point replying to that. Cherie – with her husband who changed nappies and took her on 'date nights' and cooked the dinner every night – was welcome to her moral high ground. Deb would have to make do with the basement flat instead, and cravings for the next high tide.

Sure enough, Maisie was waiting on West Beach at nine o'clock, her wetsuit and swimming cap already on. The sun was low and orange, and was just about to dip behind Sheppey for the night. They cast long shadows as they waded into the sea, which was so high and smooth it almost felt ripe. Deb didn't say that, in case Maisie thought she was weird, but she thought it.

She thought how the sea was suddenly brimming with possibility.

3

Deb was standing on Maisie's back doorstep so that she could smoke and talk at the same time. Every time she wanted to say something, she had to lean her head into the kitchen, and hold the fag as far out behind her as possible so that the smoke wouldn't come in. There would never be a moment, she realised, when Maisie would say, *Why don't you just smoke inside? It doesn't matter.* Women like Maisie didn't smoke. Instead, Deb would just have to keep on leaning out of the door, and making sure she didn't make a mess with her ash.

A fortnight after their first swim, she was a regular at Maisie's fisherman's cottage. It was part of a narrow terrace on a road behind the High Street, not far from West Beach. These were the houses that nobody wanted twenty years ago; poky really, about the width of a decent caravan, and most of them still bearing the scars of the floods of '53.

But now it had become a status symbol to lavish money on something so small. Maisie's cottage was a case in point. From the grey-green front door (which had almost certainly replaced uPVC), to the bare oak floorboards (newly laid, reclaimed wood), through to the handsome Shaker kitchen, not a single surface in that house had missed the attentions of an expensive builder. Just two bedrooms upstairs, each with its own bathroom, because Maisie said she realised that she just didn't need a third bedroom. No kids, you see. Just the odd guest to accommodate, stylishly, pristinely, separately. The message was: I could afford a big house, but I have chosen to let this be enough.

Deb wondered if she could ever let her studio flat be enough, but decided that there was a gulf of difference between the peeling pink paint on her front door (unintentional), and the paint on the Victorian cupboards in Maisie's dining room, which had been artfully sanded to reveal the gentle rainbow of paints used by previous residents. Derek would have said the decorator was on the take, but that was just another thing that he didn't have the wits to understand.

Maisie was brewing green tea in a china pot. She swished the leaves in the water, poured out a little to test the colour, tutted, and then swished again. Deb leaned out to take a drag from her cigarette, blew the smoke in the direction of the neighbour's fence, and then put her head back into the kitchen.

'You're the only person I know whose mugs match.'

Maisie poured the tea into two pure white mugs, which were almost certainly bone china. 'Thank you,' she said. 'I think.'

'It's a compliment,' said Deb. 'You like everything just-so. You know how to buy all the right things.'

'Maybe,' said Maisie. 'But my mugs didn't match in my old house. The only reason they match here is because I had to buy everything new.'

Deb stubbed out her cigarette in the flowerpot Maisie had laid on. She would have to empty it out before she went home. This was an unusual invitation into Maisie's past, and she wasn't going to miss it by hanging halfway out of the back door.

'Did your ex get custody of the mugs then?'

'It wasn't like that, really. It was my decision to leave. He'd done nothing wrong. I wanted to make it as easy for him as possible.'

'So you let him have everything?'

'I took a few things. It was easier to start afresh than to stir everything up. I wanted to be kind.'

That intention – to leave kindly and cleanly – had seemed a great deal more comforting when she was planning it. Maisie's mother had died the year before, and the two things seemed to happen at once: the decision to leave Stephen, and the sale of her mother's house finally going through. It wasn't as if the inheritance had given her the idea that she should leave; she had been wondering about that for years. But when the sum finally arrived – a giddying, almost hilarious shifting of the decimal point in her bank account – she could suddenly see an escape route that hadn't been there before. Now, she could simply leave and barely trouble him.

They would not have to sell the house in Islington or divide up the savings. There would be no need for any mess or accusation. She had enough, now, to look after herself. She could draw on her pension when she turned fifty-five (what a joke it had seemed, when she opened the account, to be planning for early retirement), and that was only three years away. She knew full well that she was settling for less than she was entitled to, but then it was no fault of Stephen's that she was leaving. He had carried on being the man she married. She was the one who had changed. It wouldn't be fair to make him sell the house, to move somewhere smaller, less central, to embark on those petty divisions of what was his and what was hers. It didn't matter. She could start afresh, with white mugs and matching plates. She wanted to make the transition so smooth for him that it was nearly painless.

She thought that perhaps, if she left quietly one morning, he wouldn't even notice. After a fortnight, he would perhaps observe that her post remained unopened on the hall shelf; and after a month, he would possibly become aware of a backlog of milk building up in the fridge, or a surfeit of weeds in the garden. But this was unfair. He would feel her absence immediately, keenly. She was part of the quiet rhythm of his day. He observed her, she suspected, from the corner of his eye as he read the *Telegraph* at breakfast, and he felt the weight of her body unbalance the mattress each night in bed. He heard the clank of her loading the dishwasher after supper, and sensed the orderliness of her mind as he unloaded the same crockery, still warm, the next morning. He was reminded of her tiny stature every time he adjusted the driver's seat of their shared Polo. He traced the indentations of her fingertips on the toothpaste tube. It was just that he never, once, thought to look up from those things and see her there, in person. He spent plenty of time with her, but it was always at a delay.

It wasn't his fault. It was his upbringing. No, she didn't need to make excuses on his behalf: it was him. It was how he liked things to be. And if she could no longer bear it – well, then that was her fault instead of his. They had made this life together. He had no reason to expect anything to change. She must do all the changing for him.

4

The high tides were on a morning shift this week. Maisie and Deb had swum at eight p.m. on Sunday, but then eight thirty a.m. on Monday, a disconcerting leap that happened once a fortnight, switching you from night swimmer to morning lark. There were a few days when you could catch both tides if you wanted to, as they were only twelve and a half hours apart, but then the late session would shift from nine, to ten, to eleven, and then into the bleary post-midnight hours when no sane person was out of the house. Both Deb and Maisie were awake, though, restless in their separate bedrooms. But they preferred not to admit that.

West Beach was covered in flowers. Clouds of pink and white valerian gathered at the top of the groynes, tangled with yellow-horned poppies, spikes of wild fennel, and ryegrass. Deb was tempted to pick a few of the marigolds for her table but thought that she probably wasn't supposed to, and didn't want to embarrass herself in front of Maisie. A couple of the beach huts were open today, showing off neat whitewashed interiors with daybeds and dressers full of striped china. Gone were the days when beach huts were glorified sheds for storing all your beach gear and sheltering from the inevitable rain. The huts here were like a row of doll's houses, all dressed up to the nines so that someone could come down from London twice a year, and pretend that everything was perfect.

You're just jealous, said Deb to herself. There was no denying it. She couldn't ever imagine having enough spare cash to lavish on something so pointless. Two men in hi-vis jackets were walking around them today, taking measurements with a theodolite on a tripod and gazing from the huts to the sheaf of plans in their hands, and back again.

'For heaven's sake,' said Maisie, watching them as she rolled on her swimming cap. 'I expect someone's installing a hot tub in there.'

'Or a turret,' said Deb.

'It's only a matter of time,' said Maisie.

'Why do you wear that cap, anyway? You haven't got any hair.'

Maisie glanced up, and for a few awful beats Deb thought she'd crossed a line, but there was amusement in her eyes.

'I don't wear it to keep my hair dry; I wear it to stay visible.'

'From space?' said Deb. The bathing cap was so Day-Glo that it could have been backlit.

'Don't come crying to me if you get run over by a windsurfer,' said Maisie. She waded thigh-deep into the water, rinsed her goggles and then snapped them over her eyes. 'See you on the other side,' she said.

Deb followed her a few metres into the sea, immediately flopping onto her back. She adjusted her ballooning bikini bra and straightened her legs to inspect her toes. The blue nail polish was chipped, but at least the brownness of her feet was satisfying. Not that there was much chance of catching the sun today: huge black clouds hung over the beach and the wind was just beginning to pick up. The sea was the colour of slate. She glanced over at Maisie, who was already nearly at the buoy that marked the furthest extent of the low tide. She would carry on further than that, whatever the weather. Maisie barely came in contact with the sea anyway. Being head-to-toe in neoprene seemed to make her invincible. Deb, on the other hand, loved the feeling of her bare shoulders catching the cold blasts of air above the waterline while the rest of her body was cocooned by the water.

She turned her gaze on the builders. They had packed up their equipment, and had struck up a conversation with one of the beach-hut owners, who was leaning on the doorframe holding a coffee in a studiedly shabby tin mug.

'How much did you pay for this, then?' said the younger of the two, whose loud voice drifted over onto the sea. 'If you don't mind me asking.'

You won't get a cuppa out of her with questions like that, thought Deb.

The woman coloured slightly and stood up straight. She shook her head.

'I've heard they go for forty grand,' said the builder, un-deterred. His companion was looking down at his feet, kicking the pebbles.

The woman laughed. Deb couldn't tell whether she found this completely ridiculous, or whether she was just embar-rassed at what she'd spent. Most likely, the builder wasn't all that far off.

He whistled, and they both waved and walked back onto the road. The words *forty grand* drifted back over towards her.

And then she noticed a woman sat on the shingle. This must be the fourth day in a row that Deb had seen her on the beach, or maybe even the fifth. She sat with her back impos-sibly upright, her knees bent, a reporter's notebook balanced on her thighs. She never wrote anything in it, but her pencil was permanently poised, as if she were moments away from a profound thought that would have to be captured immediately.

Deb had a strong suspicion that she wouldn't like the woman if she ever met her. There was something overbearing about her floral skirt and hiking sandals; the way she always wore a cloth sun-hat, even in weather like this. She was certain the woman was watching her and Maisie, although she never managed to catch her looking. She always seemed to arrive while they were swimming, though. Deb glanced over to see if Maisie had noticed the woman too, but although she had now turned inland, she was deeply engaged in a machine-like backstroke.

A great clatter of seagulls flew overhead, which usually meant a storm out at sea, and, sure enough, Deb felt a heavy splash of rain on her forehead, and then the surface of the water was pocked all over with raindrops. The air smelt cleaner already. On the beach, the woman was hastily folding up her notebook and gathering her fleece around her, ready to rush back to shelter.

Deb supposed that she ought to make her way ashore too, and before she could even begin her breaststroke, Maisie was powering past her, orange cap dipping in and out of the rising waves.

5

'Ta-ra! Don't do anything I wouldn't do!'

Deb hoisted the vast black holdall onto her shoulder, and felt her knees buckle ever so slightly under the weight.

'You sure I can't give you a lift home?' The woman teetered in the door, her face lit up by a sauvignon flush.

'No, no,' said Deb, 'my car's just round the corner. The fresh air'll do me good.'

'We're going clubbing,' the woman yelled, swaying slightly. She would no doubt be apologising to her neighbours tomorrow, once she could face getting out of bed.

'Call a taxi then, love, eh?' said Deb. 'You know what the police are like on Saturday night. They'll pull anyone over.'

The woman looked momentarily offended, and then raised her glass to Deb, sloshing the contents down the front of her blouse. Deb raised a hand and shifted the weight of the bag into the centre of her back, gripping the handle with both hands.

Of course, she didn't have a car, and a taxi would wipe out half of her evening's earnings. It didn't do, though, to let the clients know that you were heading for the nearest bus stop; it spoiled the party. Deb had got into a routine of pretending to have parked the car around the corner – silly her, she got the wrong road – before lugging her giant bag of rubber penises onto the bus back into town.

The sex toy parties hadn't exactly been a planned career move, but when she had seen the advert in the local paper, she wondered why she hadn't thought of it earlier. Deb could get on with anyone, could talk about anything, could always get the party started. She could cackle along with a few women on a night out, no problem. She could go there, when other people would blush and run out of words. One evening a week – if she could get it – paid more than a week working behind a bar, and put her in the company of a better grade of drunk. Or, at least, a kind of drunk she understood. She didn't touch a drop herself while she was working, knowing she would probably give away the marabou blindfolds and rubber bondage tape after the second glass. The imaginary car came in handy.

She dumped the bag down at the bus stop, and perched on the narrow bench in the shelter. There was no point checking the timetable; the buses had a will of their own around here. She remembered the days of taking three kids on the bus – because Derek always needed the car – and trying to stop the three of them running into the road, or pushing the bell before their stop, or kicking the back of the seat in front. You're never alone when you're a parent, and not in a good way. Everyone is always watching, and finding you wanting. Now and then, someone would say, *Can I help you with that pram?* or would chat to the kids as they rode along, giving her a few fragile minutes to draw her head together again before the next onslaught. But these moments were few and far between. Nowadays, Deb was a serial lifter of prams onto buses, but often she was met with a cold stare as if she was the sort of woman who might steal a Maclaren buggy just for the kicks.

She could see the bus around the corner now. She held out her hand, and it drew up at the kerb, hissing out air as its doors folded open. Deb thought she might be able to drag the bag up the step, but she soon realised she'd have to actually lift it. She hauled it over her shoulder again, and staggered to dump it into the luggage rack.

'You carrying bricks in that?' said the driver as she paid for her ticket.

'Soon I'll have enough for a garden wall,' said Deb. She loved making people laugh. The seat right next to the luggage rack was already taken, so she sat up on one of the high seats towards the back, next to a woman with a walking stick and a tiny dog on her lap.

'You've got the best seat on the bus,' said Deb, as she scratched the dog's head. 'The lap of luxury!'

'He only gets the best, this one,' said the woman. 'I cook him chicken every morning.'

'Chicken!' said Deb, and ruffled the slightly dribbly fur under his chin. 'You are one pampered pooch.'

'Have you got any pets?' asked the woman.

''Fraid not,' said Deb. 'Used to have a black Lab, but I had to leave him at home when I left.'

'Oh,' said the woman. 'Well.' There was nothing much to say about that, was there? Deb missed old Nemo, whose name showed that even thirteen-year-old boys can't tell the difference between a dog and a fish, but the landlord had said no pets, and she was in no position to argue. What would he do anyway, in her twenty square feet of space? He'd tear the place apart every time she went out. He was probably tearing her old place apart too – Derek's place, now – but that was at least satisfying to imagine.

'*C'est la vie*,' said Deb.

'*C'est la vie*,' said the woman. Deb stroked the dog again, but it was a closing statement this time, rather than a conversation starter. Her thoughts drifted back to Nemo and the way he used to sit on her feet as she watched *Strictly* on a Saturday night. She vaguely heard someone saying, 'Excuse me, love?' and didn't imagine it could have anything to do with her. But on the second, 'Excuse me, love?' she looked up.

It was the man sitting by the luggage rack. 'Sorry,' he said, 'but I think your bag's started buzzing?'

'Oh,' said Deb, 'thanks.' *Oh God.* She staggered down the centre aisle of the bus. She knew exactly which one it was: the Big Boy with the dodgy switch. It was always the first one the party guests grabbed. Bright green and fat as a marrow, it was simply not designed to be flicked on and off for hours a week, as hen parties and boozy office gatherings passed it around, and cracked questionable jokes, and sometimes just gazed, entranced, like babies around a mobile.

'Must've left my phone in there,' she said to the man when she got there. She unzipped the holdall just enough to fit her hand in and groped around, through a rabble of plastic and silicone, until she made contact with the head of the Big Boy, growling proudly at the bottom of the bag. *That's enough from you, mate*, she whispered under her breath as she found the switch. She clicked it to the right, but nothing happened. On. Off. On. Off. No difference. The Big Boy wasn't giving up that easily.

Sometimes a quick shake did the trick, bringing the wires back to their rightful place. Deb reached further into the bag, right up to her armpit, to get a better grip, and at that moment, she heard the driver shout, 'Can you sit down while the bus in in motion, please!'

Deb turned, meaning to shout back that she was doing the best she could to get this sorted, and she'd do it a damn sight quicker if he stopped yelling at her, but in turning, her elbow had pushed against the zip, and the bag was gaping open. At that moment, the bus swung into the stop on Harbour Street. As the doors folded open, Deb could only watch in horror as the whole sordid lot began to cascade down to her feet: the pink jelly Breathless Bunny, realistic flesh-toned dildos, the expensive purple silicone Intruder and the bizarre corkscrew Helter Skelter; fun-fur handcuffs, leopard-print blindfolds, a tangle of suspender belts and peephole bras. Enough lube to re-launch a whale. A leather Hanky Spanky paddle, cracked from demonstration use. And, still gripped in Deb's hand, the lime-green Big Boy, roaring like a lawnmower on a hot summer's day.

6

Deb was at the bottom of her third vodka and tonic before she was able find this remotely funny. She had scuttled into the first pub she saw, and found it hot, dark and full of good-humoured chatter. This was exactly what she needed; there were enough other people there to hide the fact that she was drinking alone. She was only grateful that – after she'd picked up the rainbow array of sex toys from the floor of the bus – she had the presence of mind to hand out her business cards to the remaining passengers. What the hell. *If life gives you lemons, make lemonade.* Or, in this case, slice the damned things nicely, and pile them into your slimline V&T.

Even so, from the tipsy comfort of her corner table, she was struggling to erase the memory of scrabbling to pick up all her wares from the bus floor, while the incoming customers tripped over them. There was only so much optimism one woman could manage on her own. The bedsit seemed a grim prospect tonight. One more drink. She shoved the holdall under the table with her foot and went to the bar.

'Same again?' asked the barman. She had the niggling suspicion that he went to school with Rob.

'Double,' said Deb. 'And a packet of peanuts.'

'Lots of calories in peanuts,' said a voice behind her. 'You'll have to watch your weight now.'

Deb's teeth automatically gripped together. She didn't need to turn around. 'I thought you went to The Ship on a Thursday,' she said. 'Or else I wouldn't have come here.'

'Oh, babe!' said Derek. 'I was only joking! I thought it would . . . you know . . . break the ice.'

'You thought the best way to break the ice was to tell me I was getting fat?'

'I never said that!' Derek started to sob. 'Oh darlin',' he said, 'I just miss you so much. Come home.'

Everyone was looking now. It was like that moment in a western when the whole bar goes silent, except that all the faces here were amused rather than suspicious. 'Piss off, Derek,' she said, and immediately wished she'd thought of something better to say. The men in this pub knew Derek. They thought he was an idiot, but he was *their* idiot. There was an audible sucking-in of breath, and one brave soul even managed a camp *oooooh*. Deb snapped her head around to see where it came from, but everyone was suddenly looking into their pints, sniggering.

'I'm not giving you the satisfaction,' she said, and snatched up her drink, swallowing it in three gulps. She put the peanuts in her pocket, and went over to collect her holdall so that she could get out of there. But the bag wasn't there. The space under her table was empty.

She turned to the two men sitting on the table next door. 'Where's my bag?' she said, but didn't wait for an answer. 'What have you done with my bag?' she shouted over at Derek, who faltered for a few seconds, so she shouted it louder.

'I SAID, WHAT THE FUCK DID YOU DO WITH MY FUCKING BAG?'

The room went quiet then, apart from an isolated cheer that quickly died. Deb stood there, shaking with fury, her blood singing in her ears.

The man at the table beside her stood up. 'There were some lads,' he said, 'over by the dartboard. I think they took it.'

'What?' said Deb.

'I'm sorry, love. I didn't realise it was yours.'

Deb looked from the man to Derek, from Derek to the man. 'What do you mean?' she said.

And then, before she even knew it, she had slammed the door behind her, and was running towards the sea.

Twenty-three minutes past midnight. West Beach was silent, and the sea was lapping high up on the beach. Had Deb known it was high tide? She thought not, but then here she was, at exactly the right time.

She was too drunk to swim, and too tired. She took off her sandals, rolled up her jeans, and began to paddle, crying now. The water was as smooth as silk. Deb sniffed and ran her knuckles under her eyes to clear up the spilt mascara. Force of habit, even though there was no one there to see.

But then she realised that another figure had waded into the water beside her. Derek? No. It was a woman, her skirt tucked voluminously into her knickers.

'Evening,' she said. Deb squinted. It was the woman she kept seeing on the beach, without the sun-hat and notepad this time, but recognisable by her wiry frame.

'Evening,' said Deb. She lifted her foot and kicked the water, watching it ripple in the moonlight.

'What would we do without the sea?' said the woman, and Deb snorted and smiled, just a little.

And then, a third pair of feet waded in, and Maisie's voice said, 'Can't an insomniac paddle in peace these days?'

7

Deb swam in just far enough for her feet to touch the ground, and then waded the rest of the way back to shore. She twisted her wrap into a halterneck, hauled herself up to sit on one of the groynes, and lit a cigarette. The smoke bloomed around her and wafted over the beach.

Maisie was still going, of course. Her orange bathing cap was bobbing just a few metres away from the shore, and next to her was Ann, who had introduced herself mid-paddle last night, and was quick to say how envious she was of Deb and Maisie's swims; how she wished she could do the same herself.

'You just put on your cossie and get in,' Deb had said. 'No secret to it.'

'No,' said Ann, 'I suppose there isn't. It's just . . . well, it sounds silly when I say it . . . It's been so long.'

'You don't forget how to do it,' said Deb. 'It's the same sea.'

'Probably more polluted,' said Ann.

'Probably,' said Deb. 'Try not to swallow too much of it.'

'And it's the practicalities that worry me,' said Ann. 'Where do I get changed? What do I bring? How do I make sure my stuff is safe while I'm in the water? I mean, I'd never leave my handbag on the beach normally.'

'Don't bring your handbag,' said Deb. 'Or your phone. You just need a towel and a few quid for a cup of tea afterwards, if you like. Maisie always has a lot more than that, mind.'

'It's pretty safe,' said Maisie, ignoring this. 'I just leave my things on the beach and it's always there when I get back.'

'Still,' said Ann. 'It's hard not to worry.'

'Probably best you don't swim, then,' said Deb, who had a loathing of fussy people, and got the distinct sense that Ann would attention-seek like this forever if she didn't shut it down. 'You wouldn't be able to enjoy it.'

'Why don't you swim with us tomorrow?' said Maisie, with a careful gentleness that Deb felt was an admonition. 'We can show you the ropes.'

'Is it like a club, then?' said Ann. 'Do you have certain meeting times?'

'It's not a club,' said Maisie. 'Deb and I just happen to swim on the same beach every day.' *Hang on*, Deb wanted to say, *it's more than that!* But she knew, at the same time, that it wasn't. It was just her and Maisie, who would never give each other a second thought if it weren't for the fact that they happened to both be chasing the high tide. Except that wasn't quite true. It seemed like Maisie wouldn't give Deb a second thought if they never bumped into each other again; but Deb would remember Maisie, perhaps forever. The unevenness of this friendship bit her.

After the midnight paddle, Deb had gone home and settled herself in for a restless, dry-mouthed night in her lopsided bed, telling herself that Ann was unlikely to turn up to swim the next day anyway. She knew the sort: far too worried about getting everything right to get anything done at all. Ann would be better off buying a member pass to the local swimming baths, where she could complain to the manager if the exact precision of her needs was not met. There were changing cubicles and lockers at the municipal pool, and a hot shower to rinse the chlorine out of your hair. If that was your sort of thing – each to their own – then you were welcome to it.

But here was Ann this morning, her thin white legs protruding from a one-piece bathing suit that, judging by its paintbrush splashes of colour and ruched bra cups, was at least thirty years old. She had brought a hand-luggage bag for her towel and clothes, and had not only padlocked it shut, but had also secured it to the groyne with a bicycle chain. She was wearing the key in a plastic pocket around her neck, but said that she 'might invest' in a combination lock if she decided to swim more regularly.

Despite all of this ridiculous behaviour, Maisie was looking after Ann with a level of care that she had never shown to Deb, walking alongside her until she was waist-deep, and then carefully talking her into submerging her torso, and taking her first few strokes. Deb, who thought that Ann looked like an anaemic fish flapping her mouth open and shut to protest at the cold, lost the will to live at this point and swam off on her own. She'd done what she felt was an impressive front crawl all the way out to the low tide buoy, where she had floated for a while to indicate how relaxed and free she was in the water – Maisie had noticed neither of these things. Now, Deb was back and on the beach while Maisie was still coaching Ann into leaving the part of the water where her feet could touch the ground. What was the point in spending all this time trying to be Maisie's equal, if Ann could come along and suck up all her attention, just by being helpless?

Well, Maisie was welcome to her. She would get fed up soon enough if she couldn't dip that orange cap into the saltwater and pound off towards the horizon on her own. *It won't take long for her to realise that I'm much less trouble*, thought Deb, who was never any trouble to anyone. She thought she might allow herself a second fag, under the circumstances.

Their section of the beach was noticeably busier than usual. They were only a couple of weeks away from the school summer holidays now, and some people were already taking advantage of the summer weather. In front of her, two middle-aged men in shorts and deck shoes were shucking a pile of oysters and drinking expensive bottled beer. Probably down from London, just for the day, and pleased with themselves for thinking of it. Deb wondered what their wives were like. Better than her, she supposed. Lithe and clever, with careers of their own and children who sought them out for advice on dinner-party recipes and which tiles to choose for their newly fitted kitchens. She wondered what it was like to have children that admired you. The boys showed her the same unquestioning, grateful, sloppy love as Nemo the Labrador did, because that's what boys were like. But Cherie? Cherie did nothing more than use her as a marker to measure how far she'd come.

That would all change for a few weeks, after the holidays started, and she would need her old mum again when the child minder broke up for the summer. Perhaps Nanna wouldn't have as much time this year, though, now that she had to work to keep a roof over her own head. She was already failing miserably at that. She had lost an hour on the phone this morning, listening to her area manager cooing sympathetically at the loss of all her demonstration models, saying *Awww* and *Poor you*, before stating quite firmly that they were Deb's responsibility and the company could not replace them. *Sorry, love.*

Maisie and Ann were wading back out of the sea, and they climbed up the steep shingle beach to dry off next to Deb.

'Good swim?' Deb asked.

'I'm not sure,' said Ann, who was fiddling with the bike lock, and then the key pouch around her neck, and then the padlock, just to get at a threadbare brown towel.

'She's getting there,' said Maisie. 'Perhaps she'll agree to take her feet off the ground next time.'

Deb was glad that Maisie found this funny, rather than, say, needy, childish and entirely pathetic. Ann was doing the grandmother-on-the-beach thing of trying to hold a towel with one hand and remove her swimming costume with the other. 'You should set up a cubicle,' she was saying, while squirming to inch the wet fabric down over her hips. 'It wouldn't take much. Then we could all change in privacy.'

'I just go home wet,' said Deb, 'and Maisie has her . . . whatever it is.' Maisie was already zipped into the extraordinary garment, and was serenely removing her wetsuit as if she were shrugging off a silken robe.

'What about the winter?' said Ann. 'What do you do then?'

'I'll put a dressing gown on,' said Deb, who really hadn't thought about it, but was now imagining riding her bike through Whitstable in a damp towelling robe, with her bare legs being whipped by freezing winds. 'I don't know. Or I'll get a wetsuit like Maisie.'

'Surely it would be better to change *in situ*,' said Ann, who was clearly more keen on problem-solving than making friends.

'We just don't need the hassle,' said Deb.

'Well if this were to become some kind of club . . .' said Ann.

'Who said anything about a club?'

'Oh well,' said Ann, who was now applying clouds of talc to her legs, still one-handed. 'I just meant to say that other people might like to join in too. You know: put up a card in the newsagent window; set up a page on Facebook or something. If we collected subs, we could buy things like a changing booth, which would make it a lot nicer.' She pulled on a pair of greying knickers under the towel, and then her signature floral skirt.

'No,' said Deb. 'This is not a club. This is just me and Maisie swimming.'

Ann pulled a blue t-shirt over her head, and then released the towel from underneath it. She shrugged and raised her hands defensively in front of her face, as if being attacked. 'Understood!' she said. 'Just a suggestion.'

Deb, who hated passive aggression in all its virulent forms, would have told her where to stick her stupid talcum powder (*on a beach, for God's sake*) right then and there were it not for Maisie finally emerging from her changing cocoon, and saying, 'Anyone's welcome to join us, but I'd rather not turn it into hard work.'

'Fine,' said Ann. She seemed happy once Maisie had declared on an issue. Deb wasn't, though; in fact, she was just about to say, 'No, it's *not* fine,' when she realised that Maisie was glancing over to the far side of the beach, and Deb followed her gaze. Two policemen were stalking over the shingle, looking intently at the shoreline. Each of them appeared to be carrying a plastic sack. They nodded politely to the women as they watched.

'What are you searching for?' said Maisie. 'Not body parts, I hope.'

One of the officers smirked, and they exchanged a glance. 'In a manner of speaking . . .' he said, and opened his sack.

Maisie peered in. 'Oh goodness!' she said, and reeled back, laughing. 'I wasn't expecting that!'

'What is it?' said Deb.

The policeman grinned and offered her the open mouth of the sack. 'They're all along the beach,' he said. 'No one knows how they got here. We're trying to gather them up before any kiddies find them.'

Inside the sack was a jumble of colour, and it took a few seconds for the realisation to dawn on Deb: here were the contents of her black holdall, her too-expensive-to-replace demonstration models, all waterlogged and draped with seaweed. The Big Boy was crowning up through them, still proud despite the sand clinging to its bulbous peak.

'Oh,' said Deb. She imagined those thieving bastards moving from disappointment to high humour when they opened the bag. They must have run along the beach, hurling them as they went. Or maybe they dumped the whole lot off West Quay and they all washed in overnight. She was on the verge of saying, *They're mine!* and taking the lot of them home with her, to wash their faces like children and dry them out on newspaper. None of them would work again, but she could get by with them until she could afford to replace them, one by one.

But then she felt Ann peering over her shoulder, saying, 'Disgusting!' and although she could merrily find the defiance to disagree, she couldn't be certain that Maisie wouldn't feel the same. If nothing else, it would mean saying out loud that *this* was her job, *this* was the best she could get. She hadn't been ashamed of it before, but now, well. She couldn't imagine Maisie ever having to sell sex toys to make ends meet. And God only knew what Ann did for a living, but she suspected it required more than your basic five passes at GCSE.

And besides all that, sometimes you had to know when something was over. It was over long before her whole stock was lost at sea off Reeves Beach. The truth was, it had all seemed a lark from a distance, playing the bawd to a roomful of giggling hens. But then there were the bus rides there and back, and the evenings spent pretending to be the life and soul of the party when everyone else in the room was five drinks down and not really in any fit state to concentrate on your sales patter.

There was the queasy line she had to tread, of pretending to be one of the girls while getting them to spend more than they could afford. The Power Sellers all processed their orders on the night they were made, so that when they got the inevitable calls the next day, sheepishly asking to cancel, they could say, *Sorry, hon, order's already gone through*. Deb couldn't do this to them. She gave them a good day's grace to change their minds, and so she was 'not meeting her earnings targets' as the area manager put it. In normal language that meant that she was only just scraping by.

More than anything, it all just made her feel old. She was not one of the gang; she was one of their mothers' gang, and pretending otherwise felt like staging a full West End show. The things they talked about! Until she started turning up to these parties, she thought she could keep up with the best of them, given half the chance and a partner who didn't make her recoil in horror. But now, after a couple of months at this, she thought she might give up on sex altogether – gratefully so – and maybe take up something more soothing, like Sudoku or crochet. Perhaps she wasn't leaving Derek for something better; perhaps she was just leaving him to be shot of men.

So she looked mildly over the assorted sex toys and mentally bid them farewell, while saying, aloud, 'Oh for God's sake, Ann, there are worse things!'

Ann made a huffing noise, crossed her cardigan tightly over her chest as if it were some kind of armour, and said, 'Well, time for me to go.'

Maisie walked with Deb as she wheeled her bike back to the centre of town. This, at least, was reassuring. Every now and then, there would be a jelly-coloured object on the tide-line, and Maisie would squint over and say, 'Is that another one? Yes, I think so.'

But Deb was too distracted to reply, because she was too busy trying to hold what was left of her savings account in her mind, while she subtracted her rent, and food, and treats for the grandchildren, and having a bit aside for Christmas.

Six months, she reckoned, if she was careful. Before rock bottom. Before she had to go crawling back to Derek.

8

Over the next week, the high tides shifted across the afternoon, so they swam at two, then three, then four. This was always the worst phase of the tide table, cutting the days in half and making it hard to achieve anything much. You spent all day waiting to swim, and then there was no point in starting anything once you got home. Or at least that's what Deb told herself. She really should be out looking for a job, but everything she looked at would mean that she couldn't look after Cherie's kids over the summer, and that, in turn, would mean kissing goodbye to what little time she got with them. She just couldn't bring herself to do it.

It didn't help that the sun was out now, properly out, blazing its heat through her window from early in the morning until bedtime. Unable to sleep in a warm bedroom, she was always disoriented in the summer. She thought this would get better without a hot, snoring body in the bed next to her, but somehow her churning brain conspired to wake her up anyway, dredging up anxious thoughts at two a.m., and then again at four. She tried to adopt the voice she used to use on the children, and tell herself, 'Put it out of mind, love. Can't do anything about it,' but it had no effect whatsoever. She wondered now if it ever comforted the kids, either.

The only thing that washed it all away was swimming. The beach was so dry that the shingle had turned pale, but the sea was delicious – blue and serene, and surprisingly clear. It was barely even cold any more, or perhaps Deb had finally got used to it.

Better still, there was no sign of Ann after that first, pernickety swim. Maisie didn't mention it, and neither did Deb; perhaps it was just a bump in the road. Life might be good again after all. Deb started using sun cream before she swam because her shoulders had now gone through the freckly stage and were beginning to turn leathery. Cherie had seen them last week while Deb was loading her daughter's washing machine, and had given a nod of sour disapproval and said, 'That's the fruit of *your* sunbathing,' as if sunbathing were a special, wicked invention of her own, like smoking and divorce.

Maisie was still wearing her wetsuit every day, despite the hot weather. 'It must be like a greenhouse in that thing,' said Deb one afternoon as they were getting ready.

'It is,' said Maisie, 'but to be honest, it means I don't ever have to shave anything, so I'm suffering it.'

Deb loved this about Maisie – her ability to be so suddenly, hilariously honest. It felt like there were two versions of her: the serene, controlled, distant one that existed most of the time, and then the one that only popped out sometimes, like a jack-in-the-box, to reveal sharp, gritty humour. She always folded this version back away too quickly for Deb's liking, as if she had surprised herself with its sudden truth.

They waded into the water together, and soon Maisie dived forwards and struck out to sea in her mechanical front crawl, while Deb floated, and trod water, and rolled onto her back while she felt the sun bounce off the surface of the sea and onto her face. It was like a millpond on days like this, so impossibly smooth. A herring gull drifted overhead and landed on the water next to her. Deb stayed as still as she could to avoid disturbing him, but soon she heard Maisie churning back towards them, and that was enough for the gull, who squawked and beat his enormous wings to launch into the air.

Deb watched him fly towards the shore – probably to hunt for abandoned chips on the shingle – and then her eye was drawn to the part of the beach where she had thrown down her bag. Someone was sitting there, writing in a notebook. Ann. Well, at least she was back in her skirt and cardigan, and not attempting to swim. Next to her was a someone else, a woman in a floral cossie, standing on one leg to pull on her sea shoes; and behind her, another figure, standing with arms crossed, a towel draped over her shoulders.

Ann waved stiffly at Deb, and then said something to the woman next to her, who waved too, and began to splash in. She was followed by the other figure, a teenager, who reluctantly removed the towel from her shoulders and hobbled over the stones.

Maisie swam up next to Deb and flipped her goggles over her swimming cap.

'What in God's name is that?' said Deb.

Maisie squinted. 'People swimming,' she said.

'No,' said Deb, 'it's more than that. She's up to something.'

Maisie tutted. 'You don't own the monopoly on swimming.'

'I know . . .' said Deb, but she was interrupted by the woman in the floral swimsuit, who was now wading towards them, submerged up to her neck.

'Hi!' she called out, and immediately had to spit out a mouthful of water. She broke into peals of laughter and began to doggy paddle. 'That's better,' she said. 'I'm Julie? I think you're in charge of the club?'

Deb eyed Maisie sideways. 'What club?'

'The sea-swimming club? Have I got the wrong person? Only I met up with the secretary on the beach and I thought she pointed your way.'

'Secretary?' said Deb.

'Ah,' said Maisie. 'I think there's been a bit of a misunderstanding here. We do swim – and you're more than welcome to join us – but we're not a club as such.'

'Oh,' said Julie. 'It's just that it said on the advert . . .'

'What advert?' said Deb.

'In the newsagent's window. That's why I came along.'

Just then there was a noise that sounded a lot like screaming coming from the shore, and the three women turned to see that the teenage girl was now ankle deep in the sea, and was squealing at the cold. Her body was tense, and she was hopping in the water, making an enormous, attention-hungry cacophony to announce her arrival.

'Bloody hell,' said Deb, 'don't tell me she's joined too.' She swam into the shallows, saying, 'It's not that bad,' as she passed the girl, and then stalked over to Ann, hoping that she dripped seawater onto that infernal notebook.

'What have you done?'

40

Ann looked up, blinking into the light from under her white sun-hat. 'Hello, Deb,' she said, brightly.

'Where did these people come from?'

'Well,' said Ann, 'it struck me that you can't have a club without members. And also –' she was pouring tea from an old blue flask into a plastic cup – 'I don't think I'm really much of a swimmer, to be honest. I can be far more useful organising things.'

'We don't need to be organised,' said Deb. 'We're quite alright on our own, thank you.'

There were footsteps behind her, and Maisie was by her side, peeling off her orange cap. Ann passed her a towel, and she wiped her face with it. 'It appears we have a club,' she said, her eyes half gleeful, half reproachful.

'I've been trying to think of a name,' said Ann. 'I wondered about The East Kent Ladies' Sea-Bathing Society.'

'No,' said Deb.

'If we must have a club, then we should at least keep it simple,' said Maisie.

Deb shot her a bewildered look. 'That's not the point. We didn't want a club in the first place. We don't want a stupid title. And we don't want you sitting there on the beach with your sodding notebook.'

'Well you'll need someone to collect the subs,' said Ann, 'and to look after everyone's bits and pieces. We'll be a magnet for thieves, once the word gets out.'

Deb meant to say something decisive at this point, but it just came out as an animal growl. Maisie placed her hand on Deb's elbow.

'Listen, Ann,' she said gently, 'I think it's lovely to invite other people in to swim with us. But I would personally be against collecting money. After all, it's a free resource; that's the beauty of it.'

'But I've already incurred expenses! And what about the changing booth?'

'What expenses?' said Deb, who had found her human voice again, but was disappointed that it was so shrill.

'The newsagent charged me a fiver to put a card in the window!'

'Well no one asked you to interfere!'

'All right!' said Maisie. 'Deb has a point, Ann. You took it upon yourself to place the advertisement.' Ann began to flap her mouth open. 'BUT,' continued Maisie, 'I'm happy to reimburse you the money if there was any misunderstanding from our last conversation.'

'Well . . .' began Ann.

'However,' said Maisie, 'I'm going to make it very clear now that this will be an end to the collecting of monies. If people want somewhere to change, they can do so in the public toilets, just behind the beach huts.

'Can you believe,' she said to Deb, 'that Julie has three children at home, and none of them at school yet? She says she ran out of her house as soon as her husband got home! And Chloe there is studying for GCSEs. Poor kid. What an age to be.'

Deb, who couldn't but have a twinge of sympathy for both of these things, turned back to the sea, where Julie was happily breaststroking backwards and forwards, and Chloe was still squealing, but now with delight.

9

Once she got out of the sea, Chloe had wrapped a towel around her waist, pulled on a baggy t-shirt and said, 'Bye, thanks,' all the while keeping her eyes fixed firmly on the ground.

'Would you like to join us for a coffee?' said Maisie.

Chloe shook her head, tried to thrust her hands into pockets that weren't there, and then nearly ran up the beach on embarrassed legs.

'Aw bless her,' said Deb. 'Difficult age.'

'Yeah,' said Julie. 'Mind you, it means we can go to the pub instead.'

'That's a far better idea than coffee,' said Maisie. 'If I'm out without the kids, might as well make the most of it.'

After an hour in The Neptune, the white weatherboard pub whose tables sat directly on the shingle beach, Deb began to think that a club wasn't such a bad idea after all. Perhaps it was the vodka and tonics. But perhaps, also, it was the fact that not everyone was like Ann.

They basked in the intense early evening sun while the pub garden bustled around them. Whitstable's squadrons of estate agents were out in force, sitting at the picnic sets with the sleeves of their smart shirts rolled up; holidaymakers looked dreamily across the beach, and hatched wild plans to sell up and move down here. The sky was still clear blue and the sea sparkled so invitingly that it was almost tempting to go in for a second time, although Deb knew it would be playing its most dastardly trick, inviting you to swim in it while actually being knee-deep. This was the time you sent the kids in to play, knowing that they wouldn't suddenly be out of their depth.

Julie had come back from the bar with a tray of drinks and several bags of crisps stuffed under her arms, two packets of peanuts in her pockets, and a bag of Bacon Fries 'for luck'.

Maisie had considered the idea of a drink carefully, and had settled on a scotch and soda. Ann had asked for 'just the soda' and had only surrendered to the addition of a slice of lemon under duress. Julie drank white wine from a large glass, beaded with condensation. She took a long, slow sip from it, and Deb thought she'd never seen anyone enjoy something more.

'Are we going to line up the shots then?' Julie said, and laughed when she saw everyone's horrified faces. 'Don't worry. As soon as I've finished this, I've got to get back for bedtime, or else there'll be hell to pay.'

'I have to ask,' said Maisie. 'How on earth did you manage to have three children in such quick succession?'

'Do we need to explain that to you?' grinned Deb.

'To be honest,' said Julie, 'I don't really know myself. I mean the first one was planned, but the other two just . . . happened. Minty, my youngest, was a bloody awful shock.'

'God,' said Deb. 'My three were bad enough, but there's nine years between the eldest and youngest. Every time one started school, I had another one.'

'If I can just get one of them into school,' said Julie, 'then we can start to get on top of things.'

'As long as you don't fall again in the meantime.'

'Oh don't,' said Julie, biting her bottom lip as if this were in the hands of the fates, and absolutely beyond her control.

'Have you got any children, Ann?' said Maisie.

'No,' said Ann. 'I'm afraid not.'

'Nor me,' said Maisie, rather hurriedly. 'When I hear these two talking, I feel pretty sure I couldn't have managed any, either.'

'No,' said Ann. 'Well. I never got to find that out. I live with my mother, actually.'

It was hard not to pick up the defiance in the word 'actually', as though anyone had implied something that contradicted this, although Deb wasn't sure exactly what. Perhaps that Ann wasn't loveable?

'Oh,' said Julie, 'that must be nice.'

Ann shrugged. 'It's my life,' she said. 'Not everything's a choice.'

'Amen to that,' said Julie, and drained the bottom of her glass before standing up and saying, 'It's been lovely to meet you ladies, but sadly I think I may have pushed my luck too far for one day. I'll be back when I can, I suppose.'

'We're here every day,' said Maisie. 'Come whenever you like.'

'I'll post the club times on the Facebook page,' said Ann, and Deb was just on the edge of saying, 'What Facebook page?' but she stopped herself and said, instead, 'Let me know the address for that, will you?' It took every ounce of self-restraint she had ever possessed.

'I ought to go too,' said Ann, and took a last, disinterested sip on her soda water before standing up, nodding rather stiffly and walking out towards the road.

'That was very tactful for you,' said Maisie.

'I s'pose it does no harm, really,' said Deb, rounding up the last crumbs of crisps in the open bag. 'I mean, if Ann's declaring certain nights "club nights", then I guess that means we have the sea to ourselves the rest of the time.'

'We get the weird times of day,' said Maisie. 'They're all ours.'

'And when Ann wants to sit and watch us from the beach, she declares it a club night, and everyone's happy.'

'That almost sounds workable. One for the road?'

'Why not,' said Deb. The sea was in full retreat now. It would be a couple of hours before the seabed was exposed, revealing expanses of mud and strange, gnarled oysters, too big and ugly to make their way onto the fish stands in the harbour. For now, it just looked flat and serene, turning silver in the waning light. Maisie was soon back holding glasses clinking with ice.

'You know,' she said, 'I enjoyed meeting new people today. When I moved down here, I promised I'd keep myself to myself. I suppose that was never realistic anyway, but now I see it was impossible.'

'Sounds like you were nursing a broken heart,' said Deb.

'Me? No. I have no right to a broken heart.'

'When you're the one who leaves, your heart was probably broken in the first place,' said Deb. 'For me, leaving was the only thing that seemed like it might fix it. I'd tried everything else.'

'Did it work?'

'In one way, yes,' said Deb. 'I've started to like myself again, a bit. I hated the stupid cow who stayed with that idiot, making excuses for him and smiling sweetly so as not to make any trouble.'

'Not to make any trouble?' said Maisie.

'You know what I mean. It wasn't worth the hassle after a while. But anyway, now there's a whole load of other things to worry about. I've got my freedom from Derek, but I've lost a whole load of other freedoms. For as long as you're the saintly, suffering mother, you've got the moral high ground, haven't you?'

'Oh I gave up the moral high ground long ago. I married a man who would happily live on bread and water, and never go out, and sit quietly at home every night reading a book. He would never dream of switching on the TV; he just didn't feel the need.' She let her fingers wander over the rim of her glass, and looked over at Deb. 'Sorry, I know it's not the same. I didn't have much to walk away from, by the end. But sometimes I was just desperate for some noise in the house. It was like living in a church. I would make him take me out, just so that I could drink a bottle of wine on my own while he looked desperate to leave.'

'Did he love you?' said Deb, who had never heard Maisie talk like this before and was almost high on the flow of information. 'I mean, by the time you left? Did he still love you?'

'I thought so,' said Maisie. 'I thought I was being the big, hard-headed woman, breaking his heart to save mine. But do you know what's really split me in two? He never cared in the first place. He didn't beg me to come back. He didn't come running down here after me. He didn't even bother to tell our friends. He just let me leave, and carried on with his life.'

'*God,*' said Deb, and drained the last of the tonic from her ice cubes.

'So it turns out I'm pretty bloody heartbroken after all,' said Maisie.

They almost hugged when Maisie got up to leave, but Deb thought better of it at the last moment. She had already risen to her feet by then, so she leaned over and kissed her friend on the cheek, and hoped it looked sophisticated, rather than one-too-many. Perhaps that didn't matter anyway, given that Maisie looked decidedly less sure-footed than usual as she wove her way through the tables and disappeared into the darkness of the beach.

The pub's yard was still packed with drinkers left over from a day at the beach. Red shoulders were glowing in the sodium lights, and there was talk of chips, a curry on the way home, a midnight swim. *Good luck with that, mate.* Deb thought she really ought to go home, rather than sit here on her own, but first she pushed her way through the crowded bar to the loos, where she sat in the cubicle for quite some time, gazing at the brown backs of her hands, and feeling the vodka tingling in her cheeks. Just for tonight, it didn't all feel quite so impossible, perhaps.

As she eased her way back out of the narrow corridor made by the bar, she caught the eye of every man in turn and said, *Oops, excuse me! Sorry! Coming through!* One man was blocking the door with his back to her, so she placed both her hands on his hips and gently turned him as she eased past him. 'Steady on!' he said. 'You have to buy me dinner first!'

'*You* have to buy *me* dinner for that kind of service,' said Deb, and they both smiled, and he said, 'Can I get you a drink?'

It was a cheesy line in the first place, and far too smooth, and he'd clearly pulled this trick before, but Deb was happy to fall for it tonight.

10

The thing that made Deb cringe the most – out of a fairly long list – was that she had given the man her phone number. Rick. She had given Rick her phone number. At least she knew his name; that was something. He wasn't a complete stranger. But she had passed on her now-redundant business card (*Deborah Winters – Parties with a 'bang'!*), and he had examined it, raised his eyebrows, and said, 'The whole town knows my number, babe.'

God only knew what that meant; the man was clearly an idiot. This had second place on her list of cringes: she had stayed pointlessly faithful to Derek through thirty-three years of marriage, and what did she do once she'd left him? Embark on a wild, romantic, rollercoaster affair? No, she had a one-night stand with an idiot. Way to go, Deb. That's really socking it to him.

She had also (number three) taken Rick back to her grotty flat. The only saving grace here was that the neighbouring street light, which filled the whole place with an aggressive orange glow each night, meant that she didn't need to turn on her own lights, and so perhaps – just perhaps – he might not have noticed how small it was.

And (four) she had been embarrassingly keen. It was just a long time since she had felt the urgency of sex, that desire to touch and be touched. His skin had been smooth and his arms were muscular. She wished she hadn't felt compelled to bite one of his biceps (*oh God*). But he smelt so good, the aftermath of too much aftershave on warm skin. She wanted to breathe him in. He had even let go of his big-man act, eventually, after he tried to pick her up and lean against the wall. He lost his balance and they had both slid, sideways, to the floor. He laughed then, and she felt that for a few brief moments they had actually made contact. Other than the obvious kind of contact, which happened three times.

Thank God he left when it was over. Of course, he'd been a prat about it: 'Sleepovers are for teenage girls,' he'd said, as if anyone had asked him to stay. But better that than waking up next to him the following morning. What was even the etiquette for that, these days? Did you make them a round of toast and wave them off towards the bus stop? Or were you supposed to repeat the whole business again the next morning, but without the anonymity of the night?

What rankled most of all was that she had looked forward to this moment when she left Derek. The reality was not how she'd imagined it. She thought there might be a flirtation, a slow seduction. She pictured herself sitting up in bed afterwards, like in French films, smoking a cigarette and talking about life and love, and the meaning of it all. Under the right circumstances, and received by a kind pair of ears, she thought she might be capable of some rather stylish philosophising. But perhaps that dream wasn't about the sex at all. Perhaps what she really wanted was someone to think she was worth listening to.

The tides had shifted enough to allow an early morning swim. These were normally Deb's favourite days: a six-thirty swim didn't pose her any difficulties as she rose early out of long habit, and the tide would return by seven p.m. ready to do it all over again. This morning, she was tempted to skip the early tide and wait for the evening, but then she thought how the sea seemed to make her forget life for as long as she was submerged in it, and she needed that now more than ever.

The sun was low in the sky, and the beach was shaded by the row of huts. The water was a still, dark blue, but Deb thought there was some residual heat in it from yesterday. She took a few strokes on her front, stretching her arms and legs to their furthest reaches, and then rolled onto her back to look for Maisie. No sign of her this morning, which was unusual. At least she wouldn't risk spilling out all the sordid details of her evening.

Deb hobbled out over the stones and put on her sarong and Darren's old hoodie. He had long ago rejected it when the fashion moved on, but Deb found it comforting on cold mornings. Her phone was in the pocket, and there was a text from Rob: a picture of a beach in Australia with big milky-blue waves and a tiny dot amid them. *Catching the waves, Mum,* it said. She expanded the photo and squinted. Was that him? She bloody hoped not, as she knew for a fact he'd scrimped on the travel insurance.

She found her bike propped where she'd left it against a beach hut, and was just about to carry it onto the path when something made her start.

'Oh God,' she said, bringing her hand to her chest. 'You almost made me scream.'

'I wasn't doing anything,' said Chloe, closing the book that was in her lap and jumping down from the deck of a yellow and white hut. 'I was just sitting here.'

'Of course you weren't, love. I just didn't see you. How long have you been here?'

'Not long,' said Chloe. 'You were already swimming when I arrived, so I couldn't say hello.'

'It's fine,' said Deb. 'You didn't do anything wrong.'

'I know,' said Chloe.

Deb took a breath. She remembered these kinds of conversations from Cherie's long teenage years, which she sometimes believed had yet to end. Everything she said caused offence.

'Reading something good?'

'*Carrie.*'

'Oh. That's . . . fun.'

'Not really,' said Chloe. 'But I like the way her period is a catalyst for homicidal rage.'

'Yeah, I was like a harridan on my period too.'

A flicker of disdain from Chloe. No. Not funny. Not a laughing matter.

'I think we've internalised a lot of negative messages about our menstrual cycle, invented by men to embarrass us into submission.'

'You're probably right, love,' said Deb. This girl was a terrifying robot that spat out words like bullets. 'I didn't mean to make light of it.'

Chloe shrugged, and Deb remembered it then, the feeling of trying to articulate all the serious, adult thoughts that gathered in her mind, and meeting benign mockery, or worse. Her own father would just interrupt her mid-sentence and say, 'Pipe down,' and that would be the end of it; and her mother, when she got the chance, would whisper, 'The boys will never go for you if you talk like that.'

Come to think of it, Derek had told her to pipe down a good few times too, whenever she started to have an opinion on anything he didn't want to have to think about. *I learned to pipe down all right*, she thought. *In fact, I learned to get out of your life altogether.*

And here she was, doing just the same to Chloe, making a joke of her serious thoughts to keep her quiet. She felt like she was part of a machine that churned out endless unhappy women, all identical and separate. There was another thing she would have to learn: how to resist that.

'To tell you the truth, love,' she said, 'I was never allowed to talk about anything like that when I was a girl. All had to be kept secret, see, in case the men found out about it. We were supposed to go around pretending our bellies didn't ache and then soak our knickers in a bucket at night so that no one saw. My mum didn't even say the word "period" to me; she just sort of mimed it. I had to look it all up in a book when my daughter came to that age. How's that oppression for you?'

She watched Chloe's eyes widen ever so slightly, and realised that, finally, she was impressed, if only because Deb was clearly a specimen of some bygone age, a Year Zero of the feminist battle.

'What did you tell your daughter?' she said.

'The whole lot: ovaries, vaginas, fallopian tubes. I used "uterus" instead of "womb" and told her that sex would be fun once she was old enough to enjoy it. She told me I was an embarrassment and hid in her bedroom for two days. Only came out when her father said he'd take her to Topshop to buy her some new clothes.'

'Oh,' said Chloe.

'Right,' said Deb. 'You can't win 'em all.'

'You can learn it from an app now,' said Chloe. 'Saves talking about it.'

Deb shrugged. 'I reckon we should talk about it, though. I reckon all that embarrassment is worth it. In the long term.' She thought for a while about how much it was best to say, at this stage. 'I mean, you might as well get over it at some point, because it gets a whole lot worse when you have kids.'

'I'm not having kids,' said Chloe, rather too quickly.

'Of course not, love,' said Deb, thinking, *No one thinks they will at your age.* And then, by way of changing the subject, 'What are you doing here at this time of the morning anyway?'

It was exactly the wrong way to change the subject.

'I'm on my way to school,' said Chloe.

'Clearly,' said Deb.

'I'm not bunking, if that's what you think. I'm actually bunking in the opposite direction. Dad thinks the bus leaves at six forty-five. That gives me an extra hour. I'm never late.'

'I've never heard of that one before,' said Deb.

'Yeah, well,' said Chloe. 'I'm a lark. But apparently so is my dad, so I need to get out of the house.'

'Must be cold in the winter.'

'It's all right in the bus shelter.'

'God,' said Deb, 'I don't like to think of you there, all on your own in the cold. It's like "The Little Match Girl". Will you come to mine for toast next winter? I'll let you read and not bother you.'

'Might take you up on that,' said Chloe, and for the first time there was a glint of humour there.

'What's the time now though?' said Deb, who still had an instinctive knowledge of the school bus timetable left over from her kids.

Chloe looked at her watch and said *Fuck* under her breath, then said, 'Sorry,' to Deb, and hooked her backpack over one shoulder and ran towards the town.

'Don't worry about it, love,' said Deb to the receding figure. 'Heard it all before.' She wriggled the key into her rusty bike lock (which she really must spray with WD40, if only she could remember to buy a can), and untangled the chain from the wheels of the bike. She never bothered to actually tether it to anything, because surely the only kind of idiot who would nick it was in dire need of charity. Frankly, she had pity for anyone who got the hideous old thing back to their lock-up, and then wondered who on earth would buy it. If they were that desperate, they were welcome to it. She got onto the saddle and then whispered *Bugger it*, and rang her mate at the taxi office and asked them to drive past the bus stop and take Chloe to school. There was no way she would have made that bus. Deb would settle the account later today; that's what savings were for.

She had just lifted her bike onto the tarmac path and was about to pedal towards home when she saw a familiar – and entirely stupid – truck pull up at the end of the dirt track, blocking off access to the caravan park. A fat, balding man climbed out, and said, 'Hello, love. Fancy seeing you here.'

'Piss off, Derek.'

'Oh! That's not a very nice way to speak to your old husband!'

'Ex-husband.'

'Not quite yet.'

'Did you get up early just to harass me?'

'Harass you? Nah. Me being here's got nothing to do with you. I'm on a job, in't I? Nice little earner this one. You might be seeing a bit more of me.'

'I hope not.'

Derek pretended to think for a while, a look that didn't sit naturally on his features. 'I heard a rumour,' he said, 'that you were snogging some bloke in the Neppy last night.'

'Did you now?' Deb felt her guts compress as if they were the crumple zone of her entire body and she had just slammed hard into the crash barrier. 'Don't you have anything better to do with your time than gossip about me?'

'I have friends all over town,' he said. 'They look out for me. They let me know if, say, my wife is making a display of herself and showing me up.'

'Ex-wife,' said Deb. 'I'll do what I bloody well like.'

'It's not . . .' Derek paused, clearly struggling to wrap his mouth around a word of more than one syllable '. . . dignified.'

'What would you know about dignity? I've spent my whole adult life watching you fall in and out of all the pubs in Whitstable; I've had to show my face in public knowing damned well you've slept with every tart in town. I've packed the kids into the car at all hours of the night to pick you up after you've got so drunk you've pissed yourself and passed out on the road. Believe me, I wrote the bloody book on dignity. And do you know what? I *did* meet a man in a bar last night, and I took him back to my flat, and we screwed all night. And I bloody enjoyed it. And do you want to know another thing? I'm going to do it again, and again, and again, because it's my life, and my body, and it's got nothing to do with you.'

She hadn't realised how loudly she was shouting until she stopped and heard her voice ricocheting off the beach huts. Derek had clamped his mouth shut and narrowed his eyes, which once she would have found ominous, but now, today, she could finally see it as a flesh wound that she had made, and it felt good. She straightened her bike, climbed onto the saddle, and said, 'Get out of my way, Derek. I've got better things to do than this.'

Derek stepped to one side, bowed as if she had made some kind of queenly demand, and said, 'Still, nice news about Darren's baby, eh?'

'What?' said Deb.

'About Darren's Lou, expecting. Don't tell me you didn't know.'

'Of course I knew,' said Deb, and struck off so hard that the tyres spun on the tarmac. She was damned if she would let him see her crying.

11

'You all right, Mum?'

She recognised that voice on Darren – slightly thin, minutely wavering, but full of front. She'd been hearing it since he was four years old and had decorated the bathroom wall with toothpaste because he liked the stripes; she heard it again every time he smashed her plant pots with his football, or left his PE kit at the park, or got into trouble at school for fighting in the playground and knew that she was seconds away from being called into the empty classroom by his teacher, who *just didn't understand what got into him sometimes.* She knew what had got into him: he was just like his father, subject to sudden red mists that made him angry and stupid.

She loved him, though. There was something about that voice on Darren that made her heart clench ever so slightly, because she felt for him every time he had to use it. He was always sorry in the aftermath; he just didn't think. She heard that voice all through his teens, and it never stopped pushing her buttons, because he couldn't fake it. Say what you like about Darren – and she was the first to admit that he was an utter idiot – but he was a straightforward boy, unable to hide anything. When he was sorry, he really was sorry. And he was sorry today.

'Why didn't you tell me, Darren?'

'Tell you what?' he said, but his voice squeaked at the end of the question, like the air coming out of a pinched balloon. 'Aw, Mum,' he said, 'I wasn't keeping it from you or nothing . . .'

'Or *anything*,' said Deb out of habit. He always dropped back into being a schoolboy under pressure.

'*Anything*,' mumbled Darren. 'It was just that Dad caught me at a bad time. I'd only just found out myself, and it kind of spilled out.'

'You were wetting the baby's head, no doubt,' said Deb.

'Look,' said Darren, 'it's not what you think. We had this deal, me and Lou, that we would wait until the first scan before telling anyone. And so we came back, and we'd just seen this tiny heartbeat on the screen, and we stopped off at the Cushing on our way through town. Lou was on the J2Os, and so I had a coffee. And then suddenly there was Dad, and he says, "What are you two looking so pleased about?" and so Lou says, "We're pregnant," and the minute she said it I felt bad. It only happened yesterday, Mum. I was going to ring you tonight.'

'All right,' said Deb. 'Fair enough.' She was trying very hard not to say *Why didn't you ring me last night, then?* But of course, they would have called Louisa's mum first, because that's how it works. Those little boys who think you're the whole universe, and who swear blind they'll marry you when they grow up: well, they do grow up, and they marry someone else, and then you're suddenly the mother-in-law and you have to play second fiddle to her family. She got on well with Lou, but a girl needs her own mum when she's pregnant.

'Look, Mum,' said Darren, 'now that you and Dad are . . .' He paused to choose the next word carefully. '*Separated* . . .'

'Divorced,' said Deb. 'Divorcing.'

'Okay,' said Darren. 'Well, this is how it will be, isn't it? One of you will always know things first. We can't tell you both at the same time any more. Sometimes it will be you, and sometimes it will be him.'

It should be me, thought Deb. It should always be me, every time. Because it was always me when you were growing up. I did everything for you; he only remembered you existed once a week, when he'd finally got over his Saturday morning hangover and the football was starting, and you just happened to be there at the same time as him. Everything else was me. I thought you'd at least be loyal.

'Are you pleased though, Mum? About the baby?'

'Of course I'm pleased, love. I'm over the moon for you. When's it due?'

'January. It might have the same birthday as you.'

'Poor kid,' said Deb. 'Every year its birthday will come along just as everyone's got sick of Christmas and is on a diet. But no, I *am* pleased. I don't want you to think I'm not pleased. Have you thought about where you're going to live? You can't stay where you are.'

Darren hadn't done so badly in the end. He'd got himself a proper job as the IT technician at the Community College, but although he earned a decent wage, it didn't go far in Whitstable these days. Their flat wasn't much bigger than Deb's bedsit. Lou worked as a teaching assistant in the same school, and there had been talk of doing her teacher training next year. That would be on hold now. She probably wouldn't be able to afford to go back to work for years – longer if they had more than one, which seemed likely.

'We'll have to move out of town, like everyone else does,' he said. 'We'll need a garden, and three bedrooms ideally. Now we've had the scan, we're going to start looking.'

'Well let me know if I can help, love, won't you? Is Lou keeping well? I can come round and do the washing if you like?'

Early that evening, rain broke out: big, heavy drops that almost sizzled on the concrete outside Deb's window. She could get away with skipping the seven o'clock swim, seeing as she had already swum this morning, but after bumping into Derek, and then dealing with the strange mix of joy and disappointment that Darren's news had brought, she needed to wash away the emotions of the day. Maybe Maisie would be there tonight. She got on her bike and rode over to West Beach. She loved the smell of thirsty soil drinking in the moisture, and the way the gardens glowed emerald, the feeling of water running down her face as she pedalled.

Maisie was already rolling on her swimming cap and stretching her goggles over her head.

'You're here,' said Deb.

'I'm afraid I couldn't face it this morning. I've lost my ability to drink until late and then get up early the next morning.'

'You were only out until about nine thirty.'

'What do you want me to say? I'm getting old. I suppose you were fresh as a daisy this morning.'

'I was all right,' said Deb, and immediately realised how little she wanted Maisie to know about the hours after they parted. What would she even think about a one-night stand? Maisie didn't seem the type to judge, but then Deb couldn't exactly imagine her approving, either. No matter how much time they spent together, Deb never seemed to understand her any better. They both turned to look at the sea, which was steely grey and pocked with raindrops.

'Hangovers aside, swimming in the rain always makes me feel heroic,' said Maisie.

'It's just a different way of getting wet,' said Deb.

'Barely makes any difference to me.'

The sea still had its summer warmth, but the rain had cooled the air above it. Once Deb was in shoulder-deep, she could hear the gentle rhythm it made on the surface of the water. Maisie was right: these were the moments when you felt like you were queen of the beach; like you'd earned your right to feeling possessive over it. All the tourists had run for cover and were probably drying off in one of the local pubs. But Maisie and Deb were both still here.

The shower had passed by the time they got out. Whitstable would get a good night's sleep tonight, especially once the breezes started drifting in from the sea. Deb's skin goose-pimpled for the first time in weeks, and she was looking forward to a hot bath at home, perhaps an evening wrapped up in her dressing gown, reading a novel in bed.

When she left Derek, she had promised herself that she would never let a man patronise her again, and that meant that she had to know more than they did. To this end, she was working her way methodically through the classics, and had started, randomly, with the Brontës. The language wasn't so bad, once you got into it, and she was beginning to get a feel for its rhythm, if not for its heroines, who were too easily overcome for her taste. They wouldn't last five minutes in her world. Come to think of it, she didn't think the men were worth the effort, either.

As Maisie was ensconced in her strange changing bag, Deb drifted over to the seawall where she had seen Derek that morning. There, attached to the railings with cable ties, was a piece of paper in a clear plastic envelope.

'Oh hell no!' she shouted over to Maisie.

'What?' yelled Maisie, who was in the middle of climbing out of the changing bag. 'What did you say?'

'I said, no way,' said Deb. 'Absolutely no way. Not on my bit of beach. They can bloody well keep their bloody hands off!'

'*What?*' said Maisie, who was trying to dry her face with her camping towel while stumbling up the beach towards Deb.

'I won't have it,' said Deb.

Maisie put her hand on the sign to flatten it as she read.

Canterbury City Council
PLANNING NOTICE

TOWN AND COUNTRY PLANNING (DEVELOPMENT
AND MANAGEMENT PROCEDURE) (ENGLAND)
ORDER 2010

NOTICE UNDER ARTICLE 13

The following planning application has been received,
which constitutes a major development

For: Erection of three commercial units
At: Land adjacent to West Beach, Whitstable
By: East Kent Land Management
Application number: 2017/94736/1

A copy of the application, plans, and other documents
submitted with it may be inspected at the Planning
Office, Canterbury City Council, Military Road,
Canterbury, Kent, CT1 1YW

Comments on this application are invited by 31 July

'Restaurants, I should think,' said Maisie. 'Perhaps a coffee chain.'

'Not here,' said Deb. 'They've got the whole town for that. We've got three pizza places already. We've got coffee coming out of our ears. This is the quiet bit of the beach, just where it starts to feel wild. They can't build here.'

'Well,' said Maisie. 'There's a process. This is just the application. You're allowed to make your objection. Most of these things don't ever happen.'

'MY objection?' said Deb. 'Are you seriously telling me you think it's okay?'

'Whoa,' said Maisie. 'Calm down. We don't know what it is yet. We ought to find out before we jump to any conclusions. The details will be at the planning offices.'

'We'll go tomorrow,' said Deb.

'Will we?'

'Oh, come on, Maisie. I don't speak the language like you do.'

'All right,' said Maisie. 'I tell you what, I have to go into Canterbury tomorrow anyway. I'll stop by the council offices and take a look while I'm there. That's if you trust me to report back faithfully.'

'Of course I do. It's just that I bloody knew something was up when I saw Derek here this morning. The look on his face! Sly bastard. I bet he did backflips when he realised he'd be building on my beach.'

'Well,' said Maisie. 'It hasn't happened yet.'

'And it won't,' said Deb. 'Don't you worry. He's taken everything else away from me, but he's not taking this.'

12

'I've been mulling over your comments about the naming of the club,' said Ann, who was sitting on the beach on a folding chair, notebook open in her lap.

Maisie heard Deb mutter, 'What comments?' but she was so quiet about it that hopefully Ann didn't hear. Why on earth did Deb persist with this petulant behaviour? It was entirely obvious that she and Ann were equally desperate for company.

'And in retrospect, I accept your criticisms of my original suggestion. It was perhaps a bit dated, now I look at it again. I think modern tastes are for something less formal.'

'Okay, no problem,' said Maisie, who was doing her best not to get drawn in. She looked over Ann's shoulder toward the sea, and windmilled her arms in preparation for the swim. 'How's your mother, Ann?'

Ann looked briefly confused. 'She's well, thank you. I mean, as well as you can be when you're ninety-two. I know I shouldn't generalise, really. A bit blue at the moment. She does very well, though, all things considered.'

'Does she get out much?'

'Not a great deal, no. Not since we let go of her car. Her legs aren't so good any more. But she's sharp as a tack, she really is. Bored, really, I suppose. Aren't we all?' Ann laughed, briefly, but it quickly died in the open air, and she managed, somehow, to turn it into a sort of disappointed sniff. She looked at the ground for a few moments before pushing her glasses up her nose and saying, 'So anyway, I was thinking maybe The West Beach Women's Sea-Swimming Society. I mean, I don't think it's strictly PC to say "ladies" any more, is it?'

'Well,' Maisie began to say, but her attention was distracted by someone coming onto the beach and everybody turned.

'Hi, Chloe,' said Deb, receiving the most minute wave in return, a mere flicker of the wrist.

Chloe, whispered Ann under her breath and she wrote something in her spiral notebook. 'I suppose that name's potentially exclusionary, though,' she said aloud. 'I mean, we could go with The West Beach Women's and Girls' Sea-Swimming Society. Does that sound like some kind of a club for children, though? I don't want to get caught out with any child protection issues. We would need to say something like "accompanied girls". Or perhaps it needs some kind of a legal disclaimer at the bottom: under eighteens must be accompanied by an adult.'

'But that's not fair!' said Chloe.

'At the bottom of where?' said Deb.

'Any posters we produce. And certainly on the website.'

'Website?' said Deb. 'Since when are we getting a website?'

'Well we'll need one at some point,' said Ann. 'Otherwise people will be looking for information about us, and they won't be able to find what they need.'

'I might as well just go,' said Chloe, 'if I can't swim without my parents.'

'What kind of information will people need, for God's sake?' said Deb. 'And anyway, I thought you'd already set up a Facebook?'

'Well,' said Ann, laughing her dry, knowledgeable laugh, 'I haven't set up the whole of Facebook, but I have set up a page, yes. It just carries basic information about the group. I don't think it will be enough if . . .'

'Actually, "a Facebook" is what younger people call it. They don't say "a Facebook page" or "a Facebook account". They just say "a Facebook" because they don't need to make everything like a Victorian institution for wayward girls. All right?'

'All right!' said Ann, shrinking back as if physically threatened.

'ALL RIGHT!' said Maisie, rather more firmly than she'd intended, but at least it had the desired effect of making both women fall quiet. 'Chloe,' she said to the girl, who was already stuffing her towel back into a carrier bag, 'you have no reason to leave us. Please. Ann was just thinking aloud. Weren't you, Ann?'

'Well, yes,' said Ann. 'It's nothing personal about Chloe, obviously. But I think I've raised a serious point here. Should we, for example, consider buying insurance?'

Maisie sighed. Every now and then – and it wasn't often – she missed being at work, where everybody seemed certain and steady, and people were in competition to look decisive. Decisiveness, as a quality, was not valued here, she noted. People – did she really mean women? – seemed to be in competition to be uncertain, doubtful, anxious.

It's funny what you end up missing. She had spent years railing against masculine culture at work, about the way that decisions got rushed through without anyone really considering the consequences. How ridiculous it all was, to rush around pretending that you knew everything, when it was quite clear that everyone knew nothing! Those sudden spates of late nights in the office, just so that they could all make believe that they were doing something important. She always thought she handled those times better than anyone else, because she was calmer, more measured. She could take a deep breath and think, *It's okay; this is just work*, and slog her way steadily through, while everyone else was performing a pantomime of panic and exhaustion.

So it had surprised her one night when the words she was typing started to appear on the screen as utter gibberish. She looked down and saw that her hands were shaking. No, that was not quite right. They were trying to fold themselves into tense claws, and her arms shook with the effort to control them. *I'm shutting down*, she thought. *My body is refusing to do this any more*. And at that moment, the head of her whole division had appeared behind her chair and said, far too gently, 'Are you alright, Maisie?'

'Yes,' said Maisie, 'I'm fine. I probably just need a coffee.'

She tried to laugh, but it didn't stop him from staring at her hands, which shuddered uncontrollably in her lap. 'Perhaps it's time for you to go home,' he said. 'We can take it from here. Don't worry.'

If he'd asked her to clear her desk and leave, she would have felt less shame. But no, instead she had to endure this absurd kindness. She put her handbag over her shoulder, and her manager guided her out of the building with a hand on her elbow, as though she was a confused old woman. When they got into the street, he even hailed her a taxi, and for a terrible moment she thought he was going to offer to pay. He didn't in the end, but she had to sit in the back seat and churn over the thought that all her colleagues – who panicked, and wailed, and ate junk food, and boasted that they'd worked through two solid nights without any sleep – were coping. Maisie, meanwhile, was going home in a kind of gentle disgrace, because they were afraid she would have a stroke or something, right there in the office, and they didn't want to be held responsible.

It was odd, finally, to miss them, or at least their desire to be competent. *You're just addicted to being in control,* she thought, rehearsing the words that her therapist had wrangled out of her when she was agonising over leaving Stephen. She had made the admission meekly then, because it was clear that this was the revelation that she was expected to come to, sooner or later. And, frankly, the sooner she got to it, the sooner she could be done with all this talk and get on with her life. But even now, she couldn't convince herself that it was a bad thing. After all, when she finally lost her control, what would she have left?

'We won't be buying insurance,' she said to Ann, 'because we're doing nothing more than swimming together. We shouldn't be attempting to guarantee anyone's safety in the water. We're just swimming alongside them.'

'Obviously we'd help out anyone who was drowning,' said Deb.

'That goes without saying. It's a friendly group of people who get together to swim. Nothing more.'

'But where does that leave the club?' said Ann, who had now poised her pen over the notebook as if she was readying to take a dictation. Maisie could feel the first shades of a headache gathering around her temples, and was closer than she'd like to be to telling Ann (and possibly Deb too) to shut up and leave her alone to swim in peace. Swimming was how she coped with stress. It wasn't supposed to cause it.

Instead, she sucked in a breath and said, 'If you want there to be a club, my suggestion is that it stops at the tideline. It's a social group for people who like to swim in the sea. We have nothing to do with the actual swimming. We just gather on the shore. What people do after that is up to them.'

'That's brilliant,' said Ann. 'Perfect. Elegant.'

Maisie nodded. That was one thing you could call it. The other was 'unfussy'. She had, at least, retained her talent for not saying exactly what she thought.

She was just beginning to head down the shingle and into the sea when she heard Ann say, 'So, the name . . .' and she tried not to clench her jaw as she turned back round. She had always thought that she held a profound belief in the value of community, but that belief was currently being stretched very far indeed.

'The name?' said Maisie.

'The West Beach Women's and Girls' Sea-Swimming Society.'

'Too many S's and W's,' said Chloe.

'And "West Beach" sounds a bit "West Bank",' said Deb.

Maisie sent her a look that tried to say, *Why are you getting involved?* But it didn't seem to land. Deb could be the most warm-hearted person in the world, but she turned into a school bully whenever she spoke to Ann. It was embarrassing to witness. When all was said and done, she clearly wanted a battle over Ann's ridiculous attempts at administration. Perhaps she was enjoying being part of a fight that she could win.

'But "West Beach" is correct; it's the name of the place where we swim,' said Ann.

'Where *we* swim,' said Deb. 'As far as I can see, you just take notes.'

'I watch the bags,' said Ann.

'Oh for heaven's sake,' said Maisie, and she repositioned her goggles and splashed out into the sea until she was deep enough to get her face in the water and block out the noise.

*

When she got back onto the shore, Deb and Chloe were swimming, and Julie was standing on one leg, holding on to Ann's shoulder (with Ann's expression suggesting that she hadn't consented to this), and stripping off a pair of leggings to reveal a swimming costume underneath.

'I'm late!' she said. 'I know I am. The baby puked everywhere while we were trying to do the changeover.'

'Plenty of sea left,' said Maisie, and she sat down on the beach to watch Julie tiptoeing over the shingle in bare feet, and then belly-flopping into the sea. Ann twitched her neck from side to side, and straightened her t-shirt.

'Do you work, Ann?' said Maisie.

'No,' said Ann. 'Not any more.' There was a pause while they both watched the sun sparkling on the surface of the sea. 'I used to be an archivist at the pharmaceuticals firm down in Sandwich. But then the plant shut down, and we all got made redundant. I couldn't really find anything else. And after a while – well, Mother needed me at home.'

'So you moved in with her then?'

Ann pulled her skirt over her white legs and jabbed at her glasses. 'Well, no. I'd already moved in by then. Because of . . . other reasons.'

'I see,' said Maisie.

'So anyway, this name. Deb seems adamant that the "West Beach" bit might not mean anything to some people.'

'Okay,' said Maisie.

'So I was thinking, The Whitstable and Seasalter – because actually we're nearly in Seasalter here, and I don't want anyone to feel excluded – Sea-Swimming Society, and then, in brackets underneath, For Women and Girls.'

'Say it again,' said Maisie.

'The Whitstable and Seasalter Sea-Swimming Society (For Women and Girls).'

'Well,' said Maisie, 'I think it's getting there, probably.'

'Right,' said Ann. 'Still a bit . . .?'

'Hard to pronounce.'

Ann frowned at her notebook. 'I see. Sibilant. Heavy on the S's.'

'Possibly.'

'It's funny, because I'd wondered about including Swalecliffe too.'

Maisie heard a shout from the sea, and looked up to see Julie waving her arms and shouting, 'Oi! You getting a good look, eh?'

'What?' she shouted back at the sea.

'Over there!' yelled Deb. 'We've attracted a pervert!'

At the other side of the beach a man got up and began to scramble up the steep shelf of pebbles towards the path. Maisie jumped to her feet. Running sideways along the slope, she intercepted him easily. He was clutching a backpack under his arm, and panting heavily in his effort to get away.

'Excuse me!' she called, and the man's head turned briefly to register her presence, before snapping forwards again to pretend she wasn't there. He redoubled his efforts to escape.

'Excuse me?' called Maisie again, and at this point, the man lost his footing entirely and slid onto his side. Maisie padded up and stood over him. 'Are you all right?' she said.

'Yes,' said the man, and climbed to his feet.

'In that case, can we help you at all?'

Deb was next to her now, her hair dripping over her shoulders. 'I've been watching him from the sea. He had a bloody good look at Julie while she was changing, and then he's sat and stared at us ever since.' She glared at the man, who didn't make eye contact in return.

'Is that right?' said Maisie. The man looked as though every fibre of his being wanted to run, but he knew that he couldn't defeat the treacherous gravel.

'No,' he whispered.

'What's that?' said Deb. 'I can't hear you!'

'No,' he said, slightly more loudly. 'I wanted to join the club.'

'You what?' said Deb.

'I wanted to join the club,' he said. 'But I can see I've got the wrong idea, and I'm sorry, and if you'd just let me go home now . . .' He was perhaps in his early thirties, and a little plump, with mousy hair cut short.

'Why didn't you say something?' said Deb, but then she saw the high flush on his cheeks that was spreading across his neck, and the way that his mouth was striving to form words that wouldn't come out. 'Ah,' she said. 'Not much of a talker, eh?'

Ann's footsteps crunched towards them, and she put her hands on her hips and glared at the man.

'He's not a stalker,' said Maisie. 'He just wants to join.'

'He can't join! This is a women's swimming club! And girls'. A women's and girls' swimming society.'

'Who says?' said Deb. 'Except for you, when you were writing the stupid name? I don't remember agreeing to it.' She looked around at Julie, who shrugged, and then back at Ann.

'It's patently a women's swimming club,' Ann said. 'All the members are women.'

'All five of us,' said Deb. 'One of whom doesn't bother to swim.'

'It offers a sense of safety,' said Ann. 'And besides, I'm watching the bags.'

'Which means you're not in a swimsuit, and so it's none of your business.'

'Will you both just stop this!' said Maisie. 'We don't own the sea. This man – what's your name, please?'

'Bill.'

'Bill is welcome to swim with us if he bloody well wants to. I just don't care. There may not be a beach here much longer anyway!'

She looked down and saw that, just like the time in the office, her hands were bunching into shaking, furious claws. Her first instinct was to hide them in her pockets, but the wetsuit was unforgiving, and so she tried to conceal them under each armpit instead, folding her arms across her chest. This just made her elbows shake.

'Are you all right, love?' said Julie, and Maisie tried to say, 'Yes, I'm absolutely fine,' but the words wouldn't come out properly.

'I . . . I'm ab . . . sol . . . oooot . . . ly . . .'

'Christ,' said Deb, 'let's get you home.'

Maisie wondered if perhaps this was an even greater humili-ation: not the men in the office, but these kind, concerned faces on the beach.

13

There was something shocking about seeing Maisie upset. It was probably no big thing; a slight lapse in her calm demeanour. Deb herself veered between bouts of this several times a day. But on Maisie, it was catastrophic, like witnessing a building falling down. They must have pushed her farther than they realised with their bickering. Deb was ashamed of herself. She had been treating Maisie like her mother, expecting her to smooth over the world on her behalf.

Deb had steered her off the beach, past the Windy Stores, and into Maisie's own home, with Maisie all the while saying, 'Stop it! Don't treat me like an old lady! I still have my wetsuit on!'

Maisie had vanished into the bathroom upstairs while Deb made tea. She had observed this kitchen so closely while she'd sat here with Maisie, admiring its solid, competent beauty, its luxurious simplicity. But now, her hands fumbled around it, and she was afraid that she would break one of those perfect white mugs, disrupting the whole set. Deb didn't mean to count, but Maisie had exactly twelve of everything, as if she were planning to hold one spectacular dinner party at an unspecified date in the future. Deb gazed into the caddy of green tea leaves for a while, before deciding on two mugs of Typhoo. She was pretty sure that Maisie only owned the tea bags to accommodate guests, but at least she knew what to do with them.

Maisie appeared eventually, in a linen blouse, wide trousers and bare feet, wrapping a scarf around her neck. She sat meekly at the table, sipped the tea without any complaint, and said, 'I'm sorry about earlier. I didn't mean to upset anyone.'

'You didn't,' said Deb. 'I think we upset you.'

'Don't worry about it. I forget that I have feelings at all, until they suddenly all gang up on me, and I realise I've had them all along.'

'You're a peacekeeper. You absorb everyone else's worries and forget about your own.'

'I'm a placator. It doesn't always help.'

'I don't think you placate. I think you have . . . authority.'

'Only because you and Ann squabble like children!' Maisie brought her tea to her lips, tensed her face, and then put it down again. 'Oh I'm sorry. I'm grouchy today. I'd be better off left on my own.'

'No,' said Deb, 'you're right. I don't know why she winds me up so much.'

'Same reason she winds me up. She's barged in and taken over. She didn't consider for one moment that we might not need her organisational powers.'

'There is that.'

'The difference is that I feel sorry for her. She doesn't mean to be a nuisance, but she has no idea how else to make friends.'

'She's lonely.'

'Like both of us.'

'You're not lonely,' said Deb. 'Are you?' She watched Maisie's face settle into that look of benign humour that she knew so well, and realised for the first time that it was like a mask that hid any emotion at all. Everyone would believe she was calm and wise, as long as she kept her own counsel. Deb had never thought that anything could be boiling away under that veneer.

Deb was lonely. She was lonely despite her three children, and two (and a half) grandchildren, and despite knowing the whole bloody town. She was lonely without Derek. She was lonely without resenting Derek, and scheming against him, and being disgusted by him. She was even willing to admit that bumping into Derek and starting a fight relieved the loneliness, not because it reminded her why she had left him in the first place, but because it gave her something to do. She was lonely despite having had a one-night stand, which, if nothing else, was a tiny ego boost, even if the man in question was a moron.

Maisie had moved down here away from all her friends and family, and lived like a nun as far as Deb could tell. Her husband had just kept his distance in London and hadn't made any sort of fuss at all about her leaving – how could it never have occurred to Deb that she might be lonely? But she could see it now. She could see how that face was deliberately harmless, deliberately passionless. She couldn't afford to open the floodgates, because she had no one to turn to. If she became a burden, she might be lonelier still.

'I'm lucky,' said Maisie. 'I enjoy my own company. Anyway, we need to talk about these building plans on the beach.'

'Yes,' said Deb. 'I think we do. It doesn't sound good.'

'I went to the city council this morning and read the detailed plans. You're right: it looks like they want to build a leisure complex on the caravan site, with a couple of restaurants and cafes. But there's something else, too. It's hard to interpret it clearly, but there's talk of a "temporary structure" on the beach itself.'

'A temporary structure?'

'A wooden building. It's all very carefully worded, because they're trying to make it sound like it's nothing, but it's a bar, I think – quite a big one. I spent a long time looking at the map, trying to work out where it would go, and I cross-checked today. It's on the site of the beach huts.'

'I don't understand,' said Deb. 'How can they do that? I mean, the beach is common land, surely?'

'I'm afraid not. The beach in Whitstable is privately owned. There has long been a public right of way across it, and no one has ever tried to stop people from using it, but technically they could. The people who own beach huts only own the hut itself. The beach underneath them belongs to a land-holding company. And they've clearly decided that Whitstable seafront is too lucrative to ignore.'

'But people pay forty grand for them!' said Deb. 'Are you telling me that they don't get anything more than a fancy shed for that?'

'People,' said Maisie, 'do some very silly things with their money. You know that.'

'Most of the time they're empty anyway. Even in high summer, they're all locked up.'

'I suppose it seems like a good idea when they buy their huts, and then they never get the time to actually relax in them. Same as the rest of us.'

They both sipped their tea. Deb wondered what it mattered, really. It was just a few more people on the beach; a bit more noise and bustle. Was she really just upset because Derek was the one doing the building, and his smug, officious face repelled her? Was she really that petty? 'Thing is,' she said, 'we haven't got many quiet bits on the beach. I like West Beach. It's my favourite bit. I like the way the flowers grow all over it in the summer.'

'And that you can swim there without any idiot yelling at you,' said Maisie. 'I know what you mean. For all that we sneer at Ann's insistence that she watches the bags, I must say I wouldn't leave them in plain sight nearer the town centre. The truth is that I'd feel an awful lot less comfortable swimming on that beach with a load of people watching me while they eat their pizza. I'd feel like the sideshow.'

'It's more than that, though,' said Deb. 'West Beach means something to me. It's the place I turned to when I needed to start again. I'm not done with it yet.'

'Same for me,' said Maisie. 'I've swum at West Beach since the day I moved in.'

'I suppose we could swim at Seasalter if we had to. It's nice and quiet there. We'd probably get used to it.'

'No,' said Maisie. 'You were right first time. This is our local beach. We won't stand back and let them take it.'

14

Ann's house had a front garden that was neat but entirely empty. There were a couple of ragged rose bushes marooned at the edges of a close-clipped square of lawn, but nothing else. The front door was framed by panels of textured glass that looked as though they were permanently spattered with rain.

After she opened the door, Ann stood on the threshold with her arms folded for a few moments, before saying, 'Come in,' and ushering them through a hall that was carpeted in swirling brown. It was the kind of greeting that left the obvious unspoken: we don't have many visitors. There was the smell of a cat litter tray, and boxes of what looked like medical supplies in the hall, stacked neatly under the stairs. Something about the place made Maisie's stomach lurch, perhaps in sympathy, but perhaps also in fear that one day this could be her own life.

'I hope you don't mind us inviting ourselves over,' she said. 'I wouldn't have troubled you, but there's not a lot of time.'

Ann looked up from the sink, where she was measuring the exact amount of water into the kettle, mug by mug. 'I don't mind at all,' she said. 'Do you want to sit down while I do this? I hope you don't mind instant.'

'I like it better than the other stuff,' said Deb.

Ann sniffed. 'It's own-brand,' she said.

'Great,' said Maisie. 'Shall we go through?'

They stepped into a compact dining room, where sun was streaming through patio windows. An elderly woman was sitting at the table, filling out a crossword from a large compendium. She was using a magnifying glass to gaze from the clues to the grid and back again, but was filling out the answers with almost alarming speed. She inked in the word 'ANTIMACASSAR' down the centre of the puzzle, and then slowly looked up at the two women.

'After a while, they're all the same,' she said. 'The same words come up over and over again, and you get used to the way they phrase the clues. I may have even done this one before. Who knows.' She leaned back in her chair and folded her glasses, letting them dangle from the chain around her neck. 'I take it you two are the cause of the whirlwind of tidy I've endured this morning.'

'I do hope not,' said Maisie, but there was a glint in the woman's eye that told her that she was being teased, at least to some extent. Ann came in with four mugs of coffee on a tin tray, and nearly bellowed, 'Mother! Will you have your coffee at the table?'

'I'm not deaf, you know.'

'Why is it that you don't always hear me, then?'

'Quite often because I'm not listening.' She turned to Maisie and Deb, and put out a hand. 'I'm Edith. I don't suppose I'll be introduced.'

'Of course you will. I was just putting the coffee down.'

'In case you're wondering, yes, we *are* always this cantankerous.' This jibe made Ann's hand shake as she lifted Deb's mug from the tray to a coaster, and the coffee slopped over the rim onto the lace tablecloth.

'Damn!' said Ann. 'Look what I've done now!'

'It'll need to soak,' said Edith.

This was clearly how their days proceeded: snap, snap, snap, panic. It was like walking over a field of brittle sticks. Maisie wondered if they should have come; clearly they were overwhelming Ann just by being here. But Deb was on her feet and saying, 'Not to worry, that'll come out,' and piling the mugs and coasters back onto their tray so that she could lift the whole lot up in one go. 'There you are, Ann – Edith, grab your crossword, love – bundle it up and put it in the sink.' And it was done. Deb went into the kitchen to get a cloth, wiped everything over – the mugs, the coasters and the oilcloth on the table – and somehow made everything feel right again. Maisie supposed this was a skill that came from long, bitter experience of defusing difficult moods, but admired it all the same.

'Anyway,' she said when Ann finally sat down, 'we won't keep you. It's just that I wondered if you could help us out.' She showed Ann the photographs she had taken on her phone of the planning notice, and told her what she'd read at the council offices. She tried not to make it sound too lurid, but then again they all understood the subtext. These buildings would most likely host American chains and discount pubs. Maisie wondered if she would feel differently about the whole thing if she knew for sure that an elegant local restaurant would set up there, perhaps a seafood shack that sold cold bottles of Provençal rosé and platters of seafood on crushed ice.

'You really would need to watch the bags with all that going on,' said Deb.

'Those bags need watching anyway,' said Ann. 'But never mind that. You realise that section of the beach is a habitat for wading birds? What will happen to them if a load of louts are staggering all over their territory?'

'Well,' said Maisie, 'perhaps not quite . . .'

'Right!' said Deb. 'Exactly. God only knows what types it'll attract.'

'I shudder to think,' said Ann.

'What we were wondering was whether you could help us out,' said Maisie. 'You've already set us up a Facebook page for the swimming club. Could you maybe use your expertise to set up a page for a campaign? "Save West Beach", or something like that? We need to let people know there's a public meeting coming up.'

'Well,' said Ann, 'I don't know. We'd have to find a way of communicating the detail of the information. I'm not sure I can do that on a Facebook page.'

'What she means is, she'd love to,' said Edith. 'She's in desperate need of something to do with her time.'

'I'm quite busy enough with you!' snapped Ann. 'And anyway, what I meant is that I think I should set up a blog, too. That's all.'

'Well, great!' said Maisie. 'If it's not too much trouble.'

'I suppose I could do it all with free software, but it will take a fair chunk of time to get it set up. And then I'll need to do some research into local groups we should connect with. It'll probably wipe out the rest of my week, if I'm honest.'

'I don't know how I spawned a daughter with so little grace,' said Edith.

Before they left, Maisie paused to kiss Edith and say, 'Will you join us one afternoon on the beach?'

'We couldn't manage it,' said Ann. 'It's too much trouble to get her chair down there.'

'I'll pick you up in my car,' said Maisie. 'That's if you'd like to.'

'I'd love to,' said Edith. 'I haven't been to the beach in years.'

'Are you sure?' said Ann. 'I don't want her to be a burden on anyone.'

They could hear the row continuing as they closed the front gate behind them. 'God,' said Deb as they got into the car. 'If I get too old to look after myself, just have me put down. I don't want to live out my days with Cherie talking to me like that.'

'I have a feeling that Ann needs Edith more than Edith needs Ann,' said Maisie, but Deb was already pulling a buzzing phone out of her bag and saying, 'Speak of the devil.'

'Answer it,' said Maisie. 'Don't mind me.' She pulled out of Ann's road, and decided to take the long way round so that she could drive along Tankerton Slopes and catch another glimpse of the sea. *Hello, love, are you okay?* she heard Deb say, and thought how she would struggle to carry on showing so much adoration for great big children like Deb's, who really ought to be sorting out their own problems. But then again, perhaps that's why she wasn't cut out for motherhood. She wasn't sure if she'd have all that much adoration for them when they were small, either.

After a short conversation that seemed to consist entirely of the phrases *No problem,* and *Just let me know the times, love,* Deb hung up, rolled her eyes in an exaggerated way and said, 'Well, that's my summer holiday done for. Cherie doesn't want to put the kiddies with a different child minder while hers is on holiday. Which I understand. Can't have 'em feeling abandoned, I suppose.'

'I hope she's paying you,' said Maisie.

Deb laughed. 'What do you think?' She looked into her lap, turning the phone over and over in her hands. 'It's all right,' she said. 'I'm sure she'll give me some money to cover outings and things like that. Or I'll go back to the old days, when I'd turn up at every free event going.' She paused for a while longer. 'That's what grans are for, isn't it?'

'I suppose so,' said Maisie. She parked the car in the tiny space that took up most of her back garden but which was nevertheless considered a luxury around here. Deb's bike was still there, propped against the shed.

'I'll be off home,' Deb said, and mounted her bike, but then her phone began to ring again and she mouthed, 'Bye, love,' to Maisie as she answered it.

As Maisie unlocked her back door, she could hear Deb saying, *You've found one? Well that's lovely news! How much do you need, love?*

No, thought Maisie, I was definitely not cut out for motherhood. Imagine the relentlessness of it. Imagine never being able to turn off your phone and ignore everybody. She closed her back door, turned the key in the lock, and was grateful for the silence.

15

Darren said it was such a nice house, and Deb had to admit that it sounded perfect. It was an off-plan on the estate they were building up by the supermarket, not too far from the centre of town. Three bedrooms 'for when the next one comes along' and a decent garden.

'It'll mean we can stay in Whitstable, Mum, rather than move over to Herne Bay,' he said, and for Deb this was the best part of all. She would be able to ride her bike up there on the Crab & Winkle Way, and be there to help out with the baby.

There was a catch – of course there was. He was short on some of the deposit. The firm that built the estate were offering a discount, and they'd made some money on the old flat, but there was still a bit of a shortfall. 'Do you think I could ask Dad?' said Darren. 'I mean, is there any point?'

'How much do you need, love?' said Deb.

'Seven grand,' said Darren. 'I know it's a lot.'

'All right,' said Deb, 'you can have it.'

'From you? You can't afford that, Mum!'

'I've got a bit tucked away,' said Deb. 'Don't you under-estimate your old mum!'

'I just didn't think you had any spare, that's all. You know I wouldn't have asked.'

'It's okay. I've just found myself a job, funnily enough.'

'A job? Where's that then?'

'I'll tell you another time. I'm in a bit of a rush, actually. Text me your bank details and I'll send it over.'

'Thanks, Mum. It's a lovely house.'

'Don't tell your sister.'

What else was she supposed to do? She couldn't have him going begging to Derek, and not just because he wouldn't have it anyway. No. She had to get back to the place where her children thought she could sort out anything. This was the worst thing about the divorce: it had shaken her pedestal in their eyes.

They knew all about Derek; they were under no illusions about his drunkenness or his flings. They saw him as someone to be endured, rather than adored. He was their dad, an inevitable burden that they had to carry, because that was what you did. What had shocked them, Deb now realised, was that she could no longer put up with him. They had loved her because she stayed. They loved her because it made them feel like she could absorb anything. It made them feel safe, even as the great big kids they were now. When she left, it told them nothing new about their father, but what they learned was that there was a limit to what Deb could – or was willing to – endure. It was a betrayal; they couldn't shake him off, but apparently their mother could, and when she went, they lost their buffer. There was no one left to smooth things over, to make it all right again. They were afraid.

Deb wheeled her bike over to the seafront, and climbed on, pedalling past the Oyster Stores, which was already filling up for the evening, and through the harbour. The tide was on its way up, but wouldn't be high until ten. She passed the new beach huts behind the swimming pool, and then the Hotel Continental, its huge windows framing people sucking on mussel shells and sipping beer. Along the bottom of Tankerton Slopes, her heart began to pound as she realised what she'd done. What did she have left, after Darren's money? Another month's worth, maybe six weeks if she was careful. She would have to give notice on the flat next week. Worse, she would have to tell Cherie that she couldn't look after the kids. That was a loss of face she could hardly bear, and she would be punished for it, she knew. *Well, if you don't want to spend time with them* . . . It would be yet another black mark against her name, a further piece of evidence that she was leaving them all in chaos by seeking her own freedom. She would not be forgiven.

She was nearly at Hampton now, on the edge of Herne Bay. Her old dad, who had worked on the boats, used to call it a drowned village, as though the sea had come in one day and taken everyone with it. Even as a child, she knew really that the drowning of Hampton was a slow process, a gradual creep of the sea, leaving the villagers to abandon all the things they loved, metre by metre, until they gave up altogether and left the whole lot behind. She knew how that felt. She had jettisoned every bit of herself before she was forced to surrender. But some days it still felt sudden, as though she was inundated, and everything was lost in one, overwhelming tide.

Her kids thought they knew everything. That was the problem. They thought that this was a simple failure on her part to be tolerant of Derek. They were like five-year-olds, wanting to believe that this was just a temporary breach of their cosy home life, and that Mummy and Daddy would be getting back together again soon, with all the heartbreak over. But there was a layer of heartbreak that they didn't know about, and that she would never tell them, lying there like the muddy seabed underneath it all.

They didn't know how far her tolerance had been stretched. It had taken her years to understand it herself. When she was first married, people talked about wife-beating, but Derek never once punched or kicked, so she didn't think it was happening to her. But there were the times when he was angry – when he was drunk and angry – when the light in his eyes would go out, and she would be confronted by a machine who didn't even seem to know her. The times when he gripped her wrist and wrenched back her arm until she thought it would break. The times he wrapped her hair around his fist and pulled back her head until she saw white light. The times he choked her slowly, deliberately, carefully. And all the while, they both knew she would never scream and wake the kids. They both knew she would suffer it to keep them believing in him. It was all forgotten by the morning. He slept it off. She didn't. She never could.

If any of them stopped to think, they would question why a woman has to hide her money behind a box of tampons in the bathroom cupboard just to be able to leave. But they didn't think, because for all their mortgages and jobs and babies, born and unborn, they were all still children when they were in her company, and they thought it was all about them. Deb never, ever wanted to break this for them. It was sacred, their belief that everything was really all right.

There was a band playing at The Neptune: a trio of men with Brylcreemed quiffs and open-necked shirts playing skiffle. It was hot and loud. Deb ordered a double vodka and tonic at the bar and drank it down. She was searching the crowd for a face.

A hand on her shoulder, and she turned.

'Fancy seeing you here.'

'I was about to say the same to you.'

'Come here often?'

'You might say I'm a regular.'

If this had been a different pub, she might have bumped into Derek. It would only take a few words and everything would be predictable again. She wouldn't be safe as such, but she would have a roof over her head, and the kids would be happy. She thought, sometimes, that maybe she had given him a short, sharp shock, and that this would finally be enough to make him change.

But it wasn't Derek. This was the least-worst option. There would be more decisions to make in the morning, more impossible choices. But for tonight, this would give her what she craved. She would be visible again for a couple of hours. That was the same as being alive.

Rick swallowed down his pint and grinned like an American game show host.

'So,' he said, 'liked what you saw last time and you're coming back for more?'

'Something like that,' said Deb.

He put his arm around her shoulders and said, 'Ding, ding, round two,' as they walked out across the beach towards Deb's flat.

16

The Sea Scout hut was airless and oppressively hot, full of shuffling chairs and raised voices. Maisie had waited for Deb outside for as long as she could bear, but the steady line of people shuffling in had eventually made her panic that they wouldn't get a seat and so she went in alone. She found two seats toward the back of the hall, and saved one with her bag. They would be nearly invisible back here. This was not what she had planned.

The meeting had already started by the time Deb appeared, breathless and apologising in whispers for being late.

'I lost track of time in the library,' she said. 'I was looking through the papers . . .'

'*Sssssh!* I need to listen to this.'

'Sorry.'

Deb fidgeted and folded her hands into her lap. She looked over her shoulder to check the woman behind them could see. She shuffled her chair slightly into the aisle to get a better view. Maisie tried to ignore her incessant movement as the planning officer made his opening remarks: this was the process, this was how applications were handled, these were the rules under which they worked. Yes, yes, get on with it, thought Maisie. I want to see the whites of your eyes. All of this discussion was just window-dressing. Everyone would be rehearsing arguments that the planners knew already, just to make a show of them being heard. The decision would already have been made, one way or another.

Nevertheless, people stood up one by one to have their say. A few people from nearby houses were concerned about noise. A local pressure group wanted the beach to be common land, rather than privately owned. This was not the time or the place. The Chair moved on.

'What Whitstable needs is jobs,' said one man. 'Just because the houses cost a bomb, people think we're a wealthy town.

Well, we're not. The ordinary person needs somewhere to work. If this lets a few more people make a living, I'm all for it.'

'You're missing the point,' said a man in designer denim and horn-rimmed glasses. 'This is further gentrification, and it will only push up your cost of living. The jobs you'll get in return will be the same zero-hours contracts that all the restaurant chains use. They're not the jobs you're hoping for.'

'I hate to say it,' said a woman Deb recognised from the school gates years ago. 'But some people would rather see people living on benefits than working for a living.'

And so it went on. An elderly man with a white beard directly in front of Deb stood up and talked about the beach as a wildlife habitat, and conjured up a utopia full of wading birds and wild flowers. 'Let us not indulge in fantasies,' laughed a man at the other side of the room. 'This is an industrial site, and has been for a long time. It's not a nature reserve.'

'That depends what you mean by an industrial site, though, doesn't it?' said a voice that Maisie suddenly realised was Deb's. It was calm, measured, clear. Maisie had never heard her sound so certain. 'Yes, people have always worked on the beach. But it's about the level of impact. There's business that has to happen on a beach: fishing, for example. Nobody minds that. But building an entertainment complex is . . . just different. It's taking a quiet place and making it noisy. And it's not about the local people; it's people from the outside who'll benefit.'

'Bloody DFLs!' came a shout from the front of the room.

Maisie stood up. 'I moved "Down From London" myself, about six months ago,' she said. 'That doesn't mean I don't care about the character of the place. We have a thriving community here: a high street full of independent shops, people who say hello when you pass. Have you noticed that no one complains about the aggregate works on the harbour? That's because it's real; it's part of a living town.

'What we're talking about here isn't part of a living town. It brings nothing, and takes away the quietest, wildest part of the beach. I agree that it will cause noise, mess and disruption. But

84

most of all, it will be an attack on Whitstable – its soul. Rob Whitstable of its beach huts, and the "DFLs" who fill them every summer, and you begin the process of losing everything.'

As she sat down again, there was a smattering of applause, but most of the room were busy fanning themselves against the heat, and checking their phones. The birdwatcher with the white beard turned back in his seat and said, 'Good speech. Of course, your problem is that real people don't own those beach huts any more. The land management company have been quietly buying them up for years.'

'What?' said Maisie. 'All of them?'

'Most of 'em. Everyone else will accept a decent settlement because they don't use them anyway.' He folded his arms and rolled his eyes in the manner of a world-weary campaigner, and then huffed out a laugh. 'You watch. This will all get shunted through by the council because there's no real opposition. They'll start building within a month.'

Maisie and Deb sat on West Beach for a long while after that, watching the extraordinary spectacle of the sun setting behind Sheppey, turning the sky pink, then violet, then indigo, and casting a blazing red line over the sea. The best nights of all were when you got to swim in all this colour. Tonight, they were waiting for the tide to rise.

They had stopped by at Maisie's house on the way to pick up a bottle of wine from the fridge, and were drinking it now from plastic cups.

'I suppose I knew it would be like that,' said Maisie. 'It's a done deal. Everyone's just resigned to it.'

'Yeah,' said Deb, who didn't have many words left.

'There's a kind of logic to it that you can't defeat. Nothing can just be small and quiet any more. Everything has to get bigger. It's easier to make a case for building something awful than for doing nothing to a wild place. There's no way of accounting for the comfort that people get from somewhere like this.'

'No,' said Deb, who was raking her hands through the shingle, and picking out all the mussel shells.

'Are you all right?'

'Yeah,' said Deb. 'I'm fine. Just thinking things over.'

Out of habit, Maisie picked up her phone and scrolled through the emails. She should have given this up after she'd left her job; she shouldn't even have been doing it then. But she couldn't help but notice an email from Ann.

'My God,' she said to Deb, 'apparently the Facebook page has got two hundred followers. Most of them joined tonight after the meeting. People are asking who we are.'

'Let me see that,' said Deb, and took Maisie's phone to read the email. There was a screenshot of the page, and underneath it, in a slightly panicked tone: *What should I tell them?*

Deb took out her own phone and logged in. She hadn't even joined the page herself yet. But now she did, and using her two thumbs, she drafted a post.

Hello. Thanks for all the follows.

I'd be lying if I said we had a plan to solve this. But we love West Beach like you do. I'm sure we can think of something. Let's start talking.

If anyone's interested, we actually have a swimming club that catches the high tide on West Beach once a week. The next one is tomorrow (Saturday), at midday. Anyone's welcome to join us if they fancy. The water should be nice and warm :)

She showed the message to Maisie for approval, and then pressed send. 'We really will need a name now,' she said.

'You'll make Ann's year,' said Maisie.

By the time the sea was high enough to swim in, the sky was completely dark and littered with stars. They changed on the beach because nobody was watching, and eased into the still black water. For once, Maisie didn't strike off towards Southend, but instead floated around in the shallows, as if savouring every last moment on her beach.

It was a strange feeling to swim at night. The water seemed to take on extra depth, and what lurked beneath the surface was somehow more mysterious. The slightest brush against floating seaweed was enough to make you panic. But it was also calm, and quiet, and beautiful, with the sea mirroring the stars. Best of all, it felt courageous to be there at all. This was everything: swimming in the black night-time sea, just for the joy of being brave.

17

Ann was clutching the back of the driver's seat, hissing, 'Watch out!' 'Mind that kerb!' 'Zebra crossing!' all the way to the beach, like some particularly paranoid driving instructor.

Edith, in the front, was growling back, 'Shut *up*, Ann,' every time her daughter spoke.

Maisie was trying very hard to maintain a serene expression while all this was going on, but it meant that she had to grip the steering wheel so tightly that her knuckles turned white. As she turned into the car park on Island Wall, specially chosen for its ramp onto the beach, Ann said, 'Shall I get out and guide you into a space?'

Edith glanced sideways at Maisie, who drew in a tight breath and said, 'That won't be necessary, Ann, but thank you.'

'This one,' said Edith, cocking her head to gesture towards Ann, 'managed to pass her driving test on the fifth try, and then never drove again. I drove an ambulance in the war.'

'They let anyone drive in those days,' said Ann.

'Great big thing it was too,' continued Edith, ignoring her. 'We used to nearly take off when we went over a bump.'

Maisie pulled her car into a parking space without assistance, and helped Edith into the wheelchair that had been folded in the boot. 'I could probably walk some of it,' Edith grumbled.

'Don't get over-ambitious,' said Ann. 'I'll end up driving you to A&E.'

'I'll be perfectly fine.'

'Let's get over the seawall first, and then you can make a decision when we're on the flat,' said Maisie. She wheeled Edith onto the wooden ramp, and, as they reached the highest point, watched her take in a deep breath of sea air and say, almost under her breath, 'Oh!'

Maisie was reminded of childhood trips to the seaside, that first glimpse of blue water on the horizon as the car neared the coast; and then that moment that your feet were finally on the sand, and you realised how wide-open and wild the beach was. It was hard to imagine how startling this would be for Edith after years cooped up at home.

Maisie only regretted that Edith had finally landed back on the beach in the middle of a sunny Saturday in July. The beach was packed with daytrippers, who sat on the shingle with bags of chips and polystyrene plates of oysters, clutching bottles of beer or balancing wine glasses. Men were lined up on the seawall, swigging from cans, shirts off. There were wisps of smoke rising from barbecues, and the scent of grilling sardines. Children ran along the beach, hurdling over the groynes, or tottered at the edge of the sea in swimming shoes and anti-UV suits.

'There's a lot more life here than there used to be,' said Edith. 'Good to see it.'

They walked along the path, past The Neptune, the pastel-coloured houses at Wave Crest, alongside the tennis courts where the influence of Wimbledon was still being felt in doubles matches played by couples in pristine whites. Here, Edith got out of her wheelchair and walked a few steps on her stiff legs, holding tightly to Maisie's arm, and refusing Ann's. When the seawall dog-legged at the caravan park (and it made Maisie's stomach dip, now, to see it), she got back in her chair so that she could be wheeled across the shingle, which had mercifully been flattened by many feet before them. The beach was quieter here and Edith had her eyes fixed on the sea as they bumped over stones and ruts, past the beach huts.

'Don't tip her out!' said Ann.

'Try not to worry,' said Maisie. 'I'm doing my best.'

'You are. I know.'

'It's nice to get her out.'

'Yes. It is.'

As they reached the top of the beach where they swam, the first thing Maisie saw was Julie and Deb running towards them to help manoeuvre the wheelchair down towards the sea. But there was more: about twenty new swimmers, all changed into shorts and costumes, bathing caps and goggles, milling around on the beach, raring to get into the water.

'We wanted to wait for you,' said Deb, breathlessly lifting the front of the chair with Julie.

A Jack Russell was running into the sea, and then hurtling out, barking in shock, before dashing back in again. His owner threw a stick into the water and he swam after it, returning to the shore to shake water across the stones. There were three small children being supervised by an exasperated man, who Maisie realised must be Julie's husband. Before long, he had to call for help because he couldn't seem to contain all of them at once. Maisie dashed towards the water's edge to scoop up a toddler who was already ankle-deep in the sea, and handed him back to his father, who said, 'I'd top myself if I had to do what Julie does,' and then gazed over at her with such admiration that Maisie began to understand how they had ended up with so many children in the first place.

The birdwatching man from the public meeting was there in a pair of minuscule black swimming shorts, which, he admitted, he hadn't tried on for a good few years.

'Possibly decades,' he said, and laughed, throwing his elbows backwards to stretch his chest.

Maisie already had her wetsuit on under her dress, and she was just shaking out her bathing cap when Deb was by her side again, giving her arm a squeeze. 'They're here for *us*!' she said. 'I can't quite believe it.'

'You really have warmed to the idea of a club, haven't you?'

'Yeah, well,' said Deb, 'I was never against it *in and of itself*.'

'You weren't?'

Chloe crunched up beside them and said, 'I suddenly feel like I'm part of, like, a protest movement.'

'Yes,' said Maisie, 'it seems quite sudden to me, too.' She glanced over the beach towards Ann, who had settled herself next to her mother's wheelchair, and was now talking to a mousy-haired man in neon swimming shorts and a t-shirt.

'Bill's back,' she said. 'I didn't think he'd come again.'

'I found him on Facebook and, you know . . .' said Deb.

'Apologised for nearly scaring him out of his wits?'

'I wouldn't have quite put it like that.'

'Actually,' said Chloe, 'I was thinking about Bill, and, you know, our name.' She reached into a cloth bag and pulled out a plastic folder, pushing it towards Maisie before withdrawing it again. 'I mean, I was only playing about on Photoshop. It's no big deal or anything.'

Maisie took the folder and opened it. Inside was a sheet of paper on which Chloe had printed a lifebelt with writing curling around it.

'Oh my God,' said Deb. 'It's brilliant, Chloe.'

The Whitstable High Tide Swimming Club, it said.

'I think we finally have a name,' said Maisie.

When they showed it to Ann, she said, 'Do we need some kind of committee meeting to approve this?' and then, looking up at the circle of horrified faces, smiled. 'I am capable of cracking a joke, you know.'

'Come on!' called Julie from the beach. 'Are you coming in or not?'

People began to wade into the water, and Maisie and Deb splashed after them, submerging themselves and swimming into the clear stretch of the sea while many others were still gasping at the cold. For once, they swam together, side-by-side, reaching the yellow buoy and floating there for a while to watch the water's edge fizzing with delighted people.

Bill was there, still in his t-shirt, but waist deep already; Chloe was squealing and hopping from one foot to the other; Julie was holding a child in each arm, bobbing next to her husband, who held another. The birdwatching man was floating on his back, his pink chest shining in the sun. Even Ann was ankle-deep, her skirt folded up in her hands. She caught Maisie's eye and pointed at Edith, mouthing, 'Mother's watching the bags.'

'This lot look like trouble,' said Deb, grinning.

'I have a feeling you're right,' said Maisie, and they swam back to join them.

Part Two

1

'SAVE WEST BEACH!'

As Maisie raised her placard, a woman walked past, dragging a child by the hand, and scuttled into the library with the stiff neck of someone trying not to make eye contact. You couldn't blame her. Nobody was ever recruited to a cause by being harangued.

'We need a song. Something a bit more enticing,' she said to Deb whose skin, she noticed, had begun to goose-pimple in the grey August drizzle. 'Haven't you got a cardigan?'

Deb hopped from one foot to the other and hugged her arms around her chest. 'If I wore a cardigan, it would ruin the whole effect, wouldn't it? We're supposed to look like we're on the beach.'

Maisie reluctantly agreed, but it seemed to her that you should be able to plan a protest like this at the height of summer, without the need for thermal underwear and medicinal brandy. Apparently that was too much to ask. The Whitstable High Tide Swimming Club hadn't ever meant to be a protest group in the first place, but they wanted to let the whole town know about the plans to concrete over the wildest part of the beach. Standing here today, though, it was clear that they just didn't have a clue where to start.

'Isn't Whitstable supposed to have some sort of a micro-climate?' said Maisie. 'When I moved here, the estate agent made it sound like a subtropical paradise.'

Deb snorted. 'We do. It's probably sub-zero in Canterbury today.'

Maisie looked up at the grey sky in hope of detecting a break in the blanket of cloud, but it was more of an entreaty really, a prayer to the heavens that this protest might not look as ridiculous as it seemed to in this particular moment. The sky offered her no comfort in return. If anything, it only mirrored the absurdity of the situation back at her. They were, after

95

all, a group of women – and one ruddy-faced man – standing in the centre of town in their swimwear, in broad daylight, shouting at passing strangers.

They were definitely less of a burgeoning social movement, and more of an assembled group of oddballs scaring the public. It was no wonder that the woman in the newsagent next door kept peeping her head out to glare at them. They were almost certainly deterring any passing trade. She was surprised that the local shopkeepers hadn't banded together with pitchforks to collectively eject them from the vicinity.

It had seemed like a good idea when they were planning it, but in retrospect, they were standing on the beach at the time, where the bathing suits and bikinis, goggles and swimming caps were all in their natural habitat. On the concrete pavement next to the war memorial, with parents filtering past them to attend Bounce & Rhyme, it all looked a little more, well, *weird*. And not in a good way.

The problem was that all this flesh didn't transpose well from the beach. They lacked an essential element of glamour. Maisie herself was more grateful for her wetsuit than ever, because at least she was covered from head to toe in deeply comforting neoprene. Deb had opted for a full swimsuit instead of her usual bikini, which was a wise concession, given the temperature. But she had brought along her two grandchildren, and this added an unintentionally tragic effect to the whole affair. Little Sophie was holding her placard sulkily, shifting her skinny knees underneath a pink swimming costume. Her brother writhed in his pushchair, and occasionally cried out in frustration. It wasn't exactly the joyous celebration of seaside culture that they had planned.

The others didn't help. Being fifteen, Chloe was fully clothed and had spent the entire hour on Snapchat, sending messages to an unseen cast of friends and occasionally lifting her phone to pose for a photo, before slumping her head again and whirring her thumb over the screen. Maisie would have preferred, on balance, that she hadn't chosen today to experiment with black lipstick, but she supposed that it was unwise to mention it.

Julie had turned up, briefly, but they had all been alarmed by the way that her three toddlers were endlessly drawn towards the road, and it seemed sensible for her to take them into the library after a while. Every now and then, she appeared at the sliding doors and waved supportively, which was touching, if somewhat useless.

Ann was there, trying to look at home in swimwear, but somehow you could tell that she never actually got near the water. Perhaps in compensation, she was brandishing her placard so angrily that it looked as though she was personally admonishing every passing pedestrian. Her mother sat by her side in her wheelchair, exuding a quiet dignity that might just have tipped over into mortification if you looked closely enough. Bill, now their sole male member, hadn't turned up at all, which was, on balance, a relief given how embarrassed he was by basic human contact.

Instead, they had Brian, the bird-watching enthusiast they had befriended at the public meeting to consult on the development of West Beach. Even back then, he had told them that the planning approval was a foregone conclusion, and he had proved correct. Two weeks after the meeting, a notice was posted to say that East Kent Land Management had been granted permission to build a complex of bars and restaurants on the beach, knocking down a row of beach huts in the process. Brian was, Maisie supposed, an asset to their group, with his battle-hardened wisdom and deep knowledge of the local ecology. But today, as he stood on the High Street in his tiny swimming shorts and Santa Claus beard, it was hard to imagine that he was helping. In particular, Maisie questioned his decision to paint the words 'Beach = LIFE' on his round belly.

At that moment, the woman from the newsagent marched up to them, planted her hands on her hips and yelled, 'I've called the police! You can't do this here. You're supposed to get a licence for this sort of thing.'

'No we're not,' said Deb. 'Maisie checked. You only need a licence if you're marching.'

'Yeah, well you bloody well ought to,' said the woman. 'You're scaring everyone away. I've checked with all the shops along this stretch, and none of us has had a single customer since you started.'

Maisie sighed. 'Okay, I take your point. We'll only be ten minutes more. I'm guessing the police refused to come anyway?'

'Well . . .' said the woman.

'They tend to only come if an actual crime has been reported,' said Maisie.

'Actually, they told me off for calling 999. Said it wasn't an emergency matter. The cheek of it!'

'Indeed,' said Maisie. 'Anyway, I'm sure you don't want to leave your shop for too long. We'll have this all wrapped up soon.'

They both watched the woman trot back to her shop, clearly believing she was victorious. 'For heaven's sake,' said Maisie. 'I don't know why we bother.'

'Can you watch the kids for a moment? I'm going to have a fag,' said Deb.

'Sure,' said Maisie. 'And then we'll call it a day.'

'Really?' said Deb, pulling on a long cardigan. 'I was just thinking about chaining myself to some railings.'

'That'll really upset the kids when they come out of the library,' said Maisie.

2

Deb thought that it was best to sneak into the back garden of the Coach and Horses to smoke, so that none of the other protestors could see her and disapprove. If the pub's management complained, she would point out that her ex-husband had probably contributed half their income for the last thirty years. They owed her a discreet cigarette where the grandchildren couldn't see her, and probably much more.

In any case, the pub garden was completely empty – probably due to the protest outside – and this was her last packet ever, so she wouldn't be troubling them much longer. She had weathered years of warnings about the dire consequences for her health, and was wearing pretty well, all things considered. But the cost had got her in the end. When you can't afford to pay your rent, the fags have to go. And there was a little more to it than that. More and more, her smoking was making her look like a relic. Nobody did it these days, and to this new set in Whitstable, it was an unthinkable horror. You might as well have opened the gates of hell every time you lit up, for the reaction you got. She never used to care, but recently it was beginning to prickle her; it was just another difference between herself and the women she admired, and it was, on balance, the easiest one to fix.

Just three cigarettes left now in her final box. Should she puff through all of them today and make a fresh start tomorrow, or make them last over several days, gradually withdrawing? She would miss them, her good old friends. They had never let her down. She flicked her lighter and enjoyed the faint crackle as she drew the first puff of smoke through. The authorities had done all they could to take the pleasure out of it, but they could never take away the wave of relief that came with the first drag on your favourite brand. They could make you stand out in the street all they liked. They could put stickers on the packet to tell you your breath stank, that you would get cancer, that you would look old, that your legs would fall off. None of that had ever overcome the pleasure she got from five minutes in the garden with a cigarette and a cup of coffee in the morning, or a break mid-afternoon while you tried to get your head straight; or a last one before bed, just to pack the day away. She was going to miss them. But if it was a choice between losing them and regaining Derek, there was no contest.

Goodbye, lovely fags, she thought. *I wish my children had been as loyal and obedient.*

The stupid thing was, she would still be broke without them. Now that she'd given notice on the bedsit, she had three weeks to find somewhere to live, and, seeing as she had no income to speak of, the search wasn't going very well. The problem was, she wasn't qualified to do anything, and so the paltry work she could get didn't pay enough to live on. It was all very well to make the grand, liberated gesture and leave your idiot husband, but it turned out that the world would only let you survive if you had his income as well as your own.

So now, she would be poor, homeless, *and* crabby without the fags. She would probably put on weight, too. That's what happened to everyone else. That would make the appearance of a knight in shining armour a whole lot less likely. Not that she wanted one of those anyway. She wanted the opposite, really: a chance to get by on her own. It was just that, right now, she was failing at that very badly indeed, and she didn't know how to get out of it. Push-came-to-shove, perhaps Maisie would let her stay in that pristine spare room of hers, or if she was really desperate, she could kip on Cherie's sofa bed. She wasn't sure which option was worse: revealing to Maisie just how low she was in the food chain; or giving her self-important daughter yet another stick to beat her with.

Bollocks to it, she thought, and lit another cigarette. What's the point in drawing out a long goodbye. Might as well puff through the lot of them now, and get it over with. Maybe she'd make herself sick. That was a favourite story of her Dad's: the time he was caught smoking when he was ten, and his mother made him smoke a whole packet, just to put him off for life. Didn't work on him; they had to wheel him out of the oncology ward to have a gasper every hour. Deb didn't suppose it would work for her, either.

She stubbed out the second one, and thought she might as well see the last one off with a bit of ceremony, so she stepped into the bar and bought a vodka and slimline tonic. Then she went back to the garden, perched on the edge of a picnic set, and lit the final fag of her life. She would savour this one. She tried to bring to mind a pleasant montage of all her best smoking moments, but found that, after school, they were all filled with Derek, and so weren't all that pleasant after all. Was there a single thing that he couldn't ruin? She sipped her V&T. Perhaps this was good riddance after all.

Somebody was knocking on the gate to the beer garden. Probably kids. But then it opened just a crack, and she saw Chloe's face peer in at her.

'You alright, Chlo? Come in.'

'I can't,' said Chloe. 'It's a pub.'

'It's only the garden.' For someone dressed as an undertaker's evil twin, the girl could be surprisingly proper.

'Someone's here from the radio,' said Chloe. 'You need to come.'

'The radio?' said Deb, and she leapt off the table, stubbing out the last, prized cigarette as she went. Apparently it was too much to ask to have the whole of it in peace. She swallowed down her drink and took off her cardigan as she ran out into the street.

A Coastline Radio car had pulled up in the driveway alongside the pub, and there was a man holding a microphone under Maisie's nose. She was making her point clearly and serenely, her back straight and her face relaxed. Deb adjusted the legs of her swimming costume, wondering if she should go in there at all, given that Maisie was clearly doing a better job of making their case than she ever would. But then, the group of protestors did look a bit thin on the ground without her. She ought to at least join the others.

As she walked towards them though, the man from the radio turned, and Deb said, quite audibly, 'Shit.'

'Great to see you too,' said the man. 'Lucky this isn't going out live.'

Deb clamped her hand over her mouth and then removed it to say, 'What the hell are you doing here?'

'Do you know each other?' said Maisie.

'Maybe,' said Deb. 'I'll tell you later.'

'This is 96.4 Coastline Radio, online and in your car,' said the man with practised patter. 'I'm your host Ricky Robinson, and today I'm out and about talking to a – shall we say – *lively* band of protestors, who, if I'm reading their signs correctly, are trying to save Whitstable's West Beach by wearing their swimming costumes in the middle of town.

'So, Deb, thank you for agreeing to talk to me today. You had even fewer clothes on when I last saw you. Don't worry, I'll edit that out.' Deb could feel a blush spreading upwards from the low neck of her cossie. Maisie's eyes were so wide that it looked as though she might be considering one of her interventions. This was sexual harassment, surely? Or character assassination. Or something. Surely there was a criminal offence designed solely to punish one-night stands who turned up in your everyday life, and would not go quietly. Well, okay, two-night stands. And a few texts that were, in retrospect, regrettable.

'So, Deb,' began Rick again, 'What exactly are you saving West Beach *from*?'

Deb took a breath, and tried to find the grace that Maisie had displayed. 'From the greedy bastards who want to build on it,' she said, and immediately felt the cold horror of her words. That was not what she'd meant. She should have used words like 'unwanted development' and 'ecological disaster'. That's what she had planned, when she'd imagined this and left a message on the station's Facebook page. She should, in retrospect, have had a quick look first to see who worked there. Knowing everyone in Whitstable wasn't always a benefit.

'Steady on there with the, uh, *fruity* language,' said Rick in his bouncy tone that just seemed odd in real life. 'You're obviously very angry, Deb. What's your problem with a few buildings near the beach, then? Aren't you just fighting progress?'

'It's not progress to knock down lovely old beach huts and build a bar,' said Deb, who suddenly knew, with a certainty she rarely felt about anything else, that Derek would hear this. 'We don't want idiots all over our lovely beach, watching us while we swim.'

'You don't seem so worried about that today,' said Rick. 'For the benefit of the listeners, I should explain that Deb is currently standing outside Whitstable Library on a busy Saturday lunchtime, and she's wearing a – how should I describe it – *halter-neck* bathing suit, with a nautical blue-and-white stripe, and a very revealing neckline. May I ask how old you are, Deb?'

Deb instinctively grabbed for the top line of the suit, and hitched it up, immediately regretting that she'd given him the satisfaction. 'I'm fifty-seven,' she said. 'I'm a mother and a grandmother, and I want to keep West Beach a lovely place that kiddies can play on; not somewhere full of drunk idiots throwing up on a Friday night.'

'Would you describe yourself as a killjoy, Deb? You don't seem too keen on young people having fun.' He winked as he said this, as if they were sharing an in-joke between the two of them, except that, of course, none of the listeners would see it.

'No,' she said, 'I love a bit of fun, me.'

'I bet you do,' he said into the mic, and then leaned over and whispered, 'I know you do.'

'The most important point is . . .' began Maisie, but Rick pulled the microphone back to his own mouth, and turned away as he said, 'Thank you, ladies, for a fascinating conversation. This is 96.4 Coastline Radio, with me, Ricky Robinson. What do you think about swimsuit protests – a bit of fun? Or not the kind of thing you'd want your kids to see? Call in now on 0345 . . .'

The whole town knows my number, he'd said when they met. Now Deb finally knew what he meant.

'I'm sorry,' she said to Maisie. 'I wasn't cut out for this sort of thing.'

'Not your fault,' said Maisie.

Rick looked up from his voice recorder, took off his headphones and said, 'That sounds great, ladies. Well done.'

'I'm not sure I'm happy with that,' said Deb. 'You caught me by surprise a bit. I didn't mean to say half of what ended up on your tape. Can we try again?' Surely their nights together counted for something here? He must have a bit of residual affection for her, or at least gratitude.

'Oh I'm sorry,' he said. 'There's just not enough time. I have to be back at the station by . . .' he checked his watch to concoct a suitable lie '. . . two.'

'I didn't know you were a DJ,' said Deb, and then wasn't quite sure why she said it. He was unlikely to be delighted by the information.

'Oh come *on*,' said Rick. 'I don't believe that for a minute. Everyone knows me! I'm Ricky Robinson! The moment you clocked eyes on me, I could tell you knew exactly who I was.'

'Nope,' said Deb. 'I could just see that you were as desperate as I was.'

Quite unexpectedly, Maisie burst into laughter and Deb had to bite her lip to avoid doing the same.

'Don't push your luck,' said Rick. 'I've got a tape recording of you swearing like a trooper here.'

Deb wondered briefly whether she should apologise and say that she was only joking, but then she remembered the number of times she had kept the peace with her ex-husband, and how she had vowed never to do that again for any man.

'Do your bloody worst,' she said.

3

'Not everyone can afford high-speed broadband, you know!' Ann sat in front of the computer screen, occasionally jabbing at the mouse as the radioplayer said, endlessly, *buffering* . . . Deb had gone out to the garden for a ciggie, and then realised that she no longer smoked, and so had to stand tetchily on the concrete patio, listening to the raised voices inside while she pretended she was just getting some air. Maybe she should keep this up. Maybe it was these little breaks that made the whole experience anyway, rather than the actual smoking.

No. It was definitely the smoking. Her tongue ached for it, and she felt vaguely sick, as though her body was missing some vital vitamin. She slumped against the pebbledash wall of Ann's house, and picked at the skin around her nails.

'Do you have a normal FM radio, Ann?' she heard Maisie saying in her calm, patient voice. 'We may have to listen in the old-fashioned way.'

'It's a perfectly good way to listen,' said Ann.

'It absolutely is,' said Maisie.

'But I want to be able to see the comments on their web page as we go along,' called Deb from the garden, before realising that there was absolutely no reason that she couldn't just walk back inside any more. Finally, there was something holding her back from being a complete social pariah. That had to be a good thing.

'Well,' said Maisie as Deb came in, 'perhaps we can listen on the radio and watch the comments on the screen. That would work, wouldn't it, Ann?'

'I should think so,' said Ann. She got up and switched on an ancient-looking stacking stereo. The speakers cleared their throats and then hissed with static. 'We don't have this on much,' said Ann. 'Mother sometimes plays her records, but that's about it.'

'Do you have a bit of a dance, then, Edith?' said Deb, but the elderly woman didn't reply.

'She's on that damned tablet again,' said Ann. 'We can hardly afford to keep body and soul together, but she's somehow got cash for an iPad.'

'It's not an iPad,' said Edith, without looking up. 'And I can hear everything you say, you know. I have my savings, don't you worry.'

'I wish you'd share them, then.'

'I wish you'd go out and get a job, and stop worrying around me all day.'

'I think I've got it,' said Maisie, who was on her knees in front of the tuner. They caught the tail end of the pips, and then a short news flash, in which a young-sounding woman talked about the plan to close the local maternity unit, and then heralded the crowning of Miss Herne Bay, who was apparently a veterinary nurse with a talent for street dance. A jingle kicked in:

This is 96.4 Coastline Radio. Talk, news and tunes for the North Kent Coast.

'Not exactly promising, is it?' said Ann.

'I'm more of a Radio 4 girl,' said Maisie.

'Ssshhh,' said Deb. 'It's starting.'

A voice that was unmistakeably Rick's filled the room, and Deb experienced a bizarre, dizzy sensation in her stomach that felt like badly misplaced desire. It was just mechanical though; her long-neglected loins were stirring into recognition. It was pathetic, really.

'Welcome to *Drive Time* with your faithful host, Ricky Robinson,' said the voice, and a sound effect of a panting dog kicked in. 'Go boy!' he shouted. 'Fetch!' and the sound of barking gradually faded out as Rick said, 'Well, folks, I've been a good boy this weekend . . .'

'Oh God,' said Deb, 'he has a *thing*. He must do this every day.'

'I fear so,' said Maisie.

'Lowest common denominator,' said Ann.

'Oh *God*,' said Deb again, 'what have I done?'

'Whatever it was, I hear you did it twice,' said Maisie.

'Not that!' said Deb. 'I meant the interview!' But the vision of Rick getting up from her bed the second time and saying, *Thanks for requesting an encore, babe* swam into her mind, and she felt sick. 'Oh God,' she groaned.

'Hopefully they'll use Maisie's interview,' said Ann, oblivious to the reproachful look that Maisie gave her.

'Yeah, thanks, Ann. Funnily enough I'm hoping that too,' said Deb.

'You made an important point, passionately,' said Maisie. 'You have nothing to be ashamed of.'

'We'll see,' said Deb.

Ann made four mugs of coffee, as they sat through what Rick called an 'early-doors phone-in', in which he fielded a series of calls, mainly, it seemed, from taxi drivers. 'What's put the bee in our bonnet today?' he asked each time.

'Well,' said the first man, 'I'm wondering if these roadworks will ever end. There can't be any pipes left . . .'

'As you know, Ricky mate,' began the second, 'I've had a few run-ins with traffic wardens in my time . . .'

'How often does he call in?' said Maisie. Deb could see that she was nervous too now. She was rubbing the palms of her hands together, over and over again, as if she wanted to wear them smooth.

'Well,' said Ricky, 'I see you've all got plenty to say for yourselves today,' and he started to play 'Livin' On A Prayer', before fading down the sound and speaking over the first verse. 'After this, we'll be talking about the West Beach protestors and asking, "Can Whitstable step out of the past?"'

'That's us,' said Deb, and she got up to go outside to smoke, before realising how stupid that was and sitting straight down again.

'Brace yourselves, girls,' said Maisie. 'I have a feeling this might be a bit of a bumpy ride.'

The song finished and Rick cut straight to a recording from Saturday, with the muffled rush of passing cars in the background.

This is 96.4 Coastline Radio, online and in your car. I'm your host Ricky Robinson, and today I'm out and about talking to a – shall we say – lively band of protestors . . .

The three of them listened, hardly breathing. There was not a single word of Maisie's interview, but there was plenty of Deb's. He had, she thought, elongated the beep over the word 'bastards', making it sound like Deb had unleashed a string of expletives rather than just one, fairly tame, insult.

She heard her own voice say, *We don't want idiots all over our lovely beach, watching us while we swim.*

I'm fifty-seven.

I want to keep West Beach a lovely place that kiddies can play on; not somewhere full of drunk idiots throwing up on a Friday night.

She was sure she said more than that; she was sure she had joined it all together into something a bit more coherent, even if she had opened her mouth and put her foot straight in it. But this: *this*. It just sounded like an old ranting nimby, trying to stop everyone else from having the fun that was so clearly absent from her own life.

'Oh well,' said Maisie, as the *Drive Time* jingle signalled an ad break, 'we did our best.'

'I'm so sorry,' said Deb. 'I shouldn't have said anything. I should have just kept my mouth shut and walked away. I knew I'd muck it up.'

'It's not your fault,' said Maisie. 'We were stitched up.'

'If you ask me, it was the swimming costumes,' said Ann.

'No one asked you,' said Deb.

'You might be right, Ann,' said Maisie. 'I didn't think it through. *Damn*. I wanted it to be attention-grabbing, but it was too wacky. I made us all look stupid.'

'But without the swimsuits, no one would have noticed us at all. All publicity's good publicity, right?' said Deb.

'If you want to carry on believing that, don't look at the comments,' said Ann.

Deb leaned in, and squinted, and then stood back up again and said, 'Bloody hell.'

Great interview, Ricky, said the first, followed by a row of laughing faces.

So these 'ladies' can barely string a sentence together, but they can take off their clothes in public? I think we all know the type, said another.

If they like the beach so much, we should push 'em off the harbour, said a third.

'That one doesn't even make sense,' said Maisie, with what Deb felt was impressive serenity. But even Maisie whispered, 'Oh for heaven's sake, isn't this thing moderated at all?' when she reached the one that was just a row of emoji whales and the words *dumb bitches*.

Rick's voice intruded again. 'Before the break, we were talking to the *lovely* ladies of Save West Beach . . .' – a pause to play a wolf whistle – '. . . and to respond to their points, I have on the line our local MP, and friend of the show, Charles Brinton.'

'Not *him*,' said Edith from the corner. 'I saw him on the news the other night. All mouth and no trousers.'

'Charles,' said Rick, 'what do you say to those who would prevent further building on our beaches? Is it time to say "enough's enough"?'

'Well, good afternoon, Ricky,' said a careful, plummy voice whose warmth was clearly more learned than natural. 'As you know, I have huge respect for the heritage of our beautiful town, and for the marine environment that makes it so special.'

'Won't hear any arguments from me,' said Rick.

'Quite so,' said Charles. 'And we must, of course, preserve Whitstable's unique features in order to attract the tourists that are so crucial to our economy. But we must also bear in mind that these tourists expect a certain level of – shall we say – pizzazz . . .'

'We can indeed say that,' said Rick, 'and I won't need to use my bleeper in this case.'

At this point, his producer (whose quick reflexes you had to admire, Deb supposed) played the bleeper again, a series of high-pitched signals that sounded like it was spelling something out in Morse code. Two Smug Old Men, maybe. Or, Patronising Morons. Deb couldn't be sure.

'Indeed,' said Charles. 'Well, our visitors need good places to eat and drink in the town, and we must also remember that we provide these in order to secure jobs for the townsfolk. Those who fight this are doing so for selfish reasons, because they don't want Whitstable to succeed. They want it to be kept nice and quiet and old-fashioned, because they're alright, Jack.'

'I thought nice, quiet and old-fashioned was just your kind of thing, Charles,' said Rick.

'Oh it very much is. But I also support our hard-working families who need a strong, stable local economy to keep them in work, and off the dole.'

'Thank you very much, Charles,' said Rick. 'While I've got you on the line, I'm sure you're more than aware that a General Election has to be called by the end of the year.'

'I very much am,' said Charles, and they both laughed.

'Are you confident you can keep your seat?'

'I am but a humble servant, as you know,' said Charles. 'But I am blessed with a safe seat, and I like to think that I do a pretty good job.' A peal of self-satisfied laughter.

'I wish you the best of luck,' said Rick. 'So, this is where you have your say. Should West Beach be frozen in time? Or should Whitstable move into the modern era? Call in on 0345 . . .'

'Charles Brinton got a much easier ride than we did,' said Maisie, turning down the radio and sipping her cold coffee. 'That tells you all you need to know about this Ricky Robinson. How was it you met him, Deb?'

But Deb didn't reply. She was waiting for someone to pick up the phone.

'Hello?' she said when they answered. 'I'd like to take part in the phone-in, please. My name? It's Deborah.'

4

'Whoa!' said Ricky Robinson, as feedback boomed out through the speakers. 'Someone's keen to hear themselves on the radio! We'll be available on Listen Again later, my love; turn off your set for now. In case any of you folks out there didn't know that, you can find all our shows on coastlineradio964.com, where you have a whole fortnight to catch up . . .'

Another whine of feedback filled the room as Ann and Maisie scrambled together for the switch to the stereo system, bumping heads in the process. Ann cried out, 'Ow!' but Maisie's thumb found the button, and the room fell into silence.

'Sorry about that,' Deb said into her phone, glaring at the pair of them. 'I think we're all straight now.'

Maisie sat back to rub her head, and put a hand on Ann's shoulder, mouthing, *Sorry. Are you okay?* Ann shrugged and looked away, sulkily.

Edith, from her chair in the corner, muttered, 'Just like a child.'

'Ssssshh!' hissed Ann.

Maisie raised her hand as if she were trying to stop traffic, and placed her finger over her lips. Deb was speaking in that steady, articulate voice she found sometimes.

'My name's Deb. I'm one of the Save West Beach protestors. You just broadcast your interview with me. And made me sound like an idiot, actually.'

Maisie watched Deb pause while Ricky responded, her face a picture of good-natured restraint. She must have learned this from raising her unruly sons, listening carefully to their ridiculous excuses before itemising precisely how ridiculous they were.

'Alright, Ricky,' she said, 'we won't spend a long time talking about this, because it's not the real issue, but I just think you missed the point. Of course we looked silly in our swimming costumes; we were trying to. It might surprise you to know that women don't spend their whole lives trying to make you fancy them.'

Maisie wished she could hear the response; she imagined a great deal of spluttering and some desperate attempts at repositioning. Deb caught her eye and gave a sly smile. She knew exactly what she was doing.

'I did swear a bit, Rick, you're quite right. But not nearly as much as it sounded like in your show. You were a bit naughty there, weren't you?' A pause, in which it was tempting to imagine Rick trying to form an apology. 'And anyway, in my defence I was angry – I'm *still* angry – that anyone could be allowed to build on our beautiful West Beach. I thought we'd reached an era where we looked after nature, and tried not to make the same mistakes that we used to make. But apparently it's okay to concrete over it, as long as someone promises that everyone will have a job after it's done. We both know that won't happen.'

The colour in her cheeks was high, and her neck was flushed a deep red. She winked at Maisie, just the merest twitch of an eyelid that seemed to imply that this was a tiresome routine – that she'd been through it all before, and was just rolling it out one more time for the idiots at the back of the room who couldn't keep up. Maisie had only glimpsed this version of Deb once before, when she had stood up at the planning consultation, and been as calm and fierce as she was being today. It was almost as if she had to be pushed to her furthest extent to find this magnificent clarity, but right now, she wouldn't be out of place in one of the negotiating teams that Maisie used to manage. She had every bit of the relaxed good humour and poise that those people possessed.

What had gone wrong for Deb, that she had ended up keeping house for Derek, who Maisie was certain was a selfish, ignorant lout from what little she'd seen? As soon as the thought entered her mind, Maisie corrected it: it was the worst part of her that thought like this. Nothing had gone wrong for Deb. She had chosen to look after her children, which was a decision that Maisie should respect even if she didn't understand it. She was ashamed of her own snobbery sometimes.

'I'll make a final point before I go, Ricky,' she heard Deb say. 'You just gave Charles Brinton a very easy time of it on here. Now, I was brought up to respect people like him too, but if you're going to make fun of a little group of protestors trying to keep builders off their beach, then it's just no good sucking up to the people with all the money, and all the status. It ought to be the other way round. You should look a bit more kindly on the people who are doing their best to make their home town a nice place to live, and look a bit harder at the people who take a massive salary and only turn up to Parliament when they absolutely have to. Have you checked his voting record lately?'

Deb glared at the wall as if she could see Rick squirming through it.

'Well, I have, and I think it's your job to do it too. You know the saying I always love? It's "speak truth to power". That's talking about people like Charles Brinton. We shouldn't ring him up and make chummy jokes over the radio. We should pin him under a microscope until he squirms. That's all I want to say.'

'Hear, hear,' roared Edith.

'Sssshhh,' hissed Ann.

As she hung up the phone, Ann switched on the radio again, just in time to hear Rick say, 'Well, your host got a bit of a telling-off there, folks.' Despite playing a whiplash sound effect, he sounded ever so slightly deflated, as though some of the hot air had hissed out of him. He quickly segued into 'Eternal Flame' by the Bangles.

'Oh turn it off,' said Deb. 'I've had enough of his voice.'

'That was brilliant,' said Maisie. 'You wiped the floor with him.'

'Did I?' said Deb. 'Whoops.' She sipped her coffee, and then wrinkled her nose. 'All I meant to say was that I won't be patronised by prats like Charles Brinton, who don't know what they're talking about.'

'You play yourself down,' said Edith. 'I heard you. It sounds like you've been doing your research.'

'Old habits die hard, that's all,' said Deb. 'Brinton's been in this seat for about twenty years now. He was smug when he started, and he's never been very helpful, but he's always keen to turn up if it means he's in the limelight. You know the type. I did a bit of volunteering locally when the kids were small, so I know him of old. He's just lazy.'

'Like so many of 'em,' said Edith.

'Now come on, Mother. You can't tar all MPs with the same brush,' said Ann.

'I meant men,' said Edith.

'Oh for heaven's sake,' said Ann. 'I didn't think you were one of those.'

'One of what?' said Edith.

'You know,' said Ann, 'a bra-burner.'

'Then you haven't been listening very hard,' said Edith. 'You might have noticed I brought you up all on my own, with no help from any husband.'

'How could I not notice? You've gone on about it enough times.'

'Well then,' said Edith. 'There's a difference between not knowing, and not paying any attention.'

Watching them, Maisie wondered how Edith could possibly have produced Ann, who somehow managed to be at odds with the world, while also hating to see any change in it. Edith, meanwhile, was easy-going, and funny, and bright, the epitome of good company. It was hard to fit one into the other, to see how they were linked. The only thing that seemed to bind them together was living under the same roof, by necessity rather than from familial love, and yet, at the same time, it was easy to see that Ann would be bereft without Edith.

Which will be closer than you think, thought Maisie, whose own mother had seemed a burden right up until the day she died. Just moments later, she had become something else entirely in Maisie's mind: wise, warm, long-suffering. A crucial thread that gathered together all of her history. She couldn't fathom whether grief played a terrible trick on you when it suddenly made you revise your world-view in this way, or whether it was in fact life that played the trick, burying you so deep in everyday cares that you never came to understand who you truly loved, and how, until it was too late.

'Anyway,' said Deb, clearly trying to change the subject, 'I keep an eye on Brinton. We're like old enemies, except I shouldn't think he knows I exist.'

'I had no idea you were interested in politics at all,' said Maisie, and immediately panicked because this sounded condescending in the open air, when in her head it had been a simple compliment.

'Oh,' said Deb, visibly embarrassed. 'I don't know much about the ins and outs. I pick up what I can. It's all out there for anyone to read.'

'I didn't mean to imply . . .' began Maisie.

'No,' said Deb. 'I completely understand.'

'I don't think you do,' said Maisie. 'I just hadn't seen that side of you before. It's very impressive.' This, she knew immediately, was also the wrong thing – the kind of compliment you give to a child.

'I only read the newspaper,' said Deb. 'It shouldn't be that much of a surprise.' She looked at Maisie defiantly for a few uncomfortable seconds. 'I know my place, don't worry!'

And Maisie couldn't think of a single thing to say in reply, because she was afraid that she would only dig herself deeper.

5

They swam that evening at six. Tonight was the weekly meeting of The Whitstable High Tide Swimming Club, and the numbers had carried on growing. Deb counted fifteen, including Chloe and Bill, who were already waiting when she arrived, sitting side-by-side on the beach and watching something on Bill's phone, shielding the screen from the bright sunlight with their hands.

'Evening all,' said Deb as she crunched towards them.

'Look at this!' said Chloe. 'Bill makes these, like, sick animations.'

'Wow,' said Deb, who couldn't help but cling to the old meaning of *sick*, and was now imagining that she would find images of characters vomiting all over the screen. She bent down and squinted, but the phone seemed defiantly dark against the daylight.

'It's stop-motion,' said Chloe. 'He does it with plasticine.'

'Is that what you do for a living?' said Deb, who had never thought to ask.

'No,' said Bill, who was so painfully shy that this almost came out as a whisper. 'I do something very boring for the Water Board.'

'I'm sure it's not boring,' said Deb. 'Don't put yourself down.'

'It actually is,' said Bill. Deb noticed that he never seemed quite willing to make eye contact with her. She had offended him the first time they met, chasing him across the beach and accusing him of being a peeping Tom. Perhaps she had never quite been forgiven for that. But even so, this embarrassment in her presence seemed excessive, and she got the impression that his shyness ramped up when he was talking to her. After all, he had been chatting to Chloe quite comfortably before she tried to join in, and now he was nearly frozen. *Is that where I've got to?* she wondered. *Old enough to make young men seize up in horror?*

'Ha!' she barked, too loudly. 'But it pays the rent, right?'

'Hm,' said Bill, and looked at Chloe, hovering his finger over the button of his phone to indicate that he was ready to shut it down.

'Not yet!' said Chloe. 'I want to watch a bit more.'

'It's on YouTube,' said Bill.

'No point coming to the beach to watch the telly,' said Deb, who really, really wished she could stop behaving like everyone's mother, just for a few minutes. Chloe let her eyes slide sideways and folded her arms, just like her own daughter used to, not so long ago. 'Alrighty,' said Deb, 'I'm going in. You two do what you like.'

She took off the t-shirt and shorts that were covering her bikini, and waded in up to her thighs, before diving under and surfacing into the sunshine again, the saltwater stinging her eyes. The sun was back out today, and now that they were nearing the end of August, the beach had been slowly roasted to bronze. The valerian and dandelions that sprang out of the shingle were looking crisp around the edges, and the stones were pale with dust. The sea was so warm after months of soaking up the heat of long days that it felt like she was swimming in a baby's bath. Deb was looking forward, now, to that first bite of autumn, when the water would be refreshing again. She wondered how long she would manage to swim into the winter, before the cold exiled her from her beautiful daily routine of high tides. She wondered, too, what she would do without it.

Soon, she saw Julie arrive on the beach in her usual flurry, strip off her clothes and nearly run into the water. Deb almost expected her to apologise; she was clearly used to being late for everything, or at least to arriving in a tornado of chaos, with children knocking precious things off shelves and a double buggy blocking everyone's way. Deb knew this state of mind well. The best thing to do, in every situation, was to say sorry in advance of the kids doing anything wrong, and then again while they did it, and then afterwards as well, for good measure. Everyone you encountered would still look at you as though you had failed the basic standards of being human, but at least they couldn't claim that you weren't bothered about it.

Deb was living this all over again while she was watching her grandchildren during the summer holidays. They were perfectly good kids – Leo was a bit prone to tantrums, but that was his age, and Sophie already tended towards the superior attitude that was so abundant in her mother. But that didn't make them any less perfect, and deliciously beautiful. The minute that Deb walked away from them each afternoon, she found herself dreaming about them, rolling over the funny things they said in her mind, or thinking about what she could do next to please them. When she was with them, though, it surprised her how quickly she became crabby and frustrated, barking orders at them ('Pick it up! *Pick it UP!*') or resorting to passive aggression every time they hit a barrier. 'Don't you mind Nanny,' she found herself saying to Leo one morning. 'Her feelings don't matter, do they?'

Perhaps children were better in the anticipation than in the indulgence. That was certainly how it felt: that the greatest pleasure she took in them was when they weren't actually there. Had she been like this when her own kids were young – impatient, resentful, bad-tempered? The answer was almost certainly yes, she supposed, but until these last few weeks, she had remembered it differently somehow. She had fallen into the habit of imagining herself in contrast to Cherie, light against dark. Cherie: stern, overstretched, regimented; herself, gentle, kind, indulgent, and yet also steel-willed about the important things, like good manners and untidiness. After a couple of weeks in the company of actual kids, Deb had now begun to admire Cherie's calm, distant consistency, and was beginning to think that, somewhere along the line, she had muddled her own experience as a mother with Mary Poppins. The kids watched it often enough; it was an easy mistake to make.

That was how life worked though; the passage of time wore everything smooth, until your memories were like the rounded pebbles on the beach, with all their awkward angles ground away. Everything was bearable in retrospect. It was as though your brain played a trick on you, and let you believe that you got everything right first time. Now that she was in the process of getting it wrong all over again, Deb was forced to wonder whether she ever knew what she was doing in the first place.

She watched Julie swim out into the open water and float there on her back, watching the blue sky. How old was she – thirty-five? Forty? Deb had had a gaggle of teenagers by that age, all fussing, and fighting, and worrying about things that really didn't matter, and she thought that was hard. But she couldn't imagine finding the energy to look after toddlers, as Julie did. Women waited so long to have their babies these days. She could understand it: they wanted to spend their twenties and thirties taking advantage of all the fantastic opportunities that the world offered them, and it took them a long time to want to put all that aside. But surely it also meant that they had more to lose – proper careers where you were valued and important; exotic holidays; nights out at the theatre and in glamorous restaurants. Before she had her own kids, Deb had never really got started. Which was worse: losing so much, or always wondering what it was like to have it?

As if she had forgotten how to relax, Julie was soon upright, treading water and looking at the coastline, before swimming over towards Deb.

'Gorgeous day!' she said, breathlessly. 'I really should get out here more often.'

'It's hard to make the time though, isn't it?' said Deb. 'I know I couldn't have done it until recently.' She didn't say that she had resorted to swimming at two a.m. last week, because her childminding duties had got in the way during the daytime, and she was awake, and worrying, anyway.

'It is indeed,' said Julie, and smiled as though she were an over-inflated balloon, who, at some point, would either burst or just whizz away over the horizon in a rush of air. 'It must be lovely being retired though.'

'Retired?' said Deb. 'I'm not retired. I didn't have anything to retire from. I actually need to get a job for the first time in my life, and I've got no idea how you do that.'

'I'm sorry,' said Julie. 'I didn't mean to be insensitive.'

'No, no, love,' said Deb. 'Don't be sorry. I'm just feeling a bit washed-up, that's all.'

'Sound like you could do with a glass of wine,' said Julie. 'Come on. We'll dry off and go to the Neppy.'

'Oh God, not there,' said Deb. 'Bad things always happen to me when I go there.'

'Really?' said Julie. 'What sort of bad things?'

'Only joking,' said Deb, thinking of the times when The Neptune had been hot and dark, and how she had sought Rick out, and how he had been mysteriously potent in those moments, irresistible. It was strange how that worked; he seemed like such an idiot in broad daylight.

'Fine,' said Julie. 'We'll try that new place on Harbour Street, just to be safe.'

6

The new place on Harbour Street turned out to be a pop-up bar in the old shoe shop. Deb didn't even realise it had closed down; it made her wonder where she would buy sandals now. This seemed to be the way it was going in Whitstable – all the useful shops were disappearing, and in their place things 'popped up' or were 'installed'.

She was old enough to remember there being a pub in the middle of every terrace, full of trawlermen and labourers; she was also old enough to remember those tiny backstreet pubs shutting down, one by one, as the house prices fell, and nobody seemed to want to go out any more. They all just quietly turned into homes, their signs removed, and their windows curtained. Now that Whitstable had gone up in the world again, new owners were stripping off fascias and sand-blasting paint to reveal the faded liveries of these ghost pubs, which lent the touch of authenticity they craved. Meanwhile, you could apparently set up an actual bar anywhere now, by filling a room with battered tables, stacking beer kegs at the back, and lining up bottles of obscure gin.

You couldn't get a simple vodka and slimline, though. After Deb grudgingly surrendered to trying a gin that was apparently flavoured with Icelandic herbs *(seriously)*, she was thrown all over again when she was asked to choose from a selection of tonic waters. She was previously aware of only two types of tonic: diet, and fat. Apparently, though, in this new world order, one was expected to select a mixer that mirrored the flavours of the gin. She became so flustered that the barman took pity on her and agreed to recommend his favourite combination. She tried to ignore the fact that he spoke to her like a doddery old woman in the process.

She was thankful at least that Julie picked up the bill, because a nine-quid drink – that wasn't what she'd wanted in the first place – was basically frightening if you were on Deb's budget.

They sat down on a rickety bench, and waited for the creations to arrive. Julie's had a wedge of pink grapefruit and a stick of cinnamon protruding from it; Deb's had what looked like a bouquet garni and a cluster of black balls, which she initially feared were peppercorns, but which Julie assured her were juniper berries.

'I love this place,' said Julie, thrusting her nose deep into her goldfish-bowl glass and breathing in the scents that swirled around in there before drinking blissfully from it. 'It makes me feel like I'm cool again. I hope they stay.'

'Mind that stick doesn't go in your eye, love,' said Deb, trying to find a way to avoid choking on the floating berries. She had already fished out the bunch of herbs and put them on the table.

'The thing I miss the most is going out for a drink with the girls in the office after work, without having to organise anything,' said Julie. 'No responsibilities to anyone. Worst thing that could happen was a hangover the next morning.'

'What did you used to do?' said Deb.

'Was there a life before changing nappies?' said Julie. 'I'm not sure I remember.'

'It wasn't that long ago!'

'No, you're right. I just find it hard to imagine now. I was in human resources.'

'I always fancied that myself,' said Deb. 'Looking after everyone.'

'To be honest,' said Julie, 'you spend most of your time sacking people, disciplining them or making them redundant. Or telling them that you've got to cut their salary because they've been off sick with cancer for too long. That sort of thing.'

'Oh,' said Deb.

'Yeah,' said Julie. 'After a while you feel like the worst person alive. We needed to go out on the town just to let off steam.' She sipped her drink again. Deb had never considered that, amid all the chaos and noise of her three small children, Julie might actually be escaping stress. She had assumed that everyone else was happier and more fulfilled than she had been; but perhaps, after all, the daily fireworks of family life were more soothing for Julie, because at least they allowed her to be kind.

'Anyway,' said Julie, 'that's the reason I thought you might like a drink. I've spent a lot of time telling people that they didn't have a job any more, and that means I'm a pretty good careers counsellor. I thought I might be able to help you.'

Deb stared at her for a few seconds, wondering if Julie had mistaken her for someone with qualifications and experience. She would have to break it to her gently – humiliatingly – that she was good for nothing but stacking shelves. 'Oh I don't know, love,' she said. 'I think the people you worked with were probably further up the ladder than me.'

'Well,' said Julie, 'let's see. What's your experience?'

'Nothing,' said Deb. 'I mean, none. I worked in a bank before I got pregnant, and then that's the end of it. And now I'm nearly sixty. No one in their right mind would have me.'

'Okay,' said Julie, 'you're going to have to think a bit more positively. I know you can do that. What kind of work would you want, if you could choose anything?'

'I wouldn't know where to start,' said Deb. 'I don't really know what jobs there are, if you know what I mean.'

'Think about it another way: what skills would you like to use? What environment would you enjoy? And, the flip side: what would you hate?'

'Er, okay,' said Deb, who would have preferred to be able to dodge this conversation altogether, except that Julie was proving strangely determined. 'Alright then. I don't want much. I know I'm not going to take over the world. But I like organising things, and listening to people. I like solving their problems. I think I'm quite good at . . . caring. I don't mean looking after people; I mean taking an interest. Being concerned. I can get on with anyone if I have to. And I like being with people; it helps pass the time. I hate being on my own, if I'm honest.'

'That's great,' said Julie. 'You're actually more clear than most people about what you like. You've not had the experience of sitting behind the same desk for years, and thinking that's all there is.'

'No,' said Deb, 'I'm the opposite. I've done nothing but imagine what wonderful things I might have done, if everything had turned out better.'

Julie smiled. 'Okay,' she said, 'now tell me about your education.'

'Nothing,' said Deb. 'Well, two A levels. That doesn't count for much any more, does it?'

'Well . . .' began Julie.

'But I've been working on it. I've got this funny ambition to get myself to university. I know it's ridiculous. I can't afford it anyway, so it's just a pipe dream, and I'd be a pensioner by the time I finished. But I've been going to college for a while now doing a returning-to-education course. You know, just to get my confidence up.'

'Why aren't you just going straight to university?'

'Oh no,' said Deb. 'I don't think I'm ready. I need some extra UCAS points anyway, so I'm taking English A level next year. Well I was going to. I don't think I can afford it now.'

Julie took a deep breath. 'Right,' she said. 'I'm going to weigh in with what I think. If it's completely unwanted, tell me, and I'll shut up.'

'Alright,' said Deb. 'Do your worst.'

'Well, the biggest obstacle you face is your confidence. Nothing else. I understand that you've not got much experience, and that your education was a long time ago, but those things are easily fixed. First of all, you've got to decide that you're worth it, and that you're as good as everyone else.'

'Right,' said Deb, uncertainly. She suddenly wished her glass wasn't empty. At least, then, she could hide her face behind it as she tried to drink.

'I mean it,' said Julie. 'You're smart, you're warm, and you're resilient. You've got grit. You need to start believing in yourself. It's the hardest thing in the world, I know, but you'll get nowhere without it.'

'Okay,' said Deb. 'I'll think about that.' She caught Julie's smirk, and said, 'No, really, I will. I promise.' But I don't know how, she thought. Where do you even begin?

'But I've got a couple of more tangible suggestions, too,' said Julie. 'First up, why haven't you applied to university already?'

'I told you, love, I'm not qualified. They wouldn't have me. It wasn't the same in my day – girls like me weren't expected to go to university. My mum thought I was a bit above myself for staying on at school after I turned fourteen.' Even as she said this, Deb could feel her throat getting tight. She was trying hard not to be annoyed, but she couldn't help but bristle at Julie's breezy insistence that it was straightforward. *Why hadn't she just applied already?* The implication was that she didn't have the wits – or maybe the confidence – to think of it herself.

'Have you looked into foundation courses? They're an extra year at university before you start your actual degree. You build up your skills and by the end of the course, you move on to a degree.'

'I'm sure they're not really for old ladies like me. They're for kids who failed their A levels.'

'They're exactly for people like you. I'm ignoring the old lady comment, by the way, because you know that's rubbish.'

'Well, thanks for the advice. I'll need to think it over, and save up. That'll take a few years, the way I'm going.'

'Have you looked at student loans? You won't even have to pay it back until you're earning a decent wage.'

'Yes, but I've got to live, too.'

'You can borrow money for living expenses as well.'

'That's no good! I'd just be getting into debt. I don't want that hanging over me for the rest of my life.'

'You can't see it as a debt,' said Julie. 'You need to think of it as a grant to cover your education. Realistically, at your age, you'll never have to pay it off. The government know that. They're letting you game the system.'

'Fine, love. I take your point. But it won't nearly cover it all, will it? I don't want to be living in student halls and eating baked beans out of the tin for the next four years.'

'No, you're right. It won't cover everything, but it will help. You'll need an extra job to be comfortable. And I've got an idea for that, if you're interested.'

'I need to go to the loo,' said Deb, and she stood up, making the table shake. There was just no stopping this bloody woman, and her insistence – her absolute *certainty* – that everything could be solved. Deb knew from long, hard experience that this just wasn't the case. Most things could never be solved. You just had to knuckle down and get on with it.

She found her way to the back of the room and, realising she had no idea where she was supposed to go, looked back pleadingly at the waiter, who mouthed, 'Through the back door!' Deb nodded, and went out into the summer dusk, where she found a grim outside lavvy with a barn door and a moth banging its head against the bare light bulb, over and over again. If she'd had a packet of fags in her bag, she would have given in right now. Instead, she locked the door, and closed the toilet seat so that she could sit down and indulge in one of the seeping, silent cries that were her speciality. To really pull it off, you had to fold up two squares of loo roll and hold them along the bottom lashes of your eyes, so that any dissolved mascara was caught before it could do any harm.

Stupid bloody moth. It didn't know when to give up – it just kept getting burnt, flying away, and then coming straight back for more. Deb had been behaving like that moth all her life, and she honestly had no idea how to do things differently. *Confidence*, according to Julie. Confidence was all it took. That magic fairy dust that every woman was supposed to have these days, despite being endlessly told you were fat and ugly, unfit to be a mother, stupid, slow, emotional.

She had to admit, she was doing quite a good job of the emotional bit right now.

She stood up, removed the tissues from her eyes, and blinked into the mirror. The same face, a bit saggier than it used to be, a bit more lined. Weren't you supposed to have wisdom by her age, like it downloaded with the menopause as a kind of compensation? What wisdom did she have? What did she know? Nothing much. Only how to avoid things. Only how to run away.

She always had that wisdom in spades when it came to other people. She always knew what to tell them to make them feel better.

What would you tell yourself now, Deb, if you could step back? What would you say?

She drew in a jagged breath, and looked herself in the eye.

You, she thought, *you. You're scared. You've run crying to the toilets like a little girl. You don't know what you're worth, and you're terrified to find out.*

And you don't like being told what to do.

You'd cut off your nose to spite your face, you would.

She laughed at that.

Idiot. Julie's only trying to help.

Worst thing is, she's not wrong.

Worst thing is, it all makes sense.

Worst thing is, it's all possible. And that's terrifying.

When she sat back down opposite Julie, Deb found a glass of wine in front of her.

'I thought about another gin,' said Julie, 'but I couldn't face the idea of wrestling with more foliage.'

'Yeah,' said Deb. 'One's enough for me.'

'You were gone ages,' said Julie. 'I hope I didn't upset you.'

'No,' said Deb. 'Of course not. I've just got a little way to go with that confidence thing.'

'Haven't we all,' said Julie. 'It's a lifelong mission.'

'I'll drink to that,' said Deb, and to prove she meant it, she nearly swallowed the whole glass. 'So go on then,' she said, breathlessly, 'tell me about this idea you have for my new job.'

7

Kent and Canterbury Hospital was built like a maze. The corridors had aggressively shiny floors and the stench of disinfectant, which Maisie knew would already have sunk into her clothes and would follow her home in the car. It was almost completely silent there. An elderly man shuffled past her with his head down; a woman was wheeled by on a bed, looking like she was far away in her thoughts. Maisie wandered after them, following an obscure colour-coding system that must have made sense to some senior administrator at some point, but now just seemed hard-hearted. She just wanted to get out, and go home. Surely it wasn't so hard to signpost an exit?

And then she finally found it; past the gift shop and the coffee concession – which was comforting here, a little hint that the world carried on being luxurious, even through this misery – and she was outside in the daylight, and wondering what to do next. There was a sign telling you not to smoke anywhere on the hospital premises, even out here. As if things weren't bad enough in this place, without being denied life's little comforts. She would have to tell Deb this, when she saw her. Although maybe that was cruel since she'd given up. Maybe it didn't matter. Maybe it was right to stop people doing themselves any more harm.

Not every illness was terminal. It was easy to forget that. Some things had a cure. Most things. Most people came to the hospital to get better, despite the miasma of sorrow that clung to the walls. Maisie dipped her nose into her shirt and sniffed: yes. Just as she thought: she reeked of the place. It was funny how, nowadays, the smell reminded her of her mother. It seems like a terrible trick of the memory, that a lifetime of perfume, and lily-of-the-valley soap, and the sweet tang of stewed apples could all lose their power to conjure her mother, and be replaced by the flat, brutal tang of a hospital. That was not what she wanted to remember: the slack mouth that had lost all its words, the yellowing cheeks, the hands laid across hospital bed sheets with skin like paper. But there it was, all ready to greet her as she stepped through the sliding doors.

She couldn't stand here all day. It was time to go home. First of all, she would have to find the ticket machine, and pay whatever extortionate fee they were charging these days. Or, rather, to stumble out of the consultant's office with bad news still ringing in your ears, and somehow still have to pay for the privilege of leaving.

Come on, Maisie. Enough of this.

In situations like this, when you're confused and panicky, and can't quite believe that no one is there waiting to scoop you up and make everything alright again, what you have to do is break it down into stages.

You find the ticket machine.

You insert your ticket. *Where's the ticket? I know I put it somewhere.*

You feed in a twenty-pound note.

You collect your change.

You locate the car.

You get into the driver's seat.

You put on your seatbelt, and try not to think how point-less it is; how a sudden collision with an oncoming lorry would be a mercy, compared to what you have to face, with no seatbelt to speak of.

You take a breath, and steady yourself.

You wonder about hot, sweet tea, and whether it actually works. For the shock. For bad news. Or whether it's an old wives' tale, like everything else.

You start the engine, take off the handbrake, find the point in the clutch where the bonnet rises and the car eases forward.

You drive home.

You just drive home.

Because you can't think past that.

8

Deb rang the doorbell, straightened her white blouse, and then wondered if she'd pushed the button hard enough the first time and rang again. Somewhere in the back of the house, she heard a stirring, and wondered if they'd be angry that she'd rung twice. She should have waited for longer. It was such a bad start. She took a deep breath, and tried to make her heartbeat slow down, just a little. It didn't work.

The door opened, and a woman appeared wearing jeans and a striped fisherman's shirt, and balancing a baby on her hip. 'Deb?' she said.

'That's me!'

'I'm Frances, as you know – sorry – and this is Megan. Come on in.'

Deb followed the woman through a hall in which there was a scramble of coats and boots, and a table full of unopened letters which looked as though they might once have been stacked neatly before a landslide occurred. Frances kicked a towel out of the way and said, 'Please ignore the mess. We're not usually this bad.' But then she paused in the doorway to the kitchen. 'Actually, we're always this bad. That's why we're doing this,' and she shifted the baby onto her other hip and opened the door.

The kitchen had once been beautiful; that was easy to see. It had a smart chequered floor and a butler sink, and a fridge the size of a wardrobe. But the wooden surfaces hosted crowds of mugs and glasses, boxes of organic baby food and scattered pasta shapes. The range cooker was stacked with dirty saucepans, presumably because the sink was full of plates, and the dishwasher, whose door was flipped open, was rammed with sippy cups and baking trays. The ceramic tiles were tacky beneath Deb's feet. Over on the kitchen table, there were the remnants of a family breakfast: half-empty coffee cups, discarded toast crusts, dribbles of jam, and a high chair caked in hardened Weetabix. Amid it all was a laptop, its screen still blinking.

Frances steadied the kettle with one elbow, and pulled off the lid with her free hand.

'Tea?' she said. 'Coffee?'

'I'll make it,' said Deb. 'You just sit down for a moment.'

'Really?' said Frances. 'I mean, would you mind if I changed Megan while you did it? I think she's sprung a leak. About an hour ago, actually.'

'No problem,' said Deb, and she waited until she could hear Frances's footsteps on the stairs before running fresh hot water into the sink and tackling the plates as the kettle boiled. That made space for her to wash a couple of mugs and a teaspoon. Once the coffee was made, she cleared away the breakfast things, and put them in to soak. She was just wiping the table when Frances appeared, with Megan in a different babygro.

'Oh goodness,' said Frances. 'I didn't mean for you to tidy up already.'

'I was just passing the time, love,' said Deb. 'I wasn't getting ahead of myself, don't worry.'

They both sat down at the table, and Deb reached over to tickle Megan's ear, until she giggled. 'She must have taken to you,' said Frances. 'She's been bloody miserable all morning.'

'They have their days, don't they? I think they work out when you're stressed and play up.'

Frances opened her mouth as if she was about to say something in her defence, but then her chest deflated, and she raked her fingers through her hair. 'I've got a deadline today,' she said. 'It's hopeless. There's no chance.'

'Has she napped?'

'She's refusing to. Screamed blue murder when I tried to put her down. I think she's teething.'

'Are you growing teeth?' whispered Deb to Megan, who smiled to show her bare gums and began to chew on her fist.

'They need constant attention when they're little,' said Deb, who really had no idea why women tried to do so much these days. You just had to have a little patience. It all passed eventually. 'There's no shortcut, unfortunately.'

'I have a friend – well, a colleague – well, my boss, actually – who cared for her daughter full time, and ran a magazine. Her little girl just used to sit in her pushchair and occupy herself while we had meetings. I just don't know how she did that.'

'I couldn't tell you,' said Deb. 'I never managed it with any of my three. If I turned my back for a few seconds, they'd be stripping the wallpaper and turning the settee inside-out.'

'We're just getting to that stage,' said Frances, and looked grimly around the room at all the elegant furniture. 'Look, anyway, that's why you're here, isn't it? So that we can see whether we might both be the right fit.'

'That's what I understand,' said Deb.

'I mean, we considered a nanny, but they cost about thirty grand or something, and I don't want to send Megan to nursery just yet. I really wanted her to be at home, and to spend our afternoons together on the beach, flying kites and collecting shells.' She snorted out a laugh. 'But that was unrealistic in the first place. I basically had no idea what this would be like. It's awful. I hate it. I want to get my life back.' She looked at Deb with terrified eyes for a few moments and then said, 'Sorry. I didn't mean to say that.'

'It's alright,' said Deb, who really could have laughed if that wouldn't have ruined everything. 'It's hard. No one tells you that when you get pregnant.'

'We were looking for an au pair, but I couldn't stop worrying that we'd get some useless teenage girl who didn't know one end of a washing machine from the other, and would really be trying to run off with Dylan. That's my husband. You haven't met him yet. I'm not meaning to say that he's the sort to have an affair. I just mean . . .'

'Don't worry,' said Deb, 'I get it. You need someone who you know will cope.' And good men get badly tempted when there's a baby in the house, she thought.

'So I read this article online about granny au pairs, and I happened to mention it to Julie, and the next day, she's on the phone saying, "I think I've got one for you!"'

'Like *Ghostbusters*,' said Deb, whose own children had watched the video so many times that she could probably recite the script backwards. '*We've got one!*'

'Right,' said Frances, who clearly had no idea what Deb was talking about. 'She said that she thought you might be just the right sort of person to take us on.'

'Well,' said Deb, 'I must admit that it's a new one on me, this idea of a granny au pair. But I gather it means that I'd do a bit of cleaning and cooking, and watch the baby while you're working, and maybe babysit a couple of nights a week while you go out.'

'Oh God,' said Frances, 'would you do that too?'

'And in return, you'd let me live in your spare room, and pay me a bit of pocket money.'

'I mean, we can't pay much,' said Frances. 'I gather the going rate's about a hundred pounds a week. But we'd cover your food and things.'

'That sounds fine,' said Deb. 'It's more than my husband ever paid me.'

'And Julie thought you might be studying part time as well?'

'Did she now?' said Deb.

'Was that the wrong thing to say?'

'No, love. I think I might be.'

'Great,' said Frances. 'Do you want to see your room?'

'Is that it? We're agreed? You don't want to see references or anything?'

'I probably ought to,' said Frances. 'But I'm more interested in how soon you could start.'

9

When Deb got to the beach that afternoon, Maisie was already wading into the sea.

'Hey!' she shouted from between the huts at the top of the beach. 'Wait for me!'

For a few seconds, Maisie looked like she hadn't heard and continued to walk into the waves, but then she stopped and turned round. Deb propped her bike against the sea wall and jogged down the shingle. She was bubbling over with news that had to be told, and if she let Maisie get into the water before she had the chance to spill it, then she would have to endure watching half an hour of efficient front crawl before the opportunity came around again.

'You were going in without me,' she said as she reached the edge of the water.

'I was standing here in my wetsuit already,' said Maisie, her hands on her hips. 'I thought I might as well. You might not have come.'

Deb frowned. 'But I always come. Every day.'

Maisie shrugged. 'Are you ready now then?'

'Give me a mo,' said Deb, and she stood on one leg to remove a shoe. 'I've got some amazing news,' she said as she pulled her t-shirt off over her head. 'I've got a job. A brilliant one. A perfect one.'

'Good for you,' said Maisie, and she turned back to walk towards the sea.

'Don't you want to know what it is?' said Deb.

'Yes,' said Maisie, and she rumpled her brow as if the mere thought of it gave her a headache. 'Of course I do. Sorry.'

'Right, well, I'm basically going to be an au pair. A granny au pair! Isn't that amazing?'

'A what?' said Maisie, and it sounded more bad-tempered than surprised.

'A granny au pair. I move in, and look after the baby a bit – and she's ever so sweet, little Megan – and I clean up and make sure the dinner's cooked, and they pay me!'

'Right,' said Maisie. 'Good.' Deb noticed Maisie's hands were twitching over her goggles, desperate to stretch them over her head and get away.

'And I've got a second bit of news too,' she said, although she could hear the air coming out of her voice already. This wasn't the response she had expected when she was cycling over here, running it all over and over in her head. 'I rang up the University, and do you know what they said? They can take me in to their foundation year, and I'll be able to start an actual degree after a year. And I can get a student loan to pay for it, and to cover some of my living costs, and I'll basically never have to pay it back because I'm so old and I won't earn enough money. Isn't that great? Finally there's a benefit to waiting as long as I have!'

Deb laughed, and Maisie returned a weak smile. 'Good news,' she said blandly, and then she turned and dived straight into the water, as though she could stand no more.

Deb walked in after her, but only got ankle-deep before the fury hit her. It was alright for Maisie, with her privileged career and pile of money sitting in a bank somewhere, like a massive mattress that would break any fall. Deb supposed Maisie had got her degree out of the way forty years ago, straight out of school; it probably seemed like nothing to her. But it was a big deal to Deb. Was that embarrassing, somehow – to be awed by the idea of getting a degree, of being a graduate? Well, if it was, Deb didn't care. She might look stupid to Maisie, but this was a massive achievement for her. She wasn't going to be ashamed of it.

And the job – of course, it was nothing to Maisie, who had worked in big city firms, probably earning hundreds of thousands of pounds a year. How small and pathetic it must look, to be so delighted with a few hundred quid a month and a roof over your head, and being able to take out a loan to cover the rest.

I bet she's never had to worry that she'll be made homeless, thought Deb. Maybe I never told her how close I got. But then, the reason I didn't tell her was because I knew she'd be too grand to understand. She only tolerates me when it suits her. When she can't be bothered with me, she can just brush me aside like this.

Well, thought Deb. Sod her. And she paddled back onto the shore, stepped into her shorts, picked up her sandals, and went back to find her bike at the top of the beach.

It was tempting to think that the beach huts looked sadder now that they were condemned, but the most chilling thing was that they looked just the same as ever. The same mismatched colours: candy stripes, seaside pastels, splashes of tropical pink and turquoise, all of them peeling. The same mix of smartness and decay, pride and neglect. She had thought that perhaps someone would put tape around them as soon as the planning permission was approved, but nothing had happened. They were slipping under the radar, the bastards. They were trying to pretend that nothing was going on.

The problem was that one day they would swoop in and knock down the lot, and by then it would be too late.

The phone rang in her pocket, and out of habit, she answered it without checking who was calling.

'Hello?'

'Deb! Lovely Deb.'

Deb took the phone away from her ear and looked at the screen: Rick.

'Hello,' she said coldly. 'What do you want?'

'Well, that's a charming greeting,' said Rick, full of fake jocularity.

'It's all you deserve. Don't you try to charm me. I'm not one of your phone-in people, you know.'

'Oh, but you are!' said Rick.

'Only because I had to. Only because you made me look like an idiot and I had to set the record straight.'

'Come on, babe. All's fair in love and war. I have to make local news items sound interesting, day in, day out. You can't blame me for spicing them up a bit, can you?'

'I can,' said Deb, 'and I will. What on earth did you want to pick on us for anyway? We're completely harmless.'

'That's not what Charles Brinton thinks, I'd say. I take it you've read his column?'

'What column?'

'In the local rag. He writes a monthly ramble about all the things he loves. You know: the sound of church bells ringing on summer afternoons; taking long walks by the Stour and listing all the birds he sees. You get the picture. It's boring, but the old ladies lap it up.'

'I must have missed that, sadly,' said Deb.

'Yeah, well anyway, it turns out that one of the few things he doesn't like about old-fashioned Kentish life is you.'

'Me personally?'

'It seems that way. He called you . . .' Deb could hear the shuffling of pages at the other end of the line, as Rick leafed through the paper to find the exact quote '. . . an "impertinent upstart".'

'Oh,' said Deb. 'How charming of him.'

'Hang on, there's more. "Shrill" . . . "disrespectful" . . . "would probably call herself a feminist, if one were to have the misfortune to engage her in conversation". You have to hand it to him, he's got a certain turn of phrase.'

'I'm afraid I don't admire him quite like you do,' said Deb.

'Who says I admire him?'

'Well you certainly sucked up to him when he was on the radio. It nearly made me sick.'

'Oh *that*,' said Rick. 'That was just a bit of the old charm. He's good value, is Charles. He'll always agree to a quick phone call to pass comment on . . . anything really. We have to keep him sweet.'

'He's a rent-a-gob.'

'I'm sure he wouldn't put it like that.'

'Well, I would,' said Deb. 'He'll happily rock up on the radio because it's easy. He can't even be bothered to turn up to his real job most of the time.'

'That's exactly what I'm calling you about, Deb. This is absolute gold. *You're* absolute gold. I have to admit, I underestimated you. Well, we weren't exactly doing much talking, were we?' He paused here, clearly hoping for a response, but Deb wasn't going to give it to him. 'But look,' he said, at length. 'You've got him rattled. He's been coasting along in a safe seat for years, and no one really bothers to challenge him. The assumption is that he's the MP until he chooses to give up. But you've come in and said, no, I'm not going to defer to him. And he doesn't like that one bit. We need more of you. We need more of the both of you.'

'I didn't start a protest group to get you more listeners for your crappy radio show. I did it because I don't want anyone to ruin my favourite place to swim. I know you haven't got any convictions, but I have.'

Rick sucked in a breath. 'Ouch. That was a bit savage, wasn't it?'

'It's no more than you deserve.'

'Alright. I admit it, I messed up. Look, when I turned up, I didn't realise you were going to be there, and to be honest, I panicked. And then you completely went off on one, and I thought, well . . .'

'All's fair in love and war?' said Deb.

'Maybe. Look, I couldn't go back to my producer and say, I shagged this woman last week. Can you go easy on her. Could I?'

'I don't know. Could you?'

'Christ, Deb, you're not going to make this simple for me, are you?'

'Nope,' said Deb, but there was a small smile curling at the sides of her lips now. He was so appealing when he was flustered.

'Look, I need you. Is that what you want me to say? It's no secret that listener numbers are falling. It's the same everywhere. There's so much competition. There are podcasts and digital radio stations, and streaming services where people can hear any record they want, as soon as they want it. It's getting harder and harder to find sponsors for the show. This week, after you called in and laid in to Charles Brinton like that, it was like you'd lit a fire under the whole thing. People tweeted and wrote in, and posted comments on our Facebook page. Loads of them were saying *Good on her!* I . . . look, I got it wrong, alright? I thought you'd be an easy target, and you weren't. People like you. They relate to you. I need some of that. I need you.'

'Well,' said Deb. 'Who knew, eh?'

'Who knew.'

'I'd tell you where to go, but I'm desperate to save this beach,' she said, although any fool would be able to see that this wasn't the only reason.

'*Deb*,' said Rick. 'My lovely Deb. I've upset you, and I really didn't mean to. I hope this doesn't disrupt our little arrangement?'

'Arrangement?' said Deb. 'I didn't know there was an arrangement.'

'Well,' he said, 'if I ask you nicely, do you think there might be?'

'Maybe,' said Deb, grinning. 'It depends on what exactly that arrangement might be.'

'I'm willing to negotiate on that matter.'

'I bet you are.' Deb shifted the phone onto her other ear, and glanced over to the sea, where Maisie had just turned to swim inland. Maybe, for once, Deb had better things to do than wait around for her. Maybe, finally, she'd built a life of her own, and it was good enough.

10

Deb cycled straight over to Rick's smart apartment in Tankerton. She realised that she should probably make him wait for a day or two, but then again why should she? She was meeting *her* needs, not his. Why should she pretend she was a demure little girl just to prove a point?

More than that, she was revelling in the delicious sense that Maisie would probably disapprove. It was not sensible enough for dear old Maisie, who lived a boring life and made it look like a virtue. Deb felt as though she had been suppressing a big part of herself in order to impress Maisie, and now it was time to let go of that. It simply wasn't who she was; and it never seemed to impress Maisie anyway. Deb had been playing a losing game for too long.

Not that Rick was much of an improvement, but he served a purpose. The trick was to make sure he didn't get a chance to do any talking. With that in mind, Deb made her way up to his apartment, and as soon as he closed the door behind her, she took off her bikini top, and they stumbled onto his leather corner sofa. This was exactly how she liked Rick – he smelt good, and was handsome enough close up, as long as he had his mouth occupied with something other than talking.

She wondered how quickly she could leave afterwards, before he spoiled everything. But just as she was pulling on her shorts, he emerged from the shower with a towel wrapped around his waist and said, 'So, baby, I'm glad you keep coming back for more.'

'Oh for God's sake!' said Deb, before she thought to moderate herself. 'Don't be such a twit.' Perhaps she had broken the seal of saying exactly what she thought of him now; or perhaps she had just run out of patience altogether. 'Can't you talk normally? I'm sure you're a nice chap really, underneath all that bravado.'

'Bravado?' Rick said, with great indignation, and he straightened and puffed out his chest for a few seconds before deflating again and saying, 'What do you mean, bravado?'

'I mean your *baby this* and *baby that*, and all the talking to me like you're doing me a massive favour by sleeping with me. Come on. I don't believe it. If you've got better options, then take 'em. But if you're enjoying my company, then stop being an idiot about it. We're grown-ups.'

'Blimey,' said Rick, running his fingers through his wet hair and looking for all the world like he had been hit by a falling brick. 'I don't know what to say. Do you think I come off badly when I'm talking to you?'

'Yes!' said Deb. 'You're ridiculous. You can't tell the difference between being on the radio and talking to people in real life. You treated me a like a groupie when we first met, and I had no idea who you even were. I fancied *you*, not some radio personality.'

'Well,' said Rick, 'nobody fancied me before I was on the radio.' He jutted out his bottom lip like a little boy, and Deb thought that there was a risk he would cry.

'And have women been queuing up since you've had your show?'

'Oh yes.' A pause. 'Well, no. Not exactly. I mean, one or two. I sometimes do nightclub appearances, and there's usually someone willing and able after that.'

'Willing and able? That's a pretty low bar to set for yourself.'

'Yeah, well. The company's nice sometimes.' Deb glanced around and saw, propped on his marble mantelpiece, a photo of two smiling girls, probably both in junior school.

'You've been married before?'

'Divorced three years ago. I couldn't believe it when it happened. I begged Jeanette – that's my ex-wife – to let me know what had gone wrong. I assumed she must have met someone else. But no. I slowly realised that she just didn't like me. She thought I was a bit of a knob. Like you do, apparently.'

'Well,' said Deb, who really could sympathise with Jeanette, 'I do, a bit. But I also like you, and . . .' she hesitated, because she really didn't want to say this out loud '. . . there's a funny spark between us, isn't there?'

Rick looked at her with sad eyes, and nodded.

'So how about we work on your approach a bit, eh? We could think about how you speak to women, right?'

'Oh please tell me!' said Rick, in mock horror. 'I have no bloody idea what women want. Nothing I say seems to land right.'

'Well, here's a little rule of thumb for you. Try talking to us exactly like you'd talk to a man you like and respect. It's not rocket science.'

'Fine,' said Rick, with more than a hint of sarcasm in his voice. 'Did you watch the game last night?'

'I did actually,' said Deb, carefully holding his gaze. 'Did you?'

'No,' said Rick. 'I don't like football. It just that you can ask that question to most men, and they'll start talking. All you have to do is nod and laugh sometimes.'

'So maybe you should start asking questions that you actually want to hear answered. Ask people about themselves. Tell them something you found interesting. Stop assuming that everyone's boring except you.'

'I don't!'

'Yes you do. What do you know about me? You've assumed I'm completely uninteresting, and probably an idiot.'

'Not after that phone-in. You really gave me a run for my money there. I realised I'd misjudged you very badly.'

'You did,' said Deb, 'and you wouldn't be the first, either. So, come on. Start asking.'

They talked for a long time after that, until they realised the light had dimmed outside the window and they were both hungry. So they went out and got some dinner in an Italian place where the waiters greeted Rick like an old friend. After that, they walked back to Rick's flat, and so Deb ended up missing her final night in the terrible basement flat. Instead, she slept curled up with Rick, who cooked her poached eggs on toast the next morning, and asked, hopefully, if he could see her tomorrow.

11

Maisie woke up on Thursday morning thinking that she would perhaps skip the High Tide Swimming Club that week.

She couldn't quite explain why. She had the vague sense that she had offended Deb the day before, which was incredible, really, because Maisie was the one who ought to be offended. Deb had trampled all over her own careful signals that she needed some peace. Other people would have worked this out, and left her to be quiet; or perhaps – God forbid – even asked if she was alright. But not Deb. Oh no. Deb just carried on, and on, and on, like a jackhammer. Maisie had to walk away from her in the end, just wade into the sea to stop the noise. When she came out again, Deb was gone. Perhaps that's all she was worth to Deb: a teacher to give a big tick and a 'well done' when she achieved something, without betraying any of her own emotions.

Maybe she'd drive a little way along the coast to Herne Bay or Reculver and swim there instead. She had heard that there were sandy beaches over towards Broadstairs, and even a sea-pool at Margate, and yet she had tried none of them since she moved here. The moment she arrived in Whitstable, she had fallen into such an all-encompassing routine that she had been unable to explore the new county that she lived in. Perhaps she could even just take a stroll through one of the old country towns that littered Kent, just for this afternoon. It surely wouldn't hurt to miss one day.

But the thought of doing this made her feel sick. When everything else felt like it might spiral away from her control, her daily swim gave her something to cling to. It was like putting a pin in the map: whatever else there was waiting for her out there, here was a place she knew. Even though her instincts were screaming to be alone at the moment, it did her good to spend time with other people. As it was, she was already alone too much. It was important that she didn't retreat altogether. *It's vital that somebody notices if you don't emerge for a couple of days*, she thought, and then told herself not to be morbid. It hadn't come to that yet.

Her greatest fear, greater even than becoming ever more disabled, was other people witnessing it. Most of all her friends. Those cherished people who had been equals and companions, who had laughed alongside her through life so far, who had come together to grieve life's missteps and indignities: she would become gradually more helpless and dependent in their eyes, until there was nothing left but pity. Perhaps not now, not yet. Perhaps they could still admire her black humour and her steady determination to build defiant routines. Perhaps they could still find something to laugh about together. But soon – and she could not know exactly when – they would stop seeing themselves mirrored in her, and would instead come to see an invalid, a helpless victim of a terrible disease, who was not like them at all.

Maisie didn't want to let this happen. She had tried to avoid it when she left Stephen and moved out of London. She had not told anyone, even her closest friends. In part, this was because she had wanted to leave everything to him. *You can't take it with you,* her mother used to say. Well, that counted for friends, too. Better for him to keep them, in this world. But in truth, she was really responding to a darker instinct that had overtaken her as soon as she got her diagnosis: *burn everything*. She wasn't going to let this thing flame through her life. She would do it herself. Get rid of the lot – the fancy house, the dull marriage, the coterie of clever friends – while it was still a choice that was hers for the making. Burn it all. Goodbye to all that. Time to live a simpler life, on her own. She thought that a hermit's existence would rather suit her.

There was a flaw in her plan though: she hadn't thought about what would happen once she got to Whitstable. Well, she had: she had imagined herself swimming every day (tick), and sitting quietly in her plain little sitting room, reading every morning and night (tick); she had thought that she would eat carefully, cut out the wine with dinner and the whisky before bed (tick). But she had failed to imagine a vital part of the picture: the people she would meet. It wasn't even that she hadn't intended to make friends. She had simply failed to imagine other people being there at all. In her mind's eye, Whitstable was entirely empty, or at least full of blow-ins like herself, all of them quiet, separate, and content in their own company. She hadn't thought about the people who would walk their dog past your garden every day while you took in the fleeting slant of morning sun. She hadn't considered that the woman who served the tea at your local café would come to recognise you, and ask after you, and would then strike up a conversation when she passed you in the street. She hadn't factored in the neighbours, who would lean over the back fence and offer you handfuls of chard from their allotment, and ask you to feed their cat when they went on holiday.

Most of all, she hadn't factored in Deb, and then Ann, and then Julie and Chloe and Bill and Brian, and then, after that, the whole raggle-taggle that came with them. And the politics! Oh God, the politics. She thought she had left that behind, but apparently not. Entirely by accident, she had fallen into a commu nity, and they were not willing to let her keep her anonymity.

Today, she felt exhausted by it. She didn't want to say anything to any of them. She just wanted to disappear from sight. But she remembered that she had promised to pick up Edith in her car, and drive her to the beach, and that was a promise that she wouldn't break lightly. Edith, after all, didn't get to choose her isolation from the world – it was thrust upon her by old age, and a daughter who didn't seem set up to cope with modern life.

Maisie drove over to Ann and Edith's house, and found them both waiting in the front garden, Ann gripping the handles of Edith's wheelchair as if she was afraid that her mother would escape given half the chance. This was possibly true. As Maisie opened the car door, she heard Ann saying, 'We'll be late.'

'Oh for heaven's sake,' said Edith. 'Good afternoon, Maisie, and thank you for coming to collect us. We are not completely devoid of manners in this household.'

'Hello,' said Maisie. 'Sorry, Ann, I *am* a bit late. I'm sure everyone will carry on without us, though.'

'There,' said Ann. 'See?'

Edith caught Maisie with a look of such disgruntled embarrassment that they both broke into laughter, leaving Ann crosser than ever. Maisie helped Edith into the front seat of the car, and then folded the wheelchair and placed it in the boot, while Ann slotted herself into the back seat and put on her seatbelt. They drove in silence to West Beach.

Edith walked up the steps over the seawall this time, leaning heavily on two sticks and creasing her face with the exertion. Maisie had offered to fetch some people to carry her over in her chair, but she had said a firm no. 'I'll get there myself,' she said. 'Though it might take me all day.'

'You'll do yourself a mischief,' said Ann as Edith climbed the steps one by one.

'Don't care,' said Edith under heavy breaths.

'Well I do. I don't want to spend the night in the hospital worrying over you.'

'So don't,' said Edith.

'You two,' said Maisie. 'Will you stop it for just a few moments?'

Just then, Edith hauled herself to the top of the steps, and stood on the seawall for a few seconds, catching her breath and watching the sea with the hawk-eyed focus of someone who might never see it again. 'Right,' she said at length. 'The only way is down now, and down's worse than up when you've got knees like mine.'

They seated her at the top of the beach, and she poured herself a cup of coffee from a flask while she regained her equilibrium. Meanwhile, Ann wandered from person to person asking their names, before returning to Maisie and saying, 'I've taken the register. Twenty-five people today,' as if she were reporting back to a commander on a battlefield. Maisie nodded, as she felt was her role in this game.

'That's really quite a lot,' she said.

Deb was at the other side of the beach, sitting on the groyne and talking to Bill. Maisie tried to catch her eye, but either Deb was so entranced by the few words he managed to stutter out, or she was deliberately avoiding saying hello. Nevertheless, Maisie put her hand in the air to wave to her once more, mainly so that she couldn't be accused of being aloof, rather than through any real feeling. Deb didn't respond. Fine. If that's how she wanted it, Maisie would be very glad to retreat a little from all this entanglement.

She heard a child crying, and turned to see that Julie had arrived, and was trying to drag a double buggy over the shingle towards them, a third child trailing behind her, bawling out tears of pure fury. Maisie would have got up herself, but Deb was there first. It felt like the marking of a territory – children belonged to Deb, and probably their mothers, too. Deb immediately bent down to pick up the baby and cradled him in her arms, and Maisie took it as an act of aggression. That kind of thing didn't usually bother her; she had made peace with her lack of maternal instinct long ago. She was, quite simply, incompatible with children. But today it felt as though Deb was playing the mother hen more than usual, as if to turn up the contrast between the two of them. Big-hearted, generous Deb, versus cold, formal Maisie. Deb, who would do anything for anyone – never mind that it usually meant she resented them afterwards. It was obvious who would win in this battle.

Now, Deb embarked on the complex process of offering the baby over to Bill, who was all elbows as he tried to receive the tiny body with the same competence that Deb had shown. Bill's hands were shaking, but his eyes betrayed a kind of awe that Maisie hadn't seen before. Perhaps this was the real him, once you got past his terror of talking to people. He glanced from Deb to the baby, from the baby to Deb, but Deb's attention was suddenly drawn to the top of the beach, where a man was approaching. The look on Bill's face was pure disappointment.

'Rick!' shouted Deb, and she waved both her arms in the air like a castaway spotting a distant cruise liner. 'Over here!'

Rick? thought Maisie. *What on earth would she want with Rick?*

12

Sure enough, there was Rick, every bit the provincial radio DJ in his open-necked shirt and pink chinos, which were a little too crumpled to be impressive. Overall, he had the appearance of someone who wasn't being properly looked after, which suggested to Maisie that he was the kind of man who was helpless without a mother figure to lick him into shape. His sandy hair was unkempt, and he wore his sunglasses on the crown of his head in a fruitless effort to cover a burgeoning bald spot. Because of this, he was squinting against the reflected light of the sea. When it got too much for him, he took a baseball cap out of his shoulder bag, and quickly switched it for the glasses, as if he thought there was any possibility of concealing the red patch of skin on his crown.

'Hey!' he said, clearly willing to pretend that he was the most welcome person in the world. 'Great to see you ladies again.' He turned to Bill and nodded. 'And gentlemen, sir. I do apologise.' A broad grin, revealing stained teeth.

'What's he doing here?' said Ann.

'I was about to ask the same thing,' said Maisie, who noticed that Deb was looking up at this ridiculous man with something approaching adoration.

'Now listen,' said Deb, snaking her arm into Rick's. 'I know that our last radio appearance didn't go all that well, but we've had a little talk, and I think we understand each other now.'

'We sure do,' said Rick, and Deb giggled.

'The thing is that Rick's always looking for an interesting story, and I'm afraid I gave him something a bit too interesting when I shot my mouth off like that. It was my fault really. I see that now,' said Deb. She looked to Rick for approval, and he gave it in the form of an exaggerated look of pity, which made her giggle all over again. Maisie exchanged a wary glance with Ann. This didn't seem like Deb at all. It was as if she'd been brainwashed.

'I don't think you should take the blame,' said Maisie. 'From what I saw, you – we – were pretty much stitched up to create some sensational content for his cheap show.'

'Well,' said Deb coldly, 'perhaps you just don't understand the pressure that Rick's under to get new listeners. It's up to us to give them stories that they'll find exciting, otherwise we lose control of the story. That's right, isn't it, Rick?'

Rick smiled his assent, and Deb took in the horrified faces that surrounded her, adding hurriedly, 'He *is* sorry though, aren't you, Rick?'

'Mea culpa,' said Rick, grinning. 'What can I say? This wonderful woman has set me straight.'

'I'll do more than set you straight,' whispered Deb in his ear, loud enough for everyone to hear. From the corner of her eye, Maisie saw Chloe mime sticking her fingers down her throat and vomiting all over the shingle, while Julie bit her lip and pretended not to see. Meanwhile, Rick's hand wandered across Deb's bare belly and around to her bottom, where it was reluctantly slapped away.

'Anyway,' she said, straightening her bikini top, 'the thing is that we're being given a second go. I don't know if you saw Charles Brinton's column in the paper this week, but Rick thinks we've got him rattled. He reckons there's mileage in covering our campaign in more detail, keeping up with it week by week. He's invited the director of East Kent Land Management onto the show on Monday, and he's promised that he'll question them really hard on their timeline, and ask them what exactly they're planning to build over there. Won't you, love?'

'I will,' said Rick. 'Pinky promise.' He held up his little finger to Deb, who said, 'You! Stop it!' and batted it away affectionately. This was a little too much for Chloe, who rolled her eyes into the back of her head and pretended to faint dead away. Maisie wished she could join her.

'But more importantly, in my view,' said Rick, shifting his face into seriousness, 'is that Deb invited me to come along to your club meeting tonight, so that I can produce an informal piece about you all, and what you're doing over here.'

'You can't just come along and interview us!' said Ann, who had folded her arms across her chest and was rocking back on her heels in fury. 'You have to ask permission first. We'll take it to our committee and get back to you with our decision.'

'What committee?' asked Deb, sweetly. 'I don't remember there being one, dear.'

'I accept that we don't have a formal committee structure *per se*,' said Ann, 'but up to now, these matters have been discussed between you, me and Maisie. You're riding roughshod over that. You can't just bring him along without consulting us first.'

'I can,' said Deb. 'And, actually, he's as free to join the club as anyone else. You can't stop him coming along and talking to people. They're all adults. It's up to them.'

'It just goes to show that we're in dire need of a club constitution,' said Ann. 'Which I think I've pointed out before.'

'You have,' said Deb, 'and everyone's ignored you.'

'Fine,' said Ann, raising her hands defensively. 'I'd be interested to hear what Maisie says on the matter.'

Suddenly, all eyes were on Maisie: some in high humour, some furious. Deb's were full of challenge, as if she were saying *I dare you.*

Maisie took a breath and wondered what she thought. She didn't trust Ricky Robinson – and his slimy devoted boyfriend act – as far as she could throw him. And she didn't like this moon-eyed, girlish version of Deb, either. But then, what on earth was she supposed to do about it? She didn't have the energy for a battle, and more than that, she was sick of being the arbiter for everyone's problems. These people were adults, not children. They were big enough to make their own mistakes.

'I don't think we have much choice,' she said. 'I mean, if we're supposed to be campaigning, we can't afford to turn our back on the only local radio station. We can only do our best, I suppose, to put our arguments across. Otherwise we're shouting into the void.' She looked over at Rick, who was giving her the double thumbs-up, like some idiot child who didn't know when he was in disgrace. 'We can only hope that Rick will behave more responsibly this time.'

'Hear, hear,' said Ann, who probably didn't agree with Maisie at all.

'Thank you,' said Deb, and Maisie realised that it was the only time she had actually looked at her this afternoon, even if she couldn't tell whether or not Deb was being sarcastic.

'You won't regret it,' said Rick. 'I'm absolutely behind this thing now that Deb has explained the issues for me. I was a little slow to catch up.'

'Well, I'm going in for my swim,' said Maisie. 'That is the point of this club after all, isn't it?'

'Oh,' said Rick. 'Can you just hold off for a few minutes? I want to catch an interview with you first. Then you can swim to your little heart's content.'

Maisie sighed. 'Fine,' she said. 'Where do you want me?'

'Give me a moment, will you, love? I just have to set up my equipment.'

'Right,' said Maisie. She stalked over the beach to sit down next to Edith, who was now happily ensconced in her chair, watching the seagulls wheeling over the sea. The coffee that was steaming in her hand was black, and carried the distinct whiff of brandy. Maisie smiled and leaned her head against Edith's elbow.

'Who's the slick bugger in the stupid shirt?' said Edith.

'That's Rick,' said Maisie. 'I get the sense he's the new object of Deb's affection.'

'Won't last,' said Edith, and she sniffed. 'Still, it's no bad thing for our Deb. A little fling will do her good. She's glowing like a bride on honeymoon.'

Maisie glanced over at Deb, who was holding Rick's bag while he made a great pantomime of checking the sound levels at various points on the beach. 'You're wicked, you know that?'

'I do,' said Edith. 'You mark my words, it's the last thing they'll take from me.'

'I can believe it,' said Maisie.

'Do I take it you two have had a little falling-out?'

'Oh I don't know,' said Maisie. 'Not as such. More of a cooling-off.'

'It's a shame,' said Edith. 'You're both good girls. You find a way to set it straight. Right?'

'Am I getting a telling-off?' said Maisie, smiling.

'You are. Life's too short.'

'It is indeed,' said Maisie.

'Listen,' said Edith. 'I haven't said thank you properly for taking me onto the beach these last few weeks. It means the world to me. You know that.'

'I do. It's a pleasure to see you enjoying it.'

'Well, there's one last favour I'd like to ask. I want to swim. I want one final go in the water before I pass on.'

'Don't talk like that,' said Maisie.

'If you don't talk like that at my age, you're a damned fool,' said Edith. 'I want my time in the water again, like I did when I was a girl.'

'Then we'll make it happen,' said Maisie, and she squeezed Edith's hand. Edith swigged the loaded coffee.

'Do you know what, though,' said Edith, 'it'll take the both of you to make it happen. You and Deb. You'll have to work out your differences first, whatever they are.'

From the far corner of the beach, Rick called, 'Maisie! We're ready for you!' and Maisie wondered if reviving their friendship would be possible any more.

13

Deb was perched at Cherie's breakfast bar on one of her slippery bar stools that seemed almost wilfully uncomfortable.

'Latte? Cappuccino? Cortado?' barked Cherie from the glinting chrome coffee machine by the sink.

'Just normal is fine, thanks, love,' said Deb.

'It does it all automatically, so you're really not achieving anything by being humble,' said Cherie.

'I'm not being humble, I just want an ordinary coffee with a bit of milk.'

'Fine,' said Cherie. 'An Americano.'

'That'll be lovely,' said Deb, although in truth, these Americanos tended to be far too strong for her taste, and she would have preferred a straightforward Nescafe, which wouldn't send her home with a pounding heart. 'Can you pour a bit of extra water in though? Just from the cold tap is fine.'

'Oh for heaven's sake,' said Cherie. 'You're determined to make it disgusting.'

'I'd be happy with a glass of water, to be honest,' said Deb.

'No,' said Cherie, 'don't worry. I'll put cold water in it.'

'Thanks,' said Deb. Cherie slotted a carton into the machine, and watched attentively as it dribbled out a thin stream of coffee into a waiting mug.

'It's really very good this, you know,' she said. 'The quality's gone up since the first-generation machines. These cartons' – she shook a box in front of Deb's face, as if she was trying to occupy a fractious baby – 'are made by Costa. You won't be able to tell the difference.'

'I'm sure you can't,' said Deb.

'What I'm saying,' said Cherie, with the sort of heavy-hearted sigh that Deb used to elicit from her school teachers, 'is that you could learn to use the machine yourself, so that you can have decent coffee while you're looking after the kids, rather than using instant.'

'I like instant,' said Deb. 'I'm used to it.'

'Well it's taking up space in my cupboard. We're using pods now.'

The main thing is that you don't want anyone to catch you owning a jar of instant coffee, thought Deb. As though your friends would never speak to you again if they found it. In Cherie's case, perhaps that was even true. Either way, she wouldn't have to face that embarrassment for much longer.

'Listen, love,' she said, 'I need to tell you something.'

'Mmm-hmmm,' said Cherie, who had now produced a watery-looking latte and was busy wiping down the machine with a floral microfibre cloth.

'I'm afraid,' Deb said, 'that I won't be able to look after the kids for the rest of the holiday.' She paused to wait for this to sink in. At length, Cherie paused her industrious cleaning and turned.

'What?' she said.

'I won't be able to look after the kids for the rest of the holiday. I've found myself a job. It's not much, but it'll keep me ticking over. Otherwise I'm broke.'

She tried to make kind eyes at Cherie, and hoped against hope that she would understand. But Cherie was nothing if not predictable.

'What am I supposed to do, then?' she said. 'Where will the kids go?'

'Well,' said Deb, 'I've done a bit of looking around, and there's a play scheme that'll take Sophie for the last couple of weeks of the holiday. It's only over in Swalecliffe and I hear it's ever so nice. And maybe there's a nursery that would take Leo, or a childminder. He's a good kid; he won't make a fuss.'

'All of these things cost money, Mum. Surely you realise that. How do you think I'm going to suddenly afford this, out of the blue?'

You could cut down on those coffee pods, thought Deb, although she didn't say it out loud. 'Keeping a roof over my head costs money too, love,' she said gently.

'You should have thought of that when you walked out on Dad.'

'I did,' said Deb. 'But I always knew that at some point I'd have to start earning again. It's just come a bit sooner than I expected.'

'Right,' said Cherie, who had never lost the knack for drama that she'd nurtured so carefully in her teenage years. 'Fine. So what is this bloody job anyway?'

'I'm going to be an au pair,' said Deb, deliberately dropping the word 'granny' from her job title. 'I'll be living in.'

'So you can look after someone else's kids, but not your own grandchildren? That figures!'

'You know I adore the kids,' said Deb. 'But the difference is, they're paying me. I don't run on thin air, Cherie. I'm a . . . person.'

'I'll tell you exactly what you are,' said Cherie, snatching back Deb's half-drunk coffee. 'You're selfish. Just like all your generation. You think you're entitled to do whatever you like, while your family struggles on without your help. Well, that's fine. My children and I will make our own way, thank you.'

'Alright,' said Deb. 'If that's how you want it. I've done my best.' And she slid off the stool, picked up her bag, and left.

She thought that there would be tears as soon as she closed the door behind her, but, strangely, there were none. *I don't think I've got any left,* she thought. But that wasn't quite true. No: it was time to do this. It was necessary. She wasn't playing house any more in her little flat, with money she'd saved up in a piggy bank. This was make or break, the point at which she made the transition into a life she could sustain on her own. In that moment, she realised that there was no longer the remotest possibility that she could go back to Derek. It was so far away now, that old life of hers. It seemed almost laughable to imagine it. Cherie, quite simply, would have to catch up. Holding out for mummy and daddy to get back together was no longer an option.

As she wove her way through the artificially winding streets of Cherie's estate, she pulled her phone out of her back pocket and texted Rick.

It went as badly as I thought it would

A pause.

What did?

With Cherie.

Who's Cherie?

My daughter

Oh god yes I forgot. Sorry. How did it go?

Badly

Listen, I'm at work at the moment. Can't really talk.

Okay

Why don't you come over later so I can cheer you up ;-)

Will do :)

The next morning, she knocked on Frances's door with a suitcase stuffed with her clothes, her tatty old towels, and her one set of bed-sheets, although she supposed that she wouldn't need to use them any more. It was the same suitcase that she had dragged through her own hall one evening while Derek was at the pub, and into a waiting taxi. Then, it felt like she was on the brink of something magnificent, a new, glorious phase in her life.

This time, the gesture felt slightly more practical, but it was none the worse for that. Here she was, six months on, surviving. Just like she said she would.

Frances opened the door, smiled, and said, 'Come in!' Deb hauled the case up the stairs, and followed Frances into a small bedroom with a single bed, an old pine wardrobe and a chest of drawers with a vase of flowers on the top.

After she closed the door behind her, she sat down on her new bed, and pulled up the blind. There, beyond the roofs and chimneys, was the sea, glinting in the distance.

'A sea view!' she said aloud, to nobody.

So what if Maisie thought this was nothing; if Cherie thought it was selfish. This, finally, was the fresh start she'd been hoping for. *You've finally landed on your feet, girl,* she thought.

14

Maisie carried on swimming every day, choosing the early tides at four a.m. and then five. Once upon a time, she would have also swum the evening tides until they became impossibly late, but now she left these to Deb – a simple division of a precious asset, like a divorce settlement. Or at least, she assumed that was the deal: she saw nothing of Deb. For all Maisie knew, Deb could have given up swimming altogether. Well, if she was petty enough to do that just to avoid contact, then so be it. Maisie couldn't bring herself to care any more.

She wondered if other people would notice this quiet separation. If anyone asked – and she had rehearsed this line over and over in her mind, imagining how it would land on Julie, or Ann, or Chloe – she would tell them what she'd told Edith: there hadn't been a falling-out *as such*, but maybe instead a cooling of relations. This didn't seem unfair, or vicious; it was also the straightforward truth. They had become friends earlier in the year, and for a while that had bloomed into something intense and wonderful. Perhaps by its very nature, it had over-balanced itself and left them both feeling a little overwhelmed in each other's presence, like a summer romance. It was, after all, nearly September, the point at which all summer romances must come to their bitter conclusion.

In Maisie's long experience, friendship often followed this pattern anyway – a hunger for each other's company, followed by a sudden loss of interest which was usually mutual. It was as if you both spent some time exploring all the things you liked about each other, and all the ways in which you agreed, and then, when you found a solitary point of difference, it suddenly outweighed all the good things, and the wonder stopped abruptly, like falling off a cliff. It was hard not to reflect what fragile creatures we are as human beings, completely unable to absorb the natural differences that occur between us, and instead endlessly engaged in a futile search for a perfect reflection of ourselves.

The Save West Beach campaign would be awkward, though. She thought she could perhaps discreetly move to another beach, and slowly extricate herself from the group over a period of months. It was a shame, but maybe that's how the divorce settlement would have to fall: she would take the swimming, and Deb would get custody of the politics. In any case, she had lost all faith that there was any point in the campaign; it just seemed as though she was setting herself up to be disappointed, and she couldn't face it. It was a faint-hearted attitude, she knew, but there it was. Sometimes you had to recognise when you'd had enough.

Nevertheless, she tuned in to the feature on Ricky's show to hear what mincemeat he'd made of them this time. She was driving to the supermarket at the time – she preferred Waitrose in Canterbury, which was a twenty-minute drive but made it pleasurable to buy groceries, rather than a chore – and she told herself that she wouldn't have bothered to listen otherwise.

'A couple of days ago, I had to go to the beach – but all in the line of duty, folks. It's a tough job, but someone's got to do it,' said Ricky's distinctive voice, followed by canned applause. Maisie inwardly shuddered. She had no idea what Deb saw in him; she couldn't help but find him repulsive.

'But seriously, folks, I went and spent some time with the Save West Beach protestors, and they made a compelling case for their campaign. Have a listen and see what you think.'

Okay, thought Maisie. It's not a horrifying start.

Julie's voice came on first of all, talking about how she wanted to keep the beach for her children. 'Further into town, you're close to restaurants and pubs, and when we play there I have to keep a close eye on everything they do. There's always fish-bones, or glass bottles, and you never know what sort of behaviour you're going to find. Bringing them over to West Beach, it's a bit quieter and safer, and we can set up camp for the day. If they open bars over here, it'll be the same thing all over again. We'll have to get in the car and drive to another town. I know some people will say, *So what*, but for me that's a little bit of childhood lost.'

Then Rick's voice came on again. 'Earlier this year, a company called East Kent Land Management applied for planning permission to build on Whitstable's West Beach. Despite objections from local residents, consent was granted for them to build a leisure complex in place of the picturesque beach huts, and those who use the beach fear that this will mean the end of their natural idyll.'

It took a while for Maisie to realise that the next voice was her own, because it sounded so formal and clipped. But there she was, surprisingly firm and competent. *We're not killjoys or nimbies. We don't want to stop people from having fun, and we don't want to see Whitstable preserved in aspic, looking like a Victorian fishing village forever. It's just that we don't believe that these proposals enhance the modern town that we know and love. It won't bring in local jobs, it replicates bars and restaurants that already exist elsewhere in the town, and it will destroy a wild space that currently has a huge impact on the quality of life that our residents say they moved here to capture. This is about wellbeing, and understanding how vital that is to future generations.*

There were more interviews: Brian talking about the beach as a wildlife habitat; Chloe, being billed as 'the voice of the younger generation', saying how lucky she felt to have somewhere to hang out, where everyone was welcome. And then, right at the end, Rick summed up what he had discovered. 'What I see, looking around this beach, is a community being formed. There are children playing, people of all ages mixing happily, and folk enjoying the kind of healthy lifestyle that governments spend millions promoting. It strikes me that there needs to be more of this, not less; that we should do all we can to support groups like the Whitstable High Tide Swimming Club, and therefore to look after the outside spaces that allow them to flourish. When I was a kid, growing up over in Westgate, I was free to roam over the beach, and my mum could let me do that, knowing that

I'd never be far away from a friend or neighbour who could send me back home if I strayed too far. That's something we've lost, and it's my contention that we're finding it all over again here. Surely that's too precious to throw away for another coffee shop? This is Ricky Robinson, reporting from West Beach.'

Maisie, now parked up in the Waitrose car park, was surprised to find that this made her well up. Granted, it veered towards sentimentality at the end, but somehow – and she really couldn't imagine the process by which it had happened – Ricky had hit the nail on the head. This was all about a way of life, and perhaps it was the dream of falling into a community like this that had drawn her from London to Whitstable in the first place. Despite her love of being alone, this answered the terror of isolation she felt: not the sticky, patronising prospect of being looked after by strangers, but the ability to find her place in a loose-woven collection of people, who would surely catch her if she fell too far, or at least notice that she was suffering.

She was just about to get out of the car, when the record finished 'The Final Countdown' by Europe; Ricky hadn't undergone a complete rehabilitation), and Ricky's voice faded in.

'Well,' he said, 'this is a little unexpected. I had been hoping to introduce a guest to you to comment on that last report, a Mr Luke Crichton of East Kent Land Management, the company proposing to build on Whitstable's West Beach. But he's just walked out of the studio! He told our producer Dan – Dan, can you confirm this? – that he thought my report was biased towards the protestors, and that he wasn't going to walk into – what was it, Dan? That's it, a bear trap! Well, listeners, I must say I'm rather surprised at this turn of events. Actually, I'll go further and say I've never heard the like! Maybe you'd like to let me know what you think? You know the number: 0345 . . .'

Before she even thought about what she was doing, Maisie had texted Deb:

Did you just hear that on Ricky's show?

Yeah came the reply, almost immediately. I'm in the studio. We've got 'em on the run!

15

Deb walked through the harbour into town with baby Megan strapped to her front using a long strip of fabric that had to be turned and folded in a way that she found quite mystifying. It was like an obscure form of origami: Frances wove it around her waist, over her shoulders and then knotted it at the back, all the while talking through the process as if Deb had any hope of remembering it a second time.

'I had a carrier when mine were little,' she said, as Frances drew the material together like a corset, 'but it just clipped on.'

'Nobody uses those any more,' said Frances breathlessly. 'Turns out they were terrible for babies' hips.' Then she straightened and caught Deb in a kind of terrified gaze. 'Their thighs should come out straight at the sides, like frog's legs,' she said, miming the position with two splayed hands. 'Never straight down, never dangling. Always supported. Do you understand?'

'Yes,' said Deb. 'They should look like babies' legs.'

'Right. Sorry. Yes. Their natural form. Apparently those old carriers are a time bomb for arthritis.'

'No problem,' said Deb, and she wanted, for the tenth time today, to say that she'd been around the block a few times herself, and her kids appeared to be able to stand up alright. But she kept her counsel; it was just stress talking.

That was the only language that Frances seemed to speak. After just twenty-four hours in this fraught household, Deb had already been warned about the dangers of plastic toys that wobbled too much (phthalates, apparently, whatever the hell they were); the terrible effect of antibacterial cleaning spray on the development of children's immune systems (which was a crying shame, because Deb loved a quick whizz around with a bottle of Dettol); the absolute line-in-the-sand rule that Megan must not eat any processed sugar; and the necessity of speaking to her in French for a few minutes each day in order to help her to become bilingual in later life.

This one stumped Deb. 'I don't speak French,' she said. 'I've maybe got a bit of holiday Spanish.'

An exhausted sigh from Frances. 'Fine. No problem. I'll handle the French bit. But do you know enough to count to ten occasionally? Like, maybe when you're going up the steps you could do it then?'

She looked expectantly at Deb, who said, carefully, 'Un, deux, trois, quattro . . .'

'*Quatre*,' said Frances. 'Un, deux, trois, quatre, cinq . . .'

'Six . . . sept . . .'

'Huit, neuf, dix,' said Frances impatiently. 'Alright, fine, maybe you could practise for yourself first, before we unleash that on Megan.'

'Sure,' said Deb. 'I'll look it up on the internet.'

'It really is worthwhile,' said Frances.

'Fair enough,' said Deb. None of her kids were any good at languages, so maybe this was where she went wrong. 'Is Dylan's family French then?'

'No,' said Frances. 'Why did you think that?'

'Only that you said you wanted Megan to be bilingual,' said Deb. 'That's normally because one parent speaks another language.'

'Dylan's from Somerset,' said Frances, levelly. 'We just think that it's important, that's all.'

Deb had met Dylan the previous evening. He had rolled in at eight o'clock on a folding bike, fresh from the St Pancras train. He seemed to be the opposite of Frances: relaxed, gym-fit, certain. He kissed Frances and thrust out a hand to Deb like a well-trained public schoolboy, saying, 'And you must be Deb – great to have you on board!' with the air of a man who would be barely affected by this extra person in the house. He took hold of Megan and said, 'How's my beautiful little girl? Ready for Daddy stories and bedtime?' before turning back to Frances and saying, 'Milk all ready in her room? Great!' and bounding up the stairs, flying the baby in front of him like an aeroplane.

'He's a great father,' said Frances. 'Very involved.' She must have read the doubt on Deb's face, because she quickly added,

'He would have happily been a stay-at-home dad, only he earns a bit more than me. Quite a lot, really. And of course, I'm freelance, so my work is flexible. I mean, we thought he'd be able to work from home a couple of days a week when we moved to Whitstable, but that hasn't really come off. He's just too important to the magazine, I suppose!' She smiled tightly. 'Still, he gives Megan all his attention when he's here. He's so involved.'

It's easy enough to be involved when all you have to do is feed a baby a bottle of milk, thought Deb. Particularly when your wife had to sit and express the contents of that bottle into a machine during her lunch hour.

But anyway, today she and Megan were out for a walk, while Frances tried to get enough head-space to write an article on feminist bloggers. As she crossed the road and walked up Harbour Street, Deb noticed several other women who were – what was the term? – baby-wearing. Many of them didn't look much younger than Deb. It all seemed to be a habit that was better suited to winter than summer. In the August sun, Megan was hot against her chest, and the tight sling around her waist was already damp with sweat. Surely a pushchair would be better, letting them both cool down a bit? When she had mentioned this to Frances, though, she had been told that there was evidence that babies found pushchairs 'distressing', which seemed unlikely given that it was the only way that Deb had been able to get her own children to sleep.

The cafe at the end of the street was advertising iced coffee, and it was more temptation than she could bear. Time to give them both a break. She found a table, and unravelled Megan from the wrap, not daring to untie it for fear that she would never get it back on again. 'There you go, love,' she said, placing her in a high chair. 'You cool yourself down a bit.'

She expected Megan to start crying, but actually she just looked relived. She grinned at Deb and chewed on the book that Frances had packed, and then made an assault on the daisies that stood in a milk bottle in the middle of the table. Deb leaned back gratefully into the chair. Sensing someone standing just behind her, she assumed it was the waitress and turned to apologise. But instead, there stood Bill, shifting his weight from one foot to the other in an effort to start a conversation.

'Bill!' said Deb. 'I didn't know you were here. Why didn't you say something?'

Bill shrugged silently.

'Alright, fair enough. Come and sit down.' She pulled out a chair and he sat, knocking his knees into the table so that the daisies shook.

'What brings you out today then, love? I thought you'd be at work.'

'Day off,' said Bill. 'I had a project I wanted to finish.'

'Is this your animation? Chloe told me about it. She said it was – what was the word? Oh yes, *sick*.'

Bill laughed. 'I'm not sure if it's sick,' he said, 'but it's what I love doing. When I get the chance.'

'Is it done on computers or something? I suppose it's all very technical these days.'

'No, no. It's stop-motion. I make the models myself.'

'Wow,' said Deb. It was hard to be interested in someone who was so unwilling to talk about themselves. In some men, this would have lent an air of mystery, but in Bill's case, it was just frustrating. He said the bare minimum that he could get away with without being rude, and what little he said was so quiet that she had to strain to pick it up. She found that she was asking question after question, as if she was interviewing him, because otherwise the conversation stopped entirely.

'How old are you, Bill? I know you're younger than me . . .'

'Thirty,' said Bill. 'Well, twenty-nine. But I think I might as well round it up at this stage.'

A joke? Deb laughed more in relief than in genuine humour, although it was interesting to see his wit glint through once he relaxed.

'I'd take twenty-nine for as long as you can,' she said. 'You might as well. You're still the fresh new talent at the moment.'

'Hardly,' said Bill, but at that moment the waitress arrived, and he fell silent again.

'An iced coffee for me,' said Deb, 'and would you mind chopping up some carrot sticks for the baby? Thanks.' She was about to turn to Bill to let him order, but then she realised how impossible it must be for him to manage the most simple transactions in life. 'Can I tempt you to an iced coffee too, Bill?' she said, and he nodded in some relief.

'Have you always been as shy as this?' she asked as the waitress left. 'If you don't mind me asking.'

Bill's face twisted into discomfort, and at first she thought she'd said the wrong thing entirely, as usual. But then he breathed out and said, 'Always.' A pause. 'I'm just like my mum.'

'You'll say that more and more after you hit thirty,' laughed Deb.

'I thought that was just women.'

'Oh God, love, it is! I'm sorry.' He was alright once he got going. In fact, as the conversation went on, she realised that his shyness brought about a kind of intimacy that she wasn't used to. It forced her to lean in and listen closely, and made her quieten herself. The coffee and carrots arrived, and they carried on talking as Megan chewed contentedly. It wasn't the sort of conversation she was used to, where she rattled off strings of words, apologised for them and then rattled off some more. Talking to Bill forced her to listen, and to choose her own words carefully so that they didn't trample over his. He was an interesting man, and there was plenty of humour underneath all that quiet. He liked walking and books, and had some interesting things to say about *The English Patient*, which Deb was reading at the moment. Until then, she had been wishing she'd just stuck with the film, but now she thought she might pick it up again and find new life in that labyrinthine storytelling.

Perhaps she didn't understand men at all. Perhaps she had been so used to Derek and his straightforward stupidity that she had come to believe that all men were this unsubtle. Either way, when it was time for Bill to leave, she walked away from the cafe with the same fizzy sensation in the bottom of her belly that she got from Rick.

Your wiring's gone wrong, she told herself as she wrestled a reluctant Megan back into the baby sling. *Seems like your heart will flip for any passing man these days.*

Frances had made it very clear that she didn't want Deb back in the house before six o'clock. Deb was sure that this really meant Megan, but the way she said it – 'I need you out of my hair until tea-time' – had stung somewhat. It would mean that she would miss the high tide this afternoon, for the first time in five months. She wished, now, that she had thought to bring a swimming nappy and a towel, and they could both have gone along to the indoor pool at least, which would have been a decent substitute. Deb had a feeling that Frances would not approve of her taking Megan into the sea, and as she walked through the harbour pointing out the boats, she kept herself occupied with a kind of mental parlour game that involved guessing which particular hazard or pollutant would keep Megan off the beach. Raw sewage in the water; too much salt in the sea; the ever-present risk of nasty nips from crabs. The sun, in general. Marauding seagulls. The potential for her to realise that ice-cream existed, in which case all would be ruined.

There was no harm, though, in walking along the beach – surely – as long as Deb didn't put Megan down on the shingle. The child had a sun bonnet strapped on, and was pasted white with Factor 50. She was fed, and had drunk a bottle of expressed milk, and her nappy was clean. All of these reasons aside, it was coming up for high tide. Deb thought that perhaps Maisie might be there, and, well, it had been a while.

The last time they'd really spoken, it hadn't gone well, but so much had happened since then. In retrospect, she had begun to wonder if there hadn't been something going on that day to make Maisie so distant. She didn't seem . . . quite right. Maybe Deb had pushed it a bit far; up to then, she had always waited to be invited into sharing personal things. This time, she had just poured it all out, and maybe Maisie simply wasn't ready for it. The door wasn't always open; she knew that. In any case, she thought it might be time to bump into Maisie so that she could get a sense of where things stood.

She walked Megan through the cool, shady alleyways and onto Island Wall, which eventually became a dirt track that led behind the caravan park and onto West Beach. As she got to the top of the ramp, she could see the black neoprene silhouette of Maisie standing by the seawall, already in her wetsuit. Her stomach made another little jolt at the sight of her friend – *see, it's everyone now, not just the men. You've gone wrong.*

'Hello!' she called, and Maisie looked up, shielded her eyes from the sun, and waved. Then she began to jog over to Deb.

'I'm so glad you're here,' she said. 'I'm afraid something has happened.'

'What?' said Deb. 'What is it?' She broke into a run herself then, the baby bumping up and down against her chest until she began to cry.

'Wait!' called Maisie from behind her, but it was too late. As Deb reached the row of beach huts, she saw that overnight, somebody had driven a series of stakes into the ground, and had erected a wire fence enclosing the whole terrace. At intervals along the hoardings, there were laminated signs attached with gaffer tape:

KEEP OUT
SCHEDULED FOR DEMOLITION

'Christ,' said Deb, as she unwrapped the sling and pulled the baby onto her shoulder to comfort her. 'It's revenge, isn't it? For the radio show.'

'I fear so,' said Maisie. 'And I'm afraid there's something else, too.' She pointed at a sign at the far end of the row, which appeared to have something attached to it. Deb crunched over and found an envelope addressed to Ms Deborah Evans. Her maiden name.

She unpeeled the tape and opened it. There, inside, were her divorce papers, signed in Derek's shaky writing.

She felt a hand on her shoulder, and Maisie said, 'Well, at least he's finally signed them.'

'He had to make sure I knew it was him, though, didn't he? He had to take one last thing from me.' She shifted Megan onto her left arm, so that she could balance the baby on her tummy and swing her back and forth. The child was still distraught.

'They've shown their hand,' said Maisie. 'This is no bad thing. It gives us something to really fight against, rather than just a vague idea.'

'Yeah,' said Deb. 'You're probably right. Maisie, love, can you have a look in my backpack? There's a dummy in there. We'll be alright as long as her mum doesn't find out.'

'Sounds like a very good idea to me,' said Maisie, looking grimly at Megan, and then unzipping Deb's pack and thrusting her arm into the bottom. She retrieved a packet of two orthodontic soothers, which she wrestled open before handing one to Deb. On receiving the dummy, Megan fell blissfully silent, and Deb let out a breath.

'She's hot. I really ought to get her in the cool.'

'Come on then,' said Maisie. 'I'll make us some iced coffee at home.'

As they turned to leave, they heard footsteps rushing along the beach behind them, and saw a woman running towards them.

'I can't believe this,' she said. 'I've just come to my hut and I can't get in. What's going on?'

'Maybe you should come for coffee too,' said Maisie.

16

Megan fell asleep in Deb's absurd papoose on the short walk to Maisie's house, and was now lying on a towel in the middle of the living room floor. As soon as Deb had put her down, she was on the phone to Rick. Maisie supposed that this was the way of things now, and she would have to get used to it. Her friend was in the whirlwind phase of a romance, and this, apparently, looked no different in your fifties than it did when you were a teenager. Maisie doubted whether she would personally have the capacity to get quite so excited about a man any more, but she certainly remembered the feeling. That fine line you trod between fear and pleasure in those early months, when nothing was yet fixed, and you were eternally worried that the dream would all be over. She was grateful never to have to go through it again.

As Deb talked on the phone, Maisie chatted to the woman from the beach huts. She had introduced herself as Grace, and was neat and grey-haired, with an impish, animated face. Maisie guessed she was probably in her sixties.

'So you knew nothing about this?' said Maisie. 'I mean, they hadn't written or anything?'

'Nothing at all,' said Grace. 'That beach hut has been in the family for years. I inherited it from my dad. I come down here a few times every summer, and my sister and her children use it sometimes, but that's it, really. We only live over in Sittingbourne. I can't believe I hadn't heard anything.'

'I suppose they didn't know who to contact,' said Maisie, spooning coffee into her cafetière. 'Otherwise, I expect you'd have got a letter a while back, offering you an irresistible amount of money.'

'I never say never,' said Grace, 'but it would take a lot for me to sell the hut. We've been coming since we were children. We'd drive down to Whitstable after school on a Friday and camp out in it at weekends. It's not the same hut, obviously.

Dad had the whole thing replaced about twenty years ago, and it's still holding up well. The one before that must have been forty years old.'

'That's a long history,' said Maisie.

Deb came in from the garden, where she had been talking to Rick, her phone still glowing in her hand. 'He said he'll speak to me at the top of the show, and he'll get the producer to ring East Kent Land Management as well, to try to get them to comment. He's being ever so sweet about it, bless him. He said, "I feel like this is my fault." Aw.' She clutched the phone to her chest, and wrinkled her nose. Maisie realised that she was probably expected to make this gesture in return, but instead busied herself by filling glasses with ice.

'Sugar?' she said.

'Not for me, thanks,' said Deb. 'I need to watch my figure now.'

'He might have more luck calling the MP,' said Maisie, ignoring this neon signpost to Deb's sex life. 'I mean, we could ask what he's doing to protect the interests of residents while all this is going on. If we have people like Grace saying this is the first they've heard of it, then that might mean we can ask them to account for the ownership of all the huts before anything happens. There could be valuable things locked up in those huts – or at least, things with sentimental value. They surely have to hold off until they have contacted all the owners.'

'I should hope so,' said Grace.

'Oh yeah, that's what I meant to say,' said Deb. 'Apparently the General Election was announced about an hour ago. Rick says they're frantic, trying to pull together something to say about it when they go on air.'

'There's not much to say, is there?' said Maisie. 'Brinton will be back in and it'll be business as usual.'

'I wouldn't be so sure,' said Deb. 'Times are changing.'

'Perhaps you should get a guitar out and sing that,' said Maisie, and laughed, but Deb's expression stayed fierce.

'I'm serious. I reckon if the other parties got together, we could get rid of him. Smug old bastard. I'm going to volunteer to knock on doors this time.'

'Good for you,' said Maisie, and wondered why this had become such a grudge match for Deb. It was as if, somehow, the MP had become linked to Derek in her mind – perhaps he was just one more man who had tried to put her in her place, and he had crossed the line at the wrong time. Maisie had spent her whole life trying to reassure people that she was not a political firebrand just because she was an educated black woman. She had spent her career being quiet and dressing conservatively to make it clear that she posed no threat to the corporate environment she'd chosen to work in; she had pretended not to hear a multitude of ignorant or downright vicious comments about people from the estate where she'd grown up rather than challenge them, all the while feeling like a traitor.

She had told herself that she was doing what she had to do in order to survive, and that there would come a point in her life when it was time for her to use her accumulated status to stand up for others. Perhaps now that time was coming, and yet she still couldn't find the fire that Deb seemed to access at the drop of a hat. Maybe she had left it too long. Maybe she was ashamed that she had chosen conformity over challenge. Or maybe, now that her mother's London council house had sold for a breathtaking amount of money, she had far too much to lose. Deb, who had absolutely nothing to her name – who was carrying around another woman's baby in return for a roof over her head and three square meals a day – had no further to fall, and it had liberated her.

Maisie set the iced coffees down on the kitchen table and said, 'Cheers!'

'What do we do next?' said Grace. 'I just want to go back to the beach and take that fence down.'

'I'm posting a photo on Facebook,' said Deb, 'and asking everyone to head over. People will be shocked when they actually see a fence around everything. It kind of makes it real, you know?'

'What about the baby?' said Maisie.

'The baby?' said Deb.

'Megan. Will you bring her?'

'Shit!' said Deb, looking at her watch. 'It's half past six! Oh God.'

She made to run into the living room, but then her phone rang and she answered. 'Frances! I'm so sorry, I've just realised the time! No, everything's fine, it's just that she fell asleep, and . . . No, I do know that her routine is important. Yes. I completely understand. No, you're right. I'll wake her up and head straight over.'

'Come on,' said Maisie, 'I'll give you a lift. We'll join you on the beach a little later, Grace.'

Maisie sat in the car and watched Deb stand on the doorstep and apologise to the woman who was clearly her new boss. She wondered what it must be like to have to move into a stranger's house and look after their children, and still to be spoken to like an irresponsible child when you made the tiniest mistake. She thought that she would rather walk over hot coals than put herself through that, but then, on reflection, perhaps that was true for Deb, too. Perhaps she had already walked over hot coals, and this seemed like a viable option in comparison. It made her think that she had no idea how hard it was to be Deb after all.

After a few minutes, the passenger door opened and Deb slumped in.

'Damn,' she said as she clicked on her seatbelt. 'That wasn't great.'

'I saw you getting a telling-off,' said Maisie. 'Was it alright in the end?'

'Yeah,' said Deb, 'it's okay, I think. At least I've still got a roof over my head tonight. I'm in the dog-house though.'

'It was a simple mistake,' said Maisie. 'No harm was done.'

'Thing was, she wanted me to clear off out of the house all day with the baby, and that's what I did. In this weather, too: poor kid would have been much happier in the garden with a paddling pool and a parasol. We can't tramp around Whitstable all day, carrying her on my front like that, too. I had to settle her down somewhere.'

'Did you tell Frances that?'

'No,' said Deb. 'Of course I bloody didn't. Wouldn't dare. What would I know, anyway?'

'I thought the point of a granny au pair was to feel the benefit of their experience?'

'So did I,' said Deb, looking out of the window. 'Seems it's all changed since my day.'

'Still, at least you're out now.'

'That didn't go down well, either. She wanted me to come in and cook dinner. I had to tell her that I'd gone over my agreed hours for the day as it was . . .'

'So she actually got some free overtime, then,' said Maisie.

'I'm not sure she sees it like that.' Deb went scrabbling into her handbag before throwing it into the footwell. 'Bugger. I was looking for my fags.'

They parked in Maisie's drive and walked over to the beach, where they found Brian, dressed, as usual, as if he was about to head off on a jungle expedition, including a canteen of water slung over his shoulder and a neckerchief that made him look like an overgrown boy scout. He was pacing up and down the mesh hoardings, and when he saw Maisie and Deb, he laced his fingers into one of the panels and shook it.

'This is disgusting,' he said. 'People will be horrified when they see this.'

Deb glanced at her phone and said, 'There's a lot of chat on Facebook, but no one's quite sure what to do.'

'Story of our lives,' said Maisie. 'We're never sure what to do. We're useless, really.'

'We could take 'em down easily enough,' said Brian.

'No,' said Maisie. 'We mustn't give them an easy ride like that. They'll just dismiss us as vandals.'

'I've got the feeling they're more useful to us up than down anyway,' said Deb. She opened her backpack and pulled out a tiny pair of white socks, which belonged to Megan. She was sure Frances wouldn't miss them.

'Do you remember the Greenham Common protests?' she said. 'The women tied baby clothes to the fence of an RAF base when they tried to store nuclear weapons there.' She wove the socks into the wire of the fence. 'This is what it's about, isn't it? It's about having places where children can play.'

'And grown-ups,' said Maisie, and she fished around in her swimming bag for her goggles, knotting their rubber strap onto the fence.

'You can't survive without your goggles!' said Deb.

'I have a spare pair in here. Two, actually.'

'We mustn't forget old duffers like me,' said Brian, 'who want to remember we were once little boys dipping in rock pools.' He unknotted his neckerchief and wound in into the fence. He stepped back and admired his work for a while, and then said, 'If you'll excuse me, there are a few people I'd like to inform of this.' Taking out an ancient-looking mobile phone from his bag, he dialled a number, plugged a finger into his spare ear and strolled off towards the caravan site.

As the two women were left alone together, a silence fell between them. There was a relief to being back in Deb's company that Maisie couldn't quite express. When they had been apart, her mind had played strange tricks on her, mutating Deb into a stupid, childish monster. Now, happily back by her side, she remembered how comforting Deb was: this woman who was completely unable to disguise any of her emotions, and who had therefore become the person that Maisie trusted the most in the world. And yet Maisie herself had carefully hidden everything, and then resented Deb for not knowing anything about her. She cleared her throat.

'Listen,' she said. 'There's something I need to tell you.'

'What?' said Deb.

'I . . . I know I've been a little grumpy lately.'

'Don't mention it,' said Deb. 'We all have. We got into each other's hair too much. Or I got into your hair. I didn't mean to.'

'No,' said Maisie, 'it's not that. Oh hell, you're the first person I've told this to. I've got Parkinson's disease.'

'Oh,' said Deb.

'There's not an awful lot you can say to that, is there?'

'Well,' said Deb carefully, 'what do the doctors say? I'm sure they can do a lot for you.'

'I saw the specialist last week,' said Maisie. 'I'm deteriorating already. They can't do much, really. They talk about drugs, and physio, and occupational therapy. There's an operation on your brain. But if you watch what they're actually saying, none of it will get any better. It's all about "management" and "coping", and "improving outcomes". They don't say it out loud, but it's only going to get worse.'

'I'm sorry,' said Deb. 'That's terrible.' She put her hand on Maisie's shoulder. 'I really mean it. I just haven't got the words. I'm sorry.'

'I already freeze up sometimes. There will come a time when I won't be able to swim,' said Maisie, and at that point her voice cracked and she had to clamp her lips together to stop herself from weeping right here on the beach. Nobody needed that. Instead, she let Deb draw her into a hug, allowing her wet cheek to rest against that of her dear, dear friend.

'We'll work something out,' said Deb into her ear, 'when the time comes. But it isn't here yet.'

'No, it's not,' said Maisie, wiping her leaking eyes on the back of her wrist. 'Funnily enough, Edith told me last week that she wanted to swim in the sea again. Maybe we should do something for her first.'

'We definitely should,' said Deb. 'We will.'

'We'll have to get past Ann first,' said Maisie.

'What, the two of us? She doesn't stand a chance,' said Deb.

17

At seven, Rick's radio producer phoned to ask Deb to stand by for an interview. 'East Kent Land Management refused to talk,' he said, 'but we've got Charles Brinton in the studio because he's launching his election campaign. We thought we might put you two head to head.'

'No problem,' said Deb. 'Bring it on.' Maisie was now standing by the beach huts, explaining what was going on to people out walking their dogs. Most of them looked appalled. Deb would have helped her out, but she need to settle her mind before the interview. She took out her phone, and gazed at the grid of apps, wondering what she could immerse herself in for a few minutes, to shut out the growing commotion around her. Other members of the High Tide Swimming Club were beginning to gather, arriving from work to see the fenced-off beach huts for themselves. They milled around on the beach, looking stunned. Julie had come prepared with a carrier bag of things to tie to the fence: a child's sun-hat, a minute swimming costume, and a plastic spade. Chloe unfurled a scarf covered in skulls from her wrist, and wove it into the wire. Ann frowned at the fence and said she would have to think about finding something suitable.

Deb plugged a pair of earphones into her phone and took a swig of water. She opened YouTube, planning to calm her nerves with videos of puppies. But then she recalled Chloe and Bill sitting on the same spot a couple of weeks earlier, and remembered that she had meant, vaguely, to look up his channel. She flicked over to Facebook, found his profile, and hunted around for a link. Nothing. It was just like Bill to be too modest to promote his work. She returned to YouTube and typed in his name: *Bill Keyes animation.*

A list of tiny pictures appeared on the screen, but the top one caught her eye. It was called *The Swimmers*. Deb's breath caught in her chest. She clicked through and an image filled the screen: swirling water, its overlapping shades of blues and greens carefully worked in plasticine. The camera panned out to reveal a familiar scene: a pebble beach divided by wooden wave-breaks, just like the one she was sitting on. At the edge of the sea, perched on a washed-up tyre, sat the figure of a young man. He had mousy hair and green eyes like Bill himself, and he was watching someone in the water. A woman in a mismatched bikini, with blonde hair scragged up on top of her head. She turned in the waves like an exotic fish, and then rolled onto her back to smile at the sun and wriggle her toes above the waterline. The camera lingered lovingly on her chipped nail polish. It would be hard to miss who this woman was supposed to be, and through Bill's eyes, she was a free spirit, beautiful and wild. It was as if someone, finally, had seen the version of Deb that she imagined herself. Meanwhile, the man on the beach gazed at her with such yearning that it was almost painful to watch, but every time he tried to call out to her, the wind blew and his words floated away.

Deb's phone rang, and she hurriedly closed YouTube. She took a deep breath: she needed to get this right this time. She sat behind one of the groynes to shield her from the breeze and answered the call.

'Deb, are you there? Excellent. We've just gone to a commercial break, and then when we're back, I'll patch you in.'

'Okay,' said Deb.

Maisie came to sit beside her. She grasped Deb's hand and squeezed it. After a while, the line cleared and she heard Rick's radio voice.

'Now, as you know, we've been taking a close interest in the situation on West Beach, where protestors are fighting plans to build a leisure complex. It appears that things have moved on today, with hoardings being erected around the condemned row of beach huts on the site, seemingly overnight. The company responsible, East Kent Land Management, are still unavailable for comment – make of that what you will – but we still have Charles Brinton MP with us in the studio, who's agreed to talk about the plans, and we're joined on the line by Deb Winters of Save West Beach, who I believe is actually standing by the beach huts right now. Is that right?'

'Yes,' said Deb, 'I'm on West Beach as we speak. Thanks for having me on here.'

'Can you describe what you see, Deb?'

Deb looked up, and saw that the High Tide Swimming Club had gathered around her: Julie, Chloe, Ann and Brian. She clenched her jaw and held their gaze as she spoke. 'Well, any of your listeners who visit the beach will know that it's currently covered in greenery, so that you can hardly see the shingle any more. It's a beautiful day. The sky's blue, and the tide's up. There's a few of us ready for a swim later. But then, behind me, is a horrible great big fence covering the beach huts. And the people who are arriving are beginning to make their feelings known – they're decorating the fence with things that remind them of the days they've spent here. It's like a wall of beautiful memories. That's what's being destroyed here: childhoods, time spent with loved ones, summer romances. Everyday lives. It's a crime to drive a bulldozer over all of this. It's obscene.'

'So, Charles,' said Rick, 'You're a man of the people.'

'I like to think so,' said Charles in his smooth voice.

'What do you make of this, then? Have the council maybe underestimated public feeling here? Shouldn't this whole project be scrapped?'

'I don't believe so,' said Charles. 'Look, we all have a sentimental attachment to the beach, but times move on, and we have to move with them. We can't just cave in every time rent-a-mob turns up and makes a fuss.'

'Can I come in there?' said Deb. Don't explode, she thought to herself. 'I think there's a lot of decent people here today who will resent being called "rent-a-mob". If that's what Charles Brinton thinks, then he's really misjudged what's going on here. Every single person here today – and on our Facebook page, which now has over a thousand followers – cares about saving this beach for their own, personal reasons. They have a relationship with it. They're asking that it isn't taken away from them.'

'I'm afraid,' said Brinton, 'that the world doesn't work like that. The people who own the land have a right to make a profit. That's just how it goes. It's naïve to think they'll throw away their profits – which, I might add, pay the wages of their staff – just because a few people don't like it.'

'I find that extremely patronising!' said Deb. 'Do you always talk down to your constituents like this, or is it only when you're trying to protect your mates? I've been doing a bit of googling about you, Mr Brinton. It looks to me like you're good friends with the chairman of the company who wants to destroy our beach. So tell me: do you actually represent your constituents, or do you just pocket the wages and look after your own?'

Maisie, noted Deb, was looking slightly alarmed. She heard Rick say, *Alright, folks, let's try to keep this civil*, but she was distracted, because at that moment Bill walked onto the beach, fresh from work in chinos and a shirt with the sleeves folded up to the elbows, and her stomach did that weird flip again. She raised her hand to wave at him, and tried to focus her mind on what Charles Brinton was saying.

'You may have no idea how tirelessly I work for the people of this constituency, but thankfully many others disagree with you. That's how I've come to serve four terms as your MP already, and I was told by my party just this morning that they consider my majority to be unassailable.'

'I wouldn't be so sure,' said Deb.

'What?' said Brinton, laughing. 'Is that some kind of a challenge?'

'Perhaps it is,' said Deb.

'*Deb*,' she heard Maisie whisper next to her, warily.

'Can we just be clear here,' said Rick. 'Are you suggesting that you're aware of an alternative candidate, Deb?'

Deb paused, and looked around the beach. It seemed to her that it was full of furious people who just didn't know what to do next. They needed more than a few kind words and a shoulder to cry on. They needed someone to take care of them.

'I am,' she said. 'I'm going to stand against him.' She looked over at Maisie, whose face had frozen in a look of such shock that she almost laughed, right there on air. 'Correction: *we're* going to stand. Myself and Maisie, who have led the campaign so far. We're going to meet him head on.'

For a moment, the world appeared to have stopped altogether: the gulls fell silent, the sea stopped swishing against the stones, and the wind stopped fluttering against the bric-a-brac tied to the fence around the beach huts.

'Well, all I can say is good luck to you,' laughed Brinton. Deb didn't reply.

After a few seconds of dead air, Rick's voice chimed in: 'Well, listeners, I guess you might call that an exclusive for Coastline Radio. You heard it here first. More after this.'

Bonnie Tyler began to play, and Deb hung up.

'What did she just say?' said Julie, who was holding her phone against her ear in an attempt to listen to the broadcast.

'I think,' said Maisie, glancing from Deb to Julie, and then back again, as if she was hoping to be told otherwise, 'that she's just announced we're running for Parliament.'

'Both of you?'

'Together,' said Deb. 'We'll job-share.'

'Alrighty,' said Julie brightly. 'That's what I thought I heard.' She shrugged. 'My leaflet-distribution skills are tip-top, if you need them.'

'Deb,' said Maisie, 'I can't. You know that. I'm not up to it.'

'Maybe not on your own,' said Deb, 'and I'm not up to it on my own, either. But we can do it together.'

She felt a tap on her shoulder and turned to find Bill standing behind her.

'Congratulations,' he said. 'I think.'

Deb's phone began to vibrate, and Rick's name flashed on the screen. She declined the call and stuffed it into her back pocket, where it swiftly started vibrating again.

'Thanks,' she said. 'Can I count on your support? Isn't that what politicians say?'

'Yes,' said Bill, and he broke into an unexpectedly sunny smile, his green eyes fully meeting hers for the first time. 'Of course. Always.'

Part Three

1

When Maisie came home from swimming on Friday morning, she was not entirely surprised to find a public schoolboy urinating through her letterbox.

She stood by her front gate and cleared her throat. 'I'd watch that flap if I were you,' she said. 'It's got a vicious spring.' The boy's back stiffened. He was balancing on tiptoes in an effort to reach, and now he swung his head round to see who had spoken, whispered, 'Oh goodness!' and flinched as he tried to retract his penis from the door. But he was evidently now mid-stream and unable to stop, so he peed all over his shiny black shoes instead.

'Damn!' he muttered, as he hurriedly tried to straighten his underwear and button up his camel-coloured chinos. He turned to face Maisie, the colour high in his cheeks, and said, 'I apologise for any foul language there. I would never usually speak like that in front of a lady, only, as you can see, I was under a little pressure.'

'I'd say you still are,' said Maisie, glancing down at the wet stain that was seeping across his crotch. He looked down and said, 'Damn!' again before gritting his teeth in fury and adding, 'Sorry!' while attempting to soak up the damage with the handkerchief that had been poking out of his top pocket.

Maisie, who was cold after her swim and desperate to get changed and drink a cup of tea, said, 'I think you'd better come inside and tidy up, don't you?'

It was always astonishing how quickly you adapted to new circumstances. A month ago, she would have been shaken to her core by an event like this; would have considered herself to have been grievously harassed and probably the victim of a racially motivated hate crime. But today, she couldn't seem to register anything more than mild irritation. It was an inconvenience, that was all, and one that the boy would have to rectify himself.

In the four weeks since Deb had announced that they were standing for election against Whitstable's incumbent MP, much had changed for Maisie. It had been quite a shock, Deb announcing their candidacy without consulting her, apparently spontaneously, and live on the radio. Ordinarily, Maisie would have sought a way to gracefully back out of the deal, with plenty of hard feelings; but for once, she did not.

Perhaps it was because she had only just repaired her relationship with Deb after their petty falling-out; perhaps it was because she could see that Deb was on the cusp of flourishing into the kind of woman that she'd always deserved to be; or perhaps it was because things had been changing for Maisie for a long time now. There was a little more devil-may-care in her these days, and that was partly because she was running scared from her diagnosis of Parkinson's disease, waiting for it to bite harder than it already had, and dreading the day that it would disable her. Maisie feared disability – and its sister, dependency – above all other things, and had left her husband and all her friends behind in London so that they could never see her deteriorate.

But that was no longer the whole story. Since she had moved to Whitstable, she had found that she wasn't just running away from her old life, but that she was also running towards a new life. It had been years since she had dared to try new things, to meet people outside of her own, slightly formal, circle of acquaintances, and to dabble with leisure (and perhaps even adventure) for its own sake – if, indeed, she had ever really done it at all. Because of Deb, she was seeing the world through a different lens, and finding that she rather liked it. They couldn't possibly win an election, of course; but she was enamoured with the idea of pitching rocks at authority while they failed gloriously at it. On reflection, she wished she'd done it years ago.

The sane side of Maisie hadn't gone away entirely. It was she who had checked the correct statutory procedures for registering a candidacy in a general election; she who had read up on the law and broken the news to Deb that a job share was technically impossible. It was she who had worked out an alternative solution, registering Deb as a candidate and standing on the same platform as a political advisor. It was she who had withdrawn £500 in cash from her savings account and paid the electoral deposit. Maisie, who was not a gambling woman, considered this to be the closest she had ever come to having a flutter. The odds were poor, but it felt good to throw away £500 just for the joy of aiming a potshot at the condescending Charles Brinton. There were more glamorous ways of finding your wild side in your fifties, but this method suited Maisie down to the ground.

It was Maisie, too, who had quietly submitted an appeal against the planned development on West Beach, which would knock down a row of beautiful old beach huts and replace them with what was politely termed a 'leisure complex', but which really meant a clutch of rowdy bars that would destroy the peace of her beloved wild-swimming territory. She was able to present fresh evidence that the original planning consultation hadn't seen, namely that at least one hut owner had no idea about the scheduled demolition, and would have risked losing a pile of precious family memories had she not met Maisie and Deb by chance on the beach one day. In her appeal, Maisie had argued that there might be other owners, too, who had not had their chance to object to the plans. She was awaiting a response without much hope. If that failed – short of lying down in front of the bulldozers – their final option would be a legal challenge, and Maisie was hardly relishing that prospect.

As soon as their campaign was announced, she was taken aback by the viciousness that greeted them from some quarters. It was like being thrown head first into a bear pit. Maisie wouldn't have minded a sane, reasoned critique of her plans, but what she and Deb got was a cacophony of abuse that seemed almost incoherent with rage.

There were those who simply thought that she was standing in the way of progress in her fight against the beach development. Fine. That was a matter of simple disagreement. Then there were the people who thought that she should keep her nose out of it because she wasn't a Whitstable 'native', but had instead moved 'Down From London' recently, and was therefore part of the problem in the first place. She had some sympathy with this view, until someone spray-painted *DFL GO HOME* on her back fence. Maisie felt that this – and the patchwork of graffiti that quickly grew around it – was going too far.

And then there were the anonymous voices on local chat rooms or Facebook that chimed in to say that she should pipe down and get back into the kitchen because she was female, fat, a slag, stupid, black. They posted misspelt insults, nonsensical strings of words and thinly veiled threats that any idiot could see they had no intention of carrying out. It was like reading the translated gruntings of a field of animals, but it was nevertheless disturbing to sample the nastiness that floated around inside people's minds.

In comparison, the boy who was currently scrubbing his own urine off Maisie's front door mat was a minor irritant, a mere speck in a much fiercer ocean. He was actually slightly endearing, turning up dressed – she presumed – like his own father and then choosing a form of protest that was simply beyond his ability or imagination. He was, she already knew, the leader of a ridiculous club called the Young Traditionalists, who claimed to be in the business of upholding old-fashioned common sense. They had turned up to wave placards at the most recent meetings of the Whitstable High Tide Swimming Club, all four of them, dressed in button-down shirts and blazers, their sole female member wearing an ankle-length kilt that must surely have been borrowed from her grandmother. Maisie always made a point of engaging them in conversation, and found the detail of their views strangely elusive. They were happy enough to generally disagree with the kind of thing that Maisie and Deb were doing in running for Parliament, but they would not be pinned down on exactly why. It was just Too Much, that was all; A Step Too Far.

Maisie wondered if they even knew the detail of their views themselves, or whether they were simply parroting those of some particularly domineering parents. She handed the lad a J-cloth and a bottle of multi-surface spray, and drank her coffee as she watched him wipe down the walls either side of the door, just in case of splashes.

'Shouldn't you be at school, anyway?' she said.

'Friday morning's my free period,' he said under his breath. 'I don't have to be in until eleven.'

'So you decided to waste your spare time peeing into my hall? Don't you have anything better to do?'

The boy sat up on his haunches and closed his eyes while he gripped his forehead. 'Look,' he said, 'will you please just let me know whether you intend to inform my school of this. I mean, I'm pretty sure they'll consider it to be out of character anyway . . .'

'Try harder than that,' said Maisie.

'Okay, okay . . . I'm willing to accept that this represented poor decision-making on my part, and that . . .'

'Again,' said Maisie.

The boy growled in frustration. 'Alright! It was a stupid thing to do, and I don't know what came over me, and for what it's worth I'm genuinely sorry and embarrassed, and please – *please* – don't tell my school. I'm applying to Oxbridge this year and I'm pretty sure that this won't look good on my permanent record.'

'That's better,' said Maisie. 'What's your name?'

'I'm not stupid enough to tell you that.'

'You don't have to be.' Maisie took her phone out of her pocket and snapped his photo. 'I'm sure they'll have no trouble recognising you in this.'

'For heaven's sake!' said the boy. 'Fine. It's Alfie. Alfie Marshall.' For a few brief seconds, it looked like he was going to shake her hand, but he thought better of it.

'And so, Alfie, can you give me a reason for this sudden escalation in hostilities? This is surely a bit radical for your tastes, isn't it?'

'Yes,' said Alfie, 'probably. Look, I got carried away. Charles Brinton came to address our club meeting last night. It was pretty stirring stuff – he reminded us of all that we could lose if we don't defend our traditional British values. He said we must go out and fight this plague in whatever way we can. And, well . . .'

'Did he actually suggest urinating through letterboxes?' asked Maisie.

'No,' said Alfie. 'He absolutely did not. That was an . . . imaginative leap of my own.'

'Bet you wish you'd stuck with what you know,' said Maisie, trying hard not to smile. 'You know, waving placards dressed as the Amish.'

'I can confirm that is the case, yes,' said Alfie. He stood up and dusted his hands on his trousers. 'Look, I've cleaned up your hall, so can we call it quits now? I promise not to do it again. But this doesn't change my views. I still think you're making a joke of a venerated political system, and I'll continue to bear witness against that. You can't stop me.'

'I wouldn't dream of it,' said Maisie, amused. 'I'm delighted for you to scamper off, and continue to argue against us for all you're worth. In fact, I insist on it.'

Alfie regarded her for a few seconds, unsure of whether he was being patronised. Whatever his conclusion, he evidently decided to cut his losses and run. He even paused at the door to bow slightly to Maisie, who at that point could no longer hold back a burst of laughter that echoed between the damp walls of her hallway as the door slammed behind him.

'Off you go, Alfie Marshall,' she said under her breath. 'I've got bigger fish to fry.'

2

The tide was high at ten the next morning, and for once Deb was able to join Maisie on the beach. Since she had taken her post as a granny au pair, Deb had lost the ability to follow the tides every day, and was now barely aware of whether the sea was in or out. She walked Megan along the seafront as often as she could, and made sure she turned up to The Whitstable High Tide Swimming Club once a week. But after she'd fought the ever-rising tide of Frances's untidiness, looked after the Facebook group she ran for the Save West Beach Campaign, and knocked on a few doors to talk about the election campaign, there was barely any time left to sleep. She was supposed to be tackling the reading list for her foundation degree that was starting at the end of the month. At this rate, she was going to be winging it more than the teenagers in her class.

Still, today she had made it to the beach, the sky was blue and the air was September-crisp. At the top of the beach, there were sloes and elderberries ripening on the bushes, and blackberries tangling around the path leading up to the railway line. Everything was coming to fruition, and Deb hoped that she, too, was part of that sedate, natural march of progress through which everything fulfilled its potential eventually. Perhaps she was just a slower-maturing variety, that was all.

The sea was still holding on to its summer heat. She had braced herself for a shock when she got in, but had been surprised to find it soft and still . . . not warm exactly, but certainly not biting yet. It had been her dream to keep on swimming through the tail end of the year, adjusting downwards through fractions of a degree so that she barely noticed the sea becoming cold.

But that was not to be. If she couldn't swim every day, there was no hope of gradually adjusting as the sea cooled down. She would have to start again next year – perhaps

Easter; perhaps later still. She already envied Maisie, who would carry on striking through the waves all winter, just as she was today, her neon-green bathing cap making her visible to all shipping within a three-mile radius.

Deb, meanwhile, had strayed no further than the end of the last groyne post, where she floated on her back and watched the black-headed gulls drifting above her. She wished she had the resolve to swim like Maisie did: fast, strong and rhythmic, full of stern intent. But then, maybe she was pouring all her willpower into other things at the moment, and didn't have any will left. Maybe she sometimes needed the sea to hold her up for a while, because she didn't have the energy to keep on doing it herself.

'I keep meaning to ask,' said Maisie, 'what does Frances think of you running for election?'

'None of her bloody business,' said Deb, and then she thought for a moment. 'Actually, I think she finds it funny. It's this silly little thing I'm doing. I heard her say as much to one of her mates the other day: *Deb's a bit of a character.*'

'I suspect she finds you frightfully picturesque. A bit of local colour, you know. The real Whitstable.'

'Yeah,' said Deb. 'Like she can't possibly believe I'm serious about winning.'

'You're not serious,' said Maisie. 'Are you?'

Deb shot her a fierce look and added another item to the agenda she had been drawing up. 'Well, put it this way,' she muttered, 'I'm not *not* serious. Otherwise I wouldn't be bothering with all of *this.*'

'All of this' was the pile of papers scattered between them on Ann's dining table: flyers, forms, drafts of speeches, press clippings, printouts of emails, and a mass of other things that Deb didn't even want to think about. Ann was no help: for all her love of bureaucracy, the political campaign was too fraught with discord for her liking. It wasn't so much that she hated confrontation, but rather that she liked it to only go her way. At the moment, she was making coffee, having wondered out loud if Deb and Maisie realised that the expense of laying on refreshments always fell on her. When Deb had apologised and promised to bring a replacement jar of Nescafé the following week, Ann had considered this an appalling act of aggression, and had retreated to the kitchen in order to clank the mugs and the kettle in high dander. Her mother, Edith, had glanced up from her iPad, rolled her eyes, and then returned again to her crossword.

Now Ann returned, plonking down three mugs in front of them and saying, 'I hope you don't want milk. We haven't got much left.'

'I'll take it as it comes,' said Deb, making a mental note to also bring milk the next time.

'Just right,' said Maisie. Ann sniffed, and looked down at her own drink, which Deb noted was distinctly milky.

'Are you joining us, Edith?' said Deb, who was mortified at the way the elderly woman seemed always confined to her chair in the corner while they worked together.

'She's fine,' said Ann. 'She's got her tablet on.'

'I *am* fine, thank you,' said Edith, 'but I would also rather announce it for myself.'

'Well I can't do a thing right today,' said Ann.

'Shall we start?' said Maisie, shuffling the pile of papers in front of her in an effort to break the tension in the room. 'I think Deb's been compiling an agenda?'

'It's more of a random list,' said Deb.

'I don't have a copy,' said Ann. 'This really should have been circulated in advance.'

'Well I've only just written it! How was I supposed to know what to put on it before we were all in the same room?' growled Deb.

'I believe it's common practice to email the attendees in advance, requesting agenda items,' said Ann.

'If I ever have five minutes spare, I might do that,' said Deb. 'But as it stands, I didn't hear you volunteering to help.'

'I'm up to my eyeballs with Mother,' began Ann, but she was interrupted by Maisie, who stated, with great diplomacy,

'We'll do our best with what we've got today, shall we? Perhaps Deb can read through the list and we'll note it down.'

'Alright,' said Deb gruffly. 'Item one: social media policy. Item two: online abuse. Item three: apparent leaks . . .'

'If you want my opinion,' interjected Ann, 'they're all aspects of one big problem.'

'Okay, fine, so you write the agenda next time,' said Deb.

'It doesn't really matter,' said Maisie. 'We'll discuss it all either way.'

'It just shouldn't be allowed,' said Ann. 'Have you thought of reporting it to the authorities?'

'What, that special branch of the police devoted to helping people who've been upset on Twitter?' said Deb. 'Hate to break it to you, but they don't exist.'

'Well, they ought to,' said Ann.

'Thanks for that helpful idea. But back in the real world . . .'

'I was only saying,' said Ann.

It would have killed Deb to admit it, but Ann was right. The daily wade through the swamp of insults and abuse was sucking most of the joy out of her existence. It wouldn't be so bad, but she suspected that she knew half of the men who were hiding behind online pseudonyms. In fact, she was pretty sure that one of them – the most persistent, nasty, aggressive one, who seemed to be watching her at every hour of the day and night – was her ex-husband, Derek. He used the same limited set of insults, and the same atrocious spelling. She could almost feel him there, beyond the computer screen, trying to eke out the last bits of control he had over her life. There was no point in throwing around accusations, though. She just had to endure it with as much grace as she could muster.

It was tempting to give up reading her online mentions and messages altogether, but within the cacophony, there were often friendly messages from supporters, or questions from people who were genuinely interested in the campaign. Some people, God forbid, were even trying to hold a sensible debate with her. She had to witness the rest of it to find the bits that mattered.

'You shouldn't be dealing with it all on your own,' said Maisie. 'I hold my hand up there: I've been leaving Facebook to you because I don't have a profile. I should step up to the mark.'

'Okay,' said Deb, whose first instinct was usually to refuse all offers of help. 'I'd be grateful if you would, actually. If you've got time.'

'I'll make time,' said Maisie. 'You might need to show me how.'

'Children manage it,' said Ann.

Maisie laughed. 'Point taken. I'll make the effort.'

'To be honest,' said Deb, 'what worries me more are these leaks. I mean, I don't really mind people knowing I had a go at Brinton about his little boy scout coming round to tiddle through Maisie's letterbox. Whatever he says, it's irresponsible of him to wind kids up like that. But it was a private conversation and I doubt he told the press himself. And then there were the pledges we'd drafted. The local rag knew about them before we got a chance to release them ourselves. I just don't know how it's getting out there.'

'Well don't look at me,' said Ann.

'I wasn't,' said Deb. 'I'm not suggesting that either of you would gossip.'

'Are you talking about it to anyone else?' said Maisie. 'I mean friends, family?'

The image swum into Deb's mind of the way she'd wandered from group to group at the last High Tide Swimming Club, regaling everyone with the story of her triumph over Charles Brinton and his rude response, telling her to back down and save her time and money. She'd given him a good ticking-off, and was proud of it. She supposed she might have mentioned some of the election pledges, too. Just testing them out, really – seeing how people reacted. It had seemed so harmless at the time – a relief, actually, to have a proper, human conversation. But now, apparently, she had to start being a bit more guarded. It was yet another uncomfortable transition that she couldn't avoid.

'It must be someone in the club,' she said. 'God knows who.'

'Chloe, probably,' said Ann. 'She's a youngster. I've seen her on those sites all the time. Probably thinks it gives her cachet to tell all her mates about you.'

'I don't think it's fair to assume it's Chloe,' said Maisie carefully.

'She's the most likely candidate, though,' said Ann.

'Alright, look,' said Deb. 'I don't want to start accusing anyone of anything. These people have been good to us, and we could cause a lot of offence. It's me, really. I have to start keeping my big mouth shut.'

'I suppose it's the only way to guarantee it,' said Maisie, kindly.

'Unless we've been hacked,' said Ann. 'They can do all sorts these days – get into your emails, listen to your voicemail.'

'That's not the most likely source of our leak,' said Maisie, 'although of course we shouldn't rule it out.'

'You can never be too careful,' said Ann. 'Change all your passwords.'

'That's good advice,' said Maisie. 'And I'll make more of an effort to make sure you don't feel so isolated, Deb.'

'What about me?' said Edith, suddenly. 'Are you still planning to take me in for a swim? It's getting colder out there, you know. I can't wait until next year.'

Deb glanced guiltily over to Maisie, who bit her lip in reply. The plans to get Edith into the water for the first time in thirty years had rather fallen by the wayside since the election swung into gear. It wasn't just that they had lacked the breathing space to put the plans into place; they were also facing fierce resistance from Ann, who had made it clear that they would take Edith into the water very much against her wishes. But Edith was in sound mind and was desperate to swim again. Deb didn't want to let her down. It was just another piece of bravery they would have to find, that was all.

'You are far from forgotten,' said Maisie. 'How about the Saturday after next?'

'Wait . . .' said Ann.

'Done,' said Edith.

'Do I not get a say in this then?' said Ann.

'No,' said Edith. 'It's none of your bloody business.'

'But I suppose you're expecting me to come along all the same?'

'Come or don't come. It's up to you. My friends here will see me right.'

'And how's your love life, Deb?' said Maisie, in a flagrant attempt to change the subject. 'I always like to keep abreast of events.'

Deb sighed. 'Oh, you know. Still with Rick.'

'What?' said Ann, who, to her credit, was always happy to move her outrage on to the next subject. 'I thought you were all lovey-dovey?'

'We were,' said Deb. 'But – I don't know – I don't think we've got a future together.'

'What on earth does that mean?' said Ann.

'It means that I've started to find him a bit embarrassing. He won't leave me alone, even in public. I'm trying to run a campaign, and he's always pawing at me like I'm a piece of meat.'

'Wandering hands,' said Ann, ominously.

'I'm just trying to look professional,' said Deb, 'and he treats me like a sex object. Once upon a time, I'd have been grateful for the attention. But you know what? I'm beginning to think I might be able to do better.'

'Of course you can do better,' said Maisie.

'That remains to be seen,' said Deb, who was more than aware of Maisie's low opinion of Rick.

'Nonsense,' said Maisie. 'It's just confidence. One day, you'll start believing you're worth something.' This was a step too far for Deb, yet another painful reminder of how lost she was feeling, and it must have shown on her face because Maisie took a breath and changed the subject. 'What she really means,' she said to Edith, 'is that she's got her eye on another chap.'

'Shut up!' said Deb, blushing.

'Honestly, you two carry on like a pair of schoolgirls,' said Ann.

'And long may it continue!' called Edith from the corner.

'Oh for heaven's sake!' said Ann, standing to collect up the mugs and retreat to the kitchen. 'It's like working in a nursery!'

3

That afternoon, Maisie sat down at her kitchen table and logged on to Facebook. She already had an account, having been goaded into it years ago by work colleagues who were planning an 'away weekend'. She'd never touched it since. She was left with the impression of being horrified at the number of old acquaintances who found her on there, and by how she was quickly subsumed under a mass of information about their everyday lives, their seemingly endless supply of children, and their views on every aspect of human life, from how to cook an egg, to how to achieve peace in the Middle East. She had logged in a final time to pretend to have enjoyed the team-building exercises, and then never approached the dreadful thing again.

Today, it took her several guesses at what email address she had used, a password retrieval and a round of security questions to find the dreaded blue-and-white home page, more overloaded with information than ever. She had, she noted, 167 friend requests, mostly from names she did not recognise – or names that she recalled only too well, and had no desire to ever see again. What on earth motivated these people, who surely had perfectly good friends of their own, to chase down every fleeting social contact and try to solidify it into a friendship? Or perhaps they genuinely enjoyed all this shallow noise and fuss, preferring it to the mess of real human friendship? For her own part, Maisie was mystified.

Still. She wasn't here for herself. She was here because otherwise Deb bore the brunt of everything, and Maisie needed to stand beside her and take her share of the workload. After hunting around for a while, she found the Save West Beach group, and was pleased to see how warmly they were supported by the people who cared about the town's coastline. Sure, there was criticism and sniping, but it was nothing like as bad as she'd feared. She had, she realised, been afraid of coming to this place at all, imagining it to be an arena of snarling lions. In reality, it was just like real life, except you could hear everyone talking at once.

Deb was there: Maisie could see her fingerprints all over the place, her immense passion and good humour. Punctuation was not her forte (this, Maisie noted, would have to be discreetly raised and tackled; it was inviting some nasty pockets of mockery that could easily be avoided), but she had a way of phrasing her posts that exuded just the right balance of good nature, wit and fierceness. That was Deb, though: she couldn't dissemble. She was nothing but herself, as if the essence of Deb was printed through her core like a stick of rock.

The other club members were there, too: Julie's feed consisted mainly of photos of rioting toddlers and close-ups of brimming glasses of wine. Brian ran a conservationists' forum, mainly populated by men who listed the birds they had seen and the plants they had identified, and staged debates in which they all broadly agreed on the central point, but competed to quote the detail of the argument more thoroughly than the next man. Maisie wanted to find it ridiculous, but herself knew the pleasures of a little pedantry, now and again.

Bill was there too, and with a louder, more certain voice than she had ever detected before. Here he was, announcing that he had created a new animation, and Maisie clicked through to find a whole channel of his work on YouTube, intricate clay landscapes that were brought to life with simple, poignant storylines. He was extraordinarily talented, and Maisie was slightly aghast at the extent to which she had underestimated him. She wondered, vaguely, if she had always given him enough of her time, and resolved to show more interest in the future. The most recent film was the tale of a beach on which crabs scuttled and children played, suddenly under threat from a creeping urban sprawl. At first, the population of the beach grumbled and moved a little further along the coast, but then they were pushed back again by shiny buildings and unsympathetic crowds that threw litter and trampled over the wildlife. Eventually, the camera panned out to reveal the development spreading across the whole country. The screen went black, and then a message appeared: *There is a gentler way to love the seaside*, with a link to the Save West Beach campaign.

It had already been watched 100,000 times. Surely that couldn't be right. But there were the numbers at the bottom of the screen. Maisie was even moved to hit 'share' herself, creating her first Facebook post in nearly a decade:

> Hello. I'm back on here after a long break! As many of you will know, I'm currently acting as Campaign Manager for Deborah Winters who's running to be Whitstable's new MP. We're in it together, I think! Anyway, I just watched this brilliant video from Bill Keyes and I wanted to share it with you. It says so much about what we're doing here, more elegantly than I ever could!

As soon as she posted it, she noticed the spattering of exclamation marks, which really were out of character. She just wanted to delete the whole thing and start again. It read like a teenage girl trying to sound fun to the other kids at school. It made her cringe.

No, she mustn't get too fussy. She counselled herself that she would make a pot of tea, and see if it still seemed unbearable when she sat back down at the laptop. She went to the kitchen, filled the kettle, and spooned the curled oolong leaves into the teapot. When the water boiled, she let it cool for a minute before filling the pot and inhaling the green scent that rose up. This was her ritual when the anxiety surfaced. A few simple steps, a little patience, and pristine white bone china. She couldn't count how many times it had stopped her from packing up and running back to London in the early days.

Back at the table, the post still seemed ridiculous, but she noticed that Deb had clicked 'like', and that Bill had left a comment to thank her for sharing. She couldn't delete it now. It was harmless enough, and would surely soon disappear anyway, under the weight of new information that churned into this place every minute.

She noticed, though, that a new private message had appeared at the top of the screen. *Alright*, she thought, *I suppose this is part of the deal too*. People would want to chat. She would have to be polite and hope they lost interest. She clicked on the lightning bolt, and a name appeared that made her hands go cold.

Marisa Carozza.

A tiny, circular picture of Marisa and her husband, Bruno. Maisie knew that picture. It had been taken on a quayside in Venice, just before they stepped onto a gondola for a ride that Marisa was embarrassed to take, being Venetian herself. In the original version of this photo, Maisie and Stephen were there too. Marisa and Bruno, Maisie and Stephen. Always a foursome, at theatres and restaurants, art shows and weekend breaks. They matched: two quiet, academic husbands and two busy, clever women. Money was no object. The conversation always flowed. Their friendship was easy. Convenient.

It was only after Maisie was diagnosed with Parkinson's disease that she realised that easiness wasn't the same as closeness. She had this well of thoughts and feelings inside her – many of them dumb, nonsensical, contradictory – and she wanted to flood them out to someone. But there was no one to tell. Marisa was the last person that Maisie would confide in. Their friendship had been based on an absence of politics; a lack of sticky entanglements and dependencies. They had got along because they impressed each other. This – *this* – was not part of the deal.

Marisa would have been horrified by Maisie's confusion about what to do; would have been faintly disgusted at the unruly, cold-sweat fears that assailed her. Perhaps this was what had made it so easy to just disappear: the realisation that there were no real friends to leave behind, just people you spent time with. No strings attached.

Maisie clicked on the link and read Marisa's message.

Where the hell have you been?

It could, Maisie thought, be a joke. It could be spoken in an amused, baffled, yet friendly voice, inviting an old friend to return to the fold.

It could also be an expression of fury.

Impossible to judge.

Maisie thought about closing down the computer and walking away. Perhaps forever. She would have burned the damned laptop to ashes if she thought that it would stop Marisa from ever finding her again.

How could she have been so stupid? How could she have taken all these careful precautions to make sure that she got away cleanly and permanently – she had even changed her email address, and was communicating with Stephen through a solicitor – and then forgotten that it would all be waiting for her on Facebook?

But for all her shock at colliding with her old life so suddenly, Maisie also realised that this marked the end of her disappearance. There was no point in ignoring Marisa's message now; she was visible again. She might as well face the music.

She opened her laptop and replied: *I'm sorry. I needed to get away. How are you? Hope Bruno is well.* It was, she thought, sufficiently breezy and neutral, ruefully sorry without being contrite. Marisa, she knew, would not want any emotional entanglement in this.

The reply came too quickly. *Are you kidding me? You vanish for the best part of a year and then act like you've just come back from an unplanned holiday. What's wrong with you? Have you got any idea how this has affected Stephen?*

Apparently, Marisa wasn't quite as neutral as she had imagined. Maisie, who felt disoriented by now, typed: *I suppose I have no idea how it's affected Stephen, no. I assumed he wouldn't really mind. He'd ignored me for years before I left. I'd faded out of his life.*

She hit send, and then thought to add, in a separate message, *Is he okay?*

Jesus Christ, came the reply, *you're full of shit. Stephen is not okay. Of course he's not okay. He's devastated. We've been picking up the pieces, and apparently all the while you've been swanning around some crappy seaside town, having the time of your life. We thought something had HAPPENED to you.*

Maisie didn't know what to say to this. She wanted to protest: something *had* happened to her! But really, as she tried to phrase it and re-phrase it, she could see how foolish it all sounded. Something *had* happened to her. She had learned that she was ill. And it was the final straw. She saw the light. Life was suddenly too short. All she had in her armoury were these clichés, and she knew they wouldn't rub with Marisa, even though they were the truest thing she had ever known.

While she was dithering, Marisa wrote, *Fucking hell, I cannot believe you. You're pathetic. Stephen's better off without you.*

There was no reply to that. There wasn't supposed to be. There was nothing else to be said. Maisie closed her laptop and tried to pour another cup of tea, but the pale green liquid didn't seem to offer enough comfort. Instead, she opened the cupboard in the living-room alcove, and found her neglected bottle of Talisker, saved for guests and sleepless nights. This was not a sleepless night, but a restless afternoon, the churning sense of horror overtaking her. How had she ever allowed herself to believe that she had simply left Stephen behind; that he wouldn't mind; that she was handling things kindly? She had been living out a fantasy, and now it was fading like a dream in the early morning light. It was astonishing, really, how long she had believed in it at all.

Maisie sipped her whisky and tried to comfort herself with the thought that Marisa was playing up because she was having to deal with the full force of Stephen's dependency. *Good*, she tried to think. *Now she knows what it's like.*

But it was very hard to shake the feeling that Marisa was right. And that Maisie, therefore, had done something terribly wrong.

4

Edith stood at the edge of the water, with Maisie propping her up by one elbow, and leaning heavily on a stick with her other arm. There was a storm in the air, and the sea was already stirred up in anticipation, the water brown with churned-up mud and its surface wrinkled by white-edged waves that licked at Edith's toes.

'You'll ruin your shoes,' said Ann from behind them, but it lacked conviction. Edith did exactly what she liked. Maybe her daughter was finally learning that.

Edith narrowed her eyes towards the horizon as if she were conducting a methodical inspection of the terrain. Maybe she was. 'I'll be able to walk in, I think,' she said to Deb, who was hovering beside the walking stick in case she fell. 'I don't want any special arrangements. Perhaps some of those sea-shoes. The shingle will play havoc with my bunions.'

At this point, Maisie giggled, and Edith turned to her with dancing eyes. 'Bunions are no laughing matter, young lady.' She would have waggled her finger if it didn't risk toppling her entirely.

'We can get you a pair of swimming shoes, love,' said Deb. 'But what about the actual swimming bit? Will you just wade in, or are you hoping to actually, like, *float*?'

'Floating,' said Edith, 'is definitely part of the plan.'

'Right,' said Deb, 'only . . .'

'Yes,' said Edith. 'You're quite right. I don't suppose I could swim any more. Well, not reliably, anyway.'

'We could hold you up,' said Maisie. 'I mean, we could make a kind of chair with our arms, and you could float on top of it.'

'I don't think so,' said Edith. 'That's too undignified for me.' She took in a sharp breath, pursed her lips, and interrogated the waves again. 'Right,' she said at length. 'That's me done-for. Can you help me to my chair, ladies?'

Maisie and Deb duly obliged, steering Edith across the sand until she could gratefully sit down. 'Right,' she said once she was settled. 'I need one of you to go shopping on my behalf, please.' She reached into her handbag and pulled out a bundle of folded banknotes. 'No, take it. I won't hear of you spending your own money. This is my project, and I will provision it.'

Deb reluctantly took the money, and promised that she would bring back any change. 'Makes no odds to me. Can't take it where I'm going,' said Edith. 'Except I expect my darling daughter will be counting, so I suppose you better had.' She waved at Ann, who was now marching around the beach, taking a register of the swimmers who were beginning to turn up for the weekly club meeting.

'Now,' she said, 'this is my shopping list: sea-shoes; a decent, plain bathing suit. Nothing too fancy, and a low leg please. I don't want to be worrying I'm showing too much. And,' she said with a glint in her eye, 'one more thing . . .'

Maisie seemed quiet today, although it was good to see that Edith could still make her laugh. Deb left her sitting on the shingle with her head resting on Edith's arm, as was Maisie's habit these days; she had seen that Bill had arrived, and was clutching the deck of a beach hut while he took off his trainers.

It was good to have the beach huts back again, all their colours glowing against the darkening sky. Although Deb didn't hold out much hope for the appeal Maisie had put in, at least East Kent Land Management had been ordered to take down the hoardings around them while the planning department were reviewing the case. It was clear that this was a temporary reprieve, really, but it was satisfying for the ugliness to be gone for a while.

Deb crunched up to the top of the beach to meet Bill, touched his shoulder and said, 'Hi.'

The colour rose in Bill's cheeks, but less, Deb thought, than it used to. Maybe he was beginning to feel at home in her company, finally. 'Hello,' he said.

'I was hoping to see you here,' she said. 'I wanted to talk to you about the animation you did for the campaign. I mean, I wanted to say how amazing it was, but maybe we could have a chat about how we can make sure as many people see it as possible? I just think it's so important . . .'

At that moment, she felt a pair of hands wrap around her waist, and Rick almost lifted her off the ground as he swung her around to greet him. 'Babe!' he crowed. 'I've missed you!'

'Rick!' said Deb as she squirmed in his grasp. 'Not right now, love. I was talking to Bill. And you're all stubbly.'

'Oh,' said Rick, letting go of Deb abruptly. 'Sorry. I must have taken you by surprise a bit there. Hello, Bill.' Bill nodded.

'So anyway,' continued Rick, as if Bill had only existed briefly in his imagination, and had now vanished again, 'I was thinking that after this, you and I could grab a bite to eat somewhere nice, and then you could come back to my place?' He nuzzled his face into Deb's neck, and she felt his hands slide down towards her buttocks.

Deb wriggled away from him and shot him a look that was supposed to make it clear that this was entirely inappropriate. But it just didn't land on Rick; he grinned back at her as if he'd achieved something special. 'I'm really sorry,' she said, hearing how formal the words sounded as they came out, 'but I've just agreed to go for coffee with Bill afterwards. To talk about the campaign, I mean.'

'How did my Deb suddenly become a working girl?' said Rick, before putting his hand over his mouth as if he hadn't blatantly planned the innuendo, and saying, 'Oops! I don't mean *that* kind of working girl. Unless, of course . . .'

'Rick,' said Deb more firmly. 'That's enough. Come on. You're showing me up.'

Rick's face fell into shocked disappointment. 'What . . .' he said, and then remembered Bill was there, and so steered Deb by the elbow to the other side of the beach hut. 'What's the matter, Deb? Have I upset you?'

'No,' said Deb, trying to massage away the headache that his mere presence seemed to bring about nowadays. 'You've not upset me. Not specifically anyway. It's just that . . . well listen, Rick. You can't keep talking to me like that in front of everyone. It makes me look stupid.'

'Don't be daft,' said Rick, who looked badly at risk of pawing at her again. 'It makes you look adored.'

Deb tensed her face. She needed to say something here: something clear and definitive. Something that told him, kindly and firmly, that he had to change, or else it was time to move on. But then she heard someone calling her name from the other side of the beach, and turned to see Julie and Maisie staring at something on the groyne, and waving her over.

'We'll talk about it later,' she said, and was even moved by his hangdog face to lean in and kiss him on the cheek, before running gratefully over to her friends.

'Thanks,' she whispered to Maisie. 'I owe you one.'

'No, look,' said Maisie, and she tapped her finger on a plastic sign that was screwed onto every wave-break along the whole of West Beach.

NO SWIMMING
BY ORDER OF THE LANDOWNER
This is a private beach and an active site of marine industry.
For your own safety, please refrain from swimming here.

'Bastards,' said Deb. 'They can't do this, can they?'

'They can,' said Maisie. 'East Kent Land Management own the beach. To be honest, I'm surprised they didn't do it sooner.'

'But it's the sea,' said Julie. 'It's just . . . there. People have always swum in it. What are they going to do, put up a fence around it? Post a guard every few yards? I don't see how they can stop us.'

'I don't think that's the point,' said Maisie. 'They don't want us to stop swimming. They want us to carry on against their express wishes.'

'It's smart,' said Deb. 'If we stop, we lose everything that holds us together, and look like we give in easily. If we carry on, we'll be breaking the law.'

'We will swim though,' said Julie, 'won't we?'

'Of course we will,' said Deb.

'I agree,' said Maisie. 'But we have to understand that it immediately becomes an act of civil disobedience. The stakes are raised.'

'We'll need to make sure we get our word in first,' said Deb, and then she glanced over the beach to where Rick was sitting dejectedly on the seawall.

'Rick,' she called, 'have you seen this? I reckon you might have a story here.'

'You're shameless,' said Maisie, as he got to his feet and jogged over.

'All for a good cause,' said Deb.

The only table left in the cafe was in the window, and so Deb and Bill settled there after ordering two lattes. Deb thought about suggesting a slice of cake to share, but she wasn't sure if Bill would entirely like that. So they sat at right angles to each other, with Deb's stomach rumbling, and watched people drift past from the beach.

Rick tapped on the glass as he passed, and Deb had to look pleased and surprised and definitely unavailable, all in a short space of time. What on earth was she doing here anyway? Trying to get some time alone with Bill because – what? Because she had an inkling that he might, possibly, have a tiny crush on her? Because the very thought of that made her pathetic heart sing? Because she felt like she could happily melt into the gaze of his beautiful green eyes, if only he'd let her? Because he made Rick look one-dimensional and stupid in comparison? It was ridiculous. She was out of control. And, as much as she hated the cliché, she was old enough to be his mother.

'Listen,' she said to Bill, 'thanks for going along with this. I realise we hadn't quite talked it through before I kind of landed you in it with Rick.'

'No problem,' said Bill.

'I mean, I don't really want to talk about the campaign. I just thought, you know, we could have coffee.' She cringed as she said this. It was the chat-up line of someone who was lonely enough to trick a young man into her company, as though love was nothing more than calling in a favour.

'Sure,' said Bill.

'You're very good not to ask why I did it!' Although 'good' wasn't quite the word she wanted to use – more like 'frustratingly discreet'. She wanted him to lean over, as most of the men in her life up to now would have done, and say, 'Trouble in paradise?' with a salacious look in his eye. She wanted him to push her to spill the details, to root out a vulnerable confession of her fading love affair. Not this quiet acceptance. It was so . . . so *decent* of him. She was not sure how to handle it.

Bill shrugged. 'I'm sure you have your reasons.'

'You don't like him, do you?' said Deb, hoping that this, at least, would trigger a response. But as soon as the words left her mouth, she regretted them. She felt like a TV set, its contrast turned up too high, blaring out noise. She wanted Bill to behave as badly as she would have in this situation, and the beauty of him was that he wouldn't, ever. She watched his mouth shrink into an uncertain line, like a child's, and realised that she'd done damage.

'Sorry,' she said, 'that wasn't fair. I don't expect you to answer that question.' She sipped her coffee, which was still too hot to drink and burned her throat on the way down. 'I'm just frustrated really. I've left one idiot and fallen headlong for another one. I want someone to ride in like the cavalry and tell me I'm getting it all wrong. But nobody ever does.' She sipped the coffee again, just to stop herself talking, but she still had to endure Bill's slow, careful gaze. It was like being thrown into a wide-open space and she couldn't resist chattering to fill it. 'It's almost as if everyone thinks I'm a grown-up and can make my own decisions, eh?' she laughed.

'Well,' said Bill carefully, 'that's true, isn't it?'

'I don't know,' said Deb. 'I suppose so in some ways. But I'm all over the place. I hated it when Derek controlled my whole life and made all the decisions for me. So I left him. Which was the right thing to do. I'm happier without him, don't get me wrong. It's just that I don't know what I'm doing most of the time. I'm like a kid in a sweetshop. I want to try everything out. No. No, that's not all of it. I'm just scared most of the time. I feel like I'm getting a last chance to be someone, and I don't want to mess it up.'

'Slow down a bit,' said Bill, and at first Deb thought she was talking too fast, but then she realised that he meant it generally. 'You're trying to do everything at once. Give yourself enough time.'

'I know,' said Deb. 'I know.' She was surprised, suddenly, to find those last words catch in her throat, and was worried that she might sit here and cry. It was all too much. She had to go home in a moment and keep house for Frances, all the while being treated like she was an idiot child rather than someone who knew what she was doing. And then, after everyone had eaten and baby Megan was packed off to bed, they would want her to disappear again, so she would spend hours in her room, picking fights on Facebook. She wished she could call Cherie sometimes, just to have a chat; but her daughter was still giving her the cold shoulder since Deb had given up being her unpaid nanny. She was tired of all this raw, stretched-out survival. 'And I'm starting university next week,' she said, pinning on a smile. 'That'll make it even worse.'

'I wish there was something I could do to help,' said Bill, and it made Deb realise that, no matter how much she secretly dreamed of someone coming and scooping her up and sorting everything out for her, this wasn't what she actually wanted any more. That was an old dream, born of habit. She was done with being a kept woman. She was learning to keep herself, and it was a slow process of trial and error, but it was worth it. She just had to learn to keep herself well, and kindly, rather than running herself ragged.

'Thanks,' she said. 'I just have to work it out. I'm a learner driver.'

Bill smiled. 'We all are.'

Then he did something that Deb hadn't expected. He reached out and took hold of her hand, cradling it between both of his.

And at that exact moment, Deb's phone rang and Bill let go abruptly, leaving Deb glancing between him and the phone, him and the phone, desperate to say, 'No, don't stop, it can wait!'

But Bill was now looking away, as though he had been caught in the act of something terrible. Deb picked up the phone.

'Mum!' said the voice. 'I'm home!'

'Rob?' said Deb. 'Oh my God! You're back! Where are you?' She took the phone from her ear and mouthed to Bill, *My youngest. He's been on a gap year in Australia.*

'I'm home, Mum. In Whitstable.' A pause. 'I mean, Dad's place now, I s'pose.'

5

Maisie, who hadn't cleaned a bathroom for thirty years before she left Stephen, was polishing her chrome taps. While she was working, she had always had a cleaner, who came once a week and set everything straight, so that she never had to give it a second thought. Here, in her tiny fisherman's cottage, it would have been absurd to have another woman bustle in to clean up. Alone, she touched the house so lightly that the act of cleaning seemed pointless. She left her shoes at the back door so that she didn't bring in dust; she compiled simple meals from packets and jars that were sorted neatly into the recycling bins. She misted shower spray over the bathtub every time she used it. There was nothing to do. She was barely even there.

But sometimes, she just needed to do something with her hands. Today, it was for a very specific reason. Just before lunchtime, a letter had dropped onto her doormat, containing the news she had been expecting all along. After careful consideration, it said, her appeal had been rejected. Planning permission was reinstated for East Kent Land Management to build on West Beach. It wasn't much of a surprise, but it still felt like a body blow. She would have to break the news to Deb that their only hope now was a legal challenge, and that would probably suck up all their spare time for years.

There was only one way to process the nervous energy that swilled around her. Maisie hoovered and dusted, and when the obvious things were done, ran the point of a cocktail stick into all the corners of the cooker, revealing hidden collections of grease. It was satisfyingly absorbing, an act of micro-level control over her surroundings. Living in Whitstable brought about an eternal battle with limescale, and so she also descaled the kettle with citric acid crystals, and sprayed Viakal around the bathroom fittings, scrubbing away the white crusts with a toothbrush. Now, she was rinsing it off, her hands smarting from unfamiliar contact with twenty different detergents, feeling like she had triumphed in at least one area of her life.

As she went on to change the bed, she realised that she was taking out a kind of anger on the pillowcases and the fiddly buttons of her duvet cover. It was no longer the rage she had felt against the people who would destroy her beach for their personal gain. No, it had become something much more feeble, much more exhausted. Petulant: that's how she felt. She wanted to stamp her foot and yell 'NOT FAIR!' She accepted her responsibilities, but she didn't want them any more. She just wanted everything to return to normal. She wished she could remember what normal was.

She heard the snap of her letterbox and found herself rushing down to the hall on impulse, just to make sure that nothing awful had been thrust through. She got there just in time to see a leaflet floating onto the mat, with a smiling woman on the front. *VOTE MICHELLE HUNTER*, it said. *LET'S START LISTENING.*

'Chance would be a fine thing,' said Maisie under her breath. Ordinarily, she would have read the list of pledges carefully, and probably even given this young woman her vote. But, somehow, she had found herself on the opposing side, and it didn't feel quite right. Still, there was nothing to be done. They were committed to the campaign now. She rolled the flyer into a ball and threw it into the recycling. But this felt like an act of violence, so she took it out again, and smoothed it flat against the kitchen table. She would read it properly later; if nothing else, it counted as campaign research.

But it was coming up to high tide now and Maisie was desperate to ease the aches out of her shoulders from three hours of cleaning. She pulled on her wetsuit in the bedroom, picked up her bag and stalked down to the beach in her neoprene bootees.

It was raining outside, and sharp gusts of wind were blowing water into her face as she passed down a narrow alley onto the beach. There would be more and more of these days as winter approached. She would just have to get used to it. It was all the same once you were in the sea, but then again, you had to get out again eventually. Like everything else, she would have to cross that bridge when she came to it. On the bright side, there were those cold, blue-skied autumn days to look forward to. Hopefully there would be enough of those to get by.

Despite the rain, she wasn't the only one on the beach. She passed a sodden-looking dog walker on the path at the top, and they exchanged a rueful smile. There was a figure, too, at the shoreline of her favourite part of the beach, wearing a Barbour jacket with the hood up. Approaching him, Maisie made the usual fast calculation that women made in these situations: he was tall, but thin. No dog to threaten her with. Unsuitable shoes for the beach: black brogues that would surely be ruined on the shingle. She could outrun him, no problem, if she really had to. And she didn't think she would. He didn't look remotely menacing. More sad than anything.

Stephen always wore shoes like that, whatever the situation. It would have been too much change to try a pair of trainers, just once in a while.

The man turned, and there he was. Stephen. Standing on her beach in his soaking Barbour jacket.

'Maisie,' he said. 'I was worried you wouldn't come out at all today.'

The Neptune was awash with warm yellow light, fighting against the grey outside the window. Not wanting to take Stephen to her house, Maisie had suggested coffee, and he had flinched and said, 'I'm going to need something stronger than that.' So they sat at a table in the corner and Maisie watched him pretend to find his cheap red wine tolerable. It went against the grain for him to order anything without first carefully scrutinising the grape and the terroir, but then again, it went against the grain for him to stray this far out of London. He was trying very hard, she thought, to meet her halfway.

Despite herself, her eyes were enjoying roaming around his face again. Familiar as a childhood home, it was perhaps a little thinner than when she had last explored it, perhaps a little more lined. But it was also a known territory, its movements and expressions more pleasurable to see than she could have imagined. Certainly, he was on his best behaviour today, making clipped, self-effacing jokes and talking directly to her, without the buffer of a wall of newspaper between them. But in his company, it was hard to push back the memory of all the good things any longer.

She swirled the ice cubes in her Scotch and soda. 'You gave me quite a shock,' she said.

'Sorry,' said Stephen. 'I mean, it was entirely deliberate, but sorry all the same.'

'It's just so unlike you. I'm almost flattered.'

'That's unfair,' said Stephen. 'I would have turned up months ago if only I'd known where you were.'

'Sorry,' said Maisie. 'I didn't mean to be flippant.' Basking in the glow of this familiarity, she had let her words run away with her. This was not a fond reunion of old friends. This was a reckoning.

'No,' said Stephen, 'you're right to say that I would never usually have resorted to stalking you on the internet and then tracking you down on some wind-blown provincial beach. But God knows I tried all the more conventional methods to contact you.' Maisie gazed into her drink, and nodded. 'When Marisa said that you'd just popped up on Facebook one day, acting as though nothing was amiss, I didn't believe her,' he said. 'But here you are in the flesh, making out you were playing a simple game of hide and seek. I have so many questions that I don't dare to start asking.'

'Well,' said Maisie carefully, 'I suppose the thing is that I—'

'Christ,' said Stephen, 'I'm so angry. I didn't expect to be this angry.' He threw himself back against his chair and gripped his fingers into the roots of his hair. 'At first I thought something had happened. I thought you might be lying in a gutter somewhere, or – I don't know – that you'd had a blow to the head and couldn't remember who you were. Then, when I started getting solicitor's letters, I wondered what you thought I'd done. I didn't entertain the possibility of this – that you would have just walked out without an explanation, and started again as if none of it mattered. I rang your work and they said you'd taken voluntary redundancy. Can you imagine the humiliation of that – finding out that your wife of thirty years has left her job without ever thinking to mention it? There was this slow realisation that you'd been planning it all for a long time. I felt so stupid. I accused Marisa of hiding you at one point.'

'She wasn't,' said Maisie.

'I know that now. But at the time . . . Anything was possible.' He let out a breath that made his whole chest sag. 'This isn't helping. I hadn't meant to say all of this. But, honestly, Maisie: what were you thinking?'

'I'll get us another drink,' said Maisie, and rounded up both their glasses to take to the bar. But Stephen put a hand on her wrist and said, 'No.' She sat down again. She wanted to be able to throw her head in the air and tell him that it was none of his business, that she was under no obligation to explain anything. But this would have been a cruel lie. She had never owed someone an explanation so much in her life.

She opened her mouth to speak, but couldn't muster any words at all, so she closed it again. Seeing Stephen was like waking from a fever dream. She had let herself believe that leaving him was the kindest, simplest thing to do: no fuss, no rows, just a simple severance. She had decided that he would not only understand what she was doing, but would happily go along with it. How did she expect him to know: telepathy? She could see now that she had frightened somebody she loved very much; that she had broken a sacred contract of trust and pretended to herself that it was nothing at all. It was shameful. It was a shameful, terrible thing to have done.

Tears streamed down her face as she began to tell her story, and it was a new one now, the same events pieced together in a different way to reveal a new meaning. This was not the story of a wise, sensible woman who made a necessary change in her life for the benefit of all concerned. This was the story of a woman who let grief and fear overwhelm her so much that she got lost in an irrational chain of thought that was catastrophic for those who loved and depended on her. This was the story of Maisie learning she had Parkinson's disease while her mother was dying in a hospital bed, and the two becoming intertwined in her imagination: the proximity of death, the horror of surrendering your most intimate needs to the hands of strangers; Maisie and her mother, the clock ticking for both of them.

Other things, too, being caught up in that cyclone. The increasing consciousness of her age when she worked in a room full of younger men, all of whom brimmed with boundless energy and enthusiasm. The feeling that she was losing her lustre as her skin began to dry and wrinkle; that she would never be adored again – and feeling silly for even thinking that, believing that she ought to be above that kind of concern. That old anxiety rising up yet again, that without a set of maturing children to watch over her, she was invisible to the outside world. All of those feelings being jumbled up together and spat out again as a wild, wrongheaded plan that all of it could be solved by disappearing and starting again.

'I have been running away from my own old age,' she said at last.

After she finished speaking, Stephen chewed on his thumbnail quietly for a while, and then said, 'I think I will go to the bar after all.' Maisie was left alone, in the corner of the pub, trying to stop more tears from following the previous ones. Stephen returned and placed a fresh Scotch and soda in front of her, which she drank gratefully.

'Alright,' he said, 'now listen. First of all, I didn't come down here to lay the blame at your door. I had realised already that perhaps I hadn't been paying you enough attention for a long time before you left, and it must have been dreadful. Much of what you've just told me confirms that. And I'm sorry about it, I really am. Contrite, actually.' He looked up at her from under his overgrown eyebrows, and reached out to clasp his hand over hers. Maisie shook her head. She couldn't bear for him to blame himself. It was hers to carry.

'But there's new information here, too. I . . .' He let go of her hand again. 'Why didn't you tell me you were unwell? I could have been there for your appointments. We could have talked it over. You might have gained some perspective.'

'I just thought it would go away. I thought they'd say it was stress, and that I needed to take more care of myself. I thought I'd feel silly for troubling them. So I went along to the appointments and then, by the time they told me, I was too far down the line to say anything to you. It was too late. I couldn't find the words.'

'It breaks my heart that you felt that way. It shouldn't have been like that. It's clear that things had been going very wrong, and we should have addressed it. There should have been a structure in place that caught you when you fell. That's on both of us.'

'Yes,' said Maisie. 'Maybe.'

'I should have noticed,' said Stephen. 'I should have realised you were keeping something from me.'

'I should have told you,' said Maisie. 'It's as simple as that.'

'Look,' said Stephen. 'There have been mistakes here on both sides. I want you to know that I don't feel like I'm the wronged party here. I've had a long time to think about it, and I could see my role in all of this, even before this new information. My conclusion is the same: it's not irreparable. I think we could sort this out. I'm not saying come home with me tonight, but let's work towards it. Let's start a conversation.'

'I don't know,' said Maisie. 'I have a life here now. Everything's changed.'

'So we have a weekend residence. I think I could live with that.' He smiled, and Maisie did her best to smile back. 'I can see you're tired. This has all been a shock. Let's go away and lick our wounds, and I'll come back next week and take you out for dinner. There's a surprisingly fast train from St Pancras, as it turns out.'

'I know,' said Maisie.

'Well, that's settled then.' Stephen stood up, and then paused, hovering between the table and the door. 'I can't work out if I'm allowed to give you a kiss goodbye.'

'Sure,' said Maisie, and offered her cheek, as she would to an old friend.

6

It had been a very long morning. Megan had woken at a quarter to five, and got the whole house up with her. Well, it wasn't Megan exactly; it was Dylan, who was apparently unable to do anything without broadcasting his paternal virtue at the top of his voice. At five, Deb gave in and got up too, which meant that Dylan, inevitably, said 'Would you mind?' and passed Megan to her while he went back to bed.

When he rose again at five to seven, he paused to yell, 'Can you put the coffee pot on?' down the stairs to Deb, before leaping vigorously into a shower. By five past, he was in the kitchen and 'grabbing a protein bar' while asking, plaintively, where his special insulating coffee mug might be. It was in the cupboard, where it always was, and so Deb located it, filled it with coffee, and packed him off towards his train like the ridiculous schoolboy he so clearly still was.

Frances ambled downstairs at seven thirty, complaining of a hangover, and looked almost affronted to be asked if she could perhaps watch her own daughter for half an hour while Deb got dressed. And on it went until, at ten, Frances suddenly realised that she had lost her engagement ring. No, she couldn't remember – couldn't possibly be expected to remember – when she last noticed she was wearing it. Cue tears and frantic searching, several furious calls to Dylan, and, mostly, hours spent gazing at her phone while she lamented her terrible loss to all her friends. By lunchtime, Deb realised she had done a whole day's childcare and asked if it was okay for her to go now. It was registration day at her university, and she had wanted to go in and show her face. Moreover, she was desperate to see Rob, who had been back for three days now, but might as well still have been in Australia as long as he was staying in his father's house.

'Oh,' said Frances. 'Right. Look, I absolutely understand that Dylan shouldn't have asked you to look after Megan at five this morning. I will definitely have a word about that. But, like, this morning's been taken over with *a bit of a family crisis for us*, and now I need to get some work done, as I've got a deadline tomorrow. So do you think you could *possibly* –' and here her face broke into a pretty smile – 'find some flexibility this afternoon?'

Deb sighed. 'To be quite honest with you, Frances, I haven't got any flexibility left this week.'

'I mean,' said Frances, 'we obviously pay you for thirty hours' work a week.'

'And I've done thirty-five already since Monday.'

'Right. I mean, I didn't know we were counting so exactly.'

'Well this isn't the only thing I've got on.'

The two women looked at each other for a while, until Frances pinched her temples as if she was in agony and said, 'Alright! You win. How about this: you go in to university now – and I'll even let you borrow the car, alright? – and you can maybe come back at three and I'll pay you overtime.'

'Four,' said Deb. 'And I don't want overtime. But I'll take Friday off.'

'But . . .' began Frances and then clearly thought better of it. 'Okay. Fine. I'll just have to manage myself tomorrow.'

'Great!' said Deb, brightly.

Registration was an anticlimax, nothing more than a queue to have her paltry qualifications photocopied and a startled photo taken for her student identity card. As she waited, she let her eyes roam over the ranks of teenagers, wondering which of them would be on her course. She realised she was already intimidated by the other students, even the ones in her imagination; they were supposed to be here, not her. She was just a cuckoo in the nest, coming along far too late, and with no real sense of what she was doing it for. She was already dreading the day that the first marks came back and they would all realise how stupid she was.

Rob was waiting for her by the front gate afterwards, and he was truly a sight for sore eyes: taller, she was sure, than when she'd last seen him a year ago, his face tanned and his hair grown out of its familiar crop and into sun-bleached curls that clustered at the back of his neck. Deb hugged him so hard that he squealed, then tucked her arm into his and walked him in to Canterbury, where she bought him a cream tea. This was their treat together when he was a child. The two of them would huddle round a table in a dark tearoom, and gleefully pile clotted cream and jam onto scones, Rob taking his with Diet Coke. She was happy to see that nothing had changed.

'I'm so glad you're home,' she said, as he stuffed the second scone into his mouth. 'I'd begun to think you were never coming back.'

Rob shrugged. 'Tempting,' he said. 'It's lovely over there, Mum. You should come.'

'Sounds like you're not done with it yet.'

'Maybe not. I mean, I need more qualifications before I can move out there permanently, but . . . yeah.'

'Oh,' said Deb.

'So I've signed up for teacher training. Early Years. Just to get a visa, really. The Australian government website says they need teachers.'

'Right,' said Deb, 'so you're actually emigrating? It's not just a vague idea?'

'I think so,' said Rob. 'I should have found a better way to tell you. Sorry.' He sucked down a mouthful of Coke and flinched apologetically. 'But at least we'll be students together, right?'

'Just for a year,' said Deb. 'It'll be gone in no time.'

'You're not upset, are you, Mum?'

'No,' said Deb, although it was a blatant untruth. 'Of course I'm not. I understand.'

'You could come out with me,' said Rob. 'Nothing keeping you here.'

Deb laughed. 'I'll have to think about that. How's life with your dad?'

'I don't know,' said Rob. 'Weird. I mean, it's probably just because I've come back home after a year living by myself. But, y'know. I've got my name down for a student flat.'

There was a time when she could have asked him what he meant by that, but it was long gone. There was a time, in fact, when she felt like Rob was her only ally – the only one of her children who could really see Derek for what he was. There was a time when they conspired over those scones and jam, pored over their recollections of Derek's more stupid moments, and when Rob would rehearse his spot-on impression of his father, blundering about the house like a bewildered toddler. Deb would laugh until tears flowed down her cheeks, and then would have to tell him to stop, because they really shouldn't. Now Rob was very obviously a grown-up, and they were no longer in it together. She no longer had the right. But she still got the sense that he was on her side.

When Deb got back to the house – fifteen minutes early, at a quarter to four – Frances was on the phone, presumably to Dylan. 'Oh, she's back, *finally*,' Deb heard her say.

Deb knelt on the floor next to Megan and began to stack up her blocks, *one, two, three*, so that the baby could knock them down again. Frances hung up the phone and came to stand over her.

'Any luck with the ring?' said Deb.

'No,' said Frances. 'I've turned the house upside down. But Dylan's come up with one suggestion that I thought we might pursue.'

This was how Deb came to be transferring the contents of Frances's kitchen bin from one sack to another, sifting through the coffee grounds and carrot peelings in hope of catching the glint of a diamond solitaire. It wasn't nearly as bad as Frances clearly thought it ought to be. Deb had rubber gloves on, and had now instituted a regular timetable of bin-emptying that didn't let anything rot away in the kitchen, as Frances and Dylan used to, as they packed ever more rubbish into the straining black sack, willing each other to give in and take it outside. Still, Deb resented it. She had been asked to rush home for impromptu childcare while Frances worked, not to perform the tasks that her employer couldn't stomach.

She had switched on the radio as she worked, partly for company, and partly because she felt she had to monitor Rick these days, to make sure he didn't say anything stupid. Or rather, because she couldn't stop him saying stupid things, but wanted to make sure he corrected himself if he said them about her.

Today, he was hosting one of his phone-ins, which were populated solely by irritable old men whose cage had been rattled by one thing or another: temporary traffic lights on their route to work, or some new – and mostly imagined – outcropping of 'political correctness gone mad'. It was like a crèche for all the pub poets of the world, the men who had nurtured one beautiful theory for the best years of their life, while the world carried on happily without them.

The current caller had begun with the ominous phrase, 'Now I'm not a racialist, but . . .' and had gone on to make a winding, allusive argument about jobs and immigration and overloaded boats and 'nothing against any of 'em personally' that made Deb feel tired. Rick, to his credit, didn't let him go on for too long, but neither did he disagree too much, leaving Deb thinking what a coward he was.

The next caller fell silent when Rick opened up the line.

'Hello?' said Rick. 'Are you there? Do I have a Derek on the line?'

Deb froze. Afterwards, she thought that she had probably recognised her ex-husband before he even spoke. That long, ominous pause, as his slow brain wound into gear. That deliberate, learned, macho menace. He had been drinking, she could tell. The booze erased the last fragments of his helpless, well-meaning side, and turned him mean.

'Hello, Rick,' said Derek. 'You don't know me, but I think we have a friend in common. More than a friend, you might say.'

'I know half of Whitstable,' said Rick, clearly unnerved. 'You'll have to be a bit more specific than that.'

'Alright,' said Derek. 'I'm talking about your girlfriend, Deb. Deb Winters, as I believe she still goes by. My name. Winters.'

'Right,' said Rick, and Deb imagined that he was making a fast decision about whether to cut the call there and then. But he didn't. 'Well,' he said, 'I'm sure this isn't terribly interesting for our listeners. What did you want to get off your chest today?' He played one of his ridiculous jingles, a squeaky voice saying 'and another thing . . .' but Derek was not going to relax and laugh along.

'I tell you what I want to get off my chest,' he said. 'I want to let you know something, mate – as a fellow traveller. Now, to my mind, you're more than welcome to Deb, if you like sloppy seconds, I mean. Up to you, my friend. None of my business no more. I'm only calling in because I don't want her to do to you what she did to me. We should look out for each other, see?'

My name. Sloppy seconds. He sounded like a sneering yob. Deb was already peeling off her gloves by now, but found herself shouting back to the radio as she did it. 'Not just your name! My kids' name too! They'll have it long after you're dead and buried, you bastard!'

She found her phone in her back pocket and texted Rick: *Hang up.*

But as soon as the text whistled away, it sounded as though she was trying to hide something from Rick, rather than protect him.

'Look,' said Rick, 'I'm not sure where this is going, but my impression is that it's not suitable for today's phone-in . . .'

'Are you aware,' said Derek, 'that she's been running around town with some other bloke, Rick? Chap by the name of Bill, I think? Holding hands.' He laughed, a sly, wheezy laugh. 'Young love,' he began to say, but the line was cut suddenly, mid-syllable. *Young luh—*

'Well,' said Rick, 'I'm terribly sorry about that, folks. We appear to have attracted an . . . uh . . .' and there was a terrible beat when his voice failed entirely, but his presence remained on air somehow, speechless.

A record kicked in, 'Pour Some Sugar on Me' by Def Leppard.

Running around town with some other bloke . . . Holding hands. Naming him too: Bill. Poor Bill. He would be the last person to get involved in something like this. It had been a moment, a few, brief seconds of contact. Nothing. Nothing at all.

But said out loud, it sounded like a war crime.

By the time Rick cut the line, she was already dialling his number, and he picked up as the record began to play. He didn't speak though. He just let Deb talk into a stunned silence.

'Don't listen to him, Rick. He's out to cause trouble. Don't let him drag you down with him.'

The problem was, as she spoke, she realised that it was true, really. Not in terms of what was actually happening: Derek had put two and two together and made sixteen. But in terms of her intention – in terms of what she wanted to happen – he had thrown a dart straight into the bullseye. What could she really say to Rick? That it was all a lie, that she loved him, that she couldn't bear him to think that she would ever betray him? No. It would be untrue if she reassured him now. It would be meaningless. For all his cruelty, Derek had done the job that she had been meaning to do for a while now. He had told Rick a kind of truth. The kind that mattered.

'Listen, Rick, we need to talk.'

'Christ,' said Rick. 'It's true, isn't it? You're not even going to deny it.'

'What's true,' said Deb, 'is that I think the time's up for us. Don't worry about what Derek says. He's got nothing to do with this. But we – you and me – can't go on. It's not what I want from life.'

'I've got to link to the traffic,' said Rick, and he hung up. Deb listened as his watery voice came back on air. *Well, listeners, yours truly is really going through the wringer today. Here's Bob with the latest travel.*

She switched off the radio, put her gloves back on, and transferred the last of the rubbish into its plastic sack. She tied up the top and took it outside to the wheelie bin. She swept the floor, washed the gloves and then her hands underneath them. Then she went up to her room.

When she came back downstairs, she had her old red suit-case in her hand again, stuffed with the same old tat she'd brought with her: fraying towels, a bobbled duvet cover, an empty bottle of Chanel No. 5 and a few photos of her kids. She opened the living-room door.

'I'm sorry,' she said to Frances, 'but I just don't think this is working out.'

'What do you mean?' said Frances.

'You know what I mean,' said Deb. 'Your ring's in the toothbrush mug, by the way. I saw it while I was packing up. Bye, Megan, love.'

She closed the front door behind her, and wheeled the case across town to the only place she could think of.

Maisie's front door.

7

Walking back from The Neptune, Maisie spotted someone on her doorstep and wondered if she had the heart to face off another dirty protest. She didn't think she could muster the dignity she'd managed before. Perhaps she should just call the police this time. It was no good trying to reason with these kids and keep them out of trouble if they kept on making the same mistakes over and over again. Maybe it was time to bring them into contact with their own doctrine of short, sharp shock.

But as she got closer, she saw that the figure was sitting still on what looked like a suitcase, a plume of cigarette smoke rising from her.

'Deb?' she said. 'You're early.' If she was smoking again, it was a bad sign.

'I'm more than early,' said Deb. 'Oh God, Maisie, I've done it again.' And she began to cry.

'How long have you been sitting here?'

'I dunno. An hour, I suppose.'

'Come on,' said Maisie. 'Let's get you sorted out.'

As Maisie sliced bread for sandwiches, she could hear Deb noisily unpacking upstairs. It probably wasn't actually noisy at all, she told herself. It was probably just unfamiliar to have anyone else in the house.

It was a relief, really, to have something else to focus on. But it was another reminder, too, of how far from reality she had allowed herself to live. All this time, keeping a pristine guest room that no one had ever stayed in – because how could that have happened when she had so carefully cut off all her old friends? – and simultaneously allowing herself to ignore the fact that her dearest friend was living in the most precarious poverty. It suited her, she supposed, to turn a blind eye to all of this so that she could continue to wallow in her solitude. It had seemed so precious, and yet now it was an embarrassment, a relic of her own selfishness. Deb could stay as long as she wished. It was shameful that she'd had to ask in the first place.

'Deb!' she called upstairs. 'Ten minutes and we have to go!'

They were on official business tonight, a gala dinner celebrating 'Kent's Heroes', which Maisie had judged it wise that they attend. They had to keep their names in the news, and there was the possibility of a useful association being planted here, a commonality with the other people out there who were defending their communities. But most importantly, Charles Brinton would be there, and so they had to be too. There was a risk, otherwise, that he would win by default for simply doing more glamorous things.

Deb tottered downstairs in a green shift dress and red high heels. 'It's all I've got,' she said. 'If I'd had time to think about it, I would've had a look through the charity shops for something better.'

'You look very elegant,' said Maisie.

'I look like Mrs Christmas,' said Deb.

'Here, eat this before we go.' Maisie passed Deb a plate with a single chicken sandwich.

'I thought we were having dinner there?'

'We are. This is an old campaigner's trick. You make sure you have something in your stomach before you hit the free champagne.'

'Oh God, Maisie, what would I do without you?' said Deb, as she bit into the sandwich, smearing it with peach lip gloss.

'All kinds of things,' laughed Maisie. 'Will Rick still be there tonight, do you think?'

'No idea. I bloody hope not.'

'And did you manage to get hold of Bill?'

'He didn't reply,' said Deb. 'Oh God.'

'Come on,' said Maisie. 'Too late to think about that now.'

They took a taxi over to Canterbury and arrived later than Maisie would have preferred, just in time to be seated near the back. Charles Brinton paused at their table on the way to taking his seat at the front of the room, and said, 'Well look at you two, paying to be here and *still* getting the cheap seats.'

'At least we're contributing, rather than scrounging,' said Deb.

'Oh, I'm contributing alright,' said Charles. 'I'm handing out an award. I don't suppose you are? No.' He swept onwards to the top table.

Deb drained a white wine as soon as it was poured for her, and Maisie refilled her glass with water. 'Go steady,' she whispered.

'Yes, Mum,' said Deb. 'Is he here? I can't see him.'

'Rick?' said Maisie, turning left and right to cast her eyes around the hall. 'I don't think so.'

'Good,' said Deb. 'I don't mean that badly.'

'No,' said Maisie. 'We could do without any scenes tonight.'

Other people were taking their seats at the table. There were two directors of a local charity that rehabilitated young offenders, and a woman who taught art to people with cancer. There were local councillors and the headteacher of a nearby school. They made light conversation as the starters arrived, gentle enquiries like, 'What brings you here tonight?' and, 'Do you come every year?' It was awkward, really, but the kind of awkward that Maisie had mastered long ago. She always felt that, if you could work out how to sail through nights like this, you could probably rule the world.

Maisie was surprised to see how nervous Deb looked in this environment. She was usually so easy around other people. But tonight, she fiddled with her napkin and continually tugged at the hem of her bright green dress, as if she were afraid that her thighs would escape if her attention lapsed for a few brief moments. She seemed content enough for as long as the other guests were talking about themselves, but as soon as the attention turned to her, she blushed, and stammered, and apologised for her own existence. The same old Deb: ever the barometer of who was grander than her, more worthy, or more important. 'Oh, I'm no one,' Maisie heard her say. 'I'm just here for the hot dinner,' and she blushed and gulped at her wine.

'Deb's being rather modest actually,' said Maisie. 'She's run a very successful media campaign this year to challenge a questionable planning decision in Whitstable, and she's currently standing for Parliament.'

'Oh gawd,' said Deb, 'I really haven't done that much. It's mostly Maisie here, honestly.'

'Will you excuse me?' said Maisie, and she stood up and shot Deb a look that insisted she come too.

'I ought to spend a penny,' said Deb, dropping her napkin on the floor as she rose to her feet. 'Better safe than sorry. You never know how long these speeches will last, eh!'

If Maisie could have grabbed her by the ear and dragged her to the bathroom at that point, she would have. It was all she could do to stop herself from hissing, 'What *has* got into you?' as they passed between the tables. But she knew better than that. It wouldn't help. Yet again, Deb's confidence had fallen through the floor, and telling her off would only make it worse. As the door closed behind them in the quiet of the ladies' toilet, Maisie checked that all of the stalls were empty and said, 'You're going to have to sell yourself a bit more, Deb. I know it's hard.'

Leaning over the sinks and dabbing on more lip gloss, Deb said, 'Have you listened to all of them? They've all done something with their lives. They don't want to hear about me.'

'You're wrong about that,' said Maisie. 'But listen: let's imagine you're right. Let's imagine they don't care who the hell you are at all. Let's imagine they're wrapped up in their own little world, and have come here tonight to talk about nothing but themselves. Suppose all of that's true: well, you need to push yourself harder than ever in that case, don't you? You need to go out there and sparkle.'

'Easy for you to say,' said Deb.

'No, it isn't easy for me. It's no easier for me than it is for you. The only difference is that I realised a long time ago that nobody else was going to do my PR. You may be no better than those other people, but you're no worse, either. You've got to get out there and let them know you exist.'

'Maybe I just can't,' began Deb, but the door opened, and somebody said, 'I reckon I can solve that.' Both of the women turned to see Rick, swaying slightly.

'What the hell are you doing?' said Maisie.

'Get the fuck out, Rick,' shouted Deb. 'This is a ladies' toilet.'

'You're the only ones in here,' said Rick. 'What difference does it make?' He had clearly been availing himself of the hospitality for quite some time: his face was red and his bow tie was rotated so that it was brushing under his chin as he moved his head unsteadily.

'Someone might come in,' said Deb.

Rick shrugged. 'So I'll step outside if that happens.'

'I thought you might be a bit more dignified than this,' said Deb. 'Making a scene doesn't benefit anyone.'

Rick began to laugh. 'A scene? I'm not making a scene.' He leaned in towards Deb, suddenly serious. 'I'll tell you what a *scene* is. A *scene* is being told live on air that your girlfriend is cheating on you. On your own radio show. A *scene* is having all the fucking taxi drivers in Whitstable ring up to see if you're okay.'

'I wasn't cheating on you,' said Deb, quietly. 'I almost wish I was after all this fuss. At least I'd have had some fun.'

'*Deb*,' said Maisie warily. For all her dislike of Rick, it was hard not to feel sorry for him, especially in this state. The shame he'd endured was unthinkable. 'Can we try not to escalate this situation, please?'

'Situation?' slurred Rick. 'I'm not a situation!'

'You're not a situation,' said Maisie. 'But this is. Come on, Rick. I'm sorry for you – I really am – but maybe you two can arrange to talk about this quietly tomorrow. Deb's on duty tonight.'

Rick looked from Maisie to Deb, and then back again. 'You don't get it, do you?' he said. 'Deb's nothing without me. I made her. I made this campaign. Do you remember how bad things looked for you before I changed my mind and started backing you? Everyone was laughing at you, Deb. Some dumb housewife in a cheap bikini, trying to change the world. You were a joke.' He twisted his eyes over to Maisie. 'Both of you.'

'Are you threatening us?' said Maisie.

'I'm not threatening. I'm just saying I could change my mind again. I could turn it all back against you. Just like that. Gone!'

'You wouldn't dare,' said Deb. 'Let's face it, you've not exactly been doing this out of the goodness of your heart. You've gained as much from it as we have. Take it all away. See if I care. But you'll just be a sad old man again.'

'That's big talk, Deb, but I don't think you've really thought it through. I mean, risk losing your precious beach, just to piss me off? I don't think so.' He said the last part of this in a baby voice, jutting out his bottom lip and wiping crocodile tears from his eyes. 'No. I've got a better idea. A proposal, if you like.'

'What's that?' said Deb.

'I want to join the team. To be precise, I want to be your campaign manager.'

'No,' said Maisie.

Rick didn't even look at her. 'Think about it, Deb. You made a decent start, but you're losing momentum. The public have lost interest. If you carry on as you are, you'll just hand the election over to Brinton. You need me. I can turn this around for you, make it work again. I can get you back in the limelight.'

'I didn't know you were so desperate for the attention,' said Deb.

'Oh no,' said Rick. 'It's not attention I'm after. No. I can win this for you. I can get you into Parliament. And when that happens, I want you to give me a job. Special advisor, isn't it? Something like that.'

'Special advisor?' said Deb.

'Whatever the title is. A nice fat salary and a fresh start. It's just what I'm looking for. The radio show's been losing listeners for years; it won't be long before it gets cancelled. This is my chance to move on. Come on, Deb. It makes sense, doesn't it?'

'Are you asking me or telling me?'

'Let's call it a bit of both. I'm hoping to appeal to your better nature, but if not . . . well, I've got nothing much to lose, have I? I could do a lot of damage.'

'I suppose you could,' said Deb.

'So do we have a deal?'

'Alright then,' said Deb.

'What?' said Maisie. 'We don't even get to discuss this? You just go ahead and make the decision without me?'

'We don't really have much of a choice,' said Deb.

'Nope,' said Rick. 'You don't really. Still, I'm sure we'll all have loads of fun together, eh? My girls.' He spread out his arms in an attempt to embrace both of them, but managed to only catch Deb, squashing her face into his chest before stepping back and saying, 'Anyway, we can't be hanging around toilets on a night like this. You've got to be out there, pressing the flesh. And I've got the Child Hero award to present in,' he glanced at his watch, 'ten minutes.'

'You'd better start sobering up, then,' said Maisie.

'Nah,' said Rick. 'I'll wing it. But since we're handing out orders, *you'd* better sort the source of our little leak. At least we know who he is now.'

8

The lawn was half a foot long and full of dandelions. The clematis that grew around the front door had dried out, and was now a crisp brown husk. Other changes were more subtle: the bins were no longer lined up in the side return, but instead appeared to have been left roughly where the refuse collectors had dropped them. There was a pile of dirty work boots on the front step. Even before she knocked on the door the whole place reeked of neglect.

As Deb walked up her own front path – as was, a long time ago now – she realised that she had left it too long to come back. It was like returning to a sleeping kingdom in a fairy tale. *Her* kingdom. She may have exiled herself from it, but she hadn't meant to take all the magic with her. Everything was quietly decaying, gathering cobwebs and swathes of dust.

She still had a key, when she thought about it, but it was no longer her right to open that door and walk in. Perhaps he had changed the locks anyway. She would have done, in the same situation. But then, the threat of what might happen if the locks weren't changed wasn't quite the same, was it?

After a long wait, Derek opened the door and scowled into the sunlight. Ten o'clock on a Saturday morning. He must have been out celebrating last night. He stank of stale sweat and undigested booze.

'What do you want?' he said.

'I want to ask why you're spying on me.'

'Spying on you?' Derek managed a wheezy laugh, but in all honesty it looked more like nausea. 'I'm not spying on you.'

'Oh come on, Derek. What was that phone call about then?'

Derek looked for a few seconds as though he wasn't sure what she was talking about, and then laughed. 'Oh,' he said, 'that. I thought I might have dreamt it.' He turned and began to walk away from her down the hall. 'I need a cup of tea,' he said, over his shoulder.

Deb stepped tentatively over the threshold, glancing around her to check the state of the hall. It was stacked with dirty tools and cables, carrier bags half-filled with old newspapers and polystyrene cups. She fought the urge to gather it all up and cram it into the dustbin outside. It would only take her five minutes. What must the neighbours think? But, no. This was the kind of behaviour that had tied her to Derek for so long – always wanting to cover up one last bit of his degradation. She had to leave him to it now.

'Where's Rob?' she said.

'I dunno.' Derek sniffed, and then shouted, 'ROB! YER MUM'S HERE.' No sound from upstairs. 'Must be out.'

Deb's stomach clenched a tiny bit at this. She had been hoping that Rob would be some kind of bridge now that he was back, letting her enter the house under his protection. Not that she expected him to do anything to defend her, exactly. Just having a witness. That had always been enough.

Derek, she noticed, was making one cup of tea, just for himself. She cleared her throat. 'This won't take long. I want to know why you've been watching me. It's got to stop, Derek. There are laws, you know. I can take out a restraining order.'

'I ain't spying on you,' said Derek.

'If you're not spying on me, then what was all that about? How could you know what I was doing, with who?'

'Let's just say,' said Derek, tapping his nose, 'that I've got an informant.'

'What do you mean?'

'I mean what I mean.'

'Don't talk in circles, Derek. It just makes you sound stupid.'

She watched the muscles twitch in Derek's fist as he stirred the tea. She was pushing her luck. But the old man just didn't seem to have the energy for a fight this morning. 'You've got no idea, have you?' he said without looking at her. 'I've got one over on you.'

Deb, who did not like this idea one bit, suddenly realised why the house seemed so quiet.

'Where's the dog?'

'Gave him away,' said Derek.

'You did what?'

'You heard me. Couldn't have him tearing the place to shreds all day. Mate of mine had him.'

'Who is this mate?'

'Dunno. Bloke I met down the pub.'

'You can't just give Nemo to some bloke from down the pub! He's the family pet. He's mine!'

'He's not yours any more. You left him. He was mine to do what I liked with after that.'

'Right,' said Deb. 'That's it. I've had enough of this. You can't keep acting like the only man whose wife ever left him. You've got to move on. It's over. You must know that by now. There's no going back. You're just making it worse for yourself.'

'And you,' said Derek, quietly. 'I hope it makes it worse for you, too.'

'What's the point? What's the point of making it all so difficult? We're finished. We were finished for years before I left. And you can accept that and move on, or keep dragging yourself though this . . .' Without meaning to, she swung out her hand to take in the whole scene, the kitchen with its detritus of takeaway cartons and stained mugs, the dining room beyond it with the table engulfed in dirty washing and scrunched-up receipts.

'I'm not having my wife running around with other men,' whispered Derek.

'I'm not your wife,' said Deb. 'I'm *not* your wife any more.'

'You are my wife until it's over,' said Derek, looking at her for the first time. 'And it's not over yet. *It's not over until I say so.*' He shouted the last sentence, and threw the mug of tea at her. Deb dodged sideways, so that it went crashing onto the floor, splashing scalding liquid across her feet. Without meaning to, she screamed. She'd forgotten how quickly his temper could turn, how often she'd been fooled by this quiet calm before the storm. But before the thought had even quite formulated in her mind, his hands were in her hair, and he was dragging her across the kitchen, her feet tripping through the shattered remains of the cup, her scalp feeling as though it would tear.

And today, for once, she was shouting too, clawing at his hands and kicking at his shins, and shouting 'NO, NO, NO!' as she fought him. This had been their dirty little secret for too long. She had submitted to it to protect her kids, but no more. No more. She wasn't going down without a fight this time. But he had a tight grip on her hair, and she could feel it ripping out at the roots. Her feet burned. Her shoulders ached with the effort of fighting. She watched tears – black with mascara – splash onto the floor beneath her.

This was different. This was a new shift in his anger. If she had no one to protect any more, then neither did he. The kids were gone. It was just the two of them, alone. He would kill her. This was it. She had been stupid to come back. Stupid, stupid, stupid. Always stupid.

But this was her house.

She had to come back, because this was her house.

And he was in it.

She felt her head swing back in his grasp, and a terrible crash as her skull met the side of the cupboard. Her vision went white.

Her head swung back again.

Deb braced her hands around it, ready for the next blow.

And then, nothing.

His fingers released their grip.

Deb tottered and balanced herself on two feet again.

Derek coughed and then walked out of the kitchen, brushing past a man standing in the doorway. Rob. Her youngest son, the sweet boy who persuaded her out for tea and cake, just the two of them, because he *knew,* he always *knew* that something was very wrong. And he wanted to take care of her. And he couldn't.

Because if she couldn't take care of herself, then who could?

Deb said, 'I'm sorry,' and ran past him, out into the street, and down the hill towards the sea.

9

'Christ,' said Maisie as Deb came through the door. 'What the hell's happened to you?'

Deb tried to push past her but Maisie put out an arm, almost by instinct, to catch her. She pulled Deb towards her and crouched down so that she could get a better look at her face. Deb turned away, but Maisie could see that the whole of her left cheek was swollen, and her feet seemed to be blistering.

'Let's get you into the kitchen,' said Maisie, and at that moment Deb gasped out a sob, took her hand out of her pocket, and opened her fist to reveal a clump of her own hair.

Deb sat at the table while Maisie fussed around looking for ice. She never kept frozen peas in the house, and now wished she did. Instead, she had to put ice cubes into a plastic bag and wrap it in a tea towel. It took too long. All the while, Deb's phone buzzed on the table, ignored.

'Would you like me to answer that for you?' said Maisie, as she handed Deb the ice pack and began to size up the scalds on her feet. You were supposed to douse them in cold water, but it was clearly too late. She could still, perhaps, take the heat out of them if Deb would let her.

'No,' said Deb.

Nevertheless, Maisie picked up the phone to see who was calling. 'It's Cherie,' she said, and without even thinking, she pressed the button to answer the call.

'This is Maisie speaking,' she said.

'Where's Mum?' said Cherie. 'I've been driving around with Rob for ages trying to find her.'

'She's here with me, at home,' said Maisie. 'Safe and sound.' She looked over at Deb and thought, *not quite sound. But safe, I think.*

'Tell her I'm fine,' said Deb. 'Tell her whatever Rob thought he saw, he's probably got the wrong end of the stick.'

Maisie, who was sure that Cherie could hear this, said, 'What *did* Rob see, Cherie?'

Silence on the other end of the line, except for a young man's voice, which she presumed to be Rob's, saying, 'Where is she? Is she alright?'

'I saw it myself once,' said Cherie. 'When I was a little girl. I came downstairs in the night, and there it was. His hands were round her throat. I went upstairs to bed and told myself it was a bad dream.'

Fuck! shouted Rob in the background. *Fuck fuck fuck.* There was the sound of a fist hitting the dashboard.

'He's upset,' said Cherie. 'He was too shocked to do anything.'

'Alright,' said Maisie. 'Listen. I'll give you my address, and you can both come over and talk to your mum. It sounds like there's a few things that have needed to be said for a long time.'

'No,' said Deb. 'No. Not now.'

'I used to put my pillow over my ears after that, whenever he came home at night, just to make sure. I didn't want to know. I never wanted to know.'

'Alright,' said Maisie gently.

'Did you know?' said Cherie.

'No, my love,' said Maisie. 'I didn't.'

It was strange to see Deb, finally, with the children she'd said so much about. At some point down the line, Darren had been called, and the three of them landed on Maisie's doorstep, grey with fear and remorse. For all her embarrassment, Deb was obviously delighted to see them. She stretched out her arms from the sofa and hugged them all, saying, 'Now don't you go worrying about me, I'm alright.' She let Rob curl up next to her on the sofa like a lapdog, and talked Darren down as he paced the room, threatening to carry out all kinds of atrocities in his mother's name, some of which, Maisie felt, were not entirely unjustified. Cherie, who couldn't bear to be impractical, took out a comb and brushed Deb's hair this way and that, while Deb flinched and sucked in her breath, and eventually said, 'Leave it, Cherie. I don't want a comb-over. I'll have to get it all cut off.'

Cherie sighed and sat down. 'We have to call the police,' she said.

'No,' said Deb, 'I don't want the police.'

'She's right,' said Maisie. 'This is a serious assault.'

'It's not that bad,' said Deb. 'I'll survive.'

'You're missing the point,' said Cherie.

'I don't want him to think he's got the better of me.'

'Are you joking?' said Darren. 'He's already got the better of you. How long have you put up with this shit? And in the end, you moved out of our house to get away from him. If I'd have known . . .'

'You're right about that,' said Deb. 'It's my house. It's my house, and I'm having it back.'

'So make a crime report,' said Maisie. 'If nothing else, it'll strengthen your divorce case.'

'You've got to, Mum,' said Cherie. 'God, he's my dad and even I think you should.'

'No,' said Deb. 'I'm not having any fuss,' and she folded her arms in stubborn defiance, mirroring her daughter, who took the same stance at the opposite side of the room. Maisie wondered if they knew how similar they were.

10

'It looks fine,' said Maisie, as Deb ran her fingers under the edge of her bathing cap for the fourth time. 'Leave it alone.'

'It's just not very forgiving,' said Deb. 'I feel like I'm wearing a flashing beacon on my head.' The cap dragged at her face, and seemed to be heating up alarmingly fast under the late September sun, despite the crisp air. The rest of Deb's body was freezing. On reflection, it was probably a bit late in the year for the old bikini now; maybe it was time for a smart wetsuit like Maisie's, at least until spring came again.

'To be fair, nobody forced you to buy a leopard print one.'

'Leopard print,' said Deb, 'is the best thing about it.' She patted her cheeks. 'I'm wondering if it has a bit of a face-lift effect, actually.'

'You go with that,' said Maisie. Deb, who had been avoiding mirrors for a week now, decided that her best option was to trust that an enthusiastic smile would get her through, as it had so many times before. She tried not to think about the yellowing bruise on the left-hand side of her face. It would go, eventually. But at least her sun-browned skin was covering a multitude of sins. She felt like she was finally vindicated, after years of listening to Cherie's lectures on the perils of having a tan. It was a hollow victory, but she'd take it all the same.

'It's for Edith anyway, isn't it?' she said. 'Doesn't matter what I look like.'

Her phone rang – Rob, bless him, had somehow managed to make it play 'I Will Survive' whenever someone called – and she whispered to Maisie, 'It's her,' as she pressed it to her ear. 'Yes,' she said into the phone, 'you're nearly there. Once you get to the caravans, walk up the slope and you'll be on the right part of the beach. See you in a bit.'

'Thank goodness for that,' said Maisie, as Deb hung up. 'I thought she was dropping out for a moment there.'

'Nah,' said Deb. 'She won't let us down. She's a good girl. I can tell.'

There was a commotion at the top of the beach, and she heard Maisie say, 'What on earth . . .' before she clocked it herself: Rick had arrived, and trailing behind him appeared to be a cameraman, a sound technician and a news reporter in a shirt and tie.

'Oh for pity's sake,' said Deb, and began to march over the shingle towards them.

'. . . and here's the woman herself!' said Rick with a flourish as Deb approached.

'What the hell is this?' said Deb.

'Great news!' said Rick, throwing his arms out as if he was about to embrace her, and then thinking better of it. 'I've managed to get TV coverage of Edith's swim. Wonderful human-interest story: a senior citizen takes her first swim in half a century in protest at the West Beach development.'

'That's not what this is!' said Deb. 'This is a personal thing for Edith, and the club's turned out to support her. You said we'd do the interview later.'

'But this is even better,' said Rick. 'Electoral candidate supports elderly woman's dying wish for one last swim.'

'No!' said Deb. 'I'm not doing this because of the election. I'm doing this as her friend.'

'Aha,' said Rick, 'but the great thing is that you've got me as a campaign manager, and I've got the imagination to roll the two into one.'

'That's not imagination,' said Deb.

'You'll be fine, babe,' said Rick. 'Just give a short speech at the end and it's all covered. Remember: we're in it to win it! What happened to your face, by the way?'

Deb felt the kind of growl rising in her throat that could fast turn into an act of aggression, but from the corner of her eye, she saw her guest approaching the beach.

'We'll talk about this later,' she said.

'No worries,' said Rick, happily. 'I'll just get these guys set up. You're my superstar! Don't worry about anything.'

Deb dearly wanted to set him straight, but she reasoned she'd wasted enough breath on him already. 'Thank the stars this'll be over soon,' she said to Maisie.

'So you're sure?' said Maisie. 'You're not sorry to be leaving it all behind?'

'No,' said Deb. 'You?'

'Not a tiny bit sorry,' said Maisie. 'We've made the right decision.'

'I was thinking it over last night, and I realised I've got to stop trying to look after everyone. It's time to do what's right for me. I've waited long enough for it.' She glanced over at Rick, who was showing off in front of the cameramen, perching one foot on the groyne post like a particularly lame catalogue model. 'I realised another thing too,' she said. 'I left one bastard who wants to control my life, and ran straight into the arms of another one.'

Edith arrived in Julie's people carrier which, it had been decided, was far more suitable than Maisie's tiny hatchback. Deb helped her into her wheelchair and walked with her down to the shore.

'Primed and ready for action?' said Deb.

'Oh yes,' said Edith. 'I've got it all sussed, don't you worry.' She was wearing a white towelling robe, so fluffy that it looked like she had just stepped out of the spa of an exclusive hotel. Underneath it, Deb knew, was a plain black swimming costume, and she was already wearing her sea-shoes. 'Just reach into the back pocket for me, please, and pull out that plastic bag.'

Deb did as she was told, and handed the package to Edith, who opened it and unfolded the contents.

'Blow it up, will you, Deb,' said Edith.

There was no sign of Bill. Deb was beginning to wonder if there would ever be any sign of him again. It wasn't as if he was ignoring her – he was far too polite for that. No, he'd responded to her flood of apologetic texts after Derek had casually dropped his name into the phone-in, and had been friendly but distant. *I don't want to be responsible for any heartache,* he said. *I'll just stay away for a while, until it's all blown over.* Deb didn't doubt for one minute it was true. Bill was the last person she could imagine intentionally chasing after a woman with a boyfriend. But at the same time, she knew that it was also a signal of his profound embarrassment at being thrust so brutally into the limelight. He was most likely in hiding.

Perhaps it was for the best. After all, he was pretty close to thirty years younger than her, and she wasn't much of a wall-flower. It was hard to imagine how it could survive in the long run, and Deb couldn't bear the thought of being responsible for yet another broken heart when the inevitable happened. Hers, at least, was as hard as old boot-leather now, but Bill's? No. He was a tender soul. She couldn't put him through it.

Chloe was here though, looking slightly bereft without him. But whereas she once would have stood at the edge of the beach, kicking the shingle, today she was at the centre of it all, offering a kiss to Edith and chatting with Ann. Deb waved at her, and she waved back, a sunny smile breaking across her face. It was easy to forget how different she'd been when she joined the club, displaying that odd mixture of demanding and repelling attention at the same time. Now, she looked as though she was right at home, part of a big, unruly family.

'Come on, Deb!' called Edith. 'Put some welly into it!' Deb unfolded the bundle of white plastic, and began to puff air into it. It grew larger and larger, and gradually took shape.

'Oh *Edith*,' said Deb as she paused to catch her breath. 'You've surpassed yourself with this one.'

'It's a beauty, isn't it?' said Edith, as Deb dropped an inflatable ring onto the surface of the water to make sure it floated. It glowed resplendent against the grey estuary water, a white unicorn with an upright head like a hobby horse, except with a rainbow horn jutting out like a stick of rock. 'Ann wanted me to have armbands,' she added contemptuously, glancing over at her daughter.

Ann tutted and folded her arms. 'Now, listen. There's still enough time to change your mind. Nobody will think any less of you.' She edged over to the sea, bent down and dipped in her hand. 'It's freezing in there. You'll catch your death.'

'Wouldn't be such a bad thing,' muttered Edith, but then, seeing Ann's horrified face, 'Oh stand down, Ann. I've been taking cold showers for the last month to acclimatise.'

'I should have known you'd be in training,' laughed Maisie. 'Seriously though, Edith. It is very cold in there. We'll keep it short, and if I see your teeth chattering, I'm getting you straight out.'

'We'll see about that,' said Edith.

'Are the receiving party ready?' asked Deb.

'We're ready,' said Julie. 'We'll get you warmed up as soon as you're onshore.'

'Right-o,' said Edith. 'Let's get going.'

'I'm sorry about the cameras,' said Deb. 'I really wouldn't have let it happen if I'd known.'

'And miss out on having my maiden voyage recorded for posterity?' said Edith. 'I wouldn't hear of it. As long as they don't smash a bottle of champagne against my side, I'll be alright.'

She stood up on uncertain legs and walked slowly over to the edge of the sea, where she let the water dance at her toes for a few seconds before carrying on in, supported on each side by Deb and Maisie.

'Ooh!' she gasped as the water reached her thighs. 'That's fresh! Help me on with my ring now, will you?'

Deb lifted the unicorn over Edith's head, trying to ignore the camera crew, who were suddenly very interested in the unfolding spectacle. *Just pretend they're not here,* she thought.

'Right,' said Edith. 'Here we go.'

She pitched herself forward into the sea, sucking in her breath. The unicorn bent to take her weight, and Edith floated on her front, clinging to its silver mane and tail.

'Are you alright?' said Maisie.

'Oh my God,' said Edith.

'We can get you straight out!'

'Oh my GOD,' said Edith.

'Right,' said Maisie, 'don't panic. It won't take a moment.'

'OH MY GOD,' said Edith, 'it's WONDERFUL. Don't you dare!'

'Oh thank heavens,' said Maisie, bursting into laughter. 'I thought you had hypothermia.'

Edith stretched her arms out and took a few gentle strokes out to sea. Deb swam alongside her, turning onto her back so that she could watch her friend's face. It was nine-tenths delight, and the rest was determination. There was colour in Edith's cheeks, the pink flush of a young girl, and her breath was uneven with exertion.

'Okay,' said Maisie after a while, 'time's up, I think,' and Edith said, 'Alright then,' which was the closest she would ever get to giving in. Maisie gripped the head of the unicorn, and Deb its tail, and they swam her into the shallows, where Edith found her feet again. The High Tide Swimming Club stood at the water's edge, cheering, and Julie was waiting with her robe, two hot-water bottles, a pile of blankets, and a flask of tea made to Edith's specification – that is, with whisky instead of milk.

Edith sat under her mound of bedding and smiled content-edly at the sea. Beside her, Ann stood quietly, her hand on her mother's shoulder.

'There you go,' said Deb. 'You both survived it.'

'Just about,' said Ann.

'Come on, Deb!' came a shout from across the beach, and Deb turned to see Rick standing in front of the cameraman, beckoning her over.

'Let's see who survives this one,' she said, as she squeezed Edith's hand and said, 'Best swim of the year,' before walking over to join Rick.

'As you can see,' said Rick to the interviewer, 'it's been an emotional day for us here. That's what this movement is all about – family, friendship, community. Helping each other out. Taking the rough with the smooth.'

'Bloody hell,' said Deb, 'you get worse.'

Rick laughed his chat-show laugh. 'Ha ha ha! As you can see, we have a real rapport.'

'Are we ready then?' said the interviewer, who Deb

recognised from the local news. He was only young, but had the formality of a particularly embarrassing dad, and always managed to look awkward in any social situation. Today, he was trying to stop his eyes darting downwards towards Deb's bikini. 'I mean, don't you want to get dressed first?'

Deb looked down at herself, and then back up at the presenter. 'Nah,' she said. 'I'll be fine like this, love. Will you just give me a moment to sort something out though?'

'That's Deb,' she heard Rick say. 'What you see is what you get. She's . . . unpretentious.' Deb looked around for her guest, the woman she'd met at the top of the beach this morning. She leaned in and whispered something in her ear. The woman nodded and said, 'Okay. Yes. Fine.'

'Great,' said Deb, and she jogged back over to Rick. Maisie came over and joined them just off-camera, and some of the swimmers crowded around too, to hear what she had to say. It was the most like an actual politician that Deb had ever felt.

'With the General Election just two weeks away,' began the presenter, 'I'm here on West Beach with Deb Winters, who is standing as an independent candidate. I don't think you'd disagree if I said you were something of an outside hope, Deb?' he said.

'Oh God no,' said Deb. 'I'd go further than that. I haven't got a chance in hell of actually winning.'

'I think what she means—' butted in Rick, but Deb carried on.

'I know exactly what I mean, thanks,' she said. 'Listen. This has gone far enough. I started this campaign because I wanted to draw attention to our mission here to save West Beach . . .' (a cheer from the swimmers) '. . . but also because I wanted to stick it in the eye to the MP we've got at the moment. Honestly, he's a nasty piece of work and Whitstable deserves better.' The club cheered again, and clapped, but Deb could see, at the same time, that doubt was seeping onto their faces. This was not her most sophisticated performance, and neither was it meant to be.

'But look,' she said, 'we can't win against Charles Brinton. We haven't got the time or the energy to even try. Or the talent to do the job if we won. No. I'm an old campaigner, not a politician. I'm best off shouting from the sidelines.'

'Can I get this right?' said the presenter. 'Are you announcing that you're standing down?'

'Yes,' said Deb, 'I am.'

'Hold on,' said Rick, but Deb waved him away.

'Sometimes, the greatest skill in the world is knowing when to give up. I've spent my whole life looking after other people, and being told what to do by men who think they're cleverer than me.' She threw a sharp look at Rick, who had clearly already decided to cut his losses and was slowly backing out of the shot. 'This is just more of the same. It means I haven't learned. I'm rushing in to save everyone all over again, and ignoring what *I* want to do.'

'And what is it you want to do?' asked the presenter.

'I want to go to university and get my degree. I've just finished Freshers' Week, actually. I was the oldest one there and I bloody loved it. Sorry. I hope this isn't going out live.'

'Well thank you, Deb,' said the presenter, hurriedly, 'for what has been an—'

'Hang on,' said Deb, 'I haven't finished yet. We're . . . me and Maisie, I mean . . . are really grateful for everyone's support. I honestly mean that. It's been lovely, and I hope you don't feel like we're letting you down. But I wouldn't have even thought about giving up if I hadn't come across this young woman.' She beckoned to her guest, who came over and stood at Deb's side. 'I think you'll know who this is – Michelle Hunter. She's running for election too. Maisie saw one of her leaflets last week, and we got in touch to see if we could work something out. She suggested we form a coalition.' Deb laughed. 'I said, "Sweetheart, it's all yours, and I'll do what I can to help you." So anyway, if you were thinking of voting for me, I hope you'll vote for her instead. She's brilliant, and she'll do a much better job than I ever could.'

She looked over at the presenter, who was trying to find words to form the next sentence. 'That's it, love,' she said to him, 'I'm done.' And she walked away.

11

Stephen announced his arrival with a polite knock on the front door, and when Maisie opened it, she found that he had brought flowers. He was incapable of anything so spontaneous as a last-minute buy from a petrol station along the way. These were carefully arranged and wrapped in mauve and white tissue paper, probably ordered a week ago from the florist on Harbour Street: huge, rust-coloured chrysanthemums with yellow roses and spikes of eucalyptus. As Maisie rushed them to the kitchen to put their feet in water until she got home, she thought that it felt like a homecoming. Not the romantic gesture – there had been few enough of those in her marriage – but the sense of having someone who knew her tastes so well, and whose exacting standards matched her own. They were a good fit, she and Stephen.

They walked down a narrow alleyway and onto the seafront. The sun was just beginning to dip behind the Isle of Sheppey, and the sky was the thinnest blue, but golden at the horizon. Maisie drew her coat around her and fought her compulsion to slip her arm into Stephen's. She could feel a matching tension from his side, too – that odd, stiff walk they were both affecting so that their bodies didn't touch. They had spent the best part of a lifetime sharing bathrooms and bedrooms, nursing each other when they were sick, and folding each other's laundry, but now, in less than a year, all that was left was the aftermath of intimacy, an old, fading echo.

'We'll have quite a sunset tonight,' she said.

Stephen wiped his nose with a cotton handkerchief. 'Will we?'

Such things never did concern him. Or perhaps that wasn't fair. They concerned him enough when they caught his attention. It was just that he mostly forgot to notice them. They were part of the world outside his mind, and so only faded into view every now and then. They were intermittent at best.

He had booked a table at the Oyster Stores, and when they reached the storm-sheltered door, he stood aside to usher Maisie in first. 'I suppose you eat here all the time,' he said as they sat down. 'You're probably rather sick of it.'

'Locals don't really eat here,' said Maisie, and then corrected herself: 'What would I know! I've barely eaten out at all since I've been here.'

'You've changed,' said Stephen. 'I could hardly keep pace with your insatiable desire for entertainment when we . . .' And he stopped, because it was hard to know how to phrase it, now. *When we last knew each other?* Too nostalgic. *When we were together?* The past tense didn't sit quite right, here, in this atmosphere of uncertainty and expectation. He didn't want to blow it with a simple slip of language.

'When we lived in London, I had a very different set of priorities,' said Maisie. 'I was desperate for something in my evenings that didn't feel like work. Enough of them were swept away by that bloody job.'

'I well remember it.'

'But nowadays, I'm just more content. I've found a better balance. I don't need to come down from an adrenaline high with three glasses of wine, and I don't need to fight exhaustion by leaving the house. I swim, I take long walks, and I get enough sleep. I don't need all the fancy restaurants.' She thought about leaving the next sentence unspoken, but decided that it was time to say it out loud. Nothing could change if she carried on as she always had, keeping her own needs quiet. 'I also used to make you go out so I could feel like we were still a couple.'

'Ouch,' said Stephen. 'That was well-aimed. But I don't suppose you need me to point out that you've tackled that problem by being single and never going out at all.'

'You're right,' said Maisie. 'I have.'

The sky was turning red now over the beach, streaked with glorious mauve clouds. Even Stephen couldn't ignore it: it washed the table in deep crimson light, making him look up, blink, and say, 'Wow. Will you look at that.'

Maisie dragged herself from her thoughts and looked out of the window. 'I do,' she said. 'I step out onto the beach every night if I can, just to watch the sun go down. If the tide's high, I swim in it. It doesn't sound like much of a life to you, I know, but it's the life that's finally made me happy.'

'Am I guessing,' said Stephen, 'that you won't be moving back home to London with me?'

'No,' said Maisie. 'I don't think so.'

'I see,' he said, and from the dimpling of his chin, Maisie thought he was holding back tears.

'But I realise at the same time that I love you,' she said. 'You live in your own little world, and you're stuck in your ways, but that's the deal, isn't it? That's what you are. The problem is, I've changed. I've found a better way to live, one that suits me. It wouldn't suit you. London is your natural habitat. This year, I've learned that I'm a seabird.'

'What are you saying?' said Stephen. 'It's Whitstable or bust? I've got to move down here if I want to be with you?'

'No,' said Maisie. 'I'm not saying that at all. I'm saying that you are with me. I'm saying that we're together, even in separate towns. I spent decades feeling invisible when I was with you, and yet, down here, I feel like you see me again. Who's to say we have to be in the same room to be together?'

'Right,' said Stephen slowly. 'So you're suggesting a long-distance relationship?'

'I suppose I am,' said Maisie. 'A long-distance marriage. We can each be happy knowing the other is fifty miles away, doing what they love.'

'I don't know,' said Stephen. 'That doesn't sound like a marriage at all.'

'Maybe not in the traditional sense,' said Maisie. 'But then what is a marriage anyway? Sitting in the same house every night, and sleeping in the same bed, without ever giving each other a second thought? We tried that and it was awful.'

'But you're suggesting even less than that.'

'What I'm suggesting is that when we spend time together, it will be by choice. No more tolerating each other. Instead, spending time together as good old friends, joyfully. Deliberately.'

'I feel like this is just another way of you leaving me.'

'That's just your pride talking. You won't be able to go back to your friends in triumph and say, *It's all back to normal.* It's an admission that we screwed it up in the past. We'll have some explaining to do. Both of us.'

'So what you're saying is that we both go back to our separate homes and get on with our separate lives, but call ourselves a couple?'

'Yes,' said Maisie. 'And sometimes I'll come and see you in London, and we'll go to the theatre and try out fancy new restaurants.'

'And sometimes I'll come down to the seaside, I suppose,' said Stephen.

'Yes, you will. But we'll have to get you some more sensible shoes.'

'The wine list's pretty good here, actually.'

'Yes, and we have electricity and running water too.'

'Sarcasm never suited you,' said Stephen. 'But listen. What about, you know, your health? Don't you really need someone to look after you a bit now?'

'Not yet,' said Maisie.

'And when you do? What will happen then?'

'Do you know what? I have no idea. I thought I could plan for it, but I can't. I don't know how it will play out. I don't know how I'll respond to the drugs, or whether any new treatments will come along. I'll just have to take it as it comes.'

'I was all ready to rush in and play nurse, you know,' said Stephen.

'Very gallant,' said Maisie. 'When I need you, I'll let you know.'

'Promise?' said Stephen. 'I mean, no more suffering in silence?'

'I promise,' said Maisie.

'Well, that went better than expected!' he said, topping up both of their glasses. 'I thought you were going to leave me properly this time.'

'No,' said Maisie. 'I couldn't do that again.'

'I'll just go back to keeping track of your exploits on Twitter.'

'You mean Facebook,' said Maisie. 'I'm not on Twitter.'

'Oh no!' said Stephen. 'There's a brilliant account that Marisa found a couple of weeks back. Some woman – I think she's a friend of yours – who keeps us apprised of your every movement. I'm not sure she realises that anyone can see.'

'Who?' said Maisie. 'Can you show me?'

'I should think I can,' said Stephen. He reached into his inside pocket and pulled out a phone in a kid leather case. 'Here,' he said, after prodding at it for a few moments.

Maisie stared at the screen, and then scrolled back through the timeline, her stomach suddenly clenching.

'Hold on,' she said. 'I have to make a phone call.'

Deb picked up in two rings. 'Are you okay?' she said. 'Do you need me to come and get you?'

'I'm fine,' said Maisie, 'but I think Stephen's found our leak.'

12

'We could just leave it,' said Deb as Maisie pulled the car to the kerb and yanked on the hand brake. 'We could just say we were dropping by for tea. It doesn't matter any more, does it?'

'It does matter,' said Maisie. 'Not for the campaign, but for you and me, personally. We can't carry on having our whole lives being broadcast like this.'

'She'll be so embarrassed, though,' said Deb. 'I don't want to make her feel bad.'

'She's a grown-up. It's patronising to treat her like a child. She's making a mistake, and I guarantee she'll want to know so that she can put it right.'

'Oh God,' said Deb. 'All that time she's been sitting there with her iPad and I thought she was just doing a crossword. I didn't even know she had an account.'

'We should have realised,' said Maisie, 'that it's unlike Edith to do anything completely harmless.'

'Oh *God*,' said Deb. 'What's Ann going to say?'

As soon as she got home last night, Maisie had shown Deb Edith's Twitter feed. She was only following one person, a woman by the name of Stella who seemed to be a leading light in the local bowls club. It was clearly Stella who had invited Edith onto the site, and Edith seemed unaware that what she posted was visible to anyone other than her friend. The problem was that Edith had somehow amassed eight hundred followers, presumably attracted by her complete lack of discretion. There it was, for all to see: a lot of chat about old times, the friends they'd lost and who was still going; a few waspish comments about Ann, and what looked like a running commentary on each of their campaign meetings, tweeted from the armchair in the corner of the room.

The saddest thing of all was that not a single word of it was vicious: it was instead shared in a kind of giddy, conspiratorial pride. Edith was relishing being at the centre of the action for the first time in years, and she was divulging the details to her friend. It was nothing, really: she recorded the manifesto pledges with the gravity of a foreign correspondent posting back from the White House; she recounted Deb's angry phone call to Charles Brinton with enormous glee: *My Deb wiped the floor with him. Good girl.*

And then, the most innocent scrap of gossip in the world: *Finally talked Ann into taking me out for tea. Walked in & saw Deb holding hands with young Bill, no less! Good on her. Made a swift exit.*

Derek hadn't needed to stalk Deb. He just had to turn on his phone.

'We'll handle this as gently as possible,' said Maisie. 'I'm wondering if I can just adjust her privacy settings. She won't know a thing.'

'Oh God,' said Deb, 'I hope so.'

Maisie rang the doorbell, and they both watched Ann's silhouette appear in the frosted glass. 'I feel sick,' said Deb.

The door opened a crack, and Ann's face appeared, the colour of stale milk.

'Oh,' she said. 'It's you. You'd better come in, I suppose.'

Maisie glanced at Deb, and gave the faintest flick of her eyes at this fresh retreat of Ann's social skills. 'Everything okay, Ann?' she said.

'How did you find out already? Did somebody ring you?'

'Find out what, love?' said Deb, poking her head round the living room door in the hope of finding Edith in her chair. She wasn't there. They followed Ann into the kitchen, where the kettle was already coming to the boil.

'I was just making tea,' said Ann. 'It's all I can think of to do,' and she pressed her hand over her mouth and began to cry.

'What on earth's happened?' began Deb, just as Maisie said, 'Your mum . . .?'

'This morning,' said Ann. 'Well, last night, I suppose. Passed away in her sleep.'

'Oh Ann,' said Maisie. 'I'm so terribly sorry.'

'You're sorry? What difference does it make to you? That's everything gone for me. Everything.'

13

By the time the funeral came around, it was almost November. Ann said it was ridiculous to wait three weeks to bury an old woman, and Maisie remembered feeling the same about her mother, too. 'But you'll have so much to do in that time,' she told Ann, 'that you'll end up wishing you had longer.' Maisie sat down with Ann and drew up a list of everything that would need to be arranged, all the decisions made, and all the forms to be filled. It was learned from bitter experience, but at least it finally gave her something to pass on, some wisdom gleaned from that terrible time. Perhaps it even laid some old bones to rest.

It turned out that Edith's Twitter account was useful after all. Maisie posted a short, dignified notice on it, and then checked back later that day to find pages and pages of kind words: *We've lost a wonderful character there. Always the best thing on here, RIP Edith.* Over and over again, people were sharing the clip of Edith's swim, for the sheer joy of seeing her delighted face. It felt like, finally, they had managed to make kindness go viral.

Deb received a call from the local paper, asking if they could publish the details of the funeral, and the next day there was half a page devoted to Edith, complete with a photo of that last swim. Before long, Ann was complaining about the number of cards that were being pushed through the door 'at all hours', although Maisie noted the care with which she had lined all of them up along the sideboard, spilling over onto every windowsill. The next time they swam, there was a smattering of flowers on West Beach, lined up under the 'No Swimming' signs. Someone had even left an inflatable unicorn anchored to a groyne with black ribbons.

On the morning of the funeral, Deb arrived early at Ann's house to start making sandwiches. Maisie had offered to order trays of them from Marks & Spencer, but Deb had said no, she would rather do it herself. Maisie knew it was no use arguing. There were some principles that Deb would never give up.

At half past ten, two black cars arrived, and the three women got in and followed Edith to the crematorium. Deb, who had been living in a baseball cap for the last three weeks, had reluctantly agreed to swap it for a headscarf, which she had fashioned into a turban that she hoped would remind everyone of a 1940s glamour queen, and deter them from asking questions. Tiny wisps of hair were growing back into the bald patch that Derek had left behind, but it would be a good couple of months before she could even have it cut into a decent crop. She would just have to let people talk until then.

Ann hardly said a word all the way. She dabbed at her nose with a tissue that was already at the point of collapse, and clutched her seatbelt as though she was afraid that she would disappear under the driver's seat if she didn't hold on tight.

As they drove through the gates, though, she bit her lip and said, 'Oh my goodness!' There, waiting at the chapel door, was a crowd of people. Maisie recognised some of the faces from the High Tide Swimming Club: Julie, Chloe, Brian and Bill, Grace from the beach huts, and all the other people that she was beginning to know without being able to name. Ann, she suspected, would have a note of all of them in her register. But there were others, too, people who shook Ann's hand as she got out of the car and said, 'I knew your mother before she had you', or, 'I remember how she used to whip me at poker during the war.'

Once they had all packed into the chapel, it was standing-room only at the back of the pews, and the heat of so many people warmed the room. It had not surprised Maisie to know that Edith had left very specific instructions for her funeral, itemised in a numbered list that Ann found in a file on her desk, alongside her will and details of all her bank accounts. The detail of them, however, made her raise an eyebrow. 'I want no fuss,' she had written, and underlined the last two words twice, just in case anyone thought they could be ignored.

No fuss, it turned out, was an immensely specific concept, but it was executed to the letter. As Ann blustered through the list, lambasting its eccentricities and the organisational toll they took on her days, Maisie got the sly sense that this was all part of Edith's plan, keeping her daughter occupied with highly specific tasks so that she didn't have time to think.

The 'cheerful, pragmatic vicar' who would not 'make a song and dance of the whole thing' was found by Deb, who had been to enough school concerts over the years to have an encyclopaedic knowledge of the local clergy. The congregation sang, as specified, 'one hymn only', which was 'Dear Lord and Father of Mankind', 'played at a decent clip, and not droning along as seems to be the preference these days'. There was no sermon, although they decided it was best not to pass Edith's specific instruction on to the vicar: 'I can't abide the idea of someone I don't know listing all my life achievements, and then using them to make a feeble religious point.' Unfortunately, it was not possible to shield Ann from the request that there was to be 'no eulogy either' because 'they only seem to exist to make sure everyone's sad enough', and she 'couldn't bear the thought of Ann simpering over my memory, all the while thinking what a difficult old bat I actually was'.

'I want it over and done with quickly,' she had written, and it was: there was an unsentimental efficiency to the whole event, which was underlined by the final flourish, a rousing chorus of 'For She's a Jolly Good Fellow' as the curtains closed on the coffin. It had been agreed in advance that Deb would stand up and start this, because even Maisie didn't feel equal to it, and Ann was certain that she wouldn't even join in. But in the event, they all stood up together and began. Perhaps it was the emotion of the moment driving them all to restlessness, but Maisie thought that Ann might even have been the first on her feet.

As the whole congregation sang, Maisie turned to wave at the High Tide Swimming Club: Julie, who was dabbing a tear from her eye despite Edith's best efforts to prevent it; Chloe, who was holding her hand; Brian, who was rocking on his heels and bellowing 'and so say all of us!' at every opportunity;

Bill, who was swaying along awkwardly, and almost certainly not opening his mouth enough to let actual words come out. This was exactly what she couldn't bear to leave behind for the luxuries of London.

After five rounds of the song, Ann stood up, turned to the congregation and said, 'That'll do! We'll frighten the next lot of mourners.' There was an uncertain moment of silence before everyone noticed Ann's face: she was beaming. Laughter filled the chapel. 'My mother has requested that I now invite you all back to the house for tea, sandwiches, and *The Times* crossword. The tea will be served with either milk, whisky, or both if you prefer. She says she'll let you do the quick crossword if you really can't manage the cryptic.' Again, laughter. Maisie noticed that Ann's cheeks were flushed pink, and that she looked unexpectedly relaxed, as if years had fallen from her.

There was a renewed burst of cheering from the congregation, and they began to file out of the door. Outside, each one of them seemed to want to shake Ann's hand and tell her their own, particular story about Edith. Maisie watched as Ann laughed, and accepted hugs from well-meaning strangers, and thanked people sincerely for coming along. Deb was working her way around the crowd, insisting that absolutely everybody came back, and saying over and over again that they'd had to order thirty copies of *The Times* from a bewildered newsagent. The only person whose path she didn't seem to cross was Bill's.

Maisie walked over to him and said, 'Are you coming back with us?'

'I don't know,' said Bill. 'I should get back to work, I think.'

'Bill,' began Maisie, 'you can't punish Deb for . . .' but Julie arrived at her side saying, 'Whew, that had me in floods!' and before Maisie could recover the situation, Bill had turned away.

'I suppose I'd better rescue Ann,' she said.

'She looks in her element,' said Julie. 'I didn't even know Ann had an element. Is that rude?'

'No,' said Maisie. 'I know exactly what you mean.'

She put a hand on Ann's shoulder, and said, 'Will you excuse me?' to a frail-looking woman who was reminiscing about a late-night backgammon game with a group of fishermen in the sixties.

'It's time to go, Ann. Everyone's coming back to the house, so it's only a pause, I promise.'

'Okay,' said Ann, and kissed the woman she was speaking to. 'Will I see you later?'

'Oh, certainly,' said the woman. 'I wouldn't miss it.'

They turned and walked towards the car. 'Can I just say,' said Maisie, 'that it's been wonderful to watch you today. You seem . . . different somehow. Not happy, exactly. Still grieving. But . . .'

'Free,' said Ann. 'That's how I feel: free. I've been afraid of this happening for years. I've been trying to prevent it, I think. I've been trying to hold her so close that she couldn't leave me. It was stupid of me.'

'You can't stop an old woman from dying,' said Maisie.

'She did so much,' said Ann. 'And I've done so little.'

'There's plenty of time left to change,' said Maisie.

'Yes,' said Ann. 'I could sell the house and travel the world.'

'You could,' said Maisie. 'Will you?'

'I don't know,' said Ann. 'Maybe. But maybe I'll start with this country first. I've always wanted to see the Lake District. I have a feeling I might quite like hiking.'

Maisie put her arm around Ann and squeezed her. 'I think you will,' she said. 'Now, where's Deb? People will be waiting on the front lawn.'

They both scanned the dwindling crowd for Deb, eventually spotting her standing under a tree, shouting into her phone. 'You *what*?' she was saying. 'What do you mean?'

'Here we go again,' said Maisie, as Deb hung up and ran towards them.

'That was Rick,' she said, breathless.

'He has a terrible sense of timing,' said Maisie.

'No,' said Deb, 'I think he's actually doing the right thing for once. He said he went for a walk on West Beach, and there are bulldozers there, Maisie! They're going to knock down the beach huts. They must have seen the funeral announcement in the paper, and decided to cut their losses and get on with it anyway!'

14

The hearse rattled over the speed bumps as they drove down the hill. The driver didn't seem to mind being requisitioned for a trip to the beach, but he was more prickly about being asked to go faster than the customary crawl; it gave the wrong impression, he said. So they had to endure an unbearably stately descent into town, hampered even further by the midday traffic.

'Oh God,' said Deb, partly because she was already feeling sick, and partly because she couldn't quite picture what they were driving towards. 'What will we do when we arrive? I mean, are we supposed to lie down in front of a bulldozer? I'm not sure I can do it.'

'I don't know,' said Maisie. 'I'm just concentrating on getting there.'

'There's no point,' said Ann. 'They'll just arrest us.'

'We've lost,' said Deb. 'I feel like we're heading for another funeral.'

They were dropped off at the end of Island Wall, where they found Rick waiting on the dirt track that led to the beach.

'They've blocked it off,' he said. 'Hoardings all the way around. We can't get in.' Deb could hear, in the distance, the ominous rumble of machinery, and male voices shouting instructions. They were doing this in a hurry. This wasn't a random coincidence, the scheduling of a demolition at a difficult time for the protestors; this was an act of revenge, and it was cruel.

Other funeral guests were beginning to arrive now. Julie had agreed to drive over to Ann's house and gather the people who were already waiting for their tea and sandwiches. About twenty people were milling around on the dirt track, wondering what to do.

'Right,' said Deb, 'can I have your attention for a moment? Thank you for coming along here. You must all be parched.

We're just trying to work out what we can do, but in the meantime, can you get your phones out and tell everyone you know to get out here?'

There was the shuffling of hands into pockets, and the guests began to prod at smartphones and switch on antique-looking just-for-an-emergency handsets. 'I'll nip around the pubs,' said one man, and another followed him. Deb wondered if they would ever come back.

Julie arrived. 'There were about a dozen people already at the house,' she said. 'They all said they'd come down.'

'Great,' said Maisie. 'Where's Chloe? I thought she was with you.'

'She went home,' said Julie. 'She said she couldn't bear it.'

'Poor kid,' said Maisie. 'This is all too much.'

'And Bill?' said Deb, quietly. 'I can't see him here either.'

Julie shrugged, and looked away.

'He'd left already,' said Maisie, gently. 'I think he had to get back to work. Not all employers are sympathetic, I suppose.'

'Right,' said Deb. 'I understand.' Although she didn't. It was one thing to be overcome with embarrassment, but she felt like he was punishing her for something that he had done – holding her hand – of his own free will, and in full knowledge that it was in public. It wasn't her fault that her life was a mess. Perhaps he thought it was. Perhaps he didn't want to get sucked into the chaos. When she thought about it that way, she couldn't blame him.

But then she heard Maisie say, 'Oh, I stand corrected,' and she turned to see Bill winding through the crowd of people, and for once, his face was red with exertion rather than embarrassment.

'You came!' said Deb.

'I sat down at my desk, logged on to Facebook, and then ran straight over here,' he said between exhausted gasps.

'Well, we're just trying to work out what to do,' said Maisie. 'There's no access to the beach.'

'What about the sea?' said Bill. 'They surely haven't put a fence around that.'

'You mean we charter a boat?' said Maisie.

'No,' said Deb, 'I think he means we swim.' She smiled at Bill, and he held her gaze and smiled back. 'The tide's up right about now.'

'That's what we are, isn't it? Swimmers,' he said.

'That's pretty much *all* we are,' said Deb. 'All we can rely on, anyway.' She turned around to the assembled people – there must have been thirty of them there now, perhaps even forty. 'Right,' she said, 'How many of you can swim?' Most hands went up. 'We'll get into the water by the tennis courts and swim over to the beach huts.'

'I haven't got my kit, miss,' shouted a man from the back.

'Me neither,' said Deb. 'We'll do it in our vest and pants, just like at school.'

There was a stunned silence. '*Deb* . . .' said Maisie.

'Oh come on!' said Deb. 'Who cares anyway? If you get in the water fast enough, no one will see.' Everybody's attention seemed suddenly to be caught elsewhere: the sky above, the bushes around them, the gravel at their feet. Anything but look at Deb.

'Edith would do it,' said Deb, more quietly, and she noticed at that moment that Ann was by her side.

'It's lucky I wear such enormous knickers,' she said, and laughed.

'I've got nothing to lose,' said Maisie. 'What the hell!'

'We'll all run in at once,' said Julie. 'Safety in numbers.'

'Let's get on with it, then!' said Deb, and there was a rush towards the beach, as a sudden gleeful high took over the group. Deb paused at the back, partly to return any stragglers to the flock, and partly to shout over to Rick, 'You can call your TV mates now, and tell them there's a mass skinny-dip. They'll love that.'

'No time!' shouted Rick. 'I'm coming in too.'

Sun had broken out, cool and thin compared to its full summer heat, but welcoming all the same as they hopped on the shingle and stripped off their clothes.

'Straight in!' yelled Maisie. 'It's the best way, trust me!'

A rush of feet paddling into the shallows, and then, one by one, the splash of bodies hitting the water, and gasps at the cold.

'Keep moving,' said Deb, 'it'll warm you up,' and she began to swim out towards the end of the groynes, and then westwards to the beach she knew so well, where she could see the glint of metal in the distance. Maisie was streaking ahead in sports bra and a pair of leggings; Deb, who had considerably less on, was wishing that she made such sensible decisions about what she put on under her clothes. She was struggling to keep the scarf on her head dry, and longed for her leopard-print bathing cap, which now felt like a second skin. It didn't matter. It couldn't matter. They just had to get around to the beach.

Soon they could see that, beyond the hoardings, yellow diggers were churning up the shingle as they took their place, and men in high-vis jackets and hard hats were busily directing them. Maisie began to shout at this point, keeping her head above water to yell, 'No! Stop!'

One by one, the figures stopped, raised hands to shade their eyes, and pointed out to sea.

'Stop!' shouted Deb. 'Stop! Stop!'

And then she saw Derek in the middle of it all, his arms folded across his chest, and he was laughing. As Deb reached the shallow waters and her feet found solid ground, the other builders began to laugh too. She looked round at the swimmers behind her, and noticed that more people seemed to have joined in now. It looked like there could be a hundred of them, all grinding through the water, turning it white. She didn't care about the laughter. She stood up and began to walk onto the beach, with Maisie, and Julie, and Bill, and then more and more men and women, all landing on the shingle and walking slowly towards the bulldozers and the line of huts behind them.

Derek's face began to look less certain. 'This is a building site!' he roared. 'Get out!'

Still more feet were on the shingle now, coming wet out of the sea. 'No,' said Deb. 'You've taken my house, but you're not taking my beach.' She still wasn't sure what she could possibly do. They were nearly nose-to-nose now. Her best hope was to make it too unsafe for them to continue. But then what? They would all get thrown off the site eventually, and it would all start again.

'I didn't take your house,' said Derek. 'You gave it up.'

'Only because of this,' said Deb, and she began to unwrap the scarf from her head, revealing the fist-sized patch of hair that was missing from her crown. 'Only because nobody should be expected to live with this.'

A silence fell then, as the men on the site began to look not at her, but at Derek instead. And then, from the back of the beach, there was a call of 'Guv'nor!' and the builders began to shift around, wondering what they ought to look like they were doing.

A tall man walked onto the beach, wearing expensive-looking jeans and a leather jacket. Derek trotted up to him, and began to say, 'They're protestors. I was trying to get rid of them!' At that moment, Deb noticed who was walking by the man's side. Chloe.

'Alright, alright!' The man cut off Derek mid-sentence and carried on past him, up to the tideline where Deb and Maisie were standing.

'So *you're* the club,' he said. 'I thought it might be a cult or something.'

'Pardon?' said Deb.

'This is the club that Chloe's been going to. The High Tide Swimming Club. I wondered why she was being so secretive.'

'What's going on?' said Maisie. 'Chloe? I thought you were going back to school.'

'This is my dad,' said Chloe.

The man thrust out a hand. 'Luke Crichton,' he said. 'East Kent Land Management.'

'I know,' said Deb. 'I recognise you. Unfortunately.'

Chloe was turning a silver bangle around and around her wrist. 'So you've been swimming with us all this time,' said Maisie, 'and you joined the protests and never said a thing?'

'Never said a thing to either side,' said Luke. 'I didn't have a clue she was involved.'

'I didn't know what to say,' said Chloe.

'You could have spoken to me,' said Luke. 'We could have talked it over.'

'No I couldn't,' said Chloe. 'I thought you'd hear me when I was interviewed on the radio, and that would solve it. But you stormed out of the studio.'

'I . . .' Luke breathed out heavily. 'Look,' he said, 'without airing dirty laundry in public, it's probably safe to say our relationship hasn't been great for the last few years. You've been drifting away from me, and everything I did seemed to make it worse.'

'Not surprised,' said Deb.

'Yes, alright,' said Luke. 'The point I'm trying to make is that since she's been part of your club, I've noticed the change in her. She's been no more keen on me, granted, but she's been happier and more confident, I could tell. From a distance.' He put a hand onto Chloe's shoulder, and she blushed and leaned into him. 'Look, she ran into my office half an hour ago, and told me I was about to ruin the thing she loved most in the world. It was the first I'd heard of it.'

'You've ignored all the arguments you've heard before,' said Maisie.

'Yeah, but this is his little girl,' said Deb. 'She's worth a thousand middle-aged woman in their underwear.' Maisie, she noticed, folded her arms slightly tighter. 'So, are you saying you'll call it off?'

'No, I'm not saying that. But I'm saying I'm willing to start a conversation.'

'Alright,' said Deb. 'Let's sit down and talk about it. But all the diggers and fences go in the meantime, right?'

'Right,' said Luke.

'Good,' said Deb, ''cos we're freezing. Can we go back across the beach to our clothes?'

As the swimmers all clambered out of the sea, Deb watched Derek going about his business as an ordinary citizen, just a man earning a crust. She may have shamed him in front of his workmates, but it had no effect: they were busy forgetting it already, this distasteful truth that they'd never wanted to confront in the first place. Come the weekend, he'd be spinning the whole tale down the pub, twisting the truth until it was her fault instead of his, until he was the hero. There were some things that wouldn't get sorted out by the world's natural balance. Sometimes, you had to give the world a kick to set it off in the right direction.

'When I get home,' she said to Maisie, 'I'm going to phone the police and report my assault.'

'Good,' said Maisie.

'And then I'm going to make sure I get my bloody house back.'

'I'll make sure you do,' said Maisie. She wrapped her arm around Deb's shoulder, and they both turned towards the sea.

'Hang on,' said Maisie, 'why are you still in there, Brian? Are you alright?'

Brian was still treading water a few metres offshore, his teeth visibly chattering.

'I'm alright!' he called cheerfully. 'It's just that, well, when I went to strip down to my boxers, I realised I wasn't wearing any . . .'

'Luke!' shouted Deb. 'I don't suppose you've got a spare hard hat?'

Epilogue

When the first frosts arrived, Deb decided that enough was enough: she would start swimming again in the spring, when the water was a little warmer, and there was no longer the risk of her feet freezing onto the shingle when she got out. There was talk of the High Tide Swimming Club getting together for a New Year's Day dip, and she thought, perhaps, she could stand that.

Maisie had carried on swimming every day. She had switched to a dry suit instead of a wetsuit, and was bringing a flask of hot chocolate along with her now, too. But she was loving the icy splash of the waves around her, the thrilling way it knocked the air out of her lungs. She loved this vision of herself, determined, adaptable, and hardy enough to endure the winter.

On the two weekends she had spent in London with Stephen, she swam in the Serpentine each morning, while he drank macchiatos and read the papers in the Lido Cafe. They were both left more or less content by this arrangement, although Stephen felt the coffee beans had been over-roasted, and lamented the quality of the *Telegraph*'s magazine these days. In return, he had ventured down to Whitstable twice, once to sit in Maisie's kitchen watching the election on her laptop, cheering at three a.m. when it was announced that Michelle Hunter had ousted Charles Brinton from his safe seat.

Stephen was even at risk of becoming a fixture on the table outside the Deli, where he had to admit he admired the wine list. On more than one occasion now, Maisie had caught him bragging to friends that, down in Whitstable, they bought produce at the farm door. Although she was sorely tempted to point out that he meant the greengrocer's on the High Street, she let him be. It was a good sign, she thought, and his enthusiasm for rural life (as he saw it) must surely be encouraged.

With Deb living in the spare room, there had been times when the house felt fit to burst, but Maisie had slyly enjoyed umpiring the exasperation that Stephen and Deb felt for each other. It was, she hoped, increasingly affectionate. That time was only fleeting though, because, after Deb had been interviewed by two female police officers, and Rob had corroborated her story, Derek was arrested and charged with a range of offences related to domestic abuse spanning decades. While he was in custody, Deb's kids arranged for the locks to be changed, and they were waiting for their father when he arrived home, his bags already packed. Nobody was quite sure where he was living now, but it certainly wasn't Whitstable.

While Deb buried her head in textbooks in the university library, and tried hard not to take any malnourished undergraduates into her care, Rob, Darren and Cherie worked on their childhood home, clearing out the rubbish that Derek had piled all around it, and painting the walls so that they were fresh again. Darren picked her up from Canterbury on the last day of term and drove her back home, where the front lawn was neatly clipped, and the bed was made up with new linen, a rather sheepish token of reconciliation from Cherie.

Deb stood in the middle of her living room and cried, but for once it was because she had all her children around her to hug. Rob would be staying in his old room until he finished college now, and after that – well, Deb quite fancied the odd trip to Australia. Darren and Lou were settling into their new place nicely, and the baby was now so imminent that they were keeping an overnight bag in the boot, just in case. Cherie's kids were asking when they could come for a sleepover, and in a fortnight, Deb would be cooking Christmas dinner again for all of them, and Maisie and Stephen too.

And on Boxing Day, Bill was coming over. They thought they might go out for a pub lunch, if anywhere was open. If not, they would walk along the seafront until the wind made their ears beg for mercy, or just sit and watch *The Sound of Music* on the TV. They were taking it slowly: no sleepovers, no big declarations, and certainly no talk of moving in. There was, as everyone kept telling them, a big age gap. It would probably start mattering eventually, but when and how was yet to be known. Deb was relishing the privacy of her own home far too much to give it away that easily. She wasn't sure if she would ever be willing to give it up again.

And, as promised, the lovely row of wooden huts on West Beach were still standing, even if one or two of them looked like they might dismantle themselves in the next winter storm. But Deb and Luke had been talking through a plan for that, and she was beginning to think it could work.

But that was all the business of the New Year. For now, Deb was more concerned with enjoying the shelter of her own four walls, and a distant view of the sea.

THE END

Acknowledgements

I like to think that I have my very own High Tide Swimming Club - a group of supportive, astonishingly talented and down-right kick-ass women, who (at least metaphorically) keep me afloat. Here's the list of characters:

Lucy Abrahams, who is funny, generous and passionate, with a rare gift for connecting people together. I never stop being amazed at how lucky I am to know her.

Sam Eades, a human whirlwind whose brilliant ideas and eye for detail has made this a far better book than I could have managed alone.

Madeleine Milburn, a laser-focused superhero of an agent, whose wisdom, perception and steely will I gratefully depend upon.

Huge thanks, also, to the teams behind them at Trapeze and the Madeleine Milburn Literary, Film & TV Agency, especially Hayley Steed and Marleigh Price. I'm particularly grateful to the people responsible for the gorgeous cover – Debbie Holmes, Brian Roberts and Claire Keep.

I have the privilege of my writing life being supported by a post at Canterbury Christ Church University, so thanks are due to my colleagues there, and also to my students who continue to inspire me every day.

Finally, love to the team at home: H, who quietly keeps the house running while I shut myself away with a laptop; my mum who flies over close to deadlines (mainly to tidy the insides of my cupboards); and Bertie, who now swims with me in the sea.

About the Author

Katie May writes fiction and memoir, and until recently led the Creative Writing MA at Canterbury Christ Church University. She lives in Whitstable with her husband, son and two cats, and can be mostly found walking along the beach and – yes – swimming in the sea. In her spare time, she reads, cooks and drinks gin martinis, stirred.

Katie loves to hear from her readers. Get in touch online:

Twitter: @_katherine_may_
Instagram: @katherinemay_

Five tips for wild swimmers

Inspired to take up sea-swimming after reading *The Whitstable High Tide Swimming Club*? Here are some tips for getting started.

1. Know your beach

Every beach is different. Spend some time paddling first, and get a feel for how the sea is behaving. Is the tide coming in, or going out? Are there any rocks to avoid, or shelves where the waves break suddenly? If it's a monitored beach, find the safe swimming area marked by red and yellow flags, and ask the lifeguard about any tides or currents you should take into consideration. Don't be afraid to ask local swimmers for advice.

2. Assess your ability

Put simply, it's harder to swim in the sea than in a pool. If you're a weak swimmer, spend some time in the local baths first, developing your strokes and building up strength and distance. You could even work with a coach or take adult lessons to build confidence.

3. Bring the right kit

Whether you're a bikini swimmer like Deb or a wetsuit swimmer like Maisie will be a matter of preference – and the time of year you plan to swim. But it's worth making sure you have everything you need before you get in the water. Here's a checklist:

- Swimming shoes if the beach is stony
- Goggles if you plan to put your face underwater
- A neoprene glasses retainer if, like me, you're lost without your specs
- A light towel to dry off – I'm devoted to cloth hammam towels

- Waterproof sun cream
- A bottle of water to rehydrate
- I hate to say it, but a bright bathing cap like Maisie's really can help you to stay visible

4. Acclimatise

The best way to get used to cold seawater is to start swimming in the summer, and then keep going into autumn as the sea gradually cools. Winter is up to you. If you don't have this option, it's sensible to cool down gradually rather than shocking your body. If I'm swimming in cold weather, I stand on the beach in my cossie for a few minutes before getting in. Get into the water slowly, and stay shallow so that you can get out quickly if you need to. Have warm clothing ready for when you get out, even if it's the summer. A cup of tea helps if you get really chilly.

5. Safety first

Sea-swimming is one of the great pleasures of my life, and it gives me an instant hit of happiness. However, I know my limits and carefully assess the sea every time I swim. If I'm in any doubt about safety, I don't go in; it's as simple as that. You can read up on basic survival techniques on the RNLI's excellent website, respectthewater.com. There are also some useful (and inspiring) articles for beginners on the Outdoor Swimming Society's website: go to outdoorswimmingsociety.com and select 'survive' in the top menu.

Inspired to visit Whitstable after reading the book? Here are five places you may recognise in real life.

1. West Beach

First things first: West Beach – and its lovely row of beach huts – is as glorious as it sounds in the book. Head west along the coast from the town centre, go past the sea-front houses, and you'll come to it: quiet, beautiful, and covered in wild flowers from spring to autumn. Not everyone loves shingle beaches, but it's easily solved with a pair of sea shoes and it sure keeps the sand out of your picnic. Don't forget to check the tide tables if you want to swim like Maisie and Deb. When the tide's out, you'll be lucky if you can get more than ankle-deep.

2. The Neptune

Sitting directly on the beach, The Neppy is a Whitstable institution, beloved of locals and visitors alike. With its white weatherboard exterior and picnic sets outside, it's a magnet for summer drinkers, but it's cosy in the winter, too, when sea-storms lash against the windows. If the crowds get too much for you, seek out some of Whitstable's wonderful backstreet pubs, like the New Inn or the Smack. True locals drink in the Yacht Club, but you have to be a member.

3. The Windy Corner Stores & Café

Set on a residential street not far from West Beach, the Windy Stores is the café you always dream of finding: great coffee, art on the walls, and the world's most perfect mushrooms on toast for breakfast. Whenever you turn up, it's always full of people tapping on laptops, giggling with friends over coffee or indulging in a slice of carrot cake while their kids queue for sweets. Whitstable is awash with wonderful cafés, from the classic Tea & Times to the new-fangled Blueprint Coffee and Whitstable Produce Store, and this book was written in most of them!

4. The Harbour

Whitstable has a way of reminding you that it's still a working fishing town. You only need to take a stroll into the harbour to see all the fishing boats lined up, and to buy shellfish – including the famous oysters – from the black sheds on the quay. Many tourists leave out the looming towers of the aggregates plant from their holiday snaps, but for me, this is part of what makes Whitstable so special: the collision of longstanding industry with arty 'down from London' culture. There's now a permanent market on the harbour where you can buy anything from bric-a-brac to sushi, as well as crabbing nets to dangle off the end of West Quay. Take a tip from a local: to catch the big ones, you'll need to use bacon as bait.

5. Trendy gin bars

Okay, I invented the pop-up gin bar where Julie gives Deb some unwanted career advice, but Whitstable's drinking scene is getting an awful lot cooler, and unlike Deb, I think this is a great thing. If I had to call a favourite, it would have to be the Twelve Taps with its magnificent range of gins (sorry, Deb), craft beer and prosecco on tap. But I'm also deeply fond of goth micropub The Black Dog, the chic little bar attached to the David Brown Deli for a superb wine list, and, over in Tankerton, the wonderful Jo Jos at the top of the Slopes. Wherever takes your fancy, you'll always be able to spot the locals: we're the ones in striped shirts with wind-blown hair. To blend in, you'd better dress down.

Cocktails inspired by
The Whitstable High Tide Swimming Club

My Instagram feed is testimony to the fact that I'm a bit of a cocktail fiend. Here are some suggestions to sip while you read.

West Beach Martini

A fragrant dry martini that reminds me of the beach in high summer.

50 ml gin (I love Bombay Sapphire in this)
1 tsp white vermouth
1 strip orange zest
1 sprig rosemary
1 pinch sea salt

- Half-fill a cocktail shaker with ice.
- Add all the ingredients, crushing the rosemary between your fingers as you put it in (this releases the oils).
- Shake very well, and strain into a martini glass.
- Garnish with another shred of orange zest, or an olive.

Elderflower cordial

Come high summer, West Beach is in full bloom, and this year I picked some of the lacy elderflowers from around the beach huts and made my own cordial. It was simple to make and delicious topped up with fizzy water or added to prosecco. I also shake this in equal parts with my lemon vodka to make a sherbety martini.

Make sure you don't leave your elderflowers steeping to for too long: I accidentally fermented my cordial, a mistake I only realised when the lids popped off of my first batch!